Deep In the Heart

Geron GA & Associates

Celia Hayes

Published by G&A, a division of Watercress Press

Deep In the Heart

Celia Hayes

Celia Hayes

Dedication and Acknowledgements

Thanks and acknowledgements are due to a great number of people who contributed advice, feedback, editing, and all sorts of support to the writer of this novel, beginning with fellow members of the Independent Authors Guild, especially Alice Geron of Watercress Press, for editing and encouragement, to long-time blog-fan Mary "Proud Veteran" Young for friendship and support in time of crisis, and to so many "open-air" historians and reenactors in South Texas who contributed to my knowledge and understanding of Republic-era Texas. I also owe a debt of thanks to longtime blog-fan Andrew Brooks of San Diego, California, who suggested the humorous subtitle of *Barsetshire with Cypress Trees and Lots of Side-Arms* upon reading early chapters of various recreation of mid-19th century Texas. This has since turned out to be as apt as it is foresighted, since the interlinked lives and adventures of the Becker, Vining, Steinmetz, and Richter families on the Texas frontier, as well as many of their friends and distant connections are proving to be as rich and continuing a source of stories as the original Barsetshire ever was.

This book is also dedicated with love to Mom and my daughter Jeanne, both of whom were supportive well and above the call of duty. Finally and most importantly – it is dedicated to the memory of Dad, the best alpha reader and fan ever.

Celia Hayes
San Antonio, Texas
November, 2011

Spring 1865 – Margaret Remembers

"He was a man to whom no other man could be indifferent, whether they liked him or no," Margaret mused, hardly aware that she was speaking out loud. "Although many men were his partisans, at least as many more hated him. But women liked him nearly without exception, which may seem curious. He had many faults; pride, drunkenness, lechery, even anger at times. But he did not hide them in any way, pretending to be a better man; and he never failed to be gallant to any woman. He liked women, you see. He liked them for their company and intellect, and respected them, no matter what color or degree."

"Who?" Margaret's grandson Horrie asked, with great curiosity, lifting his head from the book that he was reading. He was small-boned and wiry, with the clever hazel eyes of his father, Margaret's oldest son, fallen in the early hours of the fighting at Gettysburg. Horrie was only four years of age, yet he could already read very well. At the moment, he was systematically working his way through those books which his grandfather, Race Vining, had cherished most particularly – those very same books that Race Vining had brought to Stephen Austin's grant forty years before, in order to establish a school at San Felipe. "Who do you mean, Gran'mere? I thought you were having one of your 'thinks.'"

"I was," Margaret could barely lift her head from the pillows piled behind so that she could sit up in bed, to turn and smile at her grandson. "Little One, that is about the only thing that I can do now; lie in bed, think and remember. I cannot even play my piano! So many people, so many years! It is almost a luxury, dear little duckling – to be able to turn over in my mind all of the things that I have seen, and all of those people I have known, without interruption." This was the truth; Margaret's ailment inexorably sapped her energy, her breath and her very life! She was bedridden entirely now – no longer having the capacity to sit in a wheeled-chair and attend to the business of her household, or even to be wheeled into the next room by her loving attendants. As the fortunes of the Confederacy waned, so did Margaret's strength, although not a single iota of her will. She was indomitable, a woman of character and determination, the mother of children, who had outlived two husbands, all but one of her sons, and so many of her friends, although she was only fifty-four. "I was thinking of Sam Houston; we called him General Sam. I knew him very well and his wife also. With him, I disagreed on almost

1

as many points as we agreed. But I liked him very well, from almost the first time that I met him."

Little Horrie's eyes grew large with wonder, and curiosity. "Gran'mere . . . truly, did you know General Houston? When did you first meet him?"

Margaret coughed with some difficulty; another symptom of the degenerative paralysis that was killing her by inches. Horrie set aside the book, as Hetty, her cook, long-time friend and aide-de-camp in the business of running a boardinghouse, came into the room, her skirts and starched apron rustling. Margaret's eyes watered from the force of the cough, and Hetty poured a small draft of herbal tea from the teakettle which simmered over a spirit lamp on the dressing table. Margaret sipped of it with painful slowness, as Hetty held the cup to her lips. When she could speak again, she gasped, "Thank you, Hetty. I am all right now."

"You should rest now, Marm," Hetty looked at her with tender severity, as she took a clean handkerchief, dabbed the tears from the corners of Margaret's eyes, settled her back onto her pillows and smoothed the bedcovers into place.

"No," Margaret answered, "No, I am not tired – the time is passing and I have so many stories to tell Horrie. Don't I, Horrie my dear little duckling?"

"You were going to tell me of how you met General Houston," Horrie prompted her. He had set the book carefully aside, marking his place with a piece of ribbon, at which Margaret smiled to see. Race Vining, the father of her sons, would have been so very pleased to see the care that Horrie took with his precious books.

"Remind me to also tell you of how I buried your grandfather's library under a redbud tree to keep it safe and because we could not carry it with us," Margaret answered. "I did that, the same day that I first met the General. He came to Gonzales to take charge of the Army of Texas, to lift Lopez de Santa Anna's siege of the Alamo. Too late; it had already fallen. It was a sad time, Horrie. We had many friends who had answered the call; Almaron Dickinson, and Esteban Menchaca. James Bowie – he was a friend of your grandfathers'. And so were the men of Gonzales who rode in a body to the Alamo; the Mounted Ranging Company. Our friends and neighbors, the husbands of my friends, and some of the younger had even been your grandfather's students. Oh, those poor boys!" Margaret's eyes were once again threatened with tears.

"What about General Houston?" Horrie persisted. "You said you met him the same day that you buried the books. Why did you do that, Gran'mere?"

"The General ordered us to leave our homes and to burn them, so that the Mexicans would find nothing but desolation and wilderness. He had our own army retreat towards the east, to lure the invaders farther and farther from their own borders . . . and of course, the families of the soldiers went with them. Your father was about the age that you are now, Horrie, and your Uncle Johnny was a baby. Your grandfather was a courier. He was taking General Houston's orders to Mina – Bastrop, that is. My own father, your Opa Alois Becker, he was also away, at Washington-on-the-Brazos, where the Convention had been called to form a new independent government for Texas. Oma – my mother – she was staying with me at our house in Gonzales. I was sent for because it was known that I was a friend of Susanna Dickinson's."

"But the General, Gran'mere," Horrie persisted, "What about the general?"

"I am getting to that, Horrie. The scouts had found Susanna on the road from Bexar. She had been in the Alamo with her husband and General Lopez de Santa Anna had sent her with a message to the American settlements. All of our men were dead in the Alamo. Only a few women and children were allowed to live and Colonel Travis's slave servant, Joe. She was in a state of exhaustion, Horrie; but she was the one sent with a message. Everyone, even the General, wanted to know what had happened, the fate of their friends. That was how I met him; a kindly man thought Sue should have a woman with her, someone to comfort her. As for the General himself; he was a tall man, in a dark cloth coat."

"Did he wear a grey uniform?" Horrie asked; Margaret smiled tenderly – grey was the proper color of military uniforms to Horrie. "No, dear little duckling, he did not wear a uniform at all. None of our soldiers did; they wore what they would have put on to go hunting. The general did wear a hat with the brim turned up to make three corners and he rode a white horse. He did look like a general in that respect."

"Did you ever see a battle, Gran'mere?" Horrie breathed, with passionate interest.

"No, I did not," Margaret answered sadly. "Nor would I have wanted to, since I was too much taken up with the aftermath of them. Battles and wars are cruel things, little duckling. Even if we win in the end, they destroy our homes and take from us the people whom we have loved, treasured in our hearts. Even when we are fortunate, and they come home again to us – they are often changed forever."

Chapter 1 – *Widow's Weeds*

Early in the year of 1841, Margaret Becker Vining received condolence visits in the front parlor of the house she had come to think of as her own, since her father Alois, had long yielded up the management of it to his formidable daughter. The front parlor was a room longer than wide, with tall windows on two sides, which allowed the winter sun to fill the room with the mellow golden light of afternoon after a morning of rain. It was a plain room with clean and whitewashed walls, adorned with only the shelves of books that her late husband had prized, and yet set with comfortable chairs and a daybed piled with pillow-cushions covered with blue and yellow patchwork. Margaret – tall and slender, with hair the color of ripe wheat done in a long braid wrapped coronet-wise around her head – was dressed in unrelieved black, the weeds of a new-made widow. Her first caller was likewise dressed all in somber black, but the color of deep mourning did not flatter her as well as it did Margaret.

"The Doc came to attend on one o' my boarders," remarked Margaret's visitor, by way of commencing her call. "And he told us you had received word that your man died in Boston. Cap'n Eberly, he died while on a visit to see his chirren by his first wife. Sudden it was, no warning. I'm sorry to hear of your loss, Miz Vining. He seemed like a real nice man. I reckon you miss him something turrible. Schoolteacher, was he?"

"Yes, Mrs. Eberly," Margaret answered. "We had been married more than ten years."

"I thought I recollect him from San Felipe, when he first started a school there." Angelina Eberly sighed, reminiscently. She was dumpy, capable and shrewd, some twenty years older than Margaret, who rather liked her even though she was a rival of sorts in the business of keeping a boardinghouse in the tiny frontier capital city of Texas. "My first husband and I, we had just started our place, too. Such a dashing feller, altogether too handsome to be teaching school. Seemed to be a waste, that he didn't have no ambition a'tall."

"My husband only wanted to teach school," Margaret answered, showing no sign of the grief and resentment that still burned deep within her heart, like the coals of a fire left to smolder overnight. "He came to Texas for his health. He had a weak chest and his doctors told him that for his own sake he must live in a warm climate."

Race Vining had also been escaping a loveless marriage. That was not an uncommon thing among those young men who had rushed into Texas in the mid-1820s, seeking adventure, land and their fortunes in those American colonies in Mexican territories, those settlements set up by entrepreneurs like Stephen Austin and Green DeWitt. Unfortunately, Race Vining had omitted to obtain a divorce from his well-born and well-connected Boston wife before engaging Margaret in marriage. Margaret had loved him well and borne him four sons during the adversities of war, invasion, sickness, and separation, before inadvertently discovering the nature of his existing marriage. It was for the purpose of seeking a divorce which had finally impelled Race Vining to make that arduous return journey to the East. He died of his old malady before achieving that end. Margaret had received a settlement from his horrified family back east, and hadn't decided what she would do with it. Her husband's family appeared to have brought forth only daughters: no sons to carry on their name. But the Texas frontier was far removed from Boston, and Margaret was determined to keep the embarrassment of Race Vining's bigamy a secret from all, even her sons. She assumed that his Boston family was determined to do the same.

Mrs. Eberly continued, "Now I had just five years with Captain Eberly. He was my second husband, o'course. I was married to Mr. Peyton for sixteen year a'fore that, but we had known each other all our lives, bein' that we were cousins. Like to have broke my heart when he died, but still!" She sighed, gustily. "I just cain't see that I'll marry again, Miz Vining. I'm set in my ways, an' accustomed to running my establishment as I see fit. When you're young an' pretty, it helps to have a man around the place, stand up for ye, remind the boarders an' customers to keep a civil tongue. It don' much matter when yer as old as I am, Miz Vining. Then ye can do as yer pleases."

"I do not think I shall remarry." Margaret answered, although the old black witch woman who had told Margaret her fortune on her twelfth birthday had promised that she would marry once for love and again for friendship. The utter humiliation of Race's confession to her and the long silence after he had departed for Boston still hurt Margaret dreadfully. She had done with heartbreak, with lies told for love and for men who did things for convenience.

"A man about the place is handy to have, now and again," Mrs. Eberly conceded generously, "And you're young enough still – hain't lost any of your looks – but as long as your old Pa is around, I don't think you'd be too much bothered."

"I do not think I could endure the sorrow of love regained and then the loss of it but I have considered taking up weaving, like Penelope," Margaret answered; Mrs. Eberly looked blank and Margaret stifled a small sigh. "The wife of Ulysses, plagued by unwanted suitors in his absence; she promised to marry when her weaving was done, but she picked out at night all she had accomplished during the day." Having had the allusion explained to her, Mrs. Eberly laughed in frank amusement, which gratified Margaret. She was becoming rather tired of being treated as if she were made of spun glass, and would dissolve into a welter of tears if anyone so much as cracked a smile.

Mrs. Eberly went on, "All that Penelope woman would have needed was to have your Pa sit in the corner and glower at them. I can't help thinking now that he's a man who might have done good to marry again! It would have improved his temper, at any rate."

"I don't think so, Mrs. Eberly. He took the loss of my mother so very hard," Margaret replied. "And the death of my brother Rudi with Colonel Fannin at the Goliad . . . Pa has never been the same since. But he was always a difficult man." What Margaret would not say was that Alois Becker had always been proud and hot-tempered. He doted on the older of his two sons while scorning the younger, and quarreled frequently with men who might otherwise have been his friends. Only Margaret's mother had been able to soften his harsh nature into some pretense of amity with his fellows. Her death of the bloody flux during the terrible 'runaway scrape' had removed that effective governance on Alois Becker's ill-temper. Margaret coped by serenely ignoring his occasional bitter outburst, reasoning that Papa was what he was, and paying any mind to him was a fruitless exercise. In any case, she had the house to manage and her sons to bring up properly.

Mrs. Eberly looked ready to settle in for a good enjoyable gossip. "Have you many gentleman guests, now? There's been so much talk, about Meskin bandits raiding over the Nueces! Can you believe they have the nerve? Folk are frightened about venturing alone very far from town because of the danger, and not to mention the Comanche, taking that poor Smith boy, an' murdering poor Capn' Dolson an' Mr. Black! The only boarders I have are those come on business, and Mr. Bullock, he says the same. I can't wait until the Legislature comes back to town, and fills up my rooms good and proper. General Sam, he's staying for a few days, but if it weren't for him and the missus, I might as well turn over the mattresses and lock the doors."

"I can't blame people for being frightened," Margaret answered. "But I think it would take more than talk to drive me away. I know that it would! We left our home once before, I'd not be leaving again, and I know that my father wouldn't."

"Oh, but he was up here when it was still Waterloo, wasn't he?" Mrs. Eberly fanned herself. "Then he's accustomed to living out and away from everything. But I tell you straight enough, Miz Vining, we'd be in mortal danger of loosing our livelihood altogether, if General Sam has his way. He never liked having the Legislature meet all the way out here. It was President Lamar who was dead-set upon building a new capital city, instead of meeting at Columbia or Washington-on-the-Brazos. I have to say that I much preferred Mr. Lamar. He was ever so much a real gent, always polite, never going on a spree!"

"I still have three boarders," Margaret answered. "Mr. Hattersley the Englishman, Dr. Williamson, and Seamus O'Doyle, of course. He is contracted to build the French Legation. And that is still going ahead. I do not think General Sam would be able to move the capital city away from here, even if he wanted to now that he has been re-elected."

"Truth to tell, he's a canny man," Mrs. Eberly answered, with an air of dark warning. "Who knows what he really has his mind set on? Myself, I think his wife has something to do with it. She wishes to be settled nearest her kinfolk; she tole me her sister and husband have a big plantation on the Trinity River. Take my word on it; she's the one who doesn't wish to be always traveling around, and living all the way out here! Well, there's no fool like an old fool."

"General Sam has married?" Margaret was startled. Now that she thought on it, she recalled there had been a bit of gossip floated at her suppertable last year, but as her guests were mostly men, they had very little interest in the marriage of a public figure like Sam Houston; or if they did, their remarks would have been prurient in nature and too unseemly to voice in Margaret's presence. "I had heard mention of him courting a young lady whose family did not approve, but I thought there was an end to it."

"No, Miz Vining, she defied them, and they went ahead with marrying. Last May, it was. Who would have thought it? A little slip of a girl and that drunken old goat, even if he is the hero of San Jacinto, but they seem happy enough."

"I am very glad for them," Margaret replied with all honesty. "General Sam always appeared to me as one who would be a most devoted husband. I think he is a man who likes the company of women as friends. When we had to leave Gonzales during the war, General Sam gave orders that the Army wagons should be used to carry away the women, especially the widows of those Gonzales men who had gone to the Alamo. At that terrible time, he took the trouble to be kindly. He sat with Sue Dickinson as she told us of what had happened there, holding her hand and weeping openly. I have always had the most generous feelings towards him on that account."

"Ah," Mrs. Eberly began drawing her shawl closer around herself, and setting her bonnet at a rakish angle, preparatory to taking her leave. "Well, General Sam can be charming when he wants to be, I'll give him that. But what he does and says when he has a few drinks; I'd not want to endure being married to him, knowing what I know of life and the didoes he kicked up in Tennessee and among the Cherokee. Well, I'll be taking my leave now, Miz Vining. I just wanted to tell you again how sorry I was to hear about Mr. Vining – leaving you with the boys and all."

"Thank you, Mrs. Eberly. I appreciate your consideration more than I can say." Margaret clasped her visitor's hands briefly, feeling that it really was very kind of Mrs. Eberly to take this time from her unending daily rounds of cooking, cleaning and overseeing the care of her guests.

"That's all right, my dear," Mrs. Eberly embraced her fondly, adding, "Now you hear any rumors from your gentlemen about moving the Legislature to anywhere else – you must promise to pass them on to me! A whisper of such doings will affect your business no less than mine, and not for the better."

She walked with Mrs. Eberly to the front door, musing upon how very kind everyone had been to her since the news of Race Vining's death had come from the East. She was fortunate to have such friends. That was one of the other things that the witch-woman had promised her; many friends and a large house, aside from the two husbands – but that very few of those friends would truly know her heart. These days, Margaret sometimes felt that she didn't know it, either. She had mourned her husband and her marriage all of last year. Now what she was doing was a pretense, a sop to proprieties. Just as she was emerging from the shadow of last year, like a butterfly from a chrysalis, she must make a quiet show of her grief because everyone expected it of her. She had just decided to go change out of her good black dress, and help Morag and Hetty with supper, when Morag put her head around the parlor door saying,

"Oh, Marm, it looks like there's another visitor for ye; a trap just coming up to th' door." Morag was barely sixteen and as pretty as a wildflower. Margaret often thought of a story her own mother told her; of a princess with hair as black as ebony, skin as white as snow, and lips the red of blood – Morag looked like that. Irish to the bone, at first she had been timid and almost silent. Everything frightened her, but she had gained confidence in the months since, although she was prone to blush as pink as a primrose when men paid her a compliment. She had not realized that men did so deliberately, for the picture she made then was so very pretty. She and her older sister

Hetty worked in Margaret's house, although Margaret valued them for their companionship almost more than the work that spared her and gave time to spend with her sons . . . and to sit in the parlor of a winter afternoon and receive visitors. Really, Margaret thought with a pang of regret, Race would have been so proud of her. As she had seen to his needs and nursed him in sickness, he had schooled her in the social graces and in the contents of his books; he was an educated man and had read widely.

"Is it anyone that you recognize?" Margaret asked, as she resettled the cushions that had been somewhat disarranged by Mrs. Eberly.

"Marm, I think it is General Houston," Morag breathed, with eyes as wide as saucers. "And there is a lady with him."

"Oh, my!" Margaret peeped out of one of the parlor's long windows: yes, there was a trap drawn up on the wagon-way out in front, and her father holding the bridle of the horse that drew it, as General Sam climbed down from the seat. General Sam exchanged remarks with her father; remarks which sounded casually friendly, or as friendly as anyone could ever be with Alois Becker. It looked as if Alois Becker was about to begin spring plowing, after the morning's rain, for the team of oxen stood patiently behind him. Then the General turned to hand down a young lady; a young lady in a fashionable dark purple dress and a bonnet whose beribboned brim hid her face. Margaret drew in her breath. At least Papa appeared to be in a good mood, for he was speaking to the General and his lady with a lessening of his usual sour expression. "It is indeed! Mrs. Eberly said that he and his wife were in Austin. Don't bother with showing them in, Morag. I'll meet them at the door."

"You shall not, Marm," Hetty popped her head out of the kitchen door as Margaret came from the parlor. "'Tis fitting that you should sit in the parlor an' receive your guests there, so you should, for you are in mourning for the Young Sir." Margaret could hear the men's voices from outside, closer as General Sam approached the steps.

"Very well," Margaret yielded. Morag was having so much fun, playing the part of a 'proper maid' as Hetty had called it, although neither of the Moylan sisters had any idea of what that actually entailed, other than their long-dead mother's stories of domestic service in a grand mansion in Ireland some three or four decades since. Margaret sat in the chair that had been her husband's, her back straight and her hands folded in her lap, although she was aching to take up a piece of mending from the basket at her side.

"General and Mrs. Houston," Morag announced from the parlor door, and Margaret rose from the chair. Before she had taken more than a few steps,

General Sam was within the room, the force of his personality seeming to fill it entirely, at the expense of the woman in the fashionable purple dress clinging timidly to his arm.

At once, the General enclosed Margaret's hands in his, saying, "Mrs. Vining, we had only just heard of your sad loss! What a tragedy that you would hear of it so late and be unable to take some small crumbs of comfort in knowing that you ministered to him in his last hours. He must have longed for your loving presence as well."

"He was with his family," Margaret answered, suddenly and unexpectedly overwhelmed with the intensity of General Sam's concern. He was a tall man, with craggy features and a lion's mane of hair, and possessed of such personal vitality and energy that people were drawn towards him, like iron-filings to a magnet. His charm was of such a nature that it convinced anyone who held his regard for that moment that they were the most important and fascinating person in the world. "And he had been so often ill that I was in part prepared for the end."

"Nonetheless," General Sam gave her hands a comforting squeeze, and without letting go, turned to the lady at his side. "I know that you would have grieved nonetheless, Mrs. Vining. My dear, may I present you to another Margaret? Her late husband, Mr. Vining, was long-settled in Texas. He served as a scout all during our retreat to the East, then in the line in the San Jacinto fight; a brave man and none nobler. I confess that I oft envied him for the simple wealth of his possessions; his horse, his home and his family," the General smiled impishly, "and his Margaret, as well. But then I found a very dear Margaret of my own." He yielded Margaret's hands and turned to the lady at his side, with a proud and fond expression. Margaret thought, *Oh, General Sam, what have you done? She looks hardly older than Morag and you are more than twice her age!* The General's Margaret was slender and very, very young, with tremulous dark eyes set in pale, regular features and lips that curved in a somber and rather hesitant smile. "May I present my wife, Margaret, to you?"

"I am pleased to make your acquaintance, Mrs. Vining." Margaret Houston's voice was low and gentle, like a dove; a dove that had been sipping southern honeysuckle, Margaret thought irreverently. "I think it is very sad to do so under the circumstances of a visit of condolence. My husband has made so many friends in Texas! I am honored to make their acquaintance for myself, but so many of them are men!"

"Being in politics and having been the general of an army, he can scarcely avoid that," Margaret answered, adding the unspoken thought; *Besides good friends, he has at least as many enemies and ill-wishers, too*, while General Sam chuckled, remarking, "Never been one for sitting around the drawing room, flirting with the ladies."

"Save now and again," Margaret Houston added. She and the General exchanged a look of wry fondness, as she continued, "I shall be so very glad to make friends of my own in Texas – but there are rather more men then women here!"

Margaret thought with some relief; *Oh, good. She is not timid at all – merely reserved.* Aloud she said, "So many think of it as the far frontier, Mrs. Houston – a place more suited to men and dogs, than women and horses. I was so pleased to hear of your marriage from Mrs. Eberly. I have always thought that the General was one who well-deserved the reward of a loving marriage and a happy home – as loving and happy as my own with my husband was."

"Thank you for your good wishes." General Sam looked inordinately pleased; he and Margaret Houston exchanged another of those fond looks. "I think we're off to a good start – even if it took a good long time to find my own dear Maggie Lea, and a house of our own a-building."

"I do envy yours," Margaret Houston confided, as they sat down. "So many books – I had not expected to see so many in one house! Have you read them all, Mrs. Vining?"

Margaret restrained herself from answering snappishly, *"Of course I have!"* since she had heard this question from practically every visitor that she and Race Vining had entertained from their first days of marriage in Gonzales. Instead she replied, "I have indeed. My late husband was a schoolteacher. He needed books the way most other men require food and drink. He guided my education himself, even after our marriage."

"Marvelous," Now Margaret Houston smiled a smile of genuine pleasure which brought out a pair of dimples. "May I examine your library, Mrs. Vining? I vow I have not seen such a wealth of books since my own schooldays at the Judson Female Institute!"

"Of course," Margaret answered. Margaret Lea Houston went to the bookshelves in a rustle of purple silk, just as the door of the parlor opened again.

"I've brought the boys to see General Houston, Marm." Morag said, "for they wouldn't give us any peace, knowing that he was within the house."

Margaret's three older sons stood slightly abashed within the parlor, each of their faces alight with hero-worship: ten year-old Horace, whose likeness and character was his father's image, Johnny, who was seven and rather timid, and five-year old Jamie who wasn't. Jamie was fair-haired and big for his age, a true Becker. He was as tall as Johnny and was as bold and brash as the man he had been named after – Race Vining's friend, James Bowie, who had fallen in the Alamo siege.

"Hello, boys," General Sam's own face lit up. "I see you've brought your toy soldiers!" Jamie had an armful of his corn-husk toy soldiers. "What sort of game were you playing?"

"We weren't, sir," Horace answered with touching dignity. "We were doing chores with Opa, and Miss Hetty said you had come to pay respects on account of Papa."

"Then I am very pleased to meet you, lad." General Sam shook hands gravely with all three boys, even Johnny who looked as if he would like to go back to sucking his thumb again. "Your father was a gallant gentleman indeed. He was with us at San Jacinto, and I am sure you have heard the story many times."

"Oh, yes, but not from you, sir!" Jamie spoke up. Horace answered, "I saw you then, sir. Johnny and I did. Mama and our friends, we were camped in a wagon close to Harrisburg, and Papa and Opa were gone with Captain Smith. We saw the whole Army march by, and you on a white horse, and Mrs. Kimball and Mrs. Darst told us to look well and remember that we saw the Army of Texas on its way to do battle – but we did not see Papa."

"He was most likely on a proper scout," General Sam rumbled. "Or flanking the column at a distance . . . here, let me show you." In short order, he and the boys were down on the floor – the boys entranced as General Sam demonstrated the proper marching order across the rag rug with Jamie's corn-husk soldiers and Johnny's toy wooden horses. Margaret and Margaret Lea Houston exchanged amused glances.

"A good general," Margaret remarked, "and very good with children. He took as good a care of his soldiers as if they were his sons – or so my husband claimed."

"I know," Margaret Lea knelt in a pool of whispering silk, to examine the gilt-lettered backs of the books on the lower shelves. "And I think to myself sometimes, Mrs. Vining, that it is unfair that he will then take such little care of himself, and share his deepest confidence with so very few. Yet he has been my teacher, as much as your husband was yours."

"He is a great man," Margaret said honestly. "Perhaps one of the greatest men in Texas. But not entirely without flaws – no man truly is. Even my husband had faults, and I confess that my father has many of them. I have come to think that a wife's duty is to . . . either ameliorate such faults, or to encourage a husband to rise above them by bettering himself. "

"I agree with you that the General . . . my husband," Margaret Lea acknowledged, with earnest determination, "is a great man. And my task is to help him become greater still, as he is capable, but to do so humbly. For I do not think he would willingly accept a greater master, unless it was our Lord and Master of all."

"You have done very well so far," Margaret observed. Really, she did very much like the General's Margaret. For looking so sweet and shy, she had a spine of steel under that silk, and perhaps they were better matched than appeared so at first. "You have tamed a wily, scarred old tomcat, the veteran of many battles who has run through at least three or four of his own lives – into being a tame puss who wants nothing more than a bowl of milk and to curl up on a soft cushion before the parlor fire."

"You think?" Margaret Lea smiled sideways at her. "Oh, he is scarred; some of them dreadful, enough to break your heart to look at and think of the pain it costs him and still does. Be does have plenty of wildness left in him. You have not seen – and I pray you never do – the suit that he first wished to wear to be inaugurated in. All of green velveteen, with a hideous sort of flat Indian turban."

"All of it?" Margaret asked in disbelief and Margaret Lea nodded. "Oh, what you have spared us, my dear!" and they laughed companionably over the books. Meanwhile, the boys and General Sam were down on their knees on the rag rug. General demonstrated how the thin line attacked Santa Anna's Mexican army at San Jacinto; a single rank of corn-husk soldiers, with Johnny's horses to one side to represent the cavalry, and a pair of thread-spools from Margaret's mending basket for the two cannon, which had been cast in Cincinnati by a subscription among sympathizers to the cause of Texas freedom and sent at great expense down the river to New Orleans and by sea to Velasco. The afternoon passed with remarkable swiftness, so swift and pleasurable that Margaret was hardly aware of it, until a beaming Morag came into the parlor bearing a tray with a china coffeepot, cups, plates, and a plate of fresh-baked bread, with jam and butter. Morag had brought another plate of it for the boys, who were immediately distracted from their recreation of the great battle by the prospect of something to eat. General Sam dusted off the knees of his trousers and joined his wife and Margaret at the table.

"Fine boys," he said, with admiration and approval. "This was another reason and cause, my dear, to envy Horace Vining."

"We shall have our own, in good time." Margaret Lea answered with serene confidence, "as they are given to us."

General Sam took a healthy bite of bread and butter. "And clever, too," he added. "The youngest – Jamie is it? Now, he is the bold lad; a born soldier if I ever saw one and I know the breed well. I was such a one myself."

"He is not the youngest," Margaret said. "That is Peter – but he is only two years old. He was just a baby when my husband went back East. He will not remember his father, such a sad thing! The other boys – they recall him well and dearly, but Peter will have no recollection of him at all."

"Save in the hearts of those who thought well of him, and continue to burnish his memory," General Sam affirmed stoutly, "and will speak of him and his qualities to those who cannot remember at first hand. Dear Mrs. Vining; that is our history, the best and finest of our people, and we must recall them and their noble deeds to those lately born and still unborn! How can we remember what we are, what we may yet be called to become, if we lack the example and inspiration of our forebears? Raise your sons with the memory of their noble father and words of his most valorous deeds always on your lips!"

And leaving the memory of his most ignoble deed in my heart, Margaret thought. *It was the General himself who counseled me in this, saying that scandal will eventually die when gossip has no purchase. He did not ask the reason for my distress, that day when he met me by the riverside and I was weeping because I had just discovered that Race was married to another woman besides myself. He asked nothing, only listened, and advised that we settle it between ourselves, that it was no one's business but our own.* She met General Sam's shrewd and sympathetic eye, and knew without a doubt that he also was recalling that day.

"Good lads," General Sam remarked again. "For you, Mrs. Vining, they are the sons of a Cornelia; an ornament better than any jewels, eh?"

"They are everything to me," Margaret answered. "My daily care is to see that they are educated well, and take up a profession that their father would have approved. He did not own much property in Texas – only a small town-lot in Gonzales."

"You should apply for a grant of land in your name, as the widow of a veteran," the General suggested. Inwardly, Margaret cringed; she would have to file affidavits and statements regarding her status as her husband's widow. She could not bear the thought of a deeper inquiry and what it might reveal.

"I will consider that, when the year is up," she answered, with outward calm. "Truly, there is so much land that I fear it is not so much valued. If it were dear, I might value it altogether more. A good town-lot in a prosperous region would be of more use to me than a thousand acres of wilderness, even if the land is rich and well-watered."

"You should consider applying in any case," General Sam advised. "Even in quantities, land has a value; if not for yourself, then for the boys. It is a pity that you must be living so far out at the edge of our settlements, though. Have you never considered moving to a more settled part of Texas, to Galveston or to Harrisburg? Even to Bexar, perhaps."

"I would not," Margaret shook her head. "We lived in San Felipe for a time, then Gonzales with my husband, but this is where we made our home since and I have become so fond of it that I would never leave. After the next Legislative session, I am planning to enlarge the house once again."

"I fear that it will take a long time for this place to be truly secure," General Sam answered. For a moment, Margaret thought that a shadow passed over his face; that he would say something more, but he did not.

They talked a little while longer, the casual companionable talk of friends, Margaret realizing with some surprise that General Sam and his Margaret were both well on the way to becoming her friends, friends of the heart. At last, with the afternoon sun dropping low and touching the edges of the trees with gold and silvering the reaches of the distant Colorado, General Sam and his Margaret took their leave. They could not stay to supper, having a previous invitation. Margaret saw them to the door, thanking them again for their company.

"I think this must be a notable occasion," she confessed. "A consolation visit – and I have actually been consoled by your presence!"

"Our profound pleasure," General Sam answered, with a glint of amusement in his eyes, as he tipped his hat to her. Margaret Lea's smile once more revealed her dimples. The trap rolled away, down the long sweep of hillside, between the rows of Alois Becker's treasured apple trees, with their bare branches holding up the swelling blossom buds to the sky.

Margaret straightened her shoulders, feeling at least a little guilty for having spent the afternoon in the parlor, when there was supper to be prepared. But oh – it had been so pleasant! She had spent the last year under a shadow. Now she felt as if she had come out into the sunshine again. There was only one small speck of disquiet in her mind – which she could not quite put her finger upon. Something in General Sam's expression when she had mentioned expanding the house after the Legislature next met. He had looked . . . Margaret searched for a word, and could not find it – but his expression was so like Jamie's when he had been caught in some mischief and was considering an evasive answer. Yes, that was it; General Sam had some notion in mind, something he knew but did not want to say anything of. He was a man, as her husband had once acknowledged, who played his cards very close to his vest, taking no one into his confidence. This very day, Mrs. Eberly had mentioned rumors of the Legislature meeting elsewhere. Could General Sam, having been reelected as President, now change the capital city of Texas once again? Just by ordering it? The thought made Margaret most uneasy; General Sam had never liked having the Legislature meet in Austin – too close to the frontier, too vulnerable to Comanche raids, or from Mexico. But she and Mrs. Eberly, Seamus O'Doyle the carpenter, Mr. Bullock the innkeeper, and so many others; they had invested, built businesses in the expectation of the town of Austin growing and growing well. Margaret frowned. This was something that she should have one of her 'thinks' about; one of those matters that she must contemplate quietly and at length.

As she turned to go back into the house, her father came around from the barn and stable yard at the back of the house, a pair of his oxen clumping obediently after them; he had been at work all afternoon, plowing the first of the two cornfields he still kept in cultivation. He was scowling, as usual – a big man with thinning fair hair and an untidy beard, grubby and burned by the sun after a day working in the open.

"They gone yet?" he growled, in German, the language that Margaret and her brothers had grown up speaking. "If they had stayed much longer, I swear they would have spent the night."

"Yes, they have just departed," Margaret answered. Her father grunted. He sounded neither pleased nor unhappy. On impulse Margaret asked, "Papa, would you ever consider leaving this place, and taking up a plot of land elsewhere?"

"No, I would not," he answered, gruffly. "This is where your mother and Rudi lived and were happy; not Mexicans, Indians nor your guests would ever make me leave the hearth that I built for them."

"That is what I thought, Papa." Margaret said. She closed the door behind her. *Papa might have built the hearth,* she thought, *but I have made it into our home – and neither of us will ever leave.*

Chapter 2 – *Hearth and Home*

With so few boarders in residence, Margaret's older children had a place at the supper table that evening; Horace, Johnny and Jamie were still afire with the thrill of having met the great General Sam. Of the two boarders present when Morag brought out the soup, only Mr. Hattersley the Englishman was prepared to be indulgent with the boys. Dr. Williamson merely grunted an acknowledgement and moved the medical journal in which he was completely absorbed a little to one side so that Morag could ladle soup into his dish. Margaret was quite accustomed to Dr. Williamson spending much of suppertime engrossed in his reading, with his glasses slipping down his nose. He was a tall man, a little stooped and appallingly absentminded, who used his fork and knife with delicate precision. His features looked as if they had been roughed out with a hatchet, but his eyes were mild and light blue, under a thatch of pale brown hair only a little streaked with gray which Margaret secretly thought looked like frost-killed weeds. He was very busy, as a doctor of medicine, surgery and phrenology, although his practice had fallen off once so many people had abandoned Austin for the east. He did find time, when he remembered, to tutor Horace and Johnny in botany, anatomy, geography and what he termed as 'natural science.' He had tended her husband and had been the one to bring her the news of his death, far away in Boston. Margaret liked and trusted him, although his fits of absentmindedness often drove Hetty mad.

She was still in two minds about her second boarder, to whom Hetty referred with open scorn, as 'that la-de-dah Englishman.' Mr. Adolphus Hattersley claimed to be from London and Bristol and had come to Texas to start a newspaper. Failing that, he wrote for a number of different newspapers in England as their Texas correspondent. He frequently took extensive notes on matters of interest, which he usually explained airily were for his articles or the novel that he was writing. Margaret liked him for his company at table and in the evenings; he was gentle-spoken, but possessed an acerbic wit. In his features and dandified habits of dress he rather reminded her of Race, but for that very same likeness which attracted her very greatly, she was also inclined to be wary of trusting him as she trusted Dr. Williamson and her third regular boarder, Seamus O'Doyle.

Seamus O'Doyle was every bit as Irish as his name implied, red of hair and as talkative as the day was long. He was a skilled carpenter and cabinetmaker by trade, a master-craftsman and skilled in the art of shaping wood to every beautiful and useful purpose. In exchange for his board and

17

bed, Seamus had done the work of expanding Alois Becker's original house – a plain log blockhouse of two rooms with a loft – into the present incarnation. By degrees, he had walled in what had been the front and back verandahs to make four more rooms, adorned and lit by tall windows, and transforming what had been a simple loft into three tiny chambers accessed by a narrow staircase enclosed with simple, yet ornamental panels. He had recently contracted with the French legate to Texas to begin constructing a fine residence for him. Just that morning Seamus O'Doyle had strode whistling down the hill with a roll of sketches and plans under one arm and a copy of *The American Builder's Companion* in the other. He had shown the plans for the new Legation to Margaret; a large and airy residence, which Margaret envied wholeheartedly. She and Seamus had planned for months to expand her father's house in the same elegant style, once the next legislative session had brought enough of the right sort of boarder to town – and to her establishment, rather than to Mrs. Eberly's establishment or the Bullock's Inn – a rambling and ramshackle collection of log and sawn-plank structures at the corner of Congress Avenue and Pecan Street. He was also a distant cousin of Hetty and Morag; Margaret thought he rather styled himself as their protector and guardian.

"Where is the O'Doyle fellow tonight?" Mr. Hattersley asked, noting the empty place at the table with a lifted eyebrow. "He is usually punctilious about meals."

"I believe he is invited to dine with the French Legate tonight," Margaret answered, "to finish the plans for the house."

Mr. Hattersley snorted in open disparagement, "Business over the supper table – how very vulgar, but just what one would expect."

Dr. Williamson looked up from his book, frowning. "Well, what should one talk about then?"

"The finer things." Mr. Hattersley answered. "Art, music, the theater, and literature – even just the odd bit of gossip about the Court. Politics, as long as what is said is edifying and instructive."

"That's why I bring a book to the table," Dr. Williamson retorted. "We don't have anything of that sort in Austin." Margaret hid a smile: poor Mr. Hattersley. Sometimes she wondered why he had come to Texas, since he appeared to take very little interest or enjoyment from his life and employment. From remarks and allusions which he made now and again, she had the impression that he had once been much wealthier and reduced by some misfortune to scribbling for newspapers. He also seemed well-acquainted with the practice of law. Now Margaret ventured, "I recall that you and my husband would often monopolize the conversation when you spoke about books and other matters of the mind."

"Ah, but my dear Mrs. Vining, at present it becomes difficult – not to say impossible – to hold up both ends of a conversation across the dining table," Mr. Hattersley answered.

Jamie boldly asked, "Why can't you carry on both sides of dee convers-convers-concertation?"

"Conversation, Jamie. Don't speak with your mouth full," Margaret chided. An expression of distaste briefly crossed Mr. Hattersleys' face as Jamie repeated the question.

"Because I am on one side of the table, and I cannot get up fast enough to run to the other side and make an answer," Mr. Hattersley replied.

Jamie chewed thoughtfully and swallowed. "Why can't you?" he asked, and Margaret answered, "Because he cannot. Don't be nonsensical, Jamie."

"What's non-non-sen-sikal mean, Mama?" Lately admitted to the supper table and the company of grown-ups, Jamie took full advantage by cross-questioning any who engaged his interest until his curiosity was sated, the other party exasperated beyond recall, or Margaret called a halt to the inquisition.

"It means don't ask questions to show off." Dr. Williamson emerged from his book, as he was accustomed to do at odd and sudden intervals.

"I'm not showing off," Jamie persisted, the very picture of wounded innocence. "I really want to know."

"If you listen and pay careful observation, lad, you might not need to ask so many questions," Dr. Williamson replied. Any other five-year old might have been crushed to silence, but not Jamie.

"But you said that we should always ask questions . . . that it was the scientific meth-method."

"That is in a different context, and not over the supper table. Dr. Williamson retreated into his reading, while Mr. Hattersley grimaced and observed, "I confess that I am lately become a convert to the precept of children being seen and not heard."

Jamie opened his mouth and Margaret hastily forestalled him with a general rebuke.

"Boys – eat your supper. Recall that you have two eyes, and two ears, but only one mouth. You should look and listen four times as often as you speak."

Outside the dining room, the front door opened with a rattle of the wooden latch and a creak of hinges. In a moment Seamus O'Doyle appeared in the doorway, the *Builder's Companion* under his arm, saying, "Och, I trust that I am not too late to have a place laid for me?"

"We thought you were dining at with M'seiur Dubois's tonight," Margaret explained, as Morag emerged from the kitchen with a plate of soup in her hands.

"So I did," Seamus O'Doyle sat down, rubbing his hands in anticipation, "when I set out this foine morning, but it seems that Mr. Dubois' establishment has become disarranged, as Mr. Bullock continues taking exception with the treatment of his pigs."

"Good lord, not that again!" Mr. Hattersley exclaimed in amazed disgust. Dr. Williamson emerged from his book just long enough to opine, "Those pigs are a menace. Dubois did right in ordering his man to kill a few. Pity he didn't kill them all."

"Ah, but then Mr. Bullock would be three times as angry as he is. Last month they went at in the street, ye know. Hammer and tongs it was, with Innkeeper Bullock wi' a proper shillelagh in his hand, administering a right good thumping to M'seiur Pluyette for the killing of the pigs as he was ordered to. Gave a good account of himself, so the Frenchie did – but he could scarce see for the blood pourin' down. He ran and took shelter in t'other Frenchie's grocery store, while Mr. Bullock stood outside shoutin' the most vile abuse, th' like of which I niver thought I would hear!" Seamus O'Doyle shook his head sadly, while Mr. Hattersley drawled, "Sounds like an evening in the finest drawing room in Dublin, I'd say. What then, oh gentle backwoods Beau Brummel and arbiter of public discourse?"

"This very afternoon, Dubois, the Comte de la-de-dah or whatever the bitty little man is calling himself – went to pay a call on the American *chargie-dee-affrays.*"

Seamus O'Doyle looked expectantly around the table for their reactions, and had none until Margaret put in, "That is Colonel Flood – and he took rooms at . . . oh, dear. At Bullock's Inn." Which circumstance had rather annoyed Margaret, for she would have been well-honored to have Colonel Flood in residence, but it appeared that he preferred to overlook the pigs and the mud of Pecan Street in favoring convenience and company at Bullock's – rather than comfortable, airy rooms in her house, and the allure of Hetty's beautifully flaky biscuits. "What happened then, Mr. O'Doyle?"

"Oh, thin it was become comic, truly it did, Marm. Mr. Bullock barred the door to him, would not allow him to enter at all. There they stood, Mr. Bullock in the door and Mr. Dubois in the street, screeching that he had a perfect right to enter, in the conductin' of his duties on the pairt o' *le Francois*

– and him so angered that even his ears were gone red, until Mr. Bullock shook him as a terrier shakes a rat an' threatened to beat him to death if he ever tries to come through his door again."

"Singular way for an innkeeper to treat guests," Mr. Hattersley murmured. "Even guests of guests in the conduct of their official duties. But then, Texas is a singular place. Do continue, O'Doyle."

"Aye, so thin Mr. Dubois walks away, while Mr. Bullock shouting afther him, and who is the first pairson he meets but Secretary Chalmers – the Treasury man, don't ye know?"

"A Treasury most particularly unique for having nothing of note within it," Mr. Hattersley nodded, with apparent interest.

"Aye, well, 'tis not his fault, is it?" Seamus O'Doyle answered. "An' Dubois – thin he began to make complaint to Johnny Chalmers o'er the way he has been treated, bigod, demandin' that the full power o'the administration punish Mr. Bullock for his *'lay majesty'* as he says it. An' poor Johnny Chalmers only wants his supper, d'ye see – and here he must stand in th' street wi' Dubois screechin' in his face, so angered that he's forgettin' his English at the best of times – an' finally he says to Dubois, 'Aye, and if you had spoken so to me at the door of me own house, I would nay ha' bothered wi' me fists, I'd have gotten out my gun an' shot you down like a dog, so help me god.' You'll be perceiving Johnny Chalmers isn't anythin' of a diplomat, not least when he is starving for a bite o' supper."

"A simple yet subtle marvel of observation." Mr. Hattersley shook his head. "So, what happened then, oh Ossian of the supper-table?"

"Aye well, no much." Seamus O'Doyle began eating the soup, which had been growing cold. "Dubois was so fair angry, he'd lost all of his English. I thought better of remainin' to supper, for I did no' think his company would be congenial. Which is a pity, for his clarry is very fine, an' I was thinkin' that we might come to some decision about the fireplaces within the grand new house. Such a temperamental man!"

"Not good to be tangled up in his affairs, O'Doyle." Dr. Williamson emerged from his book, rather like a swimmer coming up to the surface to breath. "Too much talk about how Dubois de Saligny would benefit from that pet bill of his."

"The Franco-Texian bill," Mr. Hattersley agreed, "setting up another entrepreneur grant to settle the frontier with Frenchmen – just as Austin and DeWitt and how many other dreamers did with Americans. It didn't pass, did it?"

"Aye," Seamus O'Doyle shook his head sadly. "The House approved, but it never went to the Senate, for whilst General Sam approved, others did not. 'Tis an old-fashioned means of bringing in settlers, so they say. Pity of it – eight thousand of *le Francois* would fill up the empty country a treat, so it would. An' do no end o' good when it came to fine clarry an' better food . . . present company excepted, o'course." He added hastily, and Dr. Williamson grunted, "But not when it came to adding more excitable Frenchman having tantrums in the streets. Dubois and his lot are about as much as I can endure."

Spring came on, gentle and fair, adorning the meadows with wildflowers – that from a distance looked as if the hills had been splashed with swaths of color; pink primrose, pale lavender verbena, and that white-tipped blue prairie clover that some folk called blue bonnets. On a mild early spring day, Horace and his brothers were hauling buckets of muck from the pile by the stable to the garden plot and digging it well in; a pure joy, Margaret thought, for boys to play in the dirt. When the laundry was done drying, folded and put away with sachets of dried verbena and rose-petals among their folds to scent them, she would begin working in the garden plot. Farther down the gentle slope which the house and its ramble of outbuildings sat upon, Alois Becker ploughed over one of his large pastures, heedless of the flowers, as he stumped along behind the ox team laboring to draw the steel plough blade. Margaret, hanging out wet sheets to dry in the fresh breeze on clotheslines strung from the back of the house, thought that he looked not unlike an ox himself, with his head bent forward from his broad shoulders. She tried to count up the times that she had seen her father actually smile in the last five years. It was as if all pleasure in life and all natural happiness within him had been extinguished, with the lives of his oldest son and wife during one wet and bitter spring.

Margaret took up another wrung-out sheet from the basket at her feet and pegged a corner to the clothesline. In the space of five years the awful tug of grief at her heart when she thought of Mama and Rudi had lessened to a dull ache, not least because they had been superseded by a fresher and even more personal grief. Mama was buried in a meadow near Harrisburg, under a tree with four limbs reaching up like a many-branched candlestick. She fell sick in the last days of their frantic journey east, fleeing the vengeful, murderous army of Lopez de Santa Anna, fell sick with the bloody flux and died of it almost immediately. Mama – Maria Becker – was buried within the same hour that the ragged Texian army was defeating that enemy, shouting "Remember the Alamo, Remember Goliad!" and calling for a Santa Anna quarter. Race had been there and seen the carnage, had told her later that Alois Becker had fought like a madman, not even pausing to reload but using the butt of his musket like a club. *Remember the Alamo. Remember Goliad.* Her younger brothers Rudi and Carl were part of Colonel Fannin's garrison at the old citadel of La Bahia at Goliad, captured after the fight at Coleto Creek. A week later, upon orders from Lopez de Santa Anna, they and nearly four hundred of their fellows were marched out of the citadel, led into the countryside and executed at point-blank range by their guards. In the confusion of murder and black-powder smoke, sixteen-year-old Carl escaped, jumping into the nearby river, making his way home on foot and alone, traveling at night like an animal for weeks and weeks, and never daring to show himself. Margaret took a wooden pin from her apron pocket and pegged the other end of the sheet to the clothesline.

Five years ago this spring; they had returned from the east, she and Race and Papa, and the two oldest boys, stopping only long enough in Gonzales to retrieve Race's trunk of books, buried safely under the roots of a neighbors' redbud tree. There was nowhere else for them to go. Their home was burnt to the ground along with everyone else's and Race was already sickening with the consumption that would eventually kill him. Nowhere to go, save to Papa's holding at Waterloo on the upper Colorado. Some weeks after that, Carl came home to Waterloo as well . . . to a cold welcome from Papa, as Rudi had always been his favorite. Margaret took up another wrung-out sheet and pegged a corner to the clothesline, remembering. *It was not Papa's fault*, she reminded herself again. *Rudi was Papa's oldest, the son that he had put all of himself into, cherished with affection like a king cherishes the crown prince – his heir and all that matters in the kingdom, even if the kingdom is but a league and a labor of a Mexican land grant.* Rudi, vital and laughter-loving, dead in a field; his body burnt to ashes in a pit by the road between La Bahia and Victoria. If something had died in Alois Becker, something died also in his youngest son. Carl – her Carlchen, so much younger than herself that he seemed as of he were one of her sons. He remained only for a few months, silent and withdrawn, unable to endure sleeping inside walls. Then he was off to join a company of rangers raised by Erastus Smith for Texas. He had come home twice since then, and the second visit only a few moments in duration, to water the horses as he and others pursued Buffalo Hump's Comanche warriors, fleeing after their defeat at Plum Creek.

Why did these times so often feel as if they walked on a knife-edge? Margaret wondered, as she hung out another sheet. She had not felt this way when she had lived in Gonzales with her parents; nor when she had married

Race Vining – although surely there had been desperate times now and again. To remember that time before was to call up memories of a Garden of Eden for Margaret. There had always been Comanche raids, but they had bothered the Mexicans far more than the American settlers. And there sometimes had been trouble with the Mexican government, especially as the Centralists were forever grappling with the Federalists. But Texas had been far, far from all that. It was only when the Centralists had taken over rule in Mexico that troubles had begun to stalk the American settlements along the Brazos, the Colorado, and the Guadalupe. This was cause for one of her 'thinks' – a matter to ponder until she came up with a resolution or an answer. Margaret had done this since she was a child. If she sat and thought about something which had perplexed her, worried over it like a woman carefully untangling a skein of yarn – very often she could come up with a rationale or a reason, some shred of understanding.

Before she could continue puzzling over this, Hetty came from the house, bearing another heavy basket of wet sheets and laundry. "'Tis the last of it, so 'tis, I swear to ye, Marm," she puffed. Around them, the white sheets waved like banners in the light spring breeze, which brought the rich smell of turned earth to them both. Alois had been at it since before sunup. Hetty shaded her eyes with her hand. "The Old Sir has done a good few rows now, has he not? A champion hand with a plough!"

"He is that," Margaret agreed, as Hetty took the empty basket. "I believe that work is his only solace these last five years."

Margaret continued with hanging out damp laundry, and her 'think.' *When had this 'walking on a knife-edge' feeling become so marked, this sense that the world had become a threatening place, that even if the sun shone in a clear blue sky – there were still shadows in which monsters lurked, shadows like Lopez de Santa Anna and his minions?* She thought a little more on it, flipping through her memories as if she were leafing through a book. When had war come upon them? About the time of the Anahuac troubles, when Horace was a small boy and Johnny a baby; that's when her sense of danger began developing. *But why then?* She wondered . . . was it the children? Ah, yes; that was it. She and Race had children. Having children – that was what made her sense of danger so acute, then. One thought little of dangers on your own account; her brother Carlchen was a Ranger and seemed to be completely heedless of perils – in fact, to rather relish them. Margaret thought that he must care little for danger to his own person, venturing on long scouts with his fellows into the Comanche-haunted wild lands, beyond the Llano. But she had children, and having them and fearing for their safety; that made her keenly aware of perils which formerly would have been of little moment. No, Margaret thought, as she hung up the last of the sheets: there must have been dangers enough, from the moment that Papa brought her and Mama, Rudi and Carl to Texas – it was just that as a child herself, she cared little for it, and would only see the garden around. It was only in growing up and having your own children that such dangers became manifestly visible.

That summer, the house for the French legate, Mr. Dubois, the Comte-de-la-de-dah as Seamus O'Doyle called him and others termed the No-Count – was finished and entirely fitted, although Mr. Dubois had departed Austin in considerable of a dudgeon over how he had fared in the matter of what was becoming known as the Pig War. Such an altercation as the one between Mr. Dubois and Innkeeper Bullock was too public and risible to be ignored for long; others besides Mr. Hattersley wrote accounts of the dispute for many newspapers. Margaret had privately always thought that Richard Bullocks' pigs were a hazard, an ugly and aggressive hazard, foraging everywhere, without regard to cleanliness or private property, and took a small private satisfaction in that they were never tempted to roam as far as Papa's house – not even the temptation of her own lush garden would have decoyed them far from the midden-pits of town. Although she was inclined to take M. Dubois's side – in that he had been provoked by Mr. Bullock's pigs, frequently and rudely invading the garden, even venturing into the rooms of his little framed-wood rented house on Pecan Street – people the length and breadth of Texas took deep offense at Mr. Dubois' lordly insistence on special privilege for himself and his household. As if the government of Texas would take the side of a snotty, stuck-on-himself foreigner who couldn't be bothered to build a stout fence, or hire a man who would! In the end, readers cheered for the pigs, and Mr. Dubois felt the derision so keenly that he spent more time away from Austin. There was a demand for him to be recalled by his government for being so arrogant and high-handed. Another story put about was that he had hoped to profit in the entrepreneur scheme proposed by the Franco-Texian bill, and he had paid a local teamster for carting a load of lumber for his house with counterfeit money – although most people put no credence in that last bit of gossip.

"Having angered and alienated all whom he has come into contact with, now he packs up his portmanteau and has as little to do as he can with the people and government of Texas. Quite the diplomat, I must say," Mr.

Hattersley observed over the supper table. Seamus O'Doyle smiled blandly and answered, "Faith, an' you might take him for an Englishman, almost."

Seamus O'Doyle could afford to be humorous about the Comte de-la-de-dah; the house was finished and he had been well-paid for his work – work which had allowed him full range to exercise to his particular skill in carpentry and cabinet-making. The departing legate had sold it entire to a friend of his, another Frenchman, an urbane and much more tactful gentleman who was – or so Seamus O'Doyle assured them all – an archbishop, Father Odin. Margaret had met him once or twice; when he conducted Mass. Seamus, Hetty and Morag attended faithfully, and spoke very well of him. But Father Odin was often away on church business and did not actually do more than spend an odd night or two under the graceful roof of the house that the Legate had paid for. Father Odin had the whole of Texas in his care; one late summer Sunday afternoon, Seamus O'Doyle offered to show Margaret and Hetty how he had finished the house. Of the outside, they could see plainly, sitting white and colonnaded on a distant height much like the one that Alois Becker had built upon, when Waterloo was a stout timber stockade in the valley below and a straggle of farms among the hills and streamlets. Margaret eagerly agreed. She had been curious about the inside of the Legation ever since Seamus O'Doyle began drawing plans for it.

"'Tis a plain design," Seamus allowed, "like to many old houses in Louisiana – built tall from the ground, with a deep gallery across the front and long windows – to take advantage of the air, y'll see." He handed Margaret and Hetty down from the trap which he had borrowed. Dr. Williamson climbed down without any assistance, and looked around. He didn't have his glasses, so Margaret knew that all he was seeing was a green and white blur. "The house is over there, Doctor," Seamus added, helpfully.

The white house crowned the low hill, set in a scattering of oak trees. The roof of split cypress shingles sloped gently on all four sides, and then spread out like wings, with a gentle extension over the deep gallery in front. Three ornate dormers, trimmed with a low balustrade-railing hinted at an upper story. Pairs of white-painted pillars were spaced along the verandah edge; the windows that Margaret could see along the front were actually long French-style double doors, fitted with glass.

"Y'see, when the Legate entertained – an' oh, my did the Comte de la-de-dah entertain the quality an' nobility –" here, Dr. Williamson snorted, and Margaret giggled outright, "of our fair city, he planned for a bounteous o'er flowing of guests." The front door was unlocked; Seamus O'Doyle opened it and called within. An answering voice came from the back of the house. Seamus opened the door wider, to allow Margaret, Hetty and Dr. Williamson to enter a long hall, paneled in warm, yellow-painted canvas, which seemed to stretch the length of the house. The door at the back stood half-open, for the day was already hot, and the man who stood in the doorway was in his shirtsleeves with a dirty apron tied over.

"Aye, M'seiur Pluyette – the visitors I spoke of, to see the house. No need to disturb yer fine self to show us around." M. Pluyette sketched a brief salute and vanished from the door. Seamus explained, "The kitchen is out that way, separate from the house. And there is a stable, too – for the Comte de la-de-dah keeps a fine lot o' horses. There are four main rooms, y'see: parlor an' dining room in front – though if it is a grand dinner, this hall might serve, for it is all but a room in itself. 'Tis said the furniture came all the way from Paris." A pair of tall double doors faced each other in the hallway, both of them also standing open to admit air. The house retained a very pleasant airy coolness, most welcome after the afternoon's heat. Margaret looked into the nearest of them; a parlor, set with elegant furniture – a number of finely upholstered chairs and a pair of settees all in orange and trimmed in gold, which contrasted pleasingly with the walls – canvas painted in a pale grass-green. The windows – all fitted with glass, stood open to the light breeze.

"'Tis as foine as th' Hall, when Mam was a girl," Hetty breathed. "Oh, Marm – isn't it beautiful? An' this would be the dining room!" That was the room opposite. The walls in that room were light pink; the seats of the chairs arrayed at regular intervals around the table were upholstered in pale pink damask. Hetty ran her finger critically along the top of the polished wood dining table, and observed, "Dust! A pity, Marm – men would niver see t' dusting the way a woman does. But oh, 'tis grand, is it not!"

"I am indeed envious," Margaret said, wistfully. "Not for the colors so much, but the space and the elegance." She was overtaken with envy for the Legate's house; so very different from the houses she had ever lived in or seen from a distance in Texas, houses which now seemed small, crude and mean. How lovely it would be to live in these generous and airy spaces; and how marvelous to entertain graciously, never worrying about having guests accidentally tread on one of her sons' toys, or encounter her father's irascible temper. The new rooms that Seamus O'Doyle had enclosed on the front and the back – now seemed cramped and inadequate in comparison. And she had been so proud of them before!

"Th' fireplace design – that we took from Benjamin's *Builders' Companion*," Seamus O'Doyle pointed out with pride, "an' I will do the' same fer yoursel', Mrs. Vining, easy enough."

"Can you imagine how pleasant it would be to sit and have supper in a room like this, Doctor?" Margaret asked, for Dr. Williamson was busy polishing his glasses. He put them on again, and looked around the dining room, very carefully.

"It's a room," he answered. "I can't see that it would make the food taste better."

"Oh, but it's a house such as they build in the east!" Margaret exclaimed. "Without fear of war or raiding Indians – or indeed anything but the heat of summer!"

"Or the envy of neighbors," Seamus O'Doyle added, jovially. He took them around to the rest of it, the two rooms at the back, which were smaller, and less ornamental: one fitted out as a bedroom, the other as a study. Margaret and Hetty approved it all most heartily while Dr. Williamson appeared to be mildly baffled by their interest.

"Some day," Margaret said, as the trap bumped away from the Legate's house, "I shall have a house every bit as fine as that one. Not with the colored walls, though – I did not much care for the look of that."

"As you wish it, Marm," Seamus O'Doyle answered. "So will you have!"

Although Margaret took to studying the *Builder's Companion,* it soon became clear that the expansion of her father's house was not to be something that would happen soon. She had thought that when the proper year of mourning was done, when she could adorn her black dress with touches of white, or even lavender-purple – that would be the time to begin plans. After Legislature came to Austin in the spring of the next year, and filled the rooms of the house with boarders; that would be when she would have the money to build on rooms as airy and elegant as she desired, rooms with French doors set with glass and opening onto shaded galleries. She looked forward to the project nearly as much as she looked forward to the end of her year of mourning, but by early spring, rumors were flying, rumors of an invasion from Mexico.

"There are always rumors in the spring, of another invasion," Margaret said indignantly, when this rumor was first brought to her by Mrs. Eberly. Margaret had begun to think of her as a storm-crow, clad in black and always croaking of doom and gloom. Really, the other woman seemed to take a great relish in bad news.

Mrs. Eberly shook her black-bonneted head. "This time, folk are taking it serious, Miz Vining. They remember how it was when Santy-Anna came to Bexar with all his army late in winter. They say that he wants Texas back, no matter what he promised by treaty – a treaty that was tore up as soon as our back was turned. An' Austin is not that far from Bexar, as an army marches. Them as are Texians who live in Bexar, they've been getting warnings from their Meskin friends for weeks to leave while they can. I have no reason to think them wrong. They did it before, an' them Meskins over the Nueces, they hold a grudge."

"This time we have an army of our own," Margaret said, "and companies of Rangers, too. We should not be caught by surprise; still wrangling over what – if anything – we ought to do in the face of a threat, as our convention was doing then."

"So we may have," Mrs. Eberly answered, shaking her head dolefully, "but I have lost three more of my boarders in the last few weeks. That Frenchie Dulong who opened a mercantile on Pecan Street? He's closed up and gone away. If this keeps up, there won't be more than a hundred or two left in town."

"We would not leave," Margaret answered. "We fled in fear six years ago – it cost my mother her life and my husband his health. We will not be driven away again, even if we are the only ones remaining here."

Mrs. Eberly patted her knee, "Bravely said, Miz. Vining; I'm with you. I'm too plumb old to take to the road again, and I ain't afraid of Indians or Santy-Anna, neither. 'Sides, General Sam, he won't stand for any nonsense now, wouldn't he?"

She took her leave, and Margaret wondered if they both spoke from an abundance of bravado. She supposed that if she had word of the Mexicans coming again, she could bury the valuables as she had before. Papa was old and the children were young . . . but no. It would never come to that, not this time. The Mexicans would never be allowed to do more than skirmish now and again, along the contested lands, between the Rio Grande and the Nueces. No. They would be safe enough where they were, and much more secure within their own walls, under a sturdy roof than if they were to flee as they had before.

Chapter 3 – *Partnerships*

It turned out that Mrs. Eberly was at least partially right – the rumor of incursions from Mexico turned out to have some kind of basis, but whether it was just bandits and not uniformed Mexican soldiers was a matter of hot contention over hers and other supper tables, and in places such as the common parlor at Bullock's inn. To Margaret's unease, enough residents of Austin took the matter seriously enough to pack up their businesses and their trunks and leave for the greater perceived safety of the eastern lowlands, which had been long-settled by Americans taking up grants from Stephen Austin, or Green DeWitt. A neighbor, plowing his field in the middle of the day, was set upon and killed by three Indians: after that incident, Alois Becker took to carrying a rifle over his shoulder and the old single-shot pistol he had taken from San Jacinto thrust through his belt. What had been so promising a city not two years before appeared to be a town of ghosts, with many dwellings and businesses shuttered and deserted, no smoke rising from their chimneys of an evening, and the meadows beginning to reclaim the gardens and streets. A band of wandering Tonkawa Indians set up their skin lodges that spring, on the outskirts of town, welcomed for the fact that they also were enemies of the Comanche – and that they brought wild fruit, game and nuts to trade. Still, their camp did not make Austin look any more any more like the proper city that everyone had hoped for it,

"Things will pick up right enough when the Legislature meets again," Mrs. Eberly assured her one day when they happened to meet outside Simpson's general emporium.

"I wish I might be as sure as you are, Mrs. Eberly," Margaret replied and the older woman looked at her very keenly. "For one of my boarders is leaving – although not because of rumors. He said that business affairs call him back to England, and he will go at the end of this month."

"Miss him, will you?" Mrs. Eberly pursed up her lips.

Margaret sighed a little. "He had been a long time with us and a particular friend of my husband's. I feel that my business is on a knife-edge, a whisper from failing entirely. Although," she added, "the original necessity for opening our house to take in boarders is long gone. It was to secure a living for us all when my husband became so ill, and now that matter is not so urgent. But I still feel an obligation to educate my boys . . . and I would feel as if I had failed in my duty if I cannot do that through my own efforts. And I am about to lose another from household, but this was not unexpected."

"Oh? Another boarding gentleman?" Mrs. Eberly's expression was one of avid curiosity: Margaret suspected that she had taken up keeping an inn or a boardinghouse as a means of having a ready supply of gossip.

"No. Morag's young man has come to her sister and Mr. O'Doyle and I, asking our permission that they may wed this summer, since she has just turned seventeen."

"Eh, well — everyone knew that was going to happen," Mrs. Eberly commiserated. "Pretty young girl like that, she would have her pick of likely young sparks. Hers din't let the grass grow under him, anyway. Have you given permission? Is he a man with prospects and will be good to her?"

"I believe so," Margaret answered. "He and his two brothers own a saw mill near Mina. He has already built a fine house for the two of them to live in. His name is Dan Fritchie, and the only ill that Mr. O'Doyle can say of him is that he is not Irish. But he is honorable and well-spoken, and loves her very dearly. All who have known of him for a time also speak well of him; were Morag my own daughter, I would accept him as her suitor without any reservation. But," she sighed in a melancholy way that was not altogether because she would be losing the companionship of a girl of whom she and the boys were very fond. "He also is aware of the rumors. He wishes to marry her as soon as is practical so that she might be removed from such danger as he fears. I would so wish that he shared our confidence with regard to the future of this town. But he is adamant."

"Well, he has a business and a home already established." Mrs. Eberly patted her arm comfortingly. "When is the happy day planned, if I may be so bold?"

"Two Sundays from now," Margaret answered. "Father Odin is expected to return from his latest missionary journey. She is being married from our house; in the absence of any church building, he will perform the ceremony of marriage there – early enough in the morning that they will be able to travel as far as Hornsby's and take shelter there for the night." Margaret sighed again. "We barely have enough time to finish a quilt for her bride's chest. Will you come to our bee this Saturday? Hetty and I are trying to assemble as many suitable linens as we may. I have even gifted her with a fine blanket which my own mother wove."

"I will be there," Mrs. Eberly replied. "I and my stout needle, you may depend upon it. Your girl will be wed with a supply of household gifts that the Queen of England herself might envy!"

Margaret took her leave from Mrs. Eberly, reflecting that Angelina Eberly – storm-crow and inveterate gossip – was also possessed of such a stout heart that she might well have done credit to the position of sovereign Queen of England. If there was such a thing as petticoat government in Austin, then surely she was the chief executive. And she was not planning to abandon Austin any more than Alois Becker was, for which Margaret gave great credit.

Morag Moylan wed Daniel Fritchie on the day appointed, in what might have seemed like an indecent hurry to someone with a suspicious turn of mind. No, not the commonly supposed reason for hasty nuptials; Hetty guarded Morag too closely for any rumor of that sort to have gained purchase. But no one could deny the sense of panic in the air, which increased by degrees every time another man of business departed Austin. Before sunrise on a Sunday in July, young Daniel and Seamus O'Doyle, with the aid of Danny's brothers, Nicholas and Richard, loaded Morag's packed bride-chest into the back of his wagon, while upstairs Margaret and Hetty helped dress her in her best dress – which they had made for her, from deep-blue linsey-woolsey ornamented with a lace collar crocheted by Hetty from heavy silk thread.

In the parlor, Dr. Williamson and Mr. Hattersley made disjointed conversation with Father Odin, conversation made especially disjointed as Dr. Williamson was under the impression that Father Odin was a medical missionary, and kept steering the discussion back to matters medical.

"You look so pretty today, Morag," Margaret said; Morag was pink-cheeked with excitement and her eyes as bright as stars. *Oh,* Margaret wondered – *was I ever so young and trusting as dear Morag? I must have been, once, for I trusted my husband and put aside any doubts that I had of him.* "Are you ready to be married, then?" She tied the ribbons of Morag's bonnet under her chin, while Hetty put a tiny nosegay of prairie wildflowers into her hands: pink primroses and buffalo clover, the same deep-blue-trimmed-with-a-touch-of-white as Morag's dress.

"Oh, yes Marm!" she exclaimed, and Margaret patted her cheek. "As long as he is dear to you, and will be kind," she said, and then added with a sideways look at Hetty. "You do know – about marriage . . . about how a husband and wife share the same bed."

"Aye, I do that," Morag's blush deepened. "But it doesn't affright me, Marm, not at all – for I love Danny very much and it cannot be so very bad, for don't all married folk share a bed?"

"Good," Margaret answered, feeling a twinge of grief in her own breast. "The ones who truly care for each other do so, Morag."

"Aye, well then," Hetty was putting the last of Morag's clothing into a bundle. "So I'll take this down to th' lad, and tell Father Odin that yer ready." Hetty's eyelids were pink, with weariness and unshed tears, for she had stayed up late, finishing the last of the linens for Morag's new home, swearing that her younger sister should not go ill-dowered as a wife. Daniel Fritchie's kin would not have cause to think that the Moylans were a family of poor tinkers. She would go to it with the double-wedding-ring pattern quilt which the womenfolk of Austin had quilted for her and one of Margaret's precious red-wool blankets, which her own mother had rewoven from Mexican wool in the days when her family was new arrived in Texas. Margaret watched Hetty embrace her younger sister, wondering wistfully what it would be like to see a daughter married from under her roof. She would never know that bittersweet joy; her sons would no doubt bring their wives to hers. Perhaps that would be the only way she would gain a daughter.

"I hope that I will not frighten them too much." Margaret mused, unaware that she spoke aloud until Hetty asked, suspiciously, "Frighten who, Marm?"

"My sons' wives," Margaret answered, laughing a little at herself. Hetty laughed as well. "Marm, they shall be right terrified at the first, so they will indade! Morag was affrighted, that first day."

"Oh, Hetty – I was not!" Morag pinked even more, as Hetty answered briskly, "Aye, you were that afraid, when O'Doyle jumped down from the wagon, and Marm came out to the front, an' you whispered that she looked so fair an' terrible, like an avenging angel, like Queen Maeve o' the old stories. A little at first sight, Marm – you are terrifyin'," she added to Margaret. "But it passes away afther a wee while. Now, Morag, darlin' – are ye ready?"

"Yes, I am ready." Morag's face was bright with confidence, and Margaret recollected with satisfaction how she had blossomed like a rose, from the timid and frightened girl she had been when Seamus O'Doyle had brought his cousins to Austin two years ago. They had no place to go. If she had not had the keeping of her father's house, the education bequeathed to her by her husband – and the generous settlement from his horrified family – Margaret was certain that without those fortunate circumstances, she might have been in the very same desperate condition as the Moylan sisters.

There were but a handful of guests waiting downstairs in the parlor; Margaret's family and household, some of Daniel Fritchie's friends, his brothers Nicholas and Richard, Mrs. Eberly and her grown children and step-children, and Father Odin, beaming pacifically upon them all, as he intoned the first words of the sacrament of marriage, and the morning sun streamed in through the east-facing window as rich and golden as honey. Seamus

O'Doyle, with his face unaccustomedly serious and deathly pale under his freckles, stood in the place of Morag's father, as the nearest male kin; Hetty stood as her mother. It seemed to be over in a few minutes; Father Odin blessed the young couple, and then everyone partook of the wedding breakfast which Margaret and Hetty had laid out in the next room.

"That's one thing that I shall miss, when I am back in London," Mr. Hattersley remarked to Margaret; he had stood a little aside, as if he were a stranger observing from a distance. "The speed and efficiency of necessary social rituals among the less fortunate. One has hardly any time to enjoy them – but then one has no time to be bored by them. Shall they be happy, I wonder? Out in this desolate wilderness, among the savages?"

"I think they look very happy today," Margaret answered.

"Ah, but our own bard of the suppertable looks like a thundercloud," Mr. Hattersley pointed out. "I wonder what gripes at him today? Ah well, at least it's not the fear of loosing a good cook." Margaret maintained her serene expression with something of an effort. Lately, Mr. Hattersley seemed to be particularly waspish, as if he had no fear of angering any. Not for the first time, Margaret wondered what had brought him to Texas; he appeared to have little enough liking for any aspect of it whatsoever. Why would anybody come and waste two years and more of their life in a place which rubbed their skin and temper raw?

Her attention was distracted then, for young Mr. Fritchie was looking fondly at Morag, and saying, "We'd best be going now – else we'll be traveling after dark alone."

His mule team had been standing ready in harness for an hour or so already. They had planned to travel in company with others, and catch up to them on the road. A flurry of farewells, and Mrs. Eberly weeping sentimentally into a black-edged handkerchief; while Seamus O'Doyle drew Dan aside at the food of the steps and looked at him silently for a moment, with a face as dark as a storm-cloud.

"A word to ye, lad – an' then I'll hold m'peace for iver. Ye shall treat her well indade, for if I iver hear that you have made m'cousin unhappy . . . then it's m'self that shall come and take up the' matter with ye. I may be in heaven, more like in hell – but ye shall answer to me, regardless."

"No cause for worry, sir," the younger man answered bravely. "M'father told me always to treat women with all courtesy – and a wife with no less."

"See that you do, then," Seamus O'Doyle answered; still as dark as thunder, but if he had meant to say more, there was no time for it. He helped Morag up into the wagon-seat and then they were away. When Margaret thought to look around for Seamus O'Doyle, he was gone as well. She thought nothing much of it, for she had other guests for her to attend.

"If it weren't that Mr. Hattersley is leaving at the end of the month," she remarked to Hetty, as they put on their aprons in the kitchen and prepared to deal with the detritus of the wedding breakfast, "I might look to hire another girl to help . . . but since there are only the two now, I think we may handle the housekeeping between ourselves."

"Aye," and Hetty sniffed. "Oh, she looked so happy, she did, Marm. Thank you and God bless, for what you have done for her, today and all this time since. Our own Mam, God rest her soul," Hetty crossed herself hurriedly. "could not have done better, an' that's the truth of it."

"She's a dear child," Margaret answered, embarrassed by Hetty's gratitude. "But I did think she would marry sooner rather than later. I am ever surprised that you don't encourage admirers of your own, Hetty. You might be married from this house as well, given the right man."

"Och, I would not!" Hetty blushed and bridled. "I am not blind, Marm – I may look into a glass at myself an' know that my face will niver be my fortune."

"It need not be," Margaret answered briskly. "Your cooking is your fortune, and your hand with biscuits. It is often only young men who yearn after a pretty face. Truly, Hetty, yours is not unpleasing. I knew many girls and women in Gonzales whose features were plain, but they were clever enough to deploy a lively wit and character. They were loved no less for it and married just as well."

"I dinna know." Hetty looked thoughtful, as she scraped crumbs and scraps from plates into the pig-swill bucket. "Who would ye say I marry then, Marm?"

"Dr. Williamson," Margaret answered at once, for the image of the kindly but absent-minded doctor was the first older and unmarried man to pop into her head. Hetty burst out laughing. "No, do not laugh! He is an older man, steady and sober, he has a good trade, and he loves your cooking. If you put an effort into it, Hetty, you might have him tamed and eating from your hand. He might even recollect where he has left his spectacles or his hat more often. You would organize his house, his medical practice and his wardrobe, and he would in return worship you for it, everlastingly!"

Hetty was shaking her head, her face grave and contemplative. "Och, no, Marm. I do no' think I am made for marriage. Now an' again I thought o' takin' the veil, but I do no' think I have a vocation. Anyways, all that prayin' an' keepin' silent an' all? I dinna think I have the' patience for that, either. I would speak my mind to all, an' for that I would be thrown out o' enny convent I can think of."

"What would you do then?" Margaret asked. "What then would you do with your life, if not marriage or a nunnery?" Hetty paused, in her scraping of plates into the slop-bucket for Alois Becker's pigs. Her plain freckled face became suddenly thoughtful. "I dinna know, Marm. I like it foine here, the cookin' an the' housekeepin' wi' the boys an' the gentleman. It's as good a home as I have iver wanted. As long as I would earn a wage, I'd be content to stay as long as you like."

"And I'd like that as well," Margaret answered, but she was pricked by a twinge of conscience. Save for the cost of commodities such as cane-sugar and wheat flour, lamp-oil and newspaper subscriptions, Hetty's wages loomed large among her expenses. If the number of boarders fell off any farther, there would be no income at all, no way to pay Hetty what would be due to her for all her hard work. "There is a problem that I can see, though – not one that I have now," she added hastily, "but in the future. Seamus O'Doyle and Dr. Williamson will be our only boarders after Mr. Hattersley leaves in two weeks. Until the Legislature meets again, then they will be the only ones. This is a business, Hetty – for all that it looks like something that men are only due; clean sheets and good meals, the parlor dusted and the table set well with seven sweet and seven sour relishes. I am in it to earn money to provide for my sons, Hetty – being the only profitable trade that a respectable widow might take up. If the business falls off any more, I shall not be able to afford the cost of your wages. I should have no more need of a cook. You might have to seek employment elsewhere."

"Aye," Hetty nodded, her expression most somber. "I can see that, so I do, Marm. For mysel', I would be most sorry to leave this sityation, for it pleases me." Hetty looked around the kitchen – that room at the core of the house that Alois Becker had build of roughly-shaped logs when there was no town at all, merely a scattering of lonely farms. He had built his place to be a veritable blockhouse, and constructed a fireplace of stone in the German fashion, with a tall hearth and nearly large enough to roast a whole pig in it. With the first profits of the boardinghouse, Margaret had an enormous patent iron cook-stove installed within the fireplace enclosure. Alois Becker had grumbled about the expense, and about newfangled inventions, but Margaret had paid no mind, as it made cooking so much easier, and the stove even heated water in a large reservoir at the side. Bunches of drying herbs from the ceiling beams, and a row of copper pots, burnished to the color of ruddy gold hung above the stove, as they had when this had been the domain of Margaret's mother, Maria. The shelves of the corner cupboards fairly groaned beneath their burden of crockery, china and baking pans.

For two years this had been Hetty's small kingdom; Margaret read that pride of ownership in Hetty's face. Now, she had finished scraping the plates. Some of them went immediately into the pan of dishwater, and then she turned to face Margaret. "So – it's a matter o' me wages, then, is it?"

"Yes," Margaret answered. "That I could not afford them."

"Aye," Hetty frowned, deep in thought. "Might we consider a partnership thin, Marm? I would stay an' work – for a share, no matter how much or little, until you may pay wages again?"

"It might be very little," Margaret warned, although her spirits rose, jubilant; that was a solution. She had dreaded the thought of telling Hetty there was no more work for her and the thought of being without her company and help; how lonely it would be, without another woman! "You might work for nothing at all, rather than a steady wage?"

"Aye, so I would," Hetty answered, "but then I might do very well . . . when the Legislature returns. How should we share the profits, then?"

"A third to you, two thirds to me?" Margaret suggested; even with the reduced number of boarders, that would mean approximately what her regular wages would have been.

Hetty nodded assent. "Aye, when the bills are paid – that'll suit. You bring the house an' the proper manner, I bring a strong back! An' when the Legislature returns, that'll suit very well indade. One more . . ." Hetty wiped her hands dry on her apron, "If ye hire another girl I would like to keep the room t' mysel'. Befittin' my station as a partner, an' all," she added hastily, and Margaret laughed, much relieved.

"Then you shall have it, and we shall shake hands on sharing the risks of a business together!" They quickly grasped hands, while out in the little parlor the clock sweetly chimed the quarter hour. Hetty gasped, "Mother Mary, an' Joseph – it's past ten already, an' dinner not even begin! Oh, Marm – we shall have to keep an eye on business, fer sure an' all!"

"There will be none today for supper save the boys and my father," Margaret answered, "and in any case, everyone partook well of the wedding breakfast."

That night at supper, Seamus O'Doyle was not present; Margaret did not worry, for he often worked well into evening when the light held, but she did wonder what could be keeping him? No one was building anything in Austin, this nervous summer of 1842. Several men of the town and travelers on the road had lately been ambushed and murdered by Comanche marauders as they went about their business. She wondered if someone in another town might hire him to build something elsewhere. That saddened her; she would hate to also lose him as a boarder. Seamus was cheerful and merry, and made wooden toys for her sons out of scraps. He, like Hetty, had become a friend and she would feel his absence keenly.

The last vestiges of daylight had faded from the sky, when Margaret did her rounds; a habit of hers, every evening; to latch the doors, and ensure that the downstairs window-shutters were closed. Papa was already snoring on the narrow bed which he insisted on keeping in a curtained-off corner of the kitchen. Her sons were all asleep. A light burned in Mr. Hattersley's room; he was still working on his novel, Margaret presumed. Dr. Williamson was reading in the small parlor.

"Have you seen Mr. O'Doyle?" Margaret asked him, as she passed the opened door to the parlor. He looked up from his book with the usual slightly baffled expression he wore when something had pulled him out of his contemplations.

"Not lately," the doctor answered, and seemed to hesitate before continuing. "This afternoon I was called to Bullock's to attend to a traveler and I did see him in the tavern – although," he added hastily, "he was not drunk. But he had been indulging."

"Well then," Margaret answered crisply, her hand on the latch of the front door, "he may very well sleep at Bullocks. They should have room enough." In her heart, she was a little disappointed at Seamus O'Doyle. He had never been one for drinking and carousing in Richard Bullock's taproom, although he was convivial enough among company. As she was about to bar the door, she heard a small sound from outside; thinking that it was Seamus O'Doyle returning at last, she opened the door. Yes, there he was, sitting on the steps to the house, his back to the door, head resting in his hands. Margaret thought at once that he must be ill.

"Mr. O'Doyle," she called softly, "are you all right? I was just wondering where you were. I was about to bar the door for the night."

"Nay – I am no' arright," he replied. To her secret horror, he was slurring his words, as if he had drunk a very great deal, and the Irish came out so thick in his voice that she could barely understand. "Sorry I am t' say, Marm – but it is desthroyed that I am . . . she is gone, m'dear angel. I left the speakin' of m'true feelings too late . . . an' now she is gaine w'another!" he lifted his head, and by the faint starlight, Margaret saw that his face was wet, as if he had been weeping all this while.

"Mr. O'Doyle, you are drunk!" she said, more in disappointment than anger, for there was a bottle by his side and a strong reek of whiskey.

"Aye, an' I'll be drunker still," he answered, and Margaret's temper rose.

"Not in this house, you won't!" She came from the house and snatched up the bottle from beside him: it gurgled. She would have poured it out then and there, but for the waste. "Come inside then, so that I can bar the door," she commanded, but Mr. O'Doyle only groaned and dropped his head into his hands again.

"Morag, me darlin' – could not ye have waited? I was goin' t' speak up, truly I was . . . time ran out on me, for I thought t'mysel' she's a child still. I have the time . . . but no, an' now she is gone!" Margaret stood, stunned and suddenly, painfully aware of what Seamus O'Doyle meant by this. He had loved Morag, loved her deeply and yet stayed silent, waiting for . . . what? He spoke of her as a child, still. That was it; he had not wanted to take advantage of a child, but allow her time and keep her safe, to see her become a woman and to bring a proper suit to her when she was grown. Now Margaret recalled how he had spoken to her of his Moylan cousins, of how there was a man trying to force Morag to marry him, and how Hetty valiantly protected her sister from his attentions. The gallant knight-errant, with his carpenter's tool-box instead of a sword and a lance; who loved from afar and had his heart broken for it. There was a step in the doorway behind her, and Dr. Williamson spoke.

"Is that O'Doyle, then?" he asked. "Not sober, either. I expected as much, seeing him at Bullocks."

"He is drunk and maudlin," Margaret answered. Dr. Williamson took in the unedifying scene and commanded, "Up with you, Seamus; on your feet, and put one before the other." With capable strength and some sympathy, he hoisted Seamus O'Doyle to his feet, draping one of his arms over his shoulder and straightening to his full height and pulling the smaller man to his feet and beyond. The doctor was indeed so much taller that Mr. O'Doyle almost hung from his grip, like washing hanging on the clothesline. Whiskey bottle in one hand, Margaret barred the door with the other. That done, she followed the sound of their voices – Dr. Williamson's soothing and businesslike, and Mr. O'Doyle querulously asking after his bottle. The door to their room stood open. As she came in, Dr. Williamson had just dropped Seamus O'Doyle onto his cot, and was tugging off his boots. Mercifully, O'Doyle had left off weeping and begun snoring.

"You may as well have this," she said, and handed Dr. Williamson the bottle. "It's whiskey, but I don't think he'll be having any more tonight."

"No," agreed the doctor. "If anything, that panther-piss of Bullock's – sorry, Mrs. Vining – will remind him of the virtues of temperance in the morning. I'll be noisy when I rise tomorrow; that will pay him back for snoring like a grampus all night." His actions belied his unsympathetic words, for he unfolded a blanket over Mr. O'Doyle, and Margaret was moved to explain. "He was in love with Morag all this time, and never mentioned his affections to her, so she never knew. Have you ever heard the like, Dr. Williamson? A man so in love with someone that he could not bring himself to speak of it?"

"Now and again," Dr. Williamson answered, noncommittally. *"'There are more things in heaven and earth, Horatio, than are dreamt of in your philosophy.'* Good night, Mrs. Vining."

"Good night, Doctor," Margaret answered, and went to her own room, still sadly marveling. Poor Seamus O'Doyle; no wonder he had looked so like a thundercloud that morning, watching Morag wed Daniel Fritchie, and never saying a word that any fond brother or father wouldn't have said.

At breakfast the next morning, Seamus O'Doyle was pale and without an appetite, flinching at the clatter of plates from the kitchen and the sound of Margaret's sons coming noisily downstairs, but he seemed chirpily cheerful nonetheless. After he had departed, carrying his toolbox over his shoulder and saying that he had a commitment to make some tables for Mr. Bullock, Margaret and Dr. Williamson exchanged skeptical glances – but no, Seamus returned that night, covered in sawdust and quite sober.

In the meantime, Margaret talked it over with Hetty, who was sympathetic but only a little surprised. "Oh, so that was th' way of it. I wondered mesel' now an' again. But it would no' have made any difference, if he had spoken to Morag or no'. For to her, he was close kin. She an' I, we're fond of Seamus, but she would ha' no more married him thin she would ha' married our brother Frankie."

The August sun burned down from a flawlessly blue sky; another spoke in the turning of the year. In Papa's cornfield the tufts of corn-silk tipping each ear of corn turned brown as the ears themselves swelled against their husks. The boughs of the apple trees hung lower as the fruit began to ripen, blushing pink and pale yellow against the green leaves. The pecan trees along the river bore clutches of green-covered pods; they would not ripen until nearly winter. Margaret's garden was bearing nicely, although it was yet too early to begin harvesting anything but a bounty of cucumbers and pale green patty-pan squash. In the last weeks of August, Margaret and Hetty began a round of pickling, just to keep it all from going to waste. The number of boarders had been reduced to two, upon the departure of Mr. Hattersley. That very morning, Dr. Williamson had mentioned that he might go Bexar in September for the opening of the district court, for he had a civil suit to bring for payment of a fee owing to him.

"We'll be eatin' pickles until they come out o' our ears!" Hetty lamented, upon contemplating the array of crocks covered with cheesecloth. "An' next week – there will be as many as ever there was!"

"We might trade with the Bullocks," Margaret said, consolingly to Hetty. "or make a sweet from them. My mother would peel them and scoop out the seeds; thin-sliced in a crust, with pie-spice and sugar. You would think you were eating apple-pie."

Hetty groaned, "Dinna remind me, Marm – for next 'twill start with apples, until I am so tired of them!"

"Then it will be pig-butchering time, and yards and yards of sausage," Margaret added, "but Papa will do most of the heavy work of that. And it will be cooler."

"Merciful Mary!" Hetty agreed. "And we shall have another month of this heat, at least."

"It is cooler here in the hills than in Bexar," Margaret drew out her account book from the shelf where it sat behind the coffee grinder. "What should we ask Dr. Williamson to bring back from Bexar? He would do so, if we ask him."

"Fine wax candles, for best," Hetty answered. "All we have are those smelly tallow things."

"We may not be able to afford them," Margaret pointed out; they talked of it for a while, looking at the neat pages of expenditures for the household and the payments of the boarders.

Mr. Hattersley had left as he promised; Margaret thought that by this time he would be nearly across the Atlantic. She wondered idly where he would live in England and if he would rent rooms again. She hoped that he would be content in his homeland, and happier than he had seemed to be in Texas. It would be pleasant also, if he continued to write. Margaret had often enjoyed reading what he had written in the newspaper. Mr. Hattersley in newsprint was less caustic and far more congenial than Mr. Hattersley at her table. Just that very spring, Britain had officially recognized Texas as an independent and sovereign nation, so Margaret hoped that his return at that particular moment would make of him an expert among those in England who might be interested in such a far and foreign place. Perhaps he might receive invitations, on account of having lately returned from Texas. At the very least, she hoped that Mr. Hattersley might find a publisher for the book that he had spent so very many months writing.

Dr. Williamson completed his plans to attend the meeting of the district court. The session had been delayed because of the troubles with Mexico in the spring, but scheduled again for September, in order to hear those civil cases which it had not been possible to have tried. It appeared that Dr. Williamson was owed a large fee by the former mayor of Bexar – none other than Race Vining's old friend, Juan Sequin. Dr. Williamson's fee had been promised but never paid. Exasperated beyond all patience, Dr. Williamson had engaged a lawyer and intended to be in Bexar until his case was put before the judge.

"Two weeks, I believe," he said, blinking over his spectacles. "I would remain only until the case is heard and judgment rendered. I hope then to be paid, of course. Fine wax candles? Should I see any for a good price, I would procure them for you."

"Thank you," Margaret said, "I would deduct the cost from your rent, of course."

"And very glad of it, also," she added later to Hetty. "For he is the one most likely to be reading after dark this winter."

In the first week of September, Dr. Williamson rented a trap and packed a small carpet-bag. He also took his doctor's satchel, and Margaret pressed a basket of fresh apples upon him, as well as another basket full of bread, cheese, and dried sausage for the two-and-a-half-day journey to Bexar. She promised that his books and medical correspondence would be kept in order – and she could see that Dr. Williamson had a book in that hand which was not already full of reins. *I hope the horse has the wit to follow the road*, she thought irreverently, *otherwise the poor man will finish up in Nacogdoches and be wondering for days how he came there.*

"But," she added aloud to Hetty, as the cloud of pale brown dust dissipated from the wheels of the trap as it vanished down the southern road, "I said nothing about turning out his room entirely and putting it all in order; it's a mare's nest. No wonder he cannot find anything."

"Mother Mary and Joseph, might he then be angry at your presuming?" Hetty asked, with some apprehension. Some of the gentleman boarders took it ill for anything more done to their quarters and possessions than to have the sheets changed, the floor swept and the chamber pot emptied

"I very much doubt he will even notice," Margaret answered.

Chapter 4 – *The Ranger from Bexar*

Around mid-morning on a day in the second week of September, Hetty was just finishing the breakfast dishes, while Margaret was rolling out piecrust; the early apples were ripe for the harvest. Papa and the boys had brought in the first of several baskets overflowing with them, and the two women were discussing what to do with them once Margaret had made three or four pies.

"Apple-butter, I think," Margaret had just said, and Hetty agreed. "We'll start today, for there will be more by tomorrow." There came a pounding upon the door, and Margaret took her hands from the rolling pin and dusted flour from her hands on her apron. "Oh, why doesn't whoever just open it and come in – it's unlatched. Jamie! Peter!" she called, "can you see who it is at the door?" She cast a glance out of the long window at the end of the kitchen, which looked out upon the farmyard and the apple trees beyond. Her father and the two oldest boys were at work there. There was no sign of her younger sons. Just as the person outside pounded again on the door, Margaret heard Jamie's voice in the hallway, and the door opening.

Within a moment, Jamie appeared in the kitchen, wide-eyed with awe. "It's Uncle Carl," he said and Margaret gasped. It was indeed – her younger brother, filling up the doorway behind her son; a tall young man with the wheat-pale fair hair that was the mark of the Becker kin; Saxon-square to the bone. His rough work trousers and leather hunting coat were covered in trail dust, and the lines of weariness in his face made him appear older than his twenty-two years.

"H'lo, M'grete," he said only. His eyes were the same calm and placid blue that they had been when he was a child; the only feature of him which had remained entirely unchanged.

"Carlchen!" Margaret cried and flew to him, flinging her arms about him in a joyous embrace. "Oh, my – you have gotten so thin! Where have you come from this time – from Bexar? Will you stay at home with us for a bit? At least remain for supper. Hetty and I are making pies from the first of the apples – fortunate that is your favorite!"

"I can't, M'grete," he answered, and the gravity of his expression drew her attention. "Jack sent me. I rode through the night to raise the alarm. I must go, as soon as Ward and Coleman have raised the volunteers. I am tasked to guide them to our camp. The Mexes have invaded; their army holds all of Bexar. "

"Holy Mary, Mother of God!" Hetty gasped; her face was ashen, the freckles on it standing out as stark as paint splatters. A tin plate dropped from nerveless fingers and fell with a clatter to the floor. Jamie stared, his eyes as round as a baby owlet's – part hero-worship of his uncle, part distress at the reaction of the adults to this dreadful news. Margaret stepped back, gasping. "How has this happened?" she demanded. "When and how did you come to escape? You and your company, you are garrisoned in Bexar, aren't you?"

"We are," he yawned hugely, and pulled a chair aside from the table, slumping into it as if he were tired to his very bones – which he would be, if he had ridden the eighty or so miles from Bexar. "Might I have something to eat now, M'grete? I haven't eaten for two days." Hetty was turning the dish-towel into knots, between her hands, the plate still on the floor at her feet where she had dropped it. "An' what of them as were there for the court?" she asked, and Margaret's own memory seemed to leap like a startled hare.

"Yes, what of the district court in session," Margaret asked, urgently. "One of our boarders, Dr. Williamson – he was in Bexar to have a civil suit heard. He left last week."

"Then he's still there." Her brother answered in short sentences, as if he were too exhausted to do any more. "They surrounded the town. Took every white man as a prisoner. Judge, district attorney, lawyers, witnesses and the lot. Lawyer Maverick – he was caught as well. John-Will Smith, the mayor – he escaped, the only one. His wife's family helped him. He saw everything from the roof of his father-in-law's house. It's an army, right enough. Not bandits and Comancheros. They even brought a band with them. Came straight into town at dawn under cover of thick fog, set up cannon in Military Square, and fired a shot. Woke up the whole town all at once, so John-Will said." Looking at his eyes, Margaret saw that it was true. Carlchen had never lied to her. Her own anger began to smolder into open flames; anger that Lopez de Santa Anna – that vile, treacherous butcher – would send his armies into Texas once again. He would dare send his gold-braided officers and his convict armies into Texas, to pillage and murder, then accept parole and sue for peace ... and six years later presume to do it again!

"What do they intend? Are they coming here?"

Carl shook his head. "I don't know, M'grete – but not if Cap'n Jack has anything to say, and General Sam, too."

He yawned again, and Margaret abruptly returned to that matter which she could do something about. She set a plate before him, with a fork and spoon to one side of it, fetched half a loaf of bread from the pie-safe, and began cutting slices from it. There was a quarter-wheel of cheese, some fresh butter from the churning of yesterday's cream, and of course, plenty of apples. Jamie brought two from the nearest basket, with the air of a page doing service to his sworn liege lord. He lingered at Carl's elbow, a worshipful expression on his face.

"Hetty – bacon and eggs; the fire is hot enough, surely? Ham . . . Papa has just begun smoking the hams, but I am sure we have some cured sausage if you would like."

"Whatever you have in a hurry. I'm too hungry to be particular." Her brother was already wolfing bread and cheese. Margaret spared a covert look at him as she busied herself about the kitchen. He was no longer the soft-spoken boy that he had been once, a boy reserved to the point of silence in the presence of strangers. He had risen to the rank of sergeant more than a year ago; he seemed surer of himself, confident and capable, but still quiet about it. Now he took a small knife from the top of his boot to slice another piece of cheese with – not the wicked-sharp brass-backed hunting knife, which hung from a belt around his waist, along with a brace of long-barreled pistols. With his mouth full, he added, "I turned m'horse out in the paddock with old Bucephalus. The boys promised they'd rub him down, and bring him some corn. He needs a rest more'n I do." Hetty was busying herself about the stove, where bacon was already sizzling briskly in the pan. Margaret finished crimping the top of the first piecrust, and her brother added, "Can I have some of that, when it's baked, M'grete?"

"You may have all of it, if you like," she answered, "if you are staying long enough." Unbidden, Hetty opened the oven door, so that Margaret could slide in the first pie. Rolling out another round of dough, Margaret continued, "Then tell us – how did you escape the Mexicans, Carlchen?" She waited for the answer: her brother would not willingly submit to being a prisoner of the Mexicans ever again. By a merest chance and the action of their brother Rudi in stepping before the Mexican's guns, Carl had survived the massacre at the Goliad. If Margaret knew anything in the world with more certainty, it was that her brother would never endure captivity or confinement a second time.

"We didn't escape from town, if that's what you mean." He swallowed a mouthful of cheese and bread. "We had never been caught there to start with. There were rumors. Seemed that there were more than usual – and those who had heard and passed them on weren't the usual rumor-passing sort. Jack thought that was strange. He was asked to go on a scout; took me and four of the fellows. Some of us went along the Old Spanish road – half a day's ride, both directions, the same with the Sabine Road and the Gonzales Road. No sign of anything out of the ordinary, no one we spoke to had seen anything strange either. But when we returned – there were Mex soldiers at every way into town. They had not come by a known road, M'grete. They made their own, so as to come around from the west without being seen. We have a camp of our own, north of town on Salado Creek. Sometimes we don't want prying eyes to see where we are headed, what we are doing. We went there and John-Will met us at midmorning, told us what had happened. The general in charge is a Frenchie soldier of fortune. A hard case, but decent enough. He has two thousand men, John-Will said. Pioneers. Cavalry. And artillery – I don't know how many pieces. We didn't stick around long enough to take a count. There weren't but about fifty of our men in town; they came for court, not for a fight. Some of them put up one at first, but it wasn't any good. They were outnumbered, and the Mexes could have leveled the place with their cannon anyway. General Woll agreed to treat them as prisoners."

"Treat them to a Santa Anna quarter, no doubt!" Margaret felt sick at the thought of Dr. Williamson as a prisoner, sick with helpless fury, He was so kind, so gentle and absent-minded; surely they would spare a doctor from execution! "Why are they doing this to us, Carlchen? Why?"

"Because they can," her brother answered, calmly biting off another mouthful of bread and cheese. His eyes were as blue and unclouded as the skies outside the kitchen window. "What they can do, they will, sooner or later. It's like the Comanche. They talk peace when it suits and when it gets them something. I reckon they mean it sincere at the time. But when it suits them and gets what they want by going on the warpath, why, they'll do that without thinking twice. Don't mean nothing what they said last week, or last year." Carl appeared quite unruffled by this fresh Mexican treachery, of naked war and invasion brought down upon them once again by the vile dictator Santa Anna. That very serenity was bracing to Margaret.

"Of the gods we believe, and of men we know – that what they can do, they will," Margaret quoted from her husband's copy of Thucydides. "So, little brother – they have done it now. What happens next?"

Carl smiled reassuringly. "Don't worry, M'grete; Jack and General Sam will sort them out, once they get to hear of it. Jack sent us flying in all directions with messages. It'll be like the Plum Creek fight all over again."

"Yes, but in the meantime the Comanches sacked Victoria and burned Linnville to the ground even before the ranging companies gathered!" Margaret answered. "And what will happen this time? This is a proper army, not a war party of Comanche!"

"Well, the Penateka haven't come back, have they?" Carl answered, reasonably. "They learned a hard lesson. Mebbe it's time to teach Santy Anna another. Or remind him again. Really, M'grete, he's awful forgetful."

"No, I think he remembers well enough," Margaret answered, her voice bitter with anger and memory. Lopez de Santa Anna's last incursion into Texas had cost her a home, the lives of a brother, her mother and dear friends, as well as a certain peace of mind. "This time he sent a flunky rather than risk his own precious skin!"

"True enough," Carl's good-natured expression dimmed slightly. "I don't reckon he would be let live if we captured him in his drawers again. He and the nearest tree and a coil of good rope would meet up – no matter what General Sam might say." He yawned again, just as Hetty brought a clean plate and the pan of eggs and bacon, still sizzling and popping with fat. Hetty tipped them onto the plate and set it before her brother; Carl caught up a piece of bacon in his fingers, and then dropped it. "That's hot!"

"Straight from the stove," Margaret answered. "At my table, most use a fork to eat." Just at that moment, Papa came in the door, a carrying-yoke over his shoulders and a bushel basket of apples hanging from each end. Horace and Johnny followed, lugging another basket between them. Margaret's breath caught in her throat, anticipating a dreadful scene, something like the last time Carl had come home and encountered Papa; but Papa merely dropped the baskets with a groan and a grunt. He glanced at his youngest son and then looked away without a change of expression. It was as if Carl were not there at all. For his own part, Carl took up the fork that lay next to the plate and took a bite of scrambled eggs.

"Papa, the Mexicans have invaded and taken Bexar," Margaret said, her heart in her very throat. "Carlchen has brought a message from his captain."

"What's it to me?" Alois Becker grumbled, in German. "They're all Mexicans in Bexar anyway. Let them have the joy of entertaining those fatherless sons of whores. Tell me when they cross Shoal Creek. Maybe I'll give a damn. Come along, lads. There's work to be done, not stand around gawking at this wastrel son of mine." He gestured to the boys to follow him and stumped out of the room; Margaret heard the door fall closed behind them. It cost her some effort to look towards her little brother. Papa's words still had the ability to hurt, like the slash of a knife. Margaret had long willed herself to move past feeling them, to think of them as nothing more than a human sort of lightning and thunder, a cold blue Norther, or a springtime flood. His words had no more effect on her, but she was certain that it was Papa's words and the careless cruelty in them which had first driven Carlchen away and kept him away ever since. She need not have worried. From the untroubled manner in which her brother was still forking up mouthfuls of eggs and bacon, it was clear that he had also moved to that point, sometime in the last six years that he had spent as a Ranger.

He only smiled very slightly, answering in the same language, "The old man hasn't changed a bit, has he, M'grete. Nice that some things remain always the same."

"He is not 'the old man,'" Margaret insisted. "You should speak of him with respect, Carlchen. He is our father and he is not a bad man." Her brother chewed thoughtfully, as he shook his head, and swallowed another mouthful before answering.

"No? And a pool of water poisoned with alkali is not good to drink from, although it still looks like water. He got us all – you, me, Rudi – on the body of Mama, but he was no more a real father to you and me than a wild mustang is a real father to the foals he sires on any handy mare."

"But he is still our father," Margaret was shocked out of countenance, and glad that this very improper conversation was being carried on in German, that Hetty was uncomprehending, as she gathered up the clean dishes and began putting them away. "We owe him all respect for that."

Carl shrugged indifferently. "You respect him then, M'grete. To me, Race was more a father to me than the old man. So was Jacob Harrell, who taught Rudi and me how to hunt. Trap Tallmadge – the Ranger sergeant in my first company – took more pains over me than the old man ever did. He's poison, M'grete, like an alkali spring. If your boys were mine, I'd keep him far from them."

"You would have no need to worry about Papa's influence on my sons, if you came home a little oftener, gave up rangering. Perhaps if you took up a trade and settled down . . ." Margaret suggested, stung by his words. She had long believed that the company of her sons might soften Papa a little, bring him to take an interest in a younger generation, and now to have Carlchen suggest that such an influence would do them harm! In all the travails of the past few years, Carl had not been there; he did not have any idea of what she had to face, every day and every hour.

He was already shaking his head. "No, M'grete. I could not. Rangering is what I am best fit for and I like it out there. It's not complicated. Other people make things complicated."

"Ah. I see – get on your horse and ride away into the wilderness, where everything is simple. Leave someone else to raise the children, nurse the sick and dying, bake bread, build houses and look after the wellbeing of families, which makes things all so very, very complicated. Well, you have that luxury, little brother, but I do not. I must cope with the complications."

Carl shrugged, apparently little affected by her words. "Someone must fight the Indians. And now the Mexes, while you bake bread and darn Papa's shirts. May as well be me, M'grete. I'm good at it." He calmly scraped up the last of the scrambled eggs, but then his voice turned grave with sympathy. "Lawyer Maverick told me last year that Race died. Consumption, he said it was. Someone told him. A friend, I guess. He had friends all over, didn't he? Race, I mean. I'm sorry, M'grete. I heard so late, didn't make any sense to come home. Anyway, I'm sorry that you lost him. He was a good man."

"Yes, he was," Margaret answered. It was on the tip of her tongue to tell her brother about the other matter, of Race's Boston marriage, and the settlement from his family. Someone ought to know, she thought – someone of her blood, but immediately she also recalled General Sam's advice about scandal and of the matter being no ones' business but hers and Races.' Instead she said, "Do you want anything more, Carlchen. The pie will not be done for another hour, I'm afraid."

"I'll wait." He still had that sweet half-smile from his childhood, converted into another yawn. "I'm sorry, M'grete. I rode through the night. Is there a place where I might sleep for a few hours, until Coleman's volunteers are ready to ride?"

"In the front parlor," Margaret answered, "on the daybed." He rose from the table, still yawning. By the time Margaret brought a blanket from her bedroom, he was already fast asleep, sprawled on the daybed without even having taken off his boots, although he had removed the belt that held his holstered weapons, and hung it close at hand over the back of the day bed.

"What are we to do then?" Hetty asked, when she returned to the kitchen, and began rolling out pie dough. Margaret deftly turned the rolled-out crust around the rolling pin, and draped it over the next pie pan. She began cutting the edges with a pastry knife, before she answered,

"Begin making apple butter, I think. Oh, you mean – what do we do if the Mexicans come? I won't leave here, Hetty. I expect that we shall have to bury the valuables, and hide the horses and the food-stores. Papa may also take his musket and find a place in the woods to hide, if he does not want to go with the fighting militia. Surely you are not frightened of them, Hetty?"

"No Marm – I am not," Hetty answered, sturdily.

"Good," Margaret piled the piecrust full of peeled apple quarters, and emptied a measure of coarse sugar over it all, with a pinch of cinnamon and a twist of nutmeg. She rolled out another round of crust before continuing.

49

"They are eighty miles away. Before very much longer, our men will be taking up a place between us and them, among the woods and the hills and behind a river. Two thousand soldiers is not very many." She draped the top crust over the rolling pin, using that as a wand to carry and lay the tender crust over the mounded-up apples. "Besides," she added, "I am resolved never to leave my home again. I would rather face them down than take to the roads and live like a beggar in all weather. I do not think they would scruple to harm us – for any insult given will be repaid in blood. I believe Lopez de Santa Anna knows this well, or if he does not, his soldiers will learn."

The making of apple butter that afternoon was often disrupted, for there was a constant stream of men and women coming to the house. Margaret finally tasked Jamie and Peter with sitting on the front steps and to fetch her from the kitchen whenever they saw someone coming up the hill, rather than have the noise of their knocking on the door waken her sleeping brother. She need not have bothered; he slept as deeply as one nearly dead for hours, in spite of the footsteps of people coming and going, of hushed voices, and Papa tramping back and forth with baskets of apples who couldn't be bothered to pay any mind to her admonitions.

Of course, Mrs. Eberly was one of the first – the storm-crow, as Margaret had privately named her; wherever there was trouble brewing, there was Angelina Eberly, flapping her black wings. She came with a basket of fresh-baked hardtack biscuits over her elbow, puffing as she climbed the hill. Margaret, already rattled because of the news her brother had brought, showed her into the kitchen and settled her into Hetty's rocking chair. Kettles of apple slices and molasses slowly bubbled away on the stove.

Fortunately, Mrs. Eberly was amiable about this omission of conventional courtesy. "I've heard already," she announced, "and brought bread for them as are going. I must say, it sounds bad. I had two more boarders leave today, and Mr. Bullock's place will be near empty in the next week. And it's not that they are going south to fight the Meskins, either – they are just plumb running scairt, and running back east with their tails between their legs." She cast an expert eye around the kitchen, warm and redolent of cooking apples and spices, every one of the copper pots polished until it gleamed like gold. "I can tell, Miz Vining, you ain't one of them. I know you've said so, often enough – but the proof of the pudding is in the eating of it. Or in the packing of the wagon."

"I have confidence in the men of our army," Margaret said, with firm confidence. "Whereas before we were a state in rebellion, and many of our people were in disarray and disagreement – now we are a sovereign nation. And not one to be violated lightly, and in defiance of the laws which rule the conduct of nations – even such a villain as Lopez de Santa Anna must take notice of those laws now and again, lest Mexico become a pariah among nations. We are united, this time, under brave and determined commanders!"

Mrs. Eberly clapped her hands, "Oh, my dear – bravely said! And I am heartened, Miz Vining, truly I am! My family and I, we will remain, as well. There are a few of us, happy and proud to stand fast in this dark time!"

"That he which hath no stomach to this fight," Margaret quoted from that play of Shakespeare's which her husband had come to love the best of all. *"Let him depart; his passport shall be made, And crowns for convoy put into his purse; We would not die in that man's company, That fears his fellowship to die with us . . ."*

"Oh, dear, I hope that it won't come to that!" Mrs. Eberly's cheer suddenly turned to apprehension.

"It won't," Margaret's brother said, confidently as he appeared in the kitchen door, walking as silently as a ghost. It seemed that he had been refreshed by the brief hours of sleep. "Captain Jack leads us, and he is the boldest and canniest of all. Better than that, he will never surrender. Best of all, many of us have these." He unshipped one of the long pistols from the holster on his belt, a matte-metal thing with a long and slender barrel, but which had an oddly large cylindrical attachment where the trigger and flintlock should have been. Margaret, Hetty, and Mrs. Eberly looked at it with puzzled, yet curious expressions, and Carl continued with the slightly exasperated air of a man explaining something to women which he would have assumed did not need explanation. "It's a Colt repeating pistol – five shots without reloading. We fight from horseback. The State bought them for the Navy, but they work very much better for us, you see." He stowed the long pistol away, and continued his explanation. "Jack – that is, Captain Hays – he trained us to fight as the Comanche do. Like the Mex lancers did, only better. To scout and harry and ambush the enemy, to go a long way without being seen. The Mexes and the Comanche still think this land is theirs. They're wrong. We own it now, day and night, plain, river and forest. They just need reminding, now and again."

"Well, I am very glad to hear of that!" Mrs. Eberly exclaimed, and Hetty looked gratified. Margaret's spirits rose, fractionally. Perhaps there was hope after all that the prisoners would be freed, and the Mexican troops sent fleeing back over the Nueces.

51

Carl and the assembled militiamen under the command of Captain Coleman departed without ceremony late that afternoon; grim and purposeful men, their saddlebags bulging with food and ammunition, their saddle holsters bristling with arms. Margaret watched as her brother moved among them, unhurried and quietly authoritative. They were moving light and fast, with two pack mules laden with even more supplies; her brother planned that they should be at the Salado camp within three days. Margaret's heart was wrung – she had seen this so many times before! The only solace she might take in this prospect was that there were no young boys among the riders this time, only men and many of them battle-hardened and wily, veterans of the first fight for Bexar back in the beginning, of the mad scramble to withdraw from the west, after the fall of the Alamo, veterans of San Jacinto, of Plum Creek and a thousand small skirmishes with Mexicans soldiers and Indians alike. And General Sam – he would not let this insult pass, indeed he would not. With that, Margaret must be content.

It was little more than a week before Margaret and those still remaining in Austin received certain news of what had happened at Bexar. The Mexicans had withdrawn – that was the best of it. The Texian companies from the lower Colorado settlements, including Captain Hays' Rangers, had lured a large portion of the Mexican force out of Bexar, lured them into a trap among the sandy creek beds and thickets of mesquite and scrub oaks north of the town. There they fought a sharp skirmish and sent the Mexicans reeling back . . . but a company of fifty or so volunteers from La Grange, led by Captain Mosby Dawson, had just arrived, and hearing the distant sounds of the fight had advanced to the aid of their comrades. They were overrun by the Mexican cavalry before they could join the main Texian companies, safely entrenched along Salado Creek. All but fifteen or so were captured alive, the rest being killed in the fight, or upon surrendering. Within days, the Mexican general Woll and his columns of marching men, of cavalry and the heavy cannons had withdrawn from Bexar, retreating slowly back towards the Rio Grande. But he took hostages with him, those men captured in Bexar, and in the skirmishing along Salado Creek. Nonetheless, this invasion had been stopped. Margaret and her household rejoiced, until a tear-stained letter from Morag arrived; Daniel Fritchie was one of Dawson's men captured at Salado and his brother Nicholas killed.

Worse yet emerged in the next weeks; those prisoners taken in Bexar, those men who had been at the meeting of the district court, were not released on the banks of the Rio Grande, as they had been promised by General Woll.

Dr. Williamson's captivity would be of longer duration than a few weeks; Margaret fumed when she read of this new treachery in the newspapers, and Hetty wept when she re-read Morag's piteous letter.

"Oh, Marm – what will she do, then?" Hetty cried. "Is all alone now – and she writes that she is become ill very often, and she cannot rest."

"She must come home to us, of course. It's the heat," Margaret answered. She had her own suspicious about what was making Morag ill.

"And I will go to fetch her, o' course." Seamus O'Doyle looked immediately more cheerful. He had made some adjustment to Morag's marriage in the past months; Margaret thought that perhaps Hetty had spoken to him bluntly on the subject.

The final blow, when it fell was not completely unexpected: citing the constant danger of hostile incursions from Mexico and from the Indians, General Sam called the Legislature to meet at Washington-on-the-Brazos . . . not at Austin. Margaret was philosophical, at least more so than Mrs. Eberly, who predictably enough was furious. She stumped up the hill to consult with Margaret – or at least to complain angrily while Margaret listened.

"Who does General Sam think he is?" the Widow Eberly shouted. "And who do those lily-livered men think they are – afraid to come to this place, to do the business required of the nation?"

"They may rightfully fear such, seeing how the men who attended district court were dragged from Bexar as prisoners," Margaret began; a temporizing statement which was entirely wasted on Mrs. Eberly.

"Fear of a Meskin sojer jumping out of a bush has gelded every one of them!" Mrs. Eberly stormed on. "That drunken old lecher may as well have taken a knife and done it wholesale! I'll lay any roads that he has gone around talking up how dangerous it is to all! This will be the ruination of our business, Miz Vining, the ruination of it all!"

"This was a passing emergency, Mrs. Eberly, a passing emergency," Margaret said. "They were defeated and have withdrawn over the Rio Grande."

"Aye, thanks to our men, men like your brother and no thanks to General Sam this time! Leave it to our best to take up a musket and defend our homes – what has it come to, that our own leader will not take up his duty here, where we had established our city!"

"I am sure that the Legislature will meet here next time." Margaret was about to give up being soothing, as it seemed to have little effect upon Mrs. Eberly.

"They had better so," Mrs. Eberly replied. "All the offices are here, and the archives safe-guarded in the land office. How can you conduct the business of the country without the records? Tell me that, Miz Vining!"

"I am sure they cannot," Margaret sighed. "Truth to tell, Mrs. Eberly, I take it a small matter, next to the holding of our men. Poor Dr. Williamson! We shall miss him so dreadfully. Morag is with child, you see, and Daniel Fritchie is a prisoner. Mr. O'Doyle has gone to Mina with a wagon to bring her back to stay with us. We hope every day that Daniel will be freed. She is so young and alone and they had not been married all that long."

"Hard times," Mrs. Eberly said, with a grim expression, "and even harder, for it is our own leader making it harder for us. Aye well – it's lads like that brother of yours that stand guard for us; I can sleep at night, trusting in him and Captain Jack Hays and Captain Coleman and all. What have we done to deserve that devotion, Mrs. Vining?"

"I do not know," Margaret admitted, "but I think they feel it to be their duty, whether we be open in our gratitude or not."

"Well, if and when your brother and any of his comrades come to Austin again," Mrs. Eberly patted her knee fondly, "and you have not the space for them all, I'll gladly make room – and not charge a bit. It's the least we can do for our lads, isn't it?"

"The very least," Margaret answered, and left unspoken the question – *would Carlchen ever return to the family home, when business or war did not take him?*

Morag did return, and with tears of mingled joy and distress, as Seamus O'Doyle came around and handed her carefully down from the wagon seat. It was October; the days were drawing shorter, with grey-clouded skies and a chill wind from the north. She ran lightly to Hetty's embrace; there was no sign outwardly that she was with child, save for the sudden sharpness of the cheekbones in her face. *There is a difference in the face of a woman who is bearing, or has born a child,* Margaret thought; *something elemental, no matter how young she may be herself.* She had observed it in the faces of those friends of her girlhood in Gonzales, seen it in her own features – and now it was in Morag's face, when she turned from her sister to Margaret.

"Dear little girl," Margaret whispered – *what it might have been to have had a younger sister of her own, or a daughter!* "I think you have some news to tell us."

"You knew!" Morag's face fell, and then her expression danced into laughter, as she hugged Margaret. "But of course, Marm! You know everything!"

"Know of what?" Hetty looked from one to another, slightly baffled, and Margaret marveled at how she and Morag were now united in a sisterhood, despite the years between the two of them, and her long friendship with Hetty – the bond of sisterhood between the mothers of children.

"I will have a child to console me!" Morag embraced her sister again. "That Danny will return, an' I will have his son to show him! He knew, o' course. That was why he went w' Captain Dawson! 'Meggie,' he said to me – 'I must do what I must to keep us safe, now more than ever – for th' matter is most urgent!' An' I kissed him an' said that he must do what he must . . . an' oh, Marm – what was I thinkin'? For now I want him worse than I have iver wanted him, t' be at my side!" Morag dissolved into tears on Margaret's shoulder.

"Moods," Margaret explained over Morag's shoulder to the much-puzzled Hetty. "It comes with the country of children. That you will have moods and your children alike, and hope that your kin and friends may forgive you for being considerably out of sorts with the world, whilst you are in the process of bearing them."

"Oh, me ain darlin'!" Hetty cried, with sudden comprehension grown doubly fond. "Come and lie down within! This is happy news, so 'tis!" She embraced her sister and walked to the house with her arm around her waist. Meanwhile, Seamus O'Doyle had lifted down the little trunk which was all that Morag had brought with her.

"It was a good thought, to have her come home to stay with us," Margaret said to him, "and thank you for bringing her."

"Aye well, she's as dear as kin," Seamus O'Doyle replied. "And Danny is a foine lad – we'll just see about getting him back, won't we, Marm? They say in Mina that General Sam is raising a large army to strike at Mexico in hopes of freeing our boys. Is it true, now?"

"It has been in several newspapers," Margaret answered. "I think it must be. But I would have known so, even if I had not read of it. I don't believe we would tamely submit to such a provocation as the taking of Bexar and the kidnapping of our own citizens."

"No, we would not," Seamus O'Doyle agreed. He had such a thoughtful expression on his face, that Margaret knew he must have already begun thinking about this. "No, we would not, indade."

Chapter 5 – *A Brief History*

Margaret's sons were ecstatically happy to have Morag returned to Austin, for they adored her, especially Jamie and Peter. She was, Margaret thought, poised delicately halfway between a grown-up and a child herself – far enough removed from their age to be looked up to, yet close enough to it to be approachable. She made toys for them, told stories and sometimes had even joined in their play. Hetty was also joyful at her sister's return.

"For all that I am pleased that she married a foine young man," Hetty confessed, "an' that I pray for him every night – I have missed her so. We Moylans were all that we had, Frankie and Morag and I!" Even Papa softened a little, for Morag dared to tease him about tracking farmyard mud into the house on his boots: Margaret held her breath at that, for it was like seeing a tiny finch fluff its feathers and cheep at a large, gruff old dog. But Papa only grumbled under his breath, and upon it becoming obvious that Morag was carrying a child, he went and sought out scraps of fine oak planks and constructed a cradle from them.

"For the little one," he said gruffly, when he brought it to the kitchen, carrying it under his arm as if it were something of no particular account. He turned away from Morag's happy gratitude, saying, "Well, the brat can't sleep in a cheese box, can it?"

Morag's baby and her return were the only reason for hope and cheer under the roof of the house which Margaret increasingly thought of as her own. At the bottom of the hill, the town of Austin seemed to crumble a little more with every passing day. The doors and windows of those places built to do the business of government stood open to the harsh elements. Dry leaves blew across the floors; rain fell in through the unglazed windows, and the green wood of which they had been hastily built cracked and warped, opening long gaps between the planks. Of those who remained, many had chosen to spend the nights at Richard Bullock's inn. Since many of the individual buildings in his sprawling establishment were built of logs, it offered a feeling of security, especially on those nights when the moon was full – that moon which was rumored to mark the preferred hunting-time of Comanche raiders. The abandoned buildings of Austin became the abode of birds, raccoons and opossum, which came and went without fear of humans.

The lovely, airy rooms of the French Legation also stood open to all weathers; Dubois de Saligny had removed all of his fine furniture, stripping the place bare. Even Father Odin preferred to find less isolated and sturdier quarters. It pained Margaret to contemplate Seamus O'Doyle's fine work, now left to weather and decay as winter came on. It pained her also to think of Dr. Williamson. Reports and rumors had it that the captives from Bexar and the Salado Creek fight were being marched in chains, far, far into Mexico, to be imprisoned at hard labor no matter what their age or condition – not to be released on the banks of the Rio Grande, as General Woll had promised.

Morag broke down and wept openly when Horace innocently asked this of her one evening after supper, after having heard those rumors from Papa. Horace looked nearly as tearful as Morag, as she moaned, "Danny, oh Danny – where are you, now? Where are you? When will you come safely back to me?" she buried her face on her sister's shoulder, incoherent with grief, while Hetty rocked her in her arms, and Seamus O'Doyle stared hard into the fireplace, his face working with suppressed, yet powerful emotions.

It was cold, uncommonly cold this evening. Margaret, the boys and her friends – for by now Hetty, Morag, and Seamus all counted as dear friends – gathered in the old parlor after supper, that part of the house that Papa had built, together with the kitchen, which remained comfortably warm on this bitterly cold evening. Even though Margaret had seen that the walls of those rooms in the house were covered with plaster, the windows in the oldest part were small, set high in the walls. The doors into those rooms were thick and well-barred. Papa had built it as secure as a block-house – a comfort in times as troubled as these!

"Hush, my dear, hush me darlin'," Hetty crooned, and Horace's lower lip trembled. "I only asked a question, Mama," he said. "I did not mean that Meggie should start to cry!"

"I know, my dear little duckling," Margaret answered, equally wrenched by concern for both. Horace was only a boy of eleven – not comprehending how a simple question could strike so raw a nerve? Morag, young and untried in the ways of marriage, had not developed the habits of stoicism. "She is going to have a baby, Horace – a frightening thing to a woman whose' husband is far away through no fault of his own. We all wish to have Danny Fritchie back, to see his child born safe and well, and that Morag would have him safe at her side, to be her husband – her dearest friend and protector."

"I would do so, for my cousin – with ivery breath I have in me." Seamus O'Doyle said, abruptly and with such fervent determination that Margaret could only assume that he had suddenly come to a decision and resolution of a matter which he had considered long. He had been sitting, staring into the fire as it burned, as if he was seeing something far away, something that had struck him to unaccustomed silence. "Morag, me darlin' – ye know that I love ye well? Well, now I promise to ye; I'll see to bringin' Danny back. I read in the newspaper that General Sam has tasked Alex Somervell wi' setting up a punitive expedition, an' 'tis in my mind that I ought to jine. I can do me own bit, t'see that Danny an' the other lads are brought safe home – an' our own Doctor Will, too! Aye, and I would do for me own pleasure, at giving Santy-Anna a good thrashing once again, so I would."

"Would you truly, Seamus?" Morag dabbed at her eyes with the corner of Hetty's apron, and Hetty assured her, "He would – an' I am sure that even the Old Sir would volunteer, also." Seamus O'Doyle laughed recklessly, which coaxed in turn a small giggle from Morag.

"Oh, ye go too far!" he exclaimed. "The Old Sir would nay go any farther than Bullock's tap-room! Besides, if he went wi' Somervell an' I, it would leave Marm and you and Hetty an' the boys all alone. No, little cousin," he took her hands within his strong and scarred carpenter's hands, "only mysel' – an' promise on me life to see Danny back to ye, safe an' sound."

He departed the very next morning. There was a freight wagon returning to Bexar, upon which he could ride, the carter being another Irishman and an old friend. He intended to take only a haversack on one shoulder, and some blankets tied into a long roll over the other, with a hunting rifle, a bag of shot, and a flask full of black powder; all that, he said cheerfully, was what he had taken before, when he went to join General Sam's army at Groce's Crossing – and look how well that had turned out! Margaret and Hetty made him a good breakfast; Margaret being uneasy in her mind about his departure. She had slept badly, plagued by a bad dream that she could not quite recall upon waking, but which left her with a sense of foreboding.

"Aye, well – take good care o' me tool chest," he said, as he took up his blankets and haversack. "I will need it upon me return – but this, Marm," and he took a book out of the top of the haversack, his treasured copy of *The American Builder's Companion*. "'Tis too heavy to carry and besides, what need of it will I have? Ye should keep it safe wi' all the other books. Study it close, an' maybe ye can afford a new wing to th' house whin I return!"

"I will do that," Margaret answered, with a heavy heart, although she tried to keep her voice light and the worry from her face. Seamus O'Doyle was a good friend, a trusty man, but she wondered if his hopeless love for Morag had not broken his heart for once and all. A man who loved, true and fair – that was a man with something to live for, and endure much for the thought of returning. Such a love was an anchor to hold fast against the tides of misfortune, whereas a man without that security might find it all too easy to let go. She was reminded of Race's friend James Bowie; a rough and brawling man, a dangerous scoundrel who had truly loved the daughter of Veramendi and took up a place on the ramparts of the old Alamo fortress – in metaphor only, since he became desperately ill not long after arriving there to take up his command of the volunteers. His wife and their children not long in the grave, and himself sickening; no, James Bowie was indifferent to death, and so death found him effortlessly. Margaret looked at Seamus O'Doyle, and had the same conviction that she had in that early spring six years ago when James Bowie rode away towards the ferry at Gonzales on the north road to Bexar; that death would find him easily enough.

It seemed that all was dying in that autumn when the tree leaves briefly flamed in tints of red, gold, and bronze and then fell to the earth below and lost the last few bits of color as the cold wind scattered them here and there. Their bare branches were etched against the clear, ice-blue sky. Papa wore heavy gloves and wound a muffler around his neck when he went to do the chores. Below the heights on which the house in the ring of apple trees stood, it seemed to Margaret as if the town of Austin was dying also, along with the tree leaves and the year. A quarter of those who had come to settle when Austin was set to become the capital city, the queen city of Texas still remained, stubbornly convinced that a prosperous future was within reach. In the daytime a handful of chimneys sent pale columns of wood smoke into the air, and at night the scattering of lights was overwhelmed by the stars overhead. Yet another farmer – a Mr. White was caught in an Indian ambush, by the springs that fed into Shoal Creek. Unable to make it safely to his home, he took refuge against the bole of a large oak tree, where he was so savagely attacked that the tree itself bore wickedly deep scars.

With Seamus O'Doyle gone, there went the last of the boarders, even though he had paid his rent in kind, by working on expansion of the house. Poor Dr. Williamson, taken prisoner into Mexico and Mr. Hattersley returned to England; Margaret wondered sometimes if she had any justification now in calling herself a boardinghouse keeper, save in caring for those items of clothing and possessions which Seamus and Dr. Williamson had left behind.

"There is no of profits share to be made," she said to Hetty, one December morning as they washed up after breakfast.

"Aye, well – thin Morag and me, we're working for our board and keep," Hetty replied comfortably. "Could be worse, Marm," she added over her shoulder. "We could have no roof an' keep at all."

"I'm sorry, Hetty," Margaret felt most particularly wretched. Hetty had worked hard and selflessly for so many months, but with no income from boarders, there was nothing to pay her with, and with no profits – nothing to be shared.

"Dinna fret, Marm," Hetty answered, a dish in one hand and a rag in the other, as she went on washing up. "For sure an' things will get better. In the meantime, the harvest is taken in, the Old Sir has the smokehouse goin' night an' day, the roof over our heads is sound – an' the chimney draws fair, so it does. I've lived wi' worse, an' so have ye."

"Thank you," Margaret laughed a little. "You are right and right to remind me. For most of my life, I would have been content with this, or even a little less. But having tasted a little of a larger life, with a dinner table full of interesting people and a profitable venture of my own devising and work – I am ambitious, Hetty. I would like more."

"Aye then, an' so you shall have," Hetty replied. "But ever remember, Marm – ambition is a good servant but a bad master."

By early December, the matter of Austin remaining as the capital – the queen city of Texas – had devolved so badly that Margaret secretly despaired. All the hopes that she had entertained when a grand city was first surveyed and mapped out, the government offices first built, and the legislators gathered for that first session – all seemed to have come to naught. Those buildings hastily put together of sawn lumber, to serve as a temporary halls and offices, in the hopes of something more grand eventually to come – they were all falling to ruins. In another year or perhaps a little more, all would crumble to the unforgiving earth again. The young oak and cypress trees would sprout again and wild animals forage where they would, while Papa's house would be what it had once been, after Alois Becker had fought with Colonel DeWitt and with the storekeeper William Smith in Gonzales. Papa had repacked his two heavy Pennsylvania wagons, Margaret's dear mother, her two brothers, and three dozen sapling apple trees and gone to the beautiful, unsettled wilderness along the upper Colorado.

It had contented Papa to farm – to become all but a hermit – but not Margaret. Not when she had a taste of a larger world, and the possibilities offered to her, in keeping a boardinghouse. Her late husband had planned to open a school, hoping that his collection of books would be equaled by other gentlemen of education and refinement come to take part in the governance of Texas. To further her own ambitions, Margaret might have taken the settlement left to her by his family and established a boardinghouse and a home for her sons in Washington-on-the Brazos, or Columbia, or even the new city of Houston – new-built near the ruins of Harrisburg and where General Sam had won his miraculous victory on the field of San Jacinto. But in remaining, she was as stubborn as her father: here was home, in the hills of the upper Colorado. The handful of other settlers who remained were similarly stubborn, unable or disinclined to remove elsewhere, though few were as adamantly outspoken about the matter as Mrs. Eberly.

She came stumping up the hill, one afternoon when Margaret, Morag, and Hetty were busy at carding and spinning the first of several bundles of wool, which a carter from Bexar had traded to Richard Bullock in exchange for three nights' lodging for himself and his team beasts. Richard Bullock had as much use for unspun wool as he had for a ladies' corset, so he had traded the wool to Margaret in exchange for a quantity of apples from her father's trees. Being winter, this was the first opportunity Margaret and Hetty had leisure to do something about the wool, which had been bound around all those months ago in strands of damp rawhide. The rawhide shrank as it dried, compressing the wool into bales as solid as wood, and there was rather more of it than anyone would have thought at first glance. Papa, grumbling as usual, brought down Mama's old walking-wheel from the barn loft, and set it in the front parlor, where pale winter sunlight streamed in through the those tall glass windows which Margaret had bought from the profits of her first year of boardinghouse keeping.

"The boys and Papa will not lack for socks, nor you and I for stockings this winter," Margaret examined the first bale, and sneezed. "And it is well-washed. No, I don't think we shall bother with coloring the first lot. It will do well enough."

Mrs. Eberly was still breathless from either the walk or outrage; Margaret couldn't tell which. "He's sent a messenger," she puffed. "It's an outrage, I tell you, Mrs. Vining – an outrage. He must think himself a sovereign king! For what did we fight against, but the overreach of kings?"

"Who has sent a messenger?" Margaret had not really been listening.

"General Sam, of course!" Mrs. Eberly exclaimed indignantly. "He sent a messenger, asking that the state archives be dispatched to Washington-on-the-Brazos immediately!" Margaret and Hetty both looked at her, with blank faces, although Hetty's strong freckled hands hardly ceased their movements with the carding paddles, combing the packed wool into long loose rolls, which Morag coiled into another basket.

Mrs. Eberly amplified. "The records and minutes of state business, of laws and properties, and all that has been decided by the Legislature – all of which is necessary for the administration of law! They are stored safely in the Land Office at present – and that is where we are determined they shall stay. Once they would be taken from Austin ..."

"The Legislature would have no reason to return," Margaret completed Mrs. Eberly's words. A sense of indignation well-mixed with anger began to burn in her alike. Really – this was too much to be borne: who did General Sam think he was? To go against what the previous Legislature had ruled; that Austin should be the capital city, not some place chosen willy-nilly and out of his own whim and convenience. He was the hero of San Jacinto – not the emperor of Texas!

Mrs. Eberly's own indignation could scarcely be contained. "It would be the death of us all, letting the archives pass out of our hands, so we have bound and determined to keep them here, where they rightfully belong!"

"Who has decided this?" Margaret asked; her chief worry all these last months had been for poor Dr. Williamson, and then for Seamus O'Doyle.

"The gentlemen have held meetings," Mrs. Eberly clicked her tongue and shook her head, "which you might have known something of, if your father took a proper interest in public affairs. They formed a militia to guard the archives with most particular strictness, to prevent anyone from taking them from Austin under any pretext whatever. It's not as if they might be put into a pocket and carried away, either. There is a cannon loaded with powder and shot, standing ready to alert all 'gainst such an attempt!"

"Why is that, Mrs. Eberly?" Margaret asked. The gentlemen were always holding meetings about something. It had been so in the first days of her marriage to Race Vining. If it weren't the militia and raiding Comanche, it was to do with the government of the Centralists encroaching on settler rights.

Now Mrs. Eberly sat back in the best chair, saying with enormous satisfaction. "Because they would fill three wagons – or two, at the very least? Given the state o' things today, how could that pass unnoticed!" She straightened her bonnet with an emphatic gesture and laid a finger alongside her nose. "We shall keep our eyes wide open; you may depend on that, Mrs. Vining – and our gunpowder well-dried."

"That is most reassuring to hear," Margaret answered. "I will tell my father. He is in such an ill-temper these days that I am not surprised that he doesn't take part in public matters. I dread conversation with him myself, so I may hardly blame any other for being reluctant to speak so to him."

"Never you mind, then," Mrs. Eberly, in rising to take her leave, patted her comfortingly on the shoulder. "I'd sooner brave waking a grizzly bear in his winter den, myself. But remember – keep your eyes open for strangers, or anyone poking about the Land Office building who can't give a fair account of his business in doing so!"

"I will," Margaret assured her, although on reflection, she couldn't think of much business that would take her anywhere near the dilapidated frame buildings put up with so much hope not three years before.

In the dark of one early morning, some days later, the single little cannon, which sat in the street before Mrs. Eberly's establishment, woke all of Austin – and a great many residents of the wooded valley on either side of Shoal Creek at a considerable distance – with a single, mighty roar which reverberated like a crack of thunder. Margaret sat up in bed, her heart pounding. In the old kitchen, she could hear her father cursing, a series of ripe and mighty oaths which, rather fortunately were in German. Upstairs, she heard Peter crying, mingled with the voices of the other boys and Morag. She snatched up her wrapper and ran up the stairs, colliding with Hetty on her way down.

"Holy Mother Mary and Joseph," Hetty gasped, "'tis the signal-cannon! Is it the Indians attacking, then?"

"I hope not." Margaret made her voice sound steady, and calm. "The doors are barred and the windows too. Papa has his musket and plenty of powder and shot, so we need not fear anything but an attempt to set this house alight. We should go upstairs and see what we might see from the upper windows."

This turned out to be not very much at all, save the flare of a torch or two, and a clamor of voices brought to them faintly on the night breeze – nothing that sounded like the screams or war-whoops of Indians attacking, or the pop-and-crackle of gunfire.

"Perhaps someone fired the cannon by accident," Margaret finally decided, "or maybe a silly boy playing a prank. When it is well-daylight, I'll send Horace to find out what was going on."

When morning came, she was as curious as any of the children; taking up her shawl and bonnet, she walked with the boys to the muddy expanse of Pecan and Constitution. There hardly seemed to be any men about; Bullock's was half-deserted, and Margaret re-directed her steps to the Eberly House. If anyone knew what had happened in the early morning it would be Mrs. Eberly.

"They tried to take the archives," the widow exclaimed triumphantly, "just as I said they would – sneaking in under the cover of night! I looked out and saw them – and I recognized they were General Sam's men, loading the wagon. I ran out with my candle, and fired off the cannon! Oh, my stars, what a noise it makes when you are nearby! Miz Vining, I swear that my ears are still ringing."

"And there is now a hole all the way through the Land Office building," Margaret said, very dryly, and Mrs. Eberly fluffed up like an indignant hen.

"Well, that was not my fault, Mrs. Vining! Them as loaded the cannon left it pointed that way! But it put a fright into General Sam's men, for they jumped into the wagon forthwith, and lashed the team … they were away before the militia came running! Just like men, although they have gone in pursuit. I daresay they will catch up soon enough. It is a serious business," she added. "Without the archives, we haven't a reason for a town here, Mrs. Vining – and I don't see that as a laughing matter."

"No, indeed," Margaret said, although she could not keep from smiling at the sight of the Land Office building, neatly punched through from front to back with a six-pound round shot. "You are indeed more fortunate than Mr. Ware, when it comes to firing cannon." Poor Mr. Ware the mayor of Austin, who had lost a leg to a cannon-ball in the fighting to take Bexar from the Mexicans at the beginning of the war in 1835, had subsequently suffered the loss of an arm the previous year, in firing a cannon to celebrate the victory at San Jacinto. "Forgive me, Mrs. Eberly – I so respect General Sam that it grieves me no end to be on the opposite side from him in this respect."

"I am on the side of my own good fortune," Mrs. Eberly snorted, "It matters not to me who does or does not stand there with me."

For the sake of Morag and the children, late in December after the fuss over the wagon load of archives had died down, Margaret took her courage in hand and braved asking Papa to search for a Yule tree – a cut cedar sapling to be placed in the corner of the old parlor. She wished the tree to set in a heavy kettle filled with river gravel and decorated in the traditional way, with small gifts and sweets, with garlands of orange laurel berries and bright ribbons, stars cut from paper, and small candles lighting the ends of branches. Long ago, when Margaret had been a child in Pennsylvania, Opa Heinrich and Oma Katerina had done that every Christmas Eve – a custom from the Old Country to delight the children; herself, Rudi, Carlchen, and their cousins. Opa Heinrich said it was a very old custom, not much done in America save in districts where Germans from Brunswick, Hesse or the Upper Rhineland had settled. Papa appeared startled for a bare moment when she asked this of him, before he grunted noncommittally.

"We should recall to them the old ways," she said. "The boys – they do not even speak German any more, but perhaps with this, we might call a little of our customs to mind. And it would cheer us all, I think."

"Aye," Papa grumbled. "It's a waste of a half-day's work, girl – but I'll see what I can find. Now and again your mother asked for the same."

"Thank you, Papa," she said, but he only grunted again. Margaret did not dare pursue the matter further, but she and Hetty spent some afternoons making candy and sweetmeats from nuts and dried fruit, and some of her precious stock of fine white lump sugar.

On one of those afternoons, she heard a light step in the doorway at her back, and thinking that it was Horace, she said, "If you are done with your schoolwork, then come and stir this sugar-syrup for me – take care that it does not burn or boil over." She nearly leapt from her skin, when a gloved hand attached to the arm of a grown man clad in a leather-fringed hunting coat came around from behind her and took the spoon from her hand.

"I'm done with schoolwork, M'grete," said Carl, over her shoulder. "Long since done with it, save what I need to follow a cold trail over stone and water." She whirled around – half startled and half overjoyed – and wholly taken back to see once again that he was taller than she by at least half a head. And she had carried him in her arms as a baby and small child!

"Oh, my dear little Carlchen!" she gasped, and then began to laugh at the ridiculousness of that image. She flung her arms around him, regardless of the wooden spoon covered with hot sugar syrup in his hand, the saddlebags over his own shoulder and the lumpiness of those items tucked into his haversack, and the front and the pockets of his buckskin hunting coat. Tears brimmed in her eyes even as she laughed. "What are you doing here? We thought that your Captain Hays was with General Somervell on the Rio Grande, or even farther. The newspapers all talked of invading Mexico in punishment."

Her brother shook his fair head somberly, answering, "No. General Sam's orders did not carry that far and General Somervell would not disobey, although there were others who did."

Margaret fixed her brother with a stern look. "I see. I would know of what happened, little brother – and why you are home with us, rather than with your Rangers at this time, and why General Sam has no inclination to punish that villain Santa Anna as he so richly deserves." She took up a gathering of her apron, and moved the pot of sugar syrup to a cooler place on the stove top. No, she could not risk the loss of any of her precious refined sugar to carelessness. "Go on, take off your hat and coat . . . you were not born in a barn, Carlchen – though I think you must have slept in such or worse more

65

often than not. Are you hungry, if you have come all the way from . . . where have you come from this time, little brother?"

"From Bexar," he answered. In obedience to her words, he was already hanging up his coat, haversack, and hat, and dropping the heavy saddlebags in a heap by the door. He still kept the knife and the brace of repeating pistols at his belt, as if they were so familiar a part of him that he hardly noticed their presence. "Jack sent me on leave. He said since I had a family to go to for Christmas that I ought to." He smiled a slight, faint smile. "He said that if I didn't, he would clap me into irons and have me delivered."

"And you will always follow orders," Margaret said, with some asperity, and Carl shook his head. "No, I will do as Jack says; he and General Sam. Neither one of them had a liking for going any farther than the Rio Grande – they have their reasons, although only Jack shared his with me. I *am* hungry, M'grete . . ."

"There's a cured ham in the safe," Margaret relented, "and half an apple pie . . . and Hetty has pease-porridge going, on the back of the stove, with cornbread for dinner tonight. There are cold biscuits from breakfast. Why is it that whenever you come home, I am feeding you as if you did not eat at all in between time?" she added. Her brother had already ransacked the pie safe with relentless efficiency, and settled at a corner of the table to eat what he had gleaned. Margaret snatched back the cured ham from his hands as soon as he had carved off a thick slice with his horn-handled hunting knife. "I didn't say you could help yourself to all of it, Carlchen; other folk in my house eat at my table." She fixed him with a stern look. "Like Mr. O'Doyle – who also went with General Somervell? Did he not return with you?"

Carl chewed and swallowed mightily. "Red-bearded hoss; Irish and talks as if his tongue was hinged in the middle to rattle at both ends? I 'member him fine, M'grete. I know well that he was a friend of your'n. Jack an' me, we tried to talk him out of going with Bigfoot Bill Wallace an' them. We really tried – Jack said right out there weren't no hope to rescue our folk taken by General Woll. They were gone too far for us to reach, but Bill an' them were keen to take Mier, an' smash the Mexes even harder than they had smashed us at Bexar." Her brother took another bite of ham and biscuit, and regarded her with a mild, sky-blue gaze, faintly shadowed with worry. "Jack wasn't having none of it, and neither was General Somervell – the General, he said his orders from General Sam only went as far as the river, and Jack said that it wouldn't look so good for us. If we ever were to invade Mexico proper, he said that it ought to be with more than a couple of hundred militia and Rangers. They'd make us out to be nothing more than brigands and pirates.

Better to have the right of it on our side, he said. Your friend O'Doyle wouldn't listen. He said he had vowed to do all he could to rescue his friend who was married to his cousin Morag, no matter if it meant going to hell or Mexico."

"Seamus O'Doyle went with an expedition to attack Mier?" Margaret felt the hair on the back of her neck prickle. "Oh, Carlchen – I do not like the sound of that." Her brother swallowed again.

"They're a passel of wildcats, M'grete. I wouldn't worry too much about your friend. They c'n look after themselves and him, too."

Margaret regarded her brother with a stern eye. "Little Brother, don't try and talk with soothing words on such affairs, when you speak to me about wars and invasions. Men told us such comforting, reassuring lies, all during the time of the war; I have no more stomach for them at all. I would sooner have the truth – if Hetty and Morag's cousin is in dreadful peril, I would rather know now."

"They thought pretty good about their chances," Carl insisted mildly.

Margaret bit back an expression of vigorous disparagement that her husband and some of the boarders had often been wont to use. "I am not a fool, Carlchen. If those of Somervell's men have gone into Mexico and the matter were as simple as you would have me think, then you would have gone yourself, and returned already."

Her brother shrugged again. "I do as Jack orders, M'grete. He is the keenest Ranger and the best soldier I know. Over every other man, I trust his judgment – even over my own. Me, I thought their chances were pretty good. Any roads, it was a chance to dish up to the Mexes a ration of what they have served us all too often. That's what those boys were really after. I don't think General Sam himself could have held them back, once they had it in mind to take Mier." He wore a troubled expression as he added. "But I don't think they had any mind as to what would come after they took Mier or Saltillo. M'grete, it was like a cat going up a tree after a bird without any thought of coming down again. I said so to Bigfoot – he was a Ranger with us in the company – he just laughed. I don't think they thought it out proper, not like Jack did when he had a plan."

"No, I think not," Margaret agreed. Her heart remained heavy with worry for Seamus O'Doyle, even with her brother's return. Having finished off all that he had raided from the food-safe, Carl wet a finger and tidily gathered up a scattering of crumbs from the tabletop.

"I heard tell of another friend of yours," he ventured. "That Englishman, Hattersley – the one who asked me all sorts of fool questions, when I came back from the Llano with Cap'n Hardiman's company? Mike Cronican, from San Augustine was one of those who went to Mier – he used to be in the printing trade, in the East someplace. He's another one for books an' all, like Race used to be. He heard that Mr. Hattersley had written a book."

"He was writing it, when he lived here," Margaret answered. "I am so glad that it has finally been published, for he wrote so amusingly, He wrote dispatches for the newspapers, you know. The boarders were always so pleased to read his reports in the *Register* or the *Democrat*."

Carl nodded, very earnestly." Mike, he had a copy that he had bought in Galveston – he had read only a bit before he sold it, but a mercantile in Bexar had a few. I bought it for you, when I recognized the name, but I don't think the book will please anyone near as much as his newspaper dispatches did."

"Why not, Carlchen?" Margaret demanded. "Did you read his book?"

"A little," Carl admitted, and now he was evasive, in a way that he had not been when he talked of Somervell's expedition to the Rio Grande and the Mier venture into Mexico. "I don't think he was really a friend after all, M'grete. Mike said folk were mighty steamed about what he wrote in his book. "

"What did he write?" Margaret demanded; recalling how often Mr. Hattersley had waxed marvelously sarcastic over the supper table, and how she had wondered many times what he had come to Texas for. Her English boarder had appeared to find nothing at all in Texas to recommend it; not the things which other men seemed to find exhilarating or interesting or even of profit.

Her brother looked uncomfortable, again. "I can't really say, M'grete. I only looked enough at the book to see that it was that Hattersley – he had a bit about how he had lived in Austin and was conversant with many of the important men of the government, so I know it must be him. But Mike Cronican said … that he never passed up a chance to be disparaging or to belittle the folk that he met. I hope," Carl added seriously, "That he did not write anything bad about you, M'grete – for I might have to have words with him. I don't want to travel all the way to England, M'grete – it's a wicked long way to go to thrash a man."

"If what your friend said was true, about what Mr. Hattersley wrote, then you might have to take the place at the end of a long line to thrash him," Margaret answered, feeling no little heart-sore. Her husband had regarded Adolphus Hattersley as a good friend. Carl looked relieved. He got up from the table, and searching through his haversack and saddlebags, removed a small, duodecimo volume bound in dark oxblood red cloth.

"I truly hope he did not say anything bad about you or Race," he said again, earnestly. "I wish I had put a fright into him, that time – just so's I could get some satisfaction from the memory." A brief smile flickered across his face. "Still, he looked plenty worried when I showed him my knife and tole him how I followed three Comanche with it."

"And then you cut yourself a piece of pie with it and licked your fingers," Margaret sighed. "I think that shocked him most of all."

Chapter 6 – *A Prisoner in a Far Land*

Margaret set aside the slim oxblood red volume, promising herself that she would read it with attention, once the holiday was past, Christmas dinner eaten, and the boys and Morag had unwrapped their presents. Until then, it would sit on the shelf in the new parlor with all of her husband's books, those books that constituted the largest library in Austin – for which she had hardly any time these days.

In all the days that her brother Carl remained at the house – until the very last – he did not ever exchange a word or even appear to take notice of Papa, who maintained a similar silence and stone-faced reserve and made every excuse to find work in the stable. Papa even retreated there on Christmas Eve, after the boys and Morag were allowed into the parlor to look upon the decorated Christmas tree. The tree was a small one, barely as tall as Peter, but the ends of its shapely branches were adorned with tiny candles, shining as brightly as stars. The boys were awed and entranced at the sight, but Papa only watched from the door, an expression like a thundercloud upon his face.

Carl spent most of the daylight hours roaming the hills and along the riverbank, on foot sometimes, but more often in the saddle of his horse – a nimble paint-spotted Indian pony. Perhaps he was hunting; now and again he returned with a wild turkey or prairie hen. Margaret wondered if he was really just storing up enough of the out-of-doors so that he might endure sleeping inside the house. Some days he took Horace, Johnny, and Jamie with him, although Margaret must then endure black looks and harsh words from Papa.

"They do not work, they should not eat," he growled, one mid-morning, a day or so after Christmas, when he had come looking for Horace and Johnny to help muck out the ox-stalls. "You'll let them turn into wastrels and parasites, just like their father."

"No, I do not believe so, Papa," was all that Margaret could bring herself to say, with a deliberately calm expression on her face. She thought that the older boys were playing nearby the house. She could hear Peter on the porch with Morag and her brother in the kitchen, asking Hetty for some bread and cheese so that they could go hunting. Margaret was in the front parlor, spinning woolen yarn at the tall spinning wheel, turning the great wheel – as large as one of Papa's wagon wheels – absently watching the thread draw out between her thumb and finger, growing upon the spindle. Doing so made it easy to seem to let her father's remarks pass by as a piece of driftwood in the mighty Colorado River. There was no point or future in arguing with him; a spirited defense of Race Vining, her brother, or her sons would only allow Papa an opening for further disparagement. The boys would not want to help Papa muck out the ox pens. Today they would go with her permission out hunting with their young uncle.

At her back, Alois Becker grunted. "You're spoiling those brats of yours, girl."

"If it pleases you to think so, Papa." Margaret gave the wheel another vigorous turn. "Carlchen and the boys shot a deer yesterday, so we will have a haunch of venison roasted for supper tonight, Papa. Would you like to have red cabbage to go with it?"

"Don't mention that coward's name under my roof!"

Margaret stole a quick look at Papa as she stepped back to continue drawing out the woolen thread. His face was turning a particularly ugly shade of brick-red, she thought dispassionately, the veins in his neck and his forehead distended from fury. She could see the whites of his eyes all the way around – like the eyes of a frightened horse, she decided.

"Carlchen is my brother, Papa. He has always been dear to me, and I will mention his name whenever I think it fit." Such a mild remonstrance had a shattering, and completely unexpected effect upon her father.

"How dare you!" Papa snarled, his face gone suddenly animal-like in rage. "How dare you! He is no son to me, I'll . . ." Margaret was never certain of what he had said next. In that very instant Papa's hands were around her neck, tight and choking, thumbs pressing against her windpipe. She had no more care than to struggle for her next breath – but she could not. There was a roaring in her ears, as if a cataract of water falling down an endless cliff, all around her seemed grey and distant, and her last conscious thought was a tiny pleading cry – *Mama!*

Suddenly, she could breathe again, drawing in great ragged drafts of blessed air, air that scorched her aching throat. She found herself lying crumpled with her legs half-underneath her body on the floor of the parlor, her cheek pressed upon the blue rag rug and next to the toppled walking-wheel. From there she could only see the basket of carded wool strewn in one direction, the ball of spun yarn unreeling from the spindle in the other. What was she doing on the floor? Her throat hurt – and that was all that she could think of at first, that and that the floor underneath her was so terribly hard. She moved her arms – yes, she could move her arms, but her throat hurt so awfully! Now there was someone, someone who lifted her upper body from the floor, holding her by her shoulders, shaking her like a frantic child shaking a rag doll; there was the sound of a man's voice babbling, and a woman screaming. Margaret blinked, and the mist before her eyes resolved itself into Papa's face, no longer red, but gone as pale as bleached linen with horror and regret.

"Dear God, M'grete, wake up, I'm sorry. I did not mean it." Margaret closed her eyes against her fathers' contrite words. This was too confusing, a struggle to comprehend as well as a struggle to draw in another breath. She wished that he would go away. He was shaking her again and it made her head hurt. This was the world shattering into a thousand pieces. In all of those years of her life until now, observing Papa's intemperate ways and words, in all the times that he had been driven to a fury – he had never once struck out in anger towards any of them – not herself, not Mama. He might have ruled over Carl with a heavy hand and a thick willow switch, but never Rudi, and never herself. Mama would never have allowed that. Dimly she recalled her own husbands' words; *The best part of your father died with your mother.* The cataract-roaring noise diminished abruptly; a metallic click echoed in the sun-drenched parlor.

"Put hands on my sister again, and I'll shoot you down like a dog." That was Carl's voice, perfectly even, calm as if passing a remark on the weather. Margaret opened her eyes again. That was better now; no one was shaking her. She lay with her head in Hetty's lap, the silence in the parlor absolute save for Hetty whispering, "Holy Mary Mother of God, pray for us now. Marm, dear, wake up... please, wake up!"

"I'm awake," Margaret announced – or, rather, tried to speak, but her voice came out in a painful croak. "Carlchen, what are you doing?" she tried to say, at once torn between horror and a sense of how ridiculous her question was: it was quite obvious what Carl was doing. He had Papa held by one arm twisted around his back, as Papa knelt on the floor at Margaret's side, in a grip so powerful that Papa was half-lifted up from his heels and the muzzle of one of Carl's patent revolving pistols pressed hard against Papa's temple.

"Praise be!" Hetty gasped, just as Carl answered, speaking the German of their childhood, "This dog-squeeze was about to throttle you, M'grete. He's run mad like a rabid dog at last. I ought to put him out of his misery and yours, just on general principles. It's what we do with mad dogs. D'you want me to shoot him now, M'grete? I will, if you ask me."

Margaret looked upon her brother in horror. He was in earnest – dispassionate, even – his eyes a blaze of blue, as clear and intense as the winter sky, seen beyond his head through the parlor window. He would do it, too. He had been a soldier and a Ranger for near on seven years, no longer the sweet-natured little boy that she had cherished. Now she saw the soldier-face of him, the face that his Ranger comrades and Captain Jack Hays knew so very well; the casually expert dealer in violence, the single-minded hunter of enemies.

"No, Carlchen," she whispered. "No. You cannot do that."

"Why not?" Carl did not loosen his hold on Papa – in fact, he ground his pistol-muzzle even harder into Papa's temple. "Give me a good reason, M'grete."

"Because he is our father," Margaret's throat hurt, so that it brought tears to her eyes. Her brother smiled grimly. Papa now had his own eyes squeezed tight-shut. At her back, Hetty, who did not understand German, was nonetheless whispering her prayers again.

"Well, that's what Mama always said, but I've never had other cause to think so – other than Mama being truthful. *He* certainly never gave me much assurance in that respect. Another reason, M'grete?"

"Because it would make a mess in my best parlor," Margaret answered – as good a reason as any, if filial respect would not do. To her relief, her brother chuckled. He lowered the pistol, uncocking it very carefully as he did so. Papa sagged momentarily in Carl's one-handed grip, until her brother hoisted him to his feet with brutal efficiency. Papa bit back a cry of pain at that, and Margaret begged, "Carlchen – don't hurt him, he is an old man, you should have pity!"

"Not because he deserves so for himself, but because you ask it, M'grete," Carl answered, his voice faintly tinged with exasperation. "I'll not hurt him, but I will take care that he will not ever hurt you."

She was struck once again at how withered and old Papa looked, exhausted and shamed. When she was a child the age of her oldest son, she had secretly thought that Papa looked like one of those ancient heroes, tall and fair, a sword at his side, but the young lion drove out the old, the king in the golden wood was killed by a challenger who took his place. Now it was Carlchen who looked like the proud, vengeful god-king in that illustrated books of old legends that the schoolmaster in Pennsylvania had showed her long ago. The room swam a little around Margaret, and she lay back against Hetty's bony but comforting shoulder.

"You should get up from the floor," Hetty fussed. "It's cold, an' you'll catch your death, Marm." Margaret opened her eyes; they were alone in the parlor. Thin winter sunlight streamed in through the west-facing windows, tinged golden with afternoon. The only disarray within the parlor was the toppled spinning wheel and the largest of the kitchen knives lying on the floor, just out of reach. "What was said, that the Old Sir should handle ye so?

For he is a harsh man, but niver in all th' time I have been here have I seen him to strike woman or child." Margaret gathered her thoughts, as Hetty helped her to rise and totter those few steps to the day bed. In truth, she was at least as shaken as she was physically harmed.

"He – Papa forbid me to mention Carls' name under his roof, saying that he was a coward and then I answered that he was my brother and I would say his name as I wished." Margaret was diverted, as Hetty stooped to gather up the long kitchen knife. "What is that knife doing here?"

"Aye, well – as soon as you cried out, I told Morag to take Peter upstairs and bar the door. I didna know what to think, Marm. I saw that the Old Sir, he had his hands on your throat. I had the knife in me hand as quick as a wink, but there was no need, with the Young Sir." Hetty's freckled face had turned solemn. "There's no love lost between them, is there, Marm?"

"No, there is not," Margaret agreed, her voice sorrowful. She did not see how her father and her brother could remain under the same roof – not when the slightest word might send Papa into such a murderous, unconsidered rage. She felt at her throat with delicate fingers and Hetty peered closely at her.

"Oh, you will have such bruises, Marm. I should bring you some arnica, and perhaps some willow-bark tea."

"If you would also see to the boys," Margaret answered. "If they heard any of this, they will be frightened."

"They did not," Hetty answered comfortably. "They were playing on the hillside below the apple trees – they wouldno' have heard. But," Hetty lowered her voice to a whisper, "what weel ye do now, Marm, if the Old Sir is a danger to you or to them?"

"I don't know, Hetty." Margaret answered. "I just don't know. Perhaps we may hope that Papa's own temper has frightened him, at least a little." She felt her throat again, still hardly believing what had happened. "Where have they gone? Papa and my brother?"

"I dunno," Hetty answered. "Out to the farmyard, I think – they went out the back." She stepped briskly from the parlor, and Margaret lay back against the daybed pillows, baffled and heartsick. What had she done that her household turned into a scene from one of those grim Sophoclean tragedies, where vengeance and murder had become commonplace things? Not for the first time, she wished that Mama had lived, not died as they waited with the other refugee women and children in a muddy field near Harrisburg during the 'runaway scrape.' Mama had always coaxed Papa into recalling his better nature; this would have never happened if she were still alive.

In a moment, Hetty came rustling back, a heavy pottery mug in her hands. "Sip this, Marm, when it has finished steeping. The Old Sir and the Young, they are by the stable, talking. Or the Young Sir is talking, the Old – he is listening. Would that be a good sign, d'ye think?"

"I don't know, Hetty." Margaret answered. "I just don't know."

As it turned out, it was – and it was not; when Carl returned to the house, he straightaway packed up his haversack and saddled his horse.

"I'm away now, M'grete," he announced calmly.

"I thought you were to stay another week or so," Margaret remonstrated.

"I was," her brother answered. "Jack made me promise. But I can't now; not if Papa flies into such a rage at the mention of my name that he all but kills you." He smiled the fleeting and shy half-smile that she knew so well. "It would be on my conscience, M'grete. Miss Hetty says that he has never struck you or the boys in all the time she has lived here. If it's me that drives him into such a rage, I can't see any other choice than for me to leave."

"At least you are saying goodbye this time, not leaving like a thief in the night," Margaret answered, unable to keep a touch of bitterness out of her voice. "You have a convenient conscience, Carlchen; it lets you do what you wish in any case. What if you are wrong? What if Papa does fly into such a rage again? Don't you think it would be best for you to come home, to protect us as best you may?"

Her brother was already shaking his head. "It's not home to me, M'grete – and hasn't been so for a long time. As for Papa, he will not dare to lay a hand on you or the boys, ever again. Not after what I told him I would do if he did and I heard about it." Margaret stared at him, a prickle of unease running down the back of her spine; her brother looked so very assured, almost smug.

"What did you say to him?" she demanded. "What did you do that might threaten Papa, when you are miles away? Tell me, Carlchen!"

"There is no need for you to know that," her brother protested. Margaret fixed him with her very sternest look, the one which never failed to quell the most obstreperous boarder, the expression that Hetty called her "Maeve-face."

He finally shrugged. "All right, M'grete – I told Papa that if I ever heard that he had struck you, or the boys, that I would go to Ed Waller, or Richard Bullock, or certain other trusty men in Austin and I would tell them that since Mama died, and with Race being so sickly that Papa had been in the habit of forcing himself upon you, threatening harm to the boys if you did not submit to him."

"Carlchen, that is vile!" Margaret could barely speak for shock and horror. "Who would believe that Papa was capable of such a horrible, unnatural deed! How could you . . ."

"Vile it may be," Carl answered, reasonably, "but it happens. Not often, but enough. "Besides," and he smiled in complete contentment. "It does not matter what Mr. Waller, or Mr. Bullock think. What matters is that Papa believes me. He does. I told him exactly what I would say in private to those men here in Austin who know and respect you. It wouldn't come to a trial, M'grete. Papa and a rope and a stout tree limb would all come to meet, and he knows it. I have good judgment of men, M'grete – he believes me." His face went somber, as he looked at Margaret. "It's an evil thing to accuse. But threatening it is the best way that I can think of to protect you if I'm not here. I've no reason to think well of Papa, and many to think ill. You would know so best." He stooped and kissed her awkwardly upon the cheek. "Stay well, M'grete. I'll come back when you need me, but do not look for me to stay long, especially while Papa is liable to be riled so."

He was gone as swift as a hawk-shadow sweeping over the valley below, the sound of his horses' hoofs diminishing with distance into a silence that seemed to go on and on.

That silence seemed to weigh upon the three adults in the house for the remainder of winter. The boys were baffled and disappointed by Carl's abrupt departure – so much more congenial company to them than their grandfather. However, Alois retreated into his own brooding silence, for many months following his explosion of murderous anger at Margaret. Long after the bruises around her throat faded to pale yellowish marks and then to nothing at all, Papa continued to withdraw, sullen and uncommunicative. Like the old stump of the massive oak tree below the ring of apple trees, he was just there; paid notion to in order to avoid. Only Morag, wrapped up in the prospect of hers' and Danny Fritchie's child seemed completely unaffected, as winter turned slowly to spring. Early in the New Year, Margaret received a letter – amazingly enough – from Dr. Williamson.

From Perote, in the State of Vera Cruz, Mexico – January 21, 1843

To Mrs. Margaret Vining, at Austin on the Colorado, Travis County, Texas

I write these words letting you know that I am at present and after many travels and travails imprisoned with such of my friends as were taken at Bexar in Sept of last year. I am in as good health as can be expected, after being conducted here as a prisoner, on foot, the journey taking many weeks. We are to be treated, apparently, as prisoners of war, although the greater part of us were not serving under arms or in a military company at the time of our capture by Gen'l Woll. I hasten to reassure you that we are in the mai, not treated with cruel severity. However, the loss of liberty – to which we were all accustomed – weighs very deeply upon us all. This is a vile and barren place, nearly waterless and isolated . . . but even if it were comfortable and congenial – such qualities would not render the deprivation of our simple human liberty congenial to us!

All prisoners here, without exception for age and station, are made to work at heavy labor, in hauling stones and digging ditches. In effect, we are made to improve the very walls and defenses which surround us! The guards are not willfully cruel, but their superiors are implacable as regards our conditions. I have been able to retain my doctor's bag of instruments and a few simples, which have proved most useful in caring for those of our numbers who sustained injuries at the time of our capture or fell ill along the way. Young Mr. Fritchie was among them, and his brother Nicholas pitiably slain, although I hasten to reassure you that Daniel Fritchie's wounds sustained in the Salado Creek fight with Dawson's company were superficial and have healed completely. He remains in good health, although as downcast as much the rest of us are at present. I know that you will not fail to reassure his wife of his situation, and of his undying consideration and affections towards her.

I am sending this missive at the urging and in the care of Gen. W. Thompson, the American Consul to Mexico City, who has been most assiduous in tending to our welfare, although unsuccessful in obtaining our release. If you would condescend to engage in a correspondence with me, he has assured me that he will take every effort to enable a written connection between those of us held prisoner in a far land and those we hold in friendship and affection.

Very truly yours, Henry Williamson, Dtr. Medicine & Phrenology

"So he is well then?" Hetty exclaimed, "Jesus, Mary an' Joseph be praised! And the doctor is safe, bless th' dear man! You will write to him, won't you Marm?"

"Most certainly," Margaret answered. Her heart was wrung, for the doctor sounded so stoic, so very dignified – as he pled for correspondence, for some kind of gentle human connection to a world outside the cruel walls of Perote Prison. The newspapers were full of the stories of the sufferings of the men held there, and indignation that they should be held there so unjustly. "I would also endeavor to send him books and newspapers – anything that would relieve the tedium of confinement and such comforts as may be allowed."

"Aye," Hetty sighed gustily. "I will miss him, when Morag is brought to bed of her child. For all that he has always such a time recallin' where he has left his spectacles, he is a doctor. It was reassuring, indade, with 'im in the house, Marm. For a doctor to be nearby at hand – sure and one could rest easy, knowing that." She appeared worried, and Margaret made her voice seem calm and cheerful.

"Morag is well, Hetty – and I see no reason why it may not go as easier for her as it has always done so with me. She blooms like a rose." Indeed, Morag had come into full flower; she was happy in her pregnancy. She glowed with health, and looked even prettier than she had been before, although Margaret sometimes thought she looked like a child with a pillow under her dress as she played with Johnny and Jamie, tossing a ball in the meadow beyond the apple trees, or sitting on her heels on the floor as the younger boys played at soldiers or at jackstraws.

"Aye, so," Hetty's own face softened, "she does – and that Danny Fritchie is not there to see her – he would fall in love with her all o'er again, so he would! I will tell her of the Doctor's letter, Marm – and that he mentioned Danny."

"She will be glad of the news," Margaret answered. "If she will write to him, I will send her letter with mine to the American Consul. I wish, though – that there had been word of Mr. O'Doyle."

As her brother had feared would happen, those volunteers who had chosen to set aside General Somervell's commands and strike at the Mexican town of Mier, just the far side of the Rio Grande, had done just that; Carl had compared their actions to that of a cat going up a tall tree without considering how to get down again. They had struck and taken Mier – then been overwhelmed and captured by the Mexican Army at about the same time that Carl voiced his fears for them. Like their fellows in Dawson's company, and the luckless plaintiffs and lawyers taken hostage in Bexar, they had also been packed off to imprisonment in Perote, nearly two hundred men and boys. Margaret grieved silently for Seamus O'Doyle; he was as good and as trusty a friend to her as the Doctor had been. Now one was imprisoned, deep in a fortress in Mexico, and the other soon to be – and she, who had once felt safe in Papa's house, now felt nothing but apprehension.

Because there was no man but Papa left living in their house, she considered taking shelter at Bullocks whenever an alarm was sounded. The inn had been made so large and sturdily built that now it served as a refuge for those families – women and children living in the star-scattering of cabins and houses among the oak-trees and the network of what had been marked out as roads, now veiled in new-grown grass and low brush.

Papa only grunted, "Suit yourself, girl. This house was good enough for me and mine before – why should it have changed, just because some fool wanted to build a city?" He darted a look at Margaret, and added, "Go to Bullocks' if you've a mind to, girl. If I'm to be killed by the god-be-damned Comanche, it'll be over my own threshold." When she suggested that refuge to Hetty and Morag, they refused as well.

"'Tis a foine tall house," Hetty answered. "An' w' stout shutters – sure an' we can see anyone coming for miles – I'd sooner be here than caught out in the open trying to run to the Bullocks." She looked very keenly at Margaret and added, "If it comes to that, I can shoot as well as the Old Sir, while you and the lads and Morag load for us."

"Very well, then – we shall remain here," Margaret acquiesced, but her nerves remained drawn as tight as fiddle-strings all that spring and summer. She remained as wary as a doe every time that she went beyond the farmyard and the boundaries of the orchard, wondering if there were hostile Indians, watching the place with avaricious intent, especially around those times that the moon was full. There *were* Indians around, seen making their way along the creek banks, or camping near where the springs gushed out from between the rocks, and fell into cool, deep pools. The threads of smoke from their campfires rose and vanished in a few days, and the red blankets that they favored flashed amongst the green thickets like the flash of a cardinal's wings. Rumors and fears flickered and ran like lightning from household to household. During those uneasy nights, when the heat kept her awake at night, tossing under a sweat-damped sheet, and the fear of raiding Indians kept the shutters bolted tightly against the night air, Margaret often rose from her bed, and lighting a lamp, would read from her husband's books until she felt ready to sleep again. It had been long since she had the inclination or the time to do this – not since the first days of her marriage, before Horace was born and her husband kept a school in Gonzales. Certainly not since she had chosen to take up the trade of keeping a boardinghouse, but now the house was empty of boarders, and it pleased Hetty – and made her feel of use – to see to the keeping of the house.

The first book that she read during those restless night hours was the one which Carlchen had brought from the bookseller in Bexar, the one which Mr. Hattersley had written. She might have been eager to read it, but for Carlchen's words of warning. Mr. Hattersley had befriended Race Vining, and Margaret had thought well of him, although she had now and again wondered what reason he had in coming to Texas. Now she feared to find confirmation that Mr. Hattersley had been showing one face to her household – and most likely not his true face.

She opened the ox-blood red volume with some trepidation. It was entitled *A True Account of the History of The Nation of Texas to the Current Day.* Mr. Hattersley had often averred that he was writing a history of Texas, and often had carried out his interrogations over her supper table of other boarders who had particular knowledge of events.

Her fears were allayed with the beginning chapters, which spoke of the early days of the Spanish in Texas; a fair and reasonable account, as nearly as she could tell, although much of these matters had taken place decades before, when the Spanish and the French jousted for possession of those rivers and lands which fringed the coastal plain east and west of the Mississippi and the Comanche swept down from the high plains to haunt the hunting grounds of the Lipan Apache and the Karankawa. She flipped through the pages, looking for those chapters which told of events that she had some knowledge and experience of, thinking that she might better judge Mr. Hattersley's abilities as a historian by comparing his account of events and of those men who had accomplished great deeds against what she would recall from her own experience and of her own knowledge.

How many such men of nobility, courage, and character had she met in those tumultuous years? How many men who now were acclaimed as heroes had been guests in the Gonzales days, friends of her husband, or husbands of her friends, who had seemed ordinary and fallible, their faults and weaknesses merely human? Yet, their strengths led them to walk the unmarked path to immortal glory, their names written now in letters of fiery gold. James Bowie – Race had described him as having a warrior soul and frittering it away in tavern brawls, until he had been sent to command the small garrison at an old mission compound in Bexar, an old mission half-tumbled down. Dying even as he journeyed there, he had perished in his sickbed – from his ailment or Mexican gunshots – he who had once held the baby Horace on his lap and came near to weeping for the loss of his two children by Veramendi's daughter. He had never been ungallant to a woman or failed to come to the aid of the defenseless – which in a way was also true of that uncomfortable young fire-eater, Buck Travis.

When Alois Becker was arrested by the commander of the Mexican customs-post at Anahuac on a dubious charge of smuggling tobacco, Race Vining had hired Travis and his law partner to see to Papa's release, although Margaret had always privately doubted if Colonel Travis – as he later became – had been much help at all in the efforts to free Papa from the customhouse cells. Nervous, fiercely ambitious – he was one of those who yearned to perform heroic deeds; Margaret was certain that he saw himself as a veritable Leonides, commanding his tiny garrison against overwhelming odds. Just before the end, he had given his signet ring to little Angelina Dickinson, hanging it around her neck on a piece of string, and gone to meet his fate on the north wall battery, falling dead – as his slave Joe had testified – of a single shot through the head.

Margaret sat with the book lying forgotten in her hands, lost in the memories; Angelina's father Almaron was a fellow-settler in Gonzales, he and his high-spirited wife, Susannah. A big, jovial young man, ravenously curious about everything mechanical, and much else besides; he had taught himself Spanish from a book and polished his accent in making conversation in that language with Race's friends from Bexar, the Menchaca brothers and Juan Seguin. If Margaret closed her eyes, she could see them with her husband, hear their voices as they talked at leisure in the breezeway of their little home on St. Francis Street – talked of a thousand varied things that thoughtful young men talked of; the rights of man, the doings of the central government in Mexico City, the latest newspaper gossip from San Felipe, the rumored speed of a particular horse, and which of the marketplace cooks who held a stall in the Plaza Mayor in Bexar had the finest and spiciest meat stew. Had it truly been more than a hand span of years? Almaron Dickinson and Esteban Menchaca had died at their post: a gun-battery in the ruined stone church at the dawn of a fire-streaked April morning. Diego Menchaca and Juan Seguin now tasted the bitter brew of exile from the land they had once called their own – the only two left alive to remember those evenings, when the blue twilight merged with the smoke of pipe tobacco and the world seemed a place that could be easily ordered to their satisfaction.

Margaret leafed through a few more pages, but her mind was not really following her eyes on the tight-packed lines of print. Once those days and memories were called to mind they were not lightly dismissed, laid away like a folded garment in her bride's chest. They were ever there, she realized, like the lees at the bottom of a cup of wine; once those memories were stirred to life, they colored the whole of it. She recalled that blustery cold March day when Gonzales' Ranging Company assembled in the town square; they were going to the aid of the besieged garrison in Bexar, thirty-two men and too many of them boys, every one of them known and known well; fathers, sons, and brothers. They had not returned; Jacob Darst, and Isaac Milsaps, young Will King, and Jesse McCoy who had once been the sheriff. Mourning the loss of them would have been an agony for their friends and womenfolk left behind, save that on the very day that word came that the Alamo had fallen and all of its defenders put to the sword, General Houston gave orders that Gonzales be burned and everyone living in it evacuate to the east. Margaret was tempted to close the book. Should she read more of Mr. Hattersley's history tonight, and allow those faces and memories to haunt what might be left of her sleep?

No, she decided abruptly. Mr. Hattersley would have had the opportunities while living in Austin to meet other great men, who had been fortunate to survive those circumstances which attended on the birth of their perilous and fortunate nation. He would have met General Houston on many occasions, and talked with many who remembered and revered Mr. Austin, whose foresight and stubborn care of his grant and those settlers came to join it, never failed, even under the most severe provocation. He was a gentle man, as well as a gentleman, Margaret recalled, from that one meeting with him. He liked small children, treating them with affectionate respect, which is what children of a certain age craved beyond all other regard. She had been twelve years old – almost a lady, in her eyes – and Carlchen a lad of four-nearly-five. Mr. Austin came to the little house that Papa had rented for Mama and herself and Carl in San Felipe. Papa had already managed to quarrel with him, as he would later quarrel with Colonel DeWitt. Mr. Austin wished to amend his quarrel with Papa – to no avail – just has he had attempted to amend and intervene in the many quarrels between the American settlers and with those in the state capital in Monclova and the even farther-distant Mexico City.

Margaret had always thought of him as a conciliatory and diplomatic man, who prized above all else comity and accord. At the age of twelve, she had sensed his deep aversion to discord, his sense of honor with regard to the oaths that he had taken to Mexico, and his devotion to what he had built in

San Felipe . . . no, there were men who became entrepreneurs to make a profit from a longing to possess the land, but Mr. Austin was not one of them, although he might have been at the beginning. He cared for his grant and the settlers who came to take a holding in it as a mother cares for a child, watchful, tender, and protective. He came around reluctantly at last to join the rebels, to become a part of the War Party – as it was called then – a circumstance which signaled the end of any accommodation with Mexico. If even Mr. Austin could be driven along that path of rebellion – then there was no hope for others, less willing to compromise. Margaret thumbed through the pages of Mr. Hattersley's *History*, searching each of them for a mention of Mr. Austin.

When she found it at last, she could scarcely comprehend what Mr. Hattersley had written – as vile as it was untruthful. *How could they all have misjudged the man so?* Margaret no longer felt lulled into slumber – no, if what Mr. Hattersley had written in the case of Mr. Austin had fallen so short of the truth of events and men as she recalled it – what else had he covered with calumny, while abiding under her roof?

Chapter 7 – *The Viper Nourished*

Margaret turned back a few pages to a chapter heading: *Chapter III – Santa Anna, President – Measures of Clemency – Texan Land Jobbing*, and a list of topics which went nearly halfway down the page, seemingly reflective of the events that she could recall the men talking about in hushed murmurs. *Measures of Clemency?* Her eyebrows lifted almost involuntarily, and she returned to that particular passage which had completely arrested her attention. *Colonel Austin, who was himself the most crafty of the "political fanatics, political adventurers, would-be great men, and vain talkers," wrote in this bland style solely to escape from the clutches of the Mexican government, and not with a view to restore tranquility to Texas . . .*

She could scarcely comprehend how Mr. Hattersley could believe and write this of Mr. Austin, whose loyalty to Mexico and personal integrity were a byword among the settlers in the American colonies. Now she turned the pages more carefully – yes, there was mention of the various Conventions – but none of the overturn of the Constitution of 1824. It was as if it had never existed, or that men like Juan Seguin and the Menchaca brothers, or Senor De Leon, the impresario of Victoria, had ever felt the slightest of loyalties to it. Nothing of the troubles at Anahuac, of the criminals among Colonel Bradburn's men and of their depredations committed among the Anglo settlers. Nothing much of the division between *Centralistas* and *Federalistas,* save for a mention of how a desire for relative independence of the states had been rejected by the majority of the Mexican nation.

There was a brief paragraph about the rebellion in Zacatecas, without a whisper of how Santa Anna had allowed his troops to sack, pillage, and rape at will. Margaret set down the book, holding it open in one hand, while she rubbed her eyes with the other. News of how the Federalist militia of Zacatecas had fared in rebellion had electrified the settlers of Texas. There was not a man alive who did not fear to see his own family, his own home treated as Santa Anna's army had treated those men, women, and children.

She adjusted the lamp wick to give a brighter light, returned to the book, and was struck anew by such laudatory words regarding Lopez de Santa Anna, who was, as Mr. Hattersley put it, *". . . the able and energetic measures of that extraordinary man, Santa Anna, who was at once the military leader and universal and patriotic pacificator of his country . . ."* What Esteban Menchaca would have said upon hearing that Margaret could hardly fathom, save that her husband's friend from Bexar would have been quite scathing. Several pages of proclamations and letters followed, quoted entire and *verbatim* as nearly as Margaret could remember, although Mr. Hattersley put his own interpretation upon them, with an air of smug certitude that fairly wreathed up from the page. *"In order to prepare my readers for these and many other assertions of a similar character put forth by the unprincipled Texans, I have in the preceding chapter shown what their conduct was while the federal system was in force in Mexico, and never did the history of a people brand them with greater treachery or grosser ingratitude and inconsistency. Austin . . . hastened away with these documents to the United States, where . . . he succeeded in getting money, arms and men to carry on the war against Mexico."*

"A serpent," Margaret said aloud, marveling. "A serpent, with a lying tongue! How he abases himself in these scribblings, licking Santa Anna's boots while covering such as Mr. Austin with the slime from the nearest gutter! No wonder Carlchen's friend did not wish to keep this book for himself!" Still, it was with a concerted effort that she read the remainder of that chapter. No, she would not sleep after reading Mr. Hattersley's mealy-mouthed justification for the treacherous slaughter of Colonel Fannin's command. Mr. Hattersley seemed to think his name was spelled "Fanning" – although Margaret or any others among her boarders whose memories of those days was as fresh as a plate of Hetty's biscuits could have corrected him on that score. No mention of the Gonzales Rangers, yet Mr. Hattersley specifically averred that no aid was ever received in response to Colonel Travis' plea! To omit any word of those men and boys whom Margaret recalled with affection, that was a lie of omission! With increasing distaste, she wondered if indeed Mr. Hattersley had been as assiduous in his research as he had claimed to be. He described Colonel Crockett breathing his last beside Rezin Bowie, James Bowie's brother and the inventor of the famous knife – but that also could not have been the case, if Sue Dickinson's words were true and that of Colonel Travis's slave, Joe. After the battle, poor pretty Sue had seen Colonel Crockett's body in front of the chapel doors, and James Bowie had died in his sickbed in a chamber by the gateway, or so Joe had claimed, having seen it when he was conducted around the old mission to identify the bodies of those captains and officers among the garrison. Mr. Hattersley also felt obliged to disparage the fashion for large hunting knives as favored by the Texians. Margaret smiled at the memory of how her brother had brought out his own to show to Mr. Hattersley – and then carved a piece of apple pie with it, and cleaned the knife with his fingers.

She read on – a short account of how the bodies of Rezin – she could only assume he meant Colonel Bowie – and the rest of the Alamo garrison had been piled up and burned, and then the next sentence leaped from the page. *"I need scarcely apologize to the reader for this digression, as the record of the fate of all such monsters is due to the lovers of humanity."*

Abruptly, Margaret slammed the book shut with fingers that trembled from sudden fury, and the sour taste of sickness rising in the back of her throat. A monster; James Bowie, who had sat in a chair in the breezeway of her home in Gonzales with the infant Horace in his arms as he came near to weeping himself for the loss of his wife and the children she bore him. A monster – then Adolphus Hattersley had erratic taste in monsters, not realizing that he had become one himself; a sycophantic, treacherous monster, with a tongue given to voicing lies and calumny, in the guise of being an honest and faithful observer of men and events. In the guise – worse yet – of having been a friend to her family, for her husband had liked him well, since they shared much of the same cultured taste and ready wit. *Why had he written this libelous little book, and for what purpose?*

A few errant fingers of sunlight sifted through the shutters, brighter than the lamplight; Margaret realized with a start that it was already dawn. She had sat up all the rest of the night reading, and was still only halfway through Mr. Hattersley's infamous little history. It was time to help Hetty fix breakfast, and to pour into the separating-pans the bucket of milk that Papa had from the two milk cows this morning, so that the cream would rise and they might have butter to churn from it. Her mind, diverted from Mr. Hattersley's book, ran onto consideration of what they might need to make cheese. Did any of their remaining neighbors plan to slaughter a calf soon, for rennet? Margaret tucked away in her mind an intention to ask Mrs. Simpson – she was a widow with two children who lived nearby and kept a herd of cows for milk. Mrs. Simpson might intend to sacrifice one of their suckling calves in a month or so, in the interests of cheese-making. If so, they could share out a portion of the calf's stomach, or ask one of their neighbors to hunt a calf from among the herds of wild cattle which wandered the grassy uplands. But not if they must go far – Margaret's heart contracted in apprehension. It was dangerous now to go on foot very far beyond clear sight of the chimneys of Austin and the faint curls of smoke rising from them. The picture of poor Mr. White came to her mind, caught not a quarter-mile from his house beyond Shoal Creek, crumpled at the foot of the oak tree where he had taken shelter from Indians; the tree and Gideon White struck alike with arrows and slashed with hatchet blows. No, it was only safe in numbers, armed and on horseback, to venture much beyond Shoal Creek, or into the oak-starred grasslands north of town. It had become the common thing while walking along the trail that led into

Pecan Street in the morning, to see the print of moccasin-clad feet and unshod horses pressed into the tramped dust.

She put away the book, having no desire to read any more of it, but was haunted throughout the rest of the day, and for many days after: how could someone who Race Vining had liked so much and that she had considered a loyal friend, who had so many opportunities to hear firsthand of the events he had written about, still choose to write such untruths, such vile falsehoods. Try as she would, she couldn't think of any reason.

Neither could Hetty, who said impatiently, "Oh, he was a plagued Englishman, Marm – who knows why they do anything at all. They love a lord, and bow before a queen. Perhaps he thought we were unnatural for not wishing to be directed by our betters."

If Race had still been alive, Margaret might have taken her puzzlement to him; of all the delights of marriage that was the aspect which she missed the most. To have a dear and loving confidant to discuss these conundrums . . . *Well,* thought Margaret, *I might at least write of this to Doctor Williamson – he also knew Mr. Hattersley well. I suppose poor Mr. O'Doyle will soon join him in Perote – I will write to him as well. And perhaps Margaret Houston. Yes, she might know from General Sam what purpose Mr. Hattersley had for writing that dreadful book. If anyone knows – he would, the wily old tomcat!*

That afternoon she did exactly that, opening up the little brass-trimmed portable writing desk at her end of the table in the parlor-schoolroom and penning out two letters rather than working at the spinning wheel as Horace, Johnny, and Jamie sat at their lessons. *Would that Race had not fallen so ill,* she thought with regret – *we might have had a proper school by this time.* As it was, she had given them each one of her husband's books to read, with a list of questions for each to answer as soon as they had finished. She looked at the letter for Dr. Williamson when she had finished, seeing with vague astonishment that she had written five pages of close-written lines in the careful, elegant penmanship that Race had schooled her in. This would be the third letter that she had written to him since receiving his quietly dignified plea, and also much the longest. *I hope that will please him,* she thought, blotting the last page – *poor Dr. Williamson, so far away and locked up behind the cold stone walls of Perote!* She lifted up the green felt-covered writing surface, and drew out another sheet of paper from space underneath, and began her letter to Margaret Houston. The General's Margaret was expecting a child soon, according to her last letter. She and the General had settled on a holding of their own, although to Margaret Houston's sorrow the General was often away on matters of government.

That is what he does, Margaret wrote on that winter afternoon, by way of consoling her friend. The nib of her pen scratched busily away on her paper. *He has been part and parcel of public affairs in Texas for lo these ten years, and for many years in the East before that. His absorption in such matters is as much a part of him as his countenance and his scars. Disallow such expeditions and you remove a portion of those qualities which led you to hold him in such affection. Love is not love which alters when it alteration finds, or bends with the remover to remove. As the great bard advised – such love is an ever-fixed mark that looks on tempests and is never shaken.*

She continued her letter to Margaret Houston, thinking that she might very well copy out that sonnet entire, for the boys to copy tomorrow as penmanship practice. The book of sonnets she found easily; that was one of the books that she loved the best. *What magic could a poet wring out of words!* She set aside the pages of her letters for the ink upon them to dry before she folded and sealed them, and drew out a clean sheet of paper, thinking that she might wish to have something like a proper writing desk someday. Perhaps when the Legislature returned, and she had a house full of boarders again. A whole page was not necessary for a writing exercise: she folded the sheet of paper in half and slit along the fold with a penknife. She bent her head over pen and the half-sheet of paper, taking care with the elegant slant of her pen and the gracefully rounded letters; copying the lines entire, and clearly.

Thus was she absorbed, until Hetty looked into the parlor just as Papa came in through the front door. "Do ye want me to start the roast now?" Hetty asked, and a gust of wind from outdoors scattered all the papers from the table – letters and the writing-exercise and all. Margaret sighed in exasperation, and stooped to gather them all from the floor; fortunately the ink was dried so nothing was smeared. Papa looked in through the parlor doorway – as if he did not dare step over the threshold.

"There's a message for you both," he said gruffly. "From Bullock's – he sent his boy with it. He's waiting outside for you."

"What is the message then, Papa?" Margaret asked, and Papa shook his head.

"The boy didn't know. He just said for you and Miss Moylan to come with him."

"I suppose we may as well go and see what it is about." Margaret hastily folded and sealed her two letters, "I was going to put these in the post, anyway."

Bullock's lad was about fourteen – he reminded her of Carl at that age, responsible and shy. He didn't know anything of why he was sent either, only that his parents had sent him, and that the ladies should come to his mother's china parlor. The wind blew crisp from the north, and the sky was filled with scudding clouds that promised rain on the horizon, even thought the sky over their heads remained clear, with the bare branches of the apple trees etching a tangle of lines across it. There was no need, Margaret thought, for the lad to carry a rifle over his shoulder. It was only a short walk, and through the daylight hours from Papa's house – there were no Indians about, only the friendly Tonkawa camp, out at the north of town.

"Mr. Waller and Papa have the newspaper from Houston City," he explained, "and they went to Mama, and Mama said you should be sent for." Margaret and Hetty looked at each other – what could this be, which so concerned Mary Bullock and Mr. Waller, the mayor after Mr. Ward? The scattering of houses seemed to draw closer for mutual protection around the Bullock's sprawling establishment, while the capitol building sat high on a hill, rising above the flimsy palisade of earth-set timbers around the circumference. The President's house, white and gleaming, sat on it's own hill. Margaret sighed to see it. Someday General Sam and Margaret or whoever followed General Sam in office would return and take up residence in it. Now it had the forlorn look of an empty building.

Mary Bullock's china parlor was a large room and plastered on the interior walls, in the center of the Bullock's Inn, a comfortable room adorned with shelves full of fine porcelain china which Margaret did not envy half as much as she envied Mary her piano. It was the only one in Austin, and Mary Bullock half-humorously complained that she played only indifferently – but there was no other to compare her playing to. Margaret had often thought of asking for lessons from Mary, so that she might learn to play herself; such lovely music the piano made! If she could not write sonnets as well as the Bard, she might at least make music as indifferently as Mary Bullock did. Now Mary sprang up from the chair where she sat, and ran towards them; she had tears on her cheeks, and Margaret again had that cold feeling at the pit of her stomach that she had on the day that Erastus Smith came to their camp, on the muddy road between San Felipe and Groce's Crossing. He had bad news for them and dreaded to tell it – that Santa Anna's soldiers had murdered all

89

those under Fannin's command at Goliad, and that her brothers were dead. Mr. Waller was already standing, and so was Mary's husband.

"We've only just heard," Mary exclaimed. "We thought of Mrs. Fritchie at once, being in a delicate condition. We thought that she best should hear from you . . ."

"What has happened, then?" Hetty demanded, with narrowed eyes. "'Tis it to do with Danny, then?"

"Not with Mr. Fritchie," Richard Bullock answered heavily, "but to do with all those lads who tried to take Mier."

"Mr. Fritchie is in Perote," Margaret said. "I have a letter from Dr. Williamson, saying that he was recovering and fit."

"With Seamus, then?" Hetty turned pale – the freckles on her face stood out in pale orange blotches. "What is it then? What have you heard?"

"It's in the newspaper from Houston," Mr. Waller answered, with grave formality. "They were being taken deep into Mexico, on foot and under guard. Near to Saltillo, nearly two hundred overpowered their guards and escaped . . . but with little water and no food, just a few horses. Most of the lads were retaken in a week. And now that butcher Santa Anna has ordered that they be executed. All of them, as punishment." Margaret could barely speak for the shock of it, knowing that the vile dictator Lopez de Santa Anna was ordering once again the murder of prisoners. *What excuse, what justification would Mr. Hattersley make for this?*

"We thought," Mary Bullock ventured softly, "that you should know of this first and in private. Mr. O'Doyle . . . such a happy soul! He had so many good friends among us, and knowing how he lived at your place, and was dear kin to you and little Mrs. Fritchie! Miss Moylan, Mrs. Vining – I thought you should know of this, Mrs. Fritchie being so near her time."

Mary Bullock's eyes overflowed again, and Hetty answered sturdily, "Aye – well, and it's good of you to take the trouble. He's a scamp and no mistake, Marm Bullock. Ye should have nae fear for Seamus O'Doyle, for he has as many lives as a cat. 'Tis good of ye to tell us, though. Oh, Seamus, why did ye do it!" Tears trembled in Hetty's eyes. "Marm Vining's brother – he told him not to go, so he did! He's a romantic soul, and he promised my sister that he would get her man back for her. What can be done for our lads, then? Surely there can be more done than just pray for their souls?"

Mr. Waller nodded his head magisterially, answering, "It seems that this atrocity has not yet been carried out. The outcry is very great, from both the American minister to Mexico and the British as well. It may well be that the sentence will not be carried out."

"So that vile butcher will not get his way this time," Margaret breathed. "There are surely brave and decent people in Mexico and elsewhere – he will not dare to carry out this vile deed in the sunshine of the world's regard."

"The reports are weeks old," Mr. Waller added warningly, even as Hetty's face brightened with hope and Mr. Bullock nodded. "The sentence of death might already have been carried out, and we would not know of it for days . . . but while there is life there is hope."

"Thank you for telling us of this," Margaret took Hetty's hand and squeezed it. "We will find a way to break this news to Morag, then – perhaps we might just wait until we hear more." In her heart Margaret had already accepted the worst. Seamus, in his hopeless and unrequited love for Morag, was indifferent to death – and so death would find him easily enough. Death may indeed already have found him, in the hopeless fight for Laredo or Mier, along the rivers which ran through the borderlands, in the harsh desert of Mexico – or against a wall in a dusty garrison courtyard. Margaret already resolved that she would never tell Morag of how Seamus O'Doyle had loved her. That would be cruel – and she was within six weeks of bearing her child.

"We are friends," Mary Bullock embraced them both. "Friends do what we can for each other."

They took their leave then, Bullock's son walking back with them to the bottom of the hill, the hill crowned with bare apple trees. Margaret left her letters to be mailed with Mary Bullock – it already seemed as if she had written them days ago, in light of his news.

They waited for news of what would happen to the Mier prisoners; Margaret felt like one stretched on tenterhooks, dreading to hear the worst while Morag approached the day of her confinement. There was no word that the sentence of death had not been carried out on the Mier prisoners, and Margaret began to hope that the tyrant Santa Anna had relented, that the outcry against him had an effect. March went into April; Morag waddled like a duck, and began occasionally to feel the spasms of fleeting labor pains – and she could not play so freely with the boys. The care of the house and the cooking went back upon Margaret and Hetty, although Margaret didn't mind.

"It keeps your mind from things," she observed to Hetty, on one of the first balmy spring days, when it was warm enough to open the parlor windows. She and Hetty were dusting – a considerable task, for all the books in the parlor. Her sons were planting potatoes in the garden plot, under Papa's direction. When they were finished, she would give them their lessons for the day, and at that moment she recalled how she had thought of penmanship practice, and looked for the sonnet that she had copied out. "That's odd," she murmured, as she opened the writing-desk. I thought sure I had left it here. There's the other half of the paper . . ."

"Left what, Marm?" Hetty sneezed, in a rain of dust from the topmost shelf.

"I wrote out a sonnet for the boys to copy . . . *Love is not love which alters when it alteration finds, or bends with the remover to remove.* I thought I had left it in my writing desk, but I cannot find it anywhere."

"Did it fall onto the floor, then?" Hetty asked. "Perhaps it slid under the book-case – d'ye wish me to look for it there?"

"Oh, it's too much trouble to move all the books," Margaret answered. "It would be less trouble for me to write it out again."

A little past the middle of April, a letter from Dr. Williamson arrived for Margaret, a letter which she took into the front parlor and opened with much anticipation. She was glad she had done so, and read it in private. He began without any particular salutation, which was his custom. Margaret found his omission of the expected convention in letters to be very like his lack of them in person. After all, this was the man who customarily read a book at the suppertable, ignoring most conversation.

> *I fear I have the worst of news for your household, concerning our mutual friend, Mr. O'Doyle. He was executed by order of the Tyrant Santa Anna at Salado on the 25th of last month, with sixteen of his comrades of the Mier Expedition. I was first told of this by an officer of the garrison at Perote, a man who cares little for the Tyrant. We share some mutual interests in matters medical. The order was first given at the highest levels in Mexico City for those prisoners recaptured to be executed en masse. To do him honor, General Mejia, the commandant of the Northern Districts refused this directive. General Mejia was removed from his command for this defiance.*

Margaret laid the folds of the letter aside and briefly closed her eyes. This is what she had feared, so many months ago, when Seamus O'Doyle left his carpenter's tools and his copy of Benjamin's *American Builder's Companion*. She had been half-expecting to hear this, ever since she and Hetty had been sent for by Mr. Waller and Mr. Bullock. How fitting that she would be sitting in the front parlor, in the very room that Mr. O'Doyle had built for her, at hers and his design. Dry-eyed, she picked up the letter and continued reading.

I did not want to write of this until I could confirm events through a visit from General Thompson, the American Minister. The storm raised by the Tyrant's order was not confined to Mexico. The gov'ts of the United States and of Britain were particularly outraged by this cruel judgement, and their ministers spoke with such a determined voice that the Tyrant was prevailed upon to amend his decision. Being the autocrat that he is, it proved beyond the skills of simple humanity to persuade him of the wisdom of reversing his condemnation entirely. Instead he proposed to ameliorate it in the classical manner by decimation – viz one man in ten. Seventeen prisoners were selected by the means of putting seventeen black beans and a number of white beans equal to the number of remaining prisoners into a covered jar. Each prisoner was made to draw a single bean, unseen. By this lottery was our Mr. O'Doyle made one of those unfortunates, who were taken to another part of the Salado presidio. I was told by my acquaintance, whose brother is an officer serving on the staff of Colonel Huerta and witnessed these terrible proceedings that the chosen men bore themselves with admirable fortitude.

Mr. O'Doyle particularly drew his attention, for his red hair and beard. At once upon seeing that he had drawn a black bean, he made a remark to the effect that he was only robbed of a quantity of years for which he had little use. Before being taken away, he made a present of his coat and boots to a fellow prisoner whose own were worn and patched to uselessness.

If it will comfort Miss Hetty, tell her that Mr. O'Doyle and the others were offered the last rites by a priest, which Mr. O'Doyle accepted with every evidence of good cheer. They were executed in two groups, in which Mr. O'Doyle was among the first. He refused to be blindfolded. Those Mexican soldiers who were tasked with the grim duty of the firing squad were not eager to perform it, and in fact were much revolted by the prospect. Several were most sickened afterwards. My informant tells me that his brother – who was charged with witnessing the executions and obeyed with much the same reluctance – described those soldiers as being more distressed than the condemned men. Seeing that they appeared reluctant to give the final order, Mr. O'Doyle cried out, "Fuerza, damn ye all, fuerza!"

The seventeen, including Mr. O'Doyle were buried the following day. One poor wretch was merely wounded, and fell pretending to be slain. He was able to crawl away from the place of execution during the night, but alas, was speedily tracked down and dispatched. You may well imagine the distress felt by those of us confined in this dreadful place upon hearing of this. Mr. Thompson has confirmed most particulars, including the names of the slain. I believe none of those may have been known to you or to Mr. Vining, save in a desultory fashion. We are told that the remainder of the Mier prisoners will join us here.

If I may impose upon you, please convey my condolences to Miss Hetty and to Mrs. Fritchie regarding Mr. O'Doyle. I know that he was regarded by them at the very least as almost a brother. As for Mr. Fritchie, he tasks me daily with questions regarding the advent of his child and of his dearest's welfare. We both remain in fair health, and grateful for your letters, and for those items of comfort which you have sent to us through Mr. Thompson's good offices.
I remain most respectfully yours, etc, etc.

Margaret folded the single page of Dr. Williamson's letter together. Now she must go break the news to Hetty and Morag, but she lingered a while in the parlor. So odd, that if she closed her eyes and called Mr. Doyle to mind, she could almost hear his voice, the musical Irish timbre of it as he argued over the supper table with the other boarders. How he had talked, as he built this room and the others, extending the plain, tall-standing log house that Papa had built. When he had worked on the French Legate's house doubtless he had talked as well. He was an artist with his carpenters' tools, working wood to his purposes and liking as easily as she fashioned cloth to hers, when she sewed clothing for the boys or for Morag's infant. What a sad end for an artist, at the foot of a wall in Salado, coatless and barefoot, having given away the largest portion of the little he had to another in need! What would Mr. Hattersley make of that, she wondered? The last two of her loyal boarders gone in opposite directions; she pictured Mr. Hattersley at some noble supper table, amusing his fellow diners with his wasp-wit. Would he, doomed to die before a firing squad, have given away his clothes or behaved with such noble courage? No – the comparison between the two shamed Mr. Hattersley, or would have, if he had cared to know.

94

Chapter 8 - *Forted Up*

The events of which Dr. Williamson had written were confirmed within days by accounts in the newspapers which arrived from across Texas. Morag wept a little when Margaret told them of what Dr. Williamson's letter conveyed. So did Hetty, but then she dried her eyes and said, "Our old Mam would have said he was born to trouble as sparks fly upwards. But he made a brave end of it, did he? And in a state of grace, as well. A blessing, I'd say: There's many dies worse that deserves better, and many deserving worse who die well." She dabbed at her eyes again and blew her nose. "An' he did well by his kinfolk an' those he called friends. Ever so grateful I am that he brought us here."

"I wish he had drawn life from that dreadful jar," Margaret replied, feeling more than a little tearful in the face of Hetty's stoicism. "I had hoped to expand the house again someday – and I trusted him to be the one to build it! I can find another carpenter, but where do you find another cousin?"

"Oh, aye – we had cousins a'plenty in Wexford!" Hetty answered robustly, and then her eyes moistened again. "No' many like Seamus though! We shall miss him too, Marm, miss him something awful. Morag, darlin' – if the baby is a boy, you should name him after Seamus, no matter what your man says. Aye, that's what you should do!"

"But what if the baby is a girl?" Morag asked, laughing a little through her tears. "What should I do then, Marm?"

"Jemima," Margaret suggested. "Close enough to James, I think." They talked a little about a girl's name for Morag's babe, Margaret all the time thinking how much she would have loved to have a daughter. Not that she loved her sons any the less, or would have wished them to be anything more or less than they were – bumptious and growing boys in all their glory, but a daughter to share in those womanly mysteries, to talk and laugh with, as she had done with her mother and Oma Katerina! Boys became men – just as her dear baby brother Carl had grown first into a boy and departed into the world of men. Her sons would do the same and very soon. They would depart, and if not into the Llano like Carl and his Ranger comrades, then to a world of which she would ever only know a portion.

In the end, Morag and Daniel's baby arrived quite swiftly, several weeks after Margaret had received Dr. Williamson's letter. Morag shuffled into the kitchen at mid-morning, heavy and off balance with the weight of the child, taking up a dish towel to dry the breakfast dishes that Hetty was washing. Morag slept badly at night in these final weeks, resting frequently with her feet up; such were the discomforts of imminent child-bearing. Standing close to the warmth of the stove, Margaret was carefully stirring a kettle of milk curds, watching the heavy masses of cheese curds separate from the clear yellowish whey. Her sons were out with Papa, working in the garden under Papa's eyes. Although they were close enough to the house, Papa still had a loaded rifle leaning against the nearest tree.

"Och, Morag dear, you should be stayin' off your feet!" Hetty exclaimed. Margaret turned around, echoing the sentiments as soon as she saw Morag's face, pale with strain and particularly bruised-looking around her eyes.

"No – there's an ache in my legs and in my back. Truly it feels better to be walking around – oh!" she gasped, half-doubling over. "Mother Mary an' Joseph!"

"What is the matter!" Both Mary and Hetty exclaimed. Margaret dropped the long spoon into the curds and Hetty abandoned the dishpan, to come to her side.

"It . . . hurts!" Morag answered, between clenched teeth. "A sudden pain, as if – oh!" She held on to Hetty with both hands, her face crimson with embarrassment. "Hetty, I think I've pissed meself! Marm, I'm terrible sorry!"

"Not to mind," Margaret answered calmly. The floor at Morag's feet became suddenly dark with liquid, which soaked into the planks or swiftly drained between. "The pain was that of the waters breaking. The baby is coming."

"Is that what 'tis?" Morag gasped again. Her face screwed up as another pain took hold. "Och, another one – not so bad!"

"How close together?" Margaret demanded, "And how long have you been feeling them?"

"Since last night and no more than a minute or two between," Morag answered, while Hetty replied comfortably, "Just like our Mam, then." She looked across Morag's bowed head to Margaret. "Mam always had hers fast. Two shakes of a lamb's tail, Mam always said. Wi' our youngest brother, she was brought to bed after the morning milking, birthed him by the time the church clock struck ten of the hour, and was bringing supper to the reapers in the field at noon."

"How . . . energetic of her," Margaret said, thinking that Hetty was most likely saying so to cheer and encourage Morag, who now clung to Margaret's hand with such a grip that Margaret's fingers were practically numb.

"Well, Mam was married when she was only a bit of a girl," Hetty answered. "She bore twenty-three babes, an' all but four born alive and well. With th' youngest of us, all the midwife need do was sit at the bottom of the bed an' hold out her hands to catch – if there was time to go an' find her. Morag, me darlin' it may take a little longer for your first, but I swear to you, for Mam it always went easy."

"I want to lie down now," Morag demanded, her face suddenly sheened with perspiration.

They had arranged a bed in the old parlor for a lying in and Margaret shook her head. "In a little while, Morag dear – if you walk now, it will bring it on easily." She looked across at Hetty, who seemed quite calm. "Do you want me to send one of the boys for a doctor?" she asked, and Hetty shook her head.

"No need, no need, Marm." She answered. None the less, she slipped out to the garden while Hetty helped Morag remove her dress and petticoats, and quietly asked Papa to keep the boys in the garden, or set them to work in the stable for as long as possible. Papa looked grimly pleased at that, while the boys were the picture of dejection at the prospect of working all the day, instead of lessons in the afternoon.

Miraculously to Margaret, there was no need to send for the doctor or any of the women in town known to be more skilled than Hetty as a midwife. Morag's baby came as easily as a kitten to a mother cat, a crumpled pink shape with a comical crown of dark hair on it's elongated little head slipped easily from between Morag's pale thighs. Morag cried out almost involuntarily, a cry that was half a moan of relief and triumph mixed together.

Hetty, behind Morag's shoulders and bracing her into a sitting position on the bed, commanded, "Now, push one more time! Och, you've a grand wee daughter for Danny. He'll want a son the next time, I'll be bound. Is the little one all there, Marm – all of her lovely little fingers and toes?"

"She is," Margaret answered, around a lump in her throat. Morag groaned again, as the red spongy mass of the afterbirth came away. While Hetty dealt capably with it, Margaret swathed the little form in a towel that had been warming by the hearth, gently rubbing the birth-matter from it's tiny limbs and from the fluff of dark hair. How small was a newborn, how compact from being sheltered in the safe refuge of a mother's womb. The baby's flesh was pale pink with health, it drew in an astonished breath, and Margaret hastily wrapped it in the towel and put Morag's daughter into her arms, while Hetty beamed with happiness and satisfaction upon them all.

"Father Odin is away, but he left me wi' a vial of holy water so that I could baptize the wee mite myself. What name d'ye wish to call her by? Jemima for Seamus, o'course, and perhaps Marm can gi' her another name, for luck."

"Mary," Margaret answered, so moved that she could barely speak. "Mary for my own mother: I'd wished to name a daughter of mine for her."

"And for the Blessed Mother," Hetty cooed. "That will do very well, Marm – Jemima Mary Fritchie it is, then. Look you. She smiled: I think she likes her names."

"She has a little pain in her middle," Margaret answered. "It only looks like she is smiling."

"No, she is truly smiling, Marm." Morag insisted, and her own face was split by a yawn. "Oh – begging your pardon – I did no' think to be so tired!"

"Try and nurse the little one a little, before you go to sleep," Margaret suggested, "so that she may become accustomed to suck, and your milk will come the sooner." Impulsively, she bent down and kissed Morag's forehead, and kissed the baby's downy little head. "Rest now – this will be the last good rest you will see for years."

Jemima-Mary was a good baby, placid and not particularly colicky. The boys, especially Peter and Jamie were entranced but deeply disappointed that she would not be a ready playmate for a good few years. The baby took no interest at all in the boy-treasures that they brought for her from the woods and creek-banks; flowers and water-tumbled stones, and flint arrowheads, although Morag smilingly promised to keep them safe for her, until she was a little older. A week after her birth, Morag and her sister and Margaret were invited by Mary Bullock to bring Jemima-Mary to a gathering of the town's women for afternoon tea.

"To welcome our newest little settler," explained Mrs. Eberly, who bore the message, stumping fearlessly up the hill. "And she is quite the picture of an angel, isn't she?" Mrs. Eberly cooed at baby, who was awake and examining the world immediately over her head and shaking her tiny boneless fists at it, lying in the cradle that Papa had made. "A love, she is – and will her eyes stay so blue? Just the color of buffalo clover, and the very image of her mama, I am sure."

"I hope so, Marm Eberly." Morag was pink with embarrassment and pride at being with her baby the center of so much attention. "I hope so indade."

"And Mr. Fritchie," Mrs. Eberly continued, "locked up in that wretched Perote place, never laying eyes on the little mite! Well, don't you fear, Mrs. Fritchie – we'll see that you'll be looked after, just as one of our own."

"Thank you, Marm." Morag blushed even deeper, as Mrs. Eberly straightened her bonnet and prepared to take her leave.

"We will see you the day after tomorrow, then, in the china parlor at Bullocks."

"A party," Hetty exclaimed. "Och, and isna that what we need for a cheering-up? To see the other ladies for a bit, and to show off Jemima-Mary . . . what shall we bring, then – some ginger-cakes? Although," and she looked as if she was having a second thought. "No, the good white flour is all but gone."

"Apple-butter," Margaret said. "We have plenty to share."

There were about thirty women and older girls still living in Austin; Margaret tallied them up thoughtfully – most of them married – and on good terms with each other as much as they had to be. Mrs. Eberly was the oldest, the grand dame of such little society as they had. Margaret reckoned herself as the only young widow who had maintained that state for more than a year, as there were far more men in Austin, more young and daring men than there were women to be courted by them. It took a strong-minded, resolute woman to maintain a single state for very long. Of families, there were enough with children that Race Vining might have opened a school; it distressed Margaret to know that one of the reasons – besides having no schoolmaster – for not having such was that the older boys and girls were taken up with the work that needed to be done, and the danger of Indians kept the smaller ones close to their mothers. But for the sake of the community of women, it was a rare week when there was not a gathering of them at one house or another, for a round of quilting, or to talk together as they sewed or knitted, while their children played outside in the afternoon. Today, Margaret resolved to take the older boys, Horace and Johnny with her. Otherwise, Papa would have put them to work, and today would be a bit of a holiday.

"This is Jemima-Mary's debut into society," she told her sons, as they walked down the rise from Papa's house, towards the scatterings of shanties and log houses clustered around Constitution and Pecan.

Morag and Hetty laughed, as Jamie asked, "What's a day-boo, Mama?"

"Back in the East," she answered, "It's when a young lady puts up her hair and her Mama and Papa have a party for all of their friends and her friends, to let everyone know she is of an age to be courted in marriage."

"It sounds silly," Horace said gravely. "Can't they all just tell by looking?"

The three women laughed together, their voices mingling pleasantly in the glade of oak trees that the path towards town meandered through, while Jamie and Peter squabbled pleasantly over which one of them would court Jemima-Mary when she was a young lady. Morag drew Jemima-Mary closer to her with one arm, and picked up the trailing hem of her skirt with the other.

Hetty answered, still laughing, "I'll tell ye how ye can tell when you're of an age to begin courting, laddie – it's when you finally get your growth and ye are taller than the one ye like!" Horace blushed. He had just turned twelve. To his horror the two girls nearest his age in Austin both towered over him by at least half a head.

Margaret saw this discomfiture and put her arm around his shoulders, whispering, "It's only a matter of time, dear one." She nearly slipped and called him 'little one.' "Girls always get their growth first, and then the boys catch up. You'll not be as tall as Uncle Carl, but you will be as tall as your Papa, and I liked him very much as he was."

Within the far-scattering of houses on the outskirts of town, but still short of the Bullocks', they were startled by the swift urgent rattle of the alarm-drum sounding. Margaret's heart chilled like a lump of ice within her breast – *what was this?* A man shouted, then another – *Comanche!* She turned and looked over her shoulder towards the steep ridge thrust up into the blue summer sky to the north of town, a height which offered a superb view of all of Austin and the outlying houses, all the way down to the riverbank. Horror rooted her feet to the ground; the green and oak-wooded height was not green any more, but patched with seething color, of men on horseback, brilliantly painted horses, and men accoutered in bright red blankets that the Comanche favored, carrying long bows and javelins adorned with ribbons and feather. Queerly, her first impulse was to turn and run back to the refuge of Papa's house. Just as sense prevailed, a man on horseback pounded past them, reining in his horse in an uprush of dust and dancing hooves.

"To the Bullock's fort – now!" He shouted, and she recognized Mr. Coleman, elected captain of the Austin Ranger Company. He lived a little farther away, up the valley and farmed near Shoal Creek. Now he held his horses' reins in one fist, a long repeating revolver in the other, the barrel pointed upwards.

Margaret gathered up the four-year-old Peter in her arms, and commanded, breathlessly, "Morag, Hetty – run! Don't stop to look behind. Horace, take Jamie's hand! Do it – Jamie, run now!" for Jamie clamored to be allowed to go back to the house and load for Opa so he could fight the Indians.

Hetty already had Johnny by one hand, her other on Morag's shoulder. Margaret looked back again, at once wished that she hadn't and was glad that she had, for the Indians on their gaily caparisoned horses were already spilling down through the trees. Captain Coleman kept between them and the Indians, his horse dancing impatiently to and fro as he kept the reins tightly gathered. He turned his horse every few moments – himself always between the Indians pouring through the trees, and Margaret and Hetty, the children and Morag with the baby as they ran. Margaret's heart pounded painfully under the bodice of her best black dress, and the corsets that she had laced so tightly. Morag ran strongly, but she was already gasping, easily tired after the work of recent childbed and the weight of that precious child in her arms.

Hetty ran like a man; her skirts pulled with indecent efficiency past her knobby knees and tucked into the waistband of her apron, her face set and her grip on Johnny and her sister like iron and rawhide. She was pulling them after her, an undaunted force. Margaret redoubled her efforts, spurred by the memory of every horror she had ever heard of the fate of women, of babies and children – save those of a particular age – in the brutal hands of the Comanche. There were other women with their children, running from their own houses, in town and in the outlying ones, from the Harrell's old compound near the river and the confluence with Shoal Creek. They were close, close and closer still to the Bullock's – the tall house on pilings, where the lower part had been walled in to make the dining room at ground level for their inn, the stout log building ramble which had become a blockhouse and refuge. With so many having departed Austin, in an emergency Bullock's place could shelter all who remained for hours, possibly even days.

Gasping for breath, Margaret, the boys, Hetty with Morag and the baby gained the front door of Bullock's, blinded as they stumbled into the sudden dimness after the bright sunlight outside. The shutters had all been hastily drawn and bolted shut, those interconnecting rooms were now as dark as a cave, filled with the murmurs of frightened men and women, save when the door opened to admit another person seeking shelter. Before her eyes adjusted, Margaret blundered into something hard, something solid and more oddly-shaped than a table. Already the heavier furniture in the taproom and public parlor was being moved, propped against the walls to strengthen the shutters. She put out her hand to steady herself, squinting in the dimness; it seemed that someone had brought a cannon from the armory. How the men had ever managed to roll it inside – and when they had done this – she couldn't think. Morag and the boys had already gone ahead through the dark hallways to Mary Bullock's china parlor, which sat in the very heart of Bullocks' establishment, the safest and most secure room, where the women and children were accustomed to take refuge upon hearing any alarm.

"Mrs. Vining?" in the confusion, someone caught at her arm – Captain Coleman, his expression urgent, as much as she could see in the darkness. "Is everyone from your household here?"

"All but my father," she answered. Captain Coleman's lips made a thin line across his face. "Damn stubborn Dutchman," he muttered. "I guess he has decided to hole up at his place. Just when we need every man-jack who can handle a weapon here!"

"What is the matter?" Margaret demanded, and stayed him by the arm as he would have turned away. She could see better now or perhaps someone had lit a few more lanterns. "Are we so few that we are in danger, even all gathered at Bullock's?"

Captain Coleman looked as if he would rather not have answered. He was a wiry, weathered man, somewhere in his thirties; one of the many unmarried men in Austin. He still limped from a wound taken a month or two ago in a fight with yet another raiding Comanche party, which had made him unfit to ride out with his company. Margaret knew him as a neighbor, and Carl spoke of him to her as a good Ranger, reputed to be the best poker player between Austin and Hornsby's Bend – maybe even as far as Mina.

"Yes, damn the luck – sorry, Miz Vining. There are twenty good men out on a long scout with the Ranging Company. At least five more that I know of, including Ed Waller, went to Houston on the stage last week for business. There's another three or four away with a wagonload of timber yesterday to the saw-mill at Beeson's Landing, and least another dozen like your father caught by surprise and holed up in their places. I'm only here 'cause I'm still healing."

"How many men are here?" Margaret drew in her breath. Captain Coleman didn't bother to lower his voice. "I count mebbe a few more than twenty men and some boys who are fitten' to carry weapons."

Margaret was appalled – this few men of fit age in Austin and the district around? She had seen many times that number of Indians, in that fleeting glance over her shoulder. Was it the Penateka Comanche, who came down like a wolf on the fold, out of the Llano with a thousand warriors? Two years ago, they terrorized the valley of the Guadalupe, pillaging their way down to Linnville, while all the folk who lived there took refuge on boats in the harbor. Those Comanche were defeated in open battle only when all the Ranger companies had time to gather and ambush them at Plum Creek, upon their return journey to their customary hunting grounds in the untamed and unsettled Llano country. That victory was weeks in coming. It had taken no little time to assemble the volunteers, the mounted militia of all the settlements in Texas. In the meantime, Linnville burned, and the Penateka had taken, tortured, and murdered many white captives. There were no boats, no sea refuge here, only the stout walls of Bullock's Inn . . . and only if there were enough men to defend it.

"Don't ye go discounting the women, if it would serve," Hetty spoke up, at Margaret's side.

Mrs. Eberly, barely seen as a blur of pale face, in her widow-black, echoed, "I'll take up a musket, if you'll need, and some of the lads, too. If they are not old enough to aim a weapon, they are old enough to re-load."

"So will I." Margaret said. She thought of her sons, of Morag and the baby, huddled in the parlor, and those other mothers and children. Margaret would do whatever was needed, to keep them safe and alive. "Give us each a musket, Captain Coleman, or a pistol; a knife even, if that is all there is at hand."

"Do you know how to use a musket?" he asked, skeptically. "Aim and cock – and are you sure you can kill a man with it? It'ud be no use if you have a weapon if they can just take it away from you. "

"A Comanche threatening my sons?   I'd kill with my bare hands." Margaret answered firmly. "I can load, and aim. I've watched my father, my husband – even my brothers do so, since the day we came to Texas."

"What about you ladies?" Captain Coleman turned to Mrs. Eberly and Hetty. "Can you load and aim, shoot to kill?"

"It's not like there is a choice in the matter," Mrs. Eberly answered with frank honesty. Hetty added, "Aye well. Its' the narrow end pointed at them as you want to do the damage upon, isn't it?"

Captain Coleman chuckled in sour amusement, but his face sobered at once. "A good thing we're not in need of sharpshooters, Miss Moylan, but that's the general notion. When we parcel out the town arsenal, I'll see that you're supplied – I reckon that I'm in charge, with Bullock my second. Now go on into the parlor, so's I'll know where you are."

He turned away as the main door opened and shut. Margaret saw in the brief light which came in with the person admitted, that two men had already taken up a sentry position on either side of it. Mr. Ward, once the mayor of Austin and now the Land Commissioner, who walked on a peg-leg and had his right coat-sleeve pinned up after his several misadventures with artillery, was directing some of the older boys in adjusting the barrel of the cannon so that it pointed directly at the front door.

"Aye, there's always a warm welcome for guests at Bullocks Inn," Hetty observed, and Mrs. Eberly laughed in genuine amusement. Margaret thought;

Angelina Eberly must have seen nearly everything in her time – I truly think there must be nothing on earth capable of shocking her.

The china parlor was down a short corridor, past the door to the Bullocks' own private quarters and a stairway which gave access to the upper floors. The parlor, as dark now as the rest of the Inn, was crammed with women and children: with relief, Margaret noted that all the women and children in Austin were there – even Mrs. Simpson, whose house was even farther distant from town than Alois Becker's – she was there with her son and daughter. With no fresh air from the opened windows and the crush within, it was stiflingly warm inside; the odor of human bodies and dirty diapers was overlaid with the stink of fear. Margaret didn't think she could endure much time within. She was certain the war-band of Comanche she had glimpsed over her shoulder was by far the largest body of them that she had ever seen in her life. She could think of no good reason why so many would come to the valley of the Colorado all at once unless it was to attack and overwhelm the folk of Austin, or Hornsby's Bend, or even Mina.

Most Comanche raids were on outlying houses, an ambush of a few travelers and carters, or a sudden attack upon men working in the fields. Sometimes the raiders were after horses: Papa had always kept his stable padlocked at night for that reason. In the early days Papa and her brothers had ploughed the cornfield with a rifle over their shoulders; of late he had taken to doing so again. And what about Papa, now? He must have heard the alarm and taken refuge in his own house, as he always stubbornly insisted that he would, rather than risk being caught out in the open and making a run for Bullock's. Surely he must be safe, if he had time to bar the windows and doors. Margaret could hardly bear thinking about this.

Perhaps the Indians had been watching them all this time, observing how few men were around, noting with calculating eyes how many families were left living like ghosts among the decaying frame buildings, their horses, food stores, and valuables – their scalps and their human flesh too – all ready for the taking by any raiding party able to reach out and just pluck them like a ripe apple from one of Papa's trees.

Morag sat in a corner of the parlor with Jemima-Mary in her arms and Margaret's sons clustered with her, like chicks under a hen's wings. She had been telling them a story of old Erin; of Cuchulain and his magical shield and sword. As always when she told them one of these tales, the Irish in her voice came out – musical and lilting, much more so than in everyday speech. Even some of the other women and children setting near her were quiet, hanging on every word as if she wove a gold-brocade spell – a spell which could magically take them away to another world.

"For it was at the place that was called Emain-Macha, Macha-of-the-Spears they called it – so they did – that Conchubar the High King held the Assembly House of the lords of Ulster, and there was the chief of his palaces. Oh, and a fine place it was, having the three parts to it – the House of the Royals, the Speckled House . . . and finally, the House of the Red Branch. Och, and it was truly a marvel; in the House of the Royals which had three-times-fifty rooms, the walls were of red cedar-wood with copper nails. The High King Conchubar's own chamber was on the first level, the walls paneled with bronze below and silver above, adorned with golden birds, their eyes were set with shining jewels – there were nine divisions of it from the fireplace to the wall at the end, and each one of them being thirty feet tall! There was a silver scepter always before Conchubar, a silver scepter with three golden apples mounted upon it, as of bells – and when he took up that rod and made the golden apples ring, all the folk in the house would be silent, wherever they were upon hearing it . . . "

"Well, we were intending to have a party," Mrs. Eberly remarked. "Here, laddie-buck, let me have that chair. I'm too old to go charging around like this in the heat. When young Morag there is finished with her story we'll have a sing-along, won't we? And Mary can play the pianner." She sounded so normal, as if the party which had been planned was going on exactly as expected, that Margaret thought at least some of the younger women and the children were reassured. "We'll be out from underfoot, while Captain Coleman decides what's best. Go on with the story, girl – silver on the walls and golden birds with jewels for their eyes? Seems quite a place, I must say."

Morag shifted Jemima-Mary in her arms and resumed the tale. *"Now, in the House of the Red Branch, they kept the weapons of the enemies which they had defeated – and their heads, as well – and the Speckled House was for the swords and shields and spears of the heroes of Ulster. It was called so for the colors of the hilts of their swords, and the brightness of the spears, for they were trimmed and bound around with rings and bands of gold and silver; so were the bosses of the shields and the rims of them. The drinking cups were likewise trimmed with silver and gold. And it was the custom of the Men of the Red Branch, upon one of them being insulted; he would demand satisfaction at that very moment, even in the middle of the feasting hall . . . "*

"Sounds a familiar sort," Margaret whispered to Mrs. Eberly, who chuckled and answered, "Oh, the times I've had to speak up and tell them to settle it – afore they commenced to break up the furniture!"

"And Cuchulain's sword hung with his shield – and the name of it was called Cruaidin Cailidcheann. The sword had a hilt of gold, ornamented with silver, and if the point of it was bent back, even as far as the hilt, it would spring back straight at once. Indeed, it was so sharp that it could cut a hair floating in the water, a hair from the head of a man without touching the skin – and if it cut a man in two, each half would not miss the other for some considerable time . . ."

Margaret leaned her back against the doorway – there were no more chairs, and she did not want to sit on the floor with the children as the minutes and hours trickled away. It would be sundown soon. Very likely they would be spending the night here. She turned at a step in the corridor to note Richard Bullock coming down the stairs, with his arms full of muskets and rifles. He also had a grey jacket, trimmed with martial braid over one arm and a peaked cap askew upon his head, a hat that looked as if it belonged to a smaller man. His son Frank followed him, similarly burdened with powder-flasks and several small haversacks over his shoulder.

"Marm Eberly, Miz Vining?" he said in a low voice, "Cap'n Coleman said you wished to be armed, since there were too few men. Are there any other ladies who can handle a rifle, or load one? Boys, too – we have enough weapons that everyone may have two at hand. Here . . ." He dealt out two each to Margaret, Hetty, and Mrs. Eberly, as well as to several other women who stepped quietly out of the press in the china parlor.

Horace, Johnny and Tommy Simpson came forward as well, Horace saying gravely, "Me an' Johnny can load for you and Miss Hetty, Mama."

"Good boys," Margaret answered, her heart swelling with pride and fear for her sons as Horace and Johnny took two powderflasks and a single haversack from Bullock's son. "Where should we take our place, Mr. Bullock?"

"I reckon you should stay downstairs," Mr. Bullock answered, "for I don't believe the upstairs will stop a bullet. There's some shooting holes in the outside walls here, Frank here will show you where. If'n you stand on benches, you should ought to be able to cover the back. An' ma'am – don't fire wild. We got plenty of lead, but not if you go wasting it."

His arms empty of weapons, he was shrugging into the grey coat. It also did not seem to be his, for it did not fit him well. Someone called his name from the front of the Inn – a man's voice, urgent but not alarmed. Margaret wondered briefly why he was bothering with such an ill-fitting coat, but then Frank Bullock hopped down from a bench, halfway along the corridor from the door that led into the china parlor. He had a small block of wood in his hand; a square of light pierced the roughly plastered log wall, light which had the golden tint of late afternoon. Outside, the tree shadows lay long, stretching across.

"See, ma'am – each one of the shooting holes is blocked with one o'these, three or four at the same height; all the way along . . . I guess Pa thinks you each take one."

"A good idea," Margaret answered sedately. Mrs. Eberly snorted.

"May as well teach your grandmother to knit, laddie-buck. Load for me then, and help me up onto the bench, I'm not as nimble as I used to be."

Silently, Frank and the boys began loading rifles and muskets. Margaret gingerly accepted one, and stepped up onto the bench. She set her face to the shooting hole – about four inches wide, and half as tall – a space between logs deliberately left unchinked. Papa had done the same with his house. This one looked out at the back of Bullock's – she could see a little of Congress Avenue, but mostly the sides of other buildings, and various trees all robed in green leaves. The little wedge of sky that she could see was blue and cloudless, tinged with the golden-red of a sunset, but she could hear no bird-song. That very silence seemed heavy with menace.

"What's happening, Mama?" Horace asked; he was loading a musket, with careful attention, as if it were a penmanship exercise. "What do you see?"

"Nothing," she answered. Then her eye caught a movement: three men, one in advance flanked by two others – they were dark shapes and at a distance, against the dazzle of sunshine. They moved along Congress Avenue, pacing slowly. "Oh, my."

"What did you see?" Horace asked again, echoed by Hetty and Mrs. Eberly.

"I saw Captain Coleman," Margaret answered, "and he was carrying a white flag."

Chapter 9 – *The Bluff at Bullock's Inn*

"A flag of truce, aye." Hetty put her own eye to another strategic gap in the wall. "Going to parley with them red de'ils . . . much good that will do, even if he does come back wi' his own hair. Awheel then, boys – load carefully, as the man said. We'll not be short of targets, I am thinkin'."

"How many Indians did you see, Mrs. Eberly?" Margaret whispered to the older woman, who whispered in return, "More'n I'd ever like to see in one place, and that's a fact." She lowered her voice even more. "Miz Vining, you take care to save a bullet for yourself, should they break in an' it goes against us. You know the wicked way they treat white women."

"I do," Margaret drew in a breath, thinking with one part of her mind how very unreal this last quarter of the hour had been. She had meant to start another letter this evening to Doctor Williamson. Now she might not be able to do that. That thought made her angry; she could not die tonight, here at Bullock's makeshift fort. She had letters to write! At one moment, walking with her sons and Hetty and Morag, in happy anticipation of an afternoon in company with the other women, now the painful reality of sudden death stared them all in the face; either a brutal death or the burden of enduring an even more brutal captivity. There would be no escape for her, for her boys, her friends, Morag's baby daughter, if the Comanche warriors she had seen sweeping down from their hill managed to break into Bullock's fort and overwhelm those few defenders. She glanced down at her sons, who having finished loading all the weapons available, were laying out the bullet-pouch, the powder-flasks and the patch-boxes in a careful order.

Does it hurt to die, M'grete? That's what her brother Rudi had asked her once, when they were just children. And she had carefully answered him, saying with the wisdom of a twelve-year old, that perhaps it hurt a little, at first but not so much if it came fast. It had come fast for Rudi; a Mexican soldier's musket outside the Goliad citadel, just as it had been for Seamus O'Doyle at Saltillo – relatively swift and thereby merciful. The Comanche were not so inclined, and Margaret's resolve hardened. They were shielded by the stout log walls of Bullock's – the Comanche could not break in, although they might try to fire the roof. Their abilities as horsemen would do them no good if it came to them laying siege. Now she saw that the boys were looking at her, apprehensively. No doubt they had heard Mrs. Eberly's whispered words. She made herself smile in reassurance.

"We may be in a siege," she said, forcing her voice to sound cheerful. "But we are in a strong fort and if you recall from your Papa's histories, there was never a castle – a proper castle – that was taken by an army from the outside. The castle was either surrendered after a long time or betrayed from within. We will not surrender, and no one here at Bullocks would give us over to the Comanche; they have nothing anyone would want, save perhaps horses. And there are plenty of horses in Texas."

"Here, they come back again," Hetty observed, and Margaret hastily applied her eye to her peep-hole to the outside. There was Captain Coleman, and two other men of the town, walking slow and unhurried. Margaret let out her breath, only then aware that she had been holding it. The three men and the white flag – she thought it might have been a linen napkin, hastily fastened to the end of a long staff – vanished from view around the corner of Bullock's. Margaret carefully climbed down from the bench that she had been perched upon so that she could see out through the shooting hole.

"Stay here," she commanded. "I'm going to find out what they saw, and what is going on." Still with a loaded musket held carefully over her shoulder, she went down the hall towards the main entry. The taproom led off of it on one side through a pair of wide doors, and the inn's public parlor through the other. Her eyes having adjusted to the dark now, she could recognize faces. The cannon had been moved back to the rear of the hallway, where it stood veiled in shadows and attended by Mr. Ward. He was another Irishman, like O'Doyle, who had come to Texas with the New Orleans Grays back in that fall of 1835, to throw General Cos out of Bexar. He had fought with her brothers there, and lost the lower part of one leg to an errant cannon-shot. Not very much discouraged by this painful misfortune, he had been fitted with a wooden peg-leg and come to Austin with the Legislature. Unlike most of them he had stayed, been elected mayor – and then maimed again, by a celebratory cannon-shot two years before which had taken off his right arm. Margaret thought privately that a sensible man would therefore have chosen to stay as far as possible from anything to do with artillery, but Mr. Ward remained irrepressibly optimistic regarding large quantities of black powder and iron shot in combination.

"Mr. Ward, we saw Captain Coleman returning. Did he go out to parlay with the Indians?"

Mr. Ward started a little at her whispered question, and half-turned towards her, his pug-Irish face alight with the interest he always displayed when having anything to do with his beloved artillery-pieces. He held the match-holder in his one hand, the lit match glowing like a baleful red eye in the darkness, a brace of pistols thrust through his belt, and a loaded musket leaning against the wall with the other tools – the swab, the rammer, and the powder-shovel which served the cannon. He also was dressed in a soldier's coat and cap. The cannon itself was leveled, a menacing round iron mouth aimed straight at the front door.

"Aye," he answered. "Six of them came riding up Pecan Street, as bold as you please, with a flag of truce. Someone among 'em speaks English, if you can believe it."

At that moment, the outer door opened to admit Captain Coleman and his fellows. The door was barred shut behind them with a brisk rattle, and the men gathered in the hallway and in the taproom quieted at a gesture from him. He appeared utterly calm, unruffled, and raised his voice just enough so as to be heard throughout those rooms. Instantly, everyone else hushed.

"They want to parley a mite more," he said. "They also claim that they are coming in peace, only hunting the buffalo. They say they have tracked a large herd and moved so fast in doing so that they have left their women and the old folk behind on the trail."

A chorus of denigration and disbelief rose from those gathered in the taproom.

"What kind of fools to they take us for?" demanded Richard Bullock, the borrowed grey coat straining over his shoulders. "They're no hunting party – painted for war, head to toe!"

"Aye, pull the other one." Mr. Ward shook his head. "It's wooden and I've hung bells on it!"

Captain Coleman merely held up his hand again. "In any case, they wish to come into this place for their parley. It may be that they really want to see how many or how few folk are forted up in here, so I'd advise you to stay out of sight, in the main – but to make as much noise as you can, bluff them into thinking there are three or four times as many within these walls. Have Mrs. Bullock play the piano and send some boys upstairs to walk as loud as they can in the hallway upstairs. Walk around, talk loudly." He smiled, a sharp smile which showed his teeth, and laughed, a quick bark of laughter like a wolf. "Bluff as if your lives all depended on it. It will."

"Aye, the cheek of him," Mr. Ward laughed also, and then he looked sideways at Margaret, adding in a soberer voice. "Ye may as well know, Miz Vining – if they really want to put their backs into it and take this place, we'll not be able to fight them off for long wi' as few as we have – even with m'dear old iron girl, here."

"I knew that, very well – since some of us were given muskets. In the china parlor, Mrs. Fritchie is telling the children the story of Cuchulain." Margaret said breathlessly.

Mr. Ward nodded in approval. "Very well – for he was as clever as he was brave. If Captain Coleman's plan works, then you will have no need of that musket. Go ye now; when the story is finished, tell Miz Bullock to play her pianna an' the ladies to sing, the lads to make a bit o' noise, as if they're playing, like."

Margaret nodded, in acknowledgement. Captain Coleman had gathered by the door with Richard Bullock and a handful of others for a brief conversation. One or two others had also donned soldier's coats and taken up a sentry position on either side of the door. Margaret, accepting that she had been given an errand, went to relay what she could to Hetty and Mrs. Eberly and those women waiting in the parlor.

"Oh?" Mrs. Eberly immediately appeared much cheered. "A bluff, so he says . . . better than fighting it out with those savages, is what I say. Nothing ventured, and nothing gained – is that right, Miz Vining?"

"Indeed." Margaret pulled Horace and Johnny to her in a swift embrace. "Boys, you should get Jamie and some of your other friends to run upstairs. Go up and down the stairs and play. Play as noisily as you like."

"But what about the Indians, Mama – what about loading for you an' Miss Hetty?" Johnny looked bewildered, and Margaret forced herself to smile, as if they had nothing to fear.

"Because the Indians want to parley, some of them: The men think that if they think this fort is full of soldiers and armed men, then they will not dare attack. If we make as much noise as we can, and make them think this place is too much of a bother to attack, they may go away and leave us all alone."

"Yes, Mama – I see." Johnny nodded in grave understanding. "But I will come back and load for you if we have to fight." Margaret briefly embraced him and ruffled his hair.

"We hope there will be no need for it. Mr. Ward has his cannon aimed right at Bullock's front door," Margaret added. "I think they hope if the Indians see that they will think better of attacking."

Behind her, Mrs. Eberly snorted. "I'm hoping he'll take care with firing it. He's not had the best luck in the world with those infernal machines. And mark my words – we'll not be able to see a hand in the front of our face for the smoke if'n he does – an' I should know the truth of that!" Both Margaret and Hetty laughed quietly, which oddly enough, appeared to reassure the boys.

Within the china parlor all was quiet and tense; the smaller children mostly entranced by Morag's voice, while their mothers listened with one ear to her and another straining to hear any noise from outside. Margaret found Mary Bullock and whispered to her the suggestion for the women sing to the music of her piano, and that the Indians had asked for a parley and claimed to be peaceful.

"Do you truly think so, Margaret?" Mary Bullock asked, the expression of pleading in her eyes so naked that Margaret wished to reassure her immediately, almost without thinking of it. This very day she had again become the captain of ladies, the leader which she had been to her friends in Gonzales during that wearisome and heartbreaking retreat to Harrisburg, the so-called "runaway scrape" after the fall of the Alamo and the burning of Gonzales.

"I do, Mary," she answered, in a confident voice. "They would wish otherwise to attack something easy, which would offer them much gain and little cost to themselves. If we can suggest to them that they would pay a great cost then I think all would be well. The Comanche," Margaret paused to think on this for a second, as she chose her words with care, "are not warrior-gods, Mary, which no one might defeat unless they are another warrior-god like Cuchulain. They are only men – of a bestial and degraded nature. Their way is of war and loot and horses, gotten in the manner which is of most convenience to them. A thief given a choice of two houses to rob will rob the one that is empty, rather than the one where the family is at home. Such will always take the easy way, seeing an opportunity. And Captain Coleman thinks that we may make Fort Bullock look like a very hard nut, not worth the bother of cracking. Or at least, to make a semblance of a house where all the family is at home, with cannon aimed out of the front door." Margaret put a confident smile on her face – that is what leaders did, she reminded herself. *That is what General Sam did; he kept his fears to himself, did what he thought necessary, and never gave way to them in public.*

She left the parlor, having given another smile over her shoulder to Peter, curled up next to Morag and rubbing a fold of her shawl between his thumb and first finger, a gesture that looked to be a comforting substitute for sucking his thumb – a habit which his older brothers had teased him from doing. She stood in an angle of wall behind Mr. Ward and his iron lady, from which post she could see what took place in the hall, and a little into the public parlor – which was now lit with so many candles that it looked like a stage in comparison with the darkened hallway. From where she stood, veiled in the shadows and her own black dress, she could see, but not herself be seen by any coming into the hall from the outside. Margaret was resolved not to withdraw into the farther corridor or wait in the china parlor with the other women, even if any of the men attempted to bid her do so. She was the leader of the women as much as Captain Coleman was of the men on this dangerous evening. She must know what was going on. If no one would tell her, she would find out by her own means.

With dusk falling outside, the main hallway into Bullocks' seemed even gloomier within, lit as it was only by a few flickering tin lanterns. The main door swung slowly open, admitting Captain Coleman, with his flagstaff in hand.

"Halt, ye," commanded Mr. Ward. "Who goes there, friend or foe?"

It had the sound of a ritual, well-rehearsed, and Margaret intuited that it was for the benefit of those following after Captain Coleman, who answered, "Friend."

"Advance and be recognized." Captain Coleman stepped into the dim light, and Mr. Ward continued. "Give the passwords for the day, friend. A crowded hour of glory."

"Is worth an age without a name," answered Captain Colman, with much the same staged air, and in as loud a voice as could be heard by those behind him outside in the darkness.

"Pass, friend." Mr. Ward straightened to a position of attention. "And who is that, with you?"

"Six men of the Comanche with an interpreter," answered Captain Coleman. "They say they have come to parley with our leaders. They want a truce, to trade with us for sugar and sweet potatoes and such." He raised his voice at the last. It looked to Margaret as if he exchanged a significant look with Mr. Ward.

"They are waiting for you in the public parlor," answered Mr. Ward, with emphatic clarity. "The commanders of the local Army garrison, and the mayor and selectmen of Austin – as many of them as were present at the time, Captain sor – and do not keep them waiting, for supper will be served soon."

"I'll keep that in mind," Captain Coleman answered, with dry emphasis upon the words. He stepped farther into the hallway, and Margaret drew in her breath. Following silently in his footsteps were half a dozen other men; the Comanche.

This was the closest that Margaret had ever been to a Comanche warrior, and the first time she had ever seen one within walls, where she could observe at leisure and with some measure of security. They were not very like the Lipan Apache, or the friendly tribe of Tonkawa Indians who had camped nearby Austin for several seasons of late, save in the dark color of their hair, and the ruddy, sunburnt tint to their skin. To her increasing astonishment, they were short. Only one of them was anything like as tall as Captain Coleman, and Captain Coleman was of only middling height. But they were powerfully-built men nonetheless, with slightly bowed legs which marked them as having spent much time on horseback. They were not a handsome and cleanly breed of folk, as she often thought the Lipan Apache and the Tonkawa were. These men; their features were heavy and set in a permanent scowl, thin lips pressed together, their countenances daubed with streaks and bands of black paint. All but one was naked above the waist, their bare shoulders and breasts adorned with paint, or ornaments made of bead and shell. Their hair streamed down, coarse like the manes of horses, and they walked on silent, moccasin-clad feet, glancing around them with wary eyes. Margaret was confident that she was invisible to them in the dark hallway behind Mr. Ward and his cannon. They noted the cannon, though – as they passed into the public parlor. The door to the taproom opposite stood half-closed, shedding a little more light and the low mutter of men's voices into the hallway. The last of the Comanches . . . Margaret looked at him again. Half-naked, and with a red blanket wrapped toga-fashion around his shoulders, he did not have the features in the same cast as the others, and his hair appeared a lighter color than black, although she could not be certain, because of the darkness within the hall. A pair of benches had been set in the public parlor, facing each other at some little distance; from her vantage point she could see the end of one, with Richard Bullock sitting on it, the borrowed military coat barely meeting across his chest.

"I did not know that we had an Army garrison here," she murmured, a breath above a whisper to Mr. Ward, who grinned cheerily. "Aye, so we do." Then his face sobered. "Did ye note that last fellow, Miz Vining, with the red cape?"

"I did," Margaret answered. "He does not look so much like the others . . . perhaps he is from another tribe."

"Oh, he is that, indade," Mr. Ward chuckled. "He's a white man, a renegade by the name of John Loflin. I recognized him right away. He vanished from town just at the same time that some fine horses vanished as well. Looks to me like he's a bird of the same feather, in choosing to take up wi' the Comanche."

Within the parlor, she could hear Captain Coleman's voice; it sounded like he was explaining who the other Anglo men were, to the Indians. Then he said, quite loudly, "I see that you are painted for the warpath, and there are no women and children with you. We ask again that you tell us what you have come to Austin for, if not for war?" Another voice answered him, too low for Margaret to hear, first speaking a guttural language that she did not understand, then louder and in English.

"My friends, they are hunting buffalo, as I told you before. They wish only a truce between us, so that we may hunt. The families, the women, they follow us slowly."

"We'll see about that," Captain Coleman answered. He sounded grim, and skeptical. "Gentlemen – we must confer." Now Margaret could see a little of him, and of Richard Bullock with their heads together just inside the public parlor. The sound of the voices coming from the taproom masked whatever confabulation was going in parlor; indeed.

Suddenly, a loud voice brayed, "I tell you what, boys – we'd be fools to let a single damn one of those Injuns get away! What with all the soldiers we'll have and two companies of Rangers arriving within two hours . . . we can surround the hill. When daylight comes, we'll wipe them off the face of the Earth!"

"Hush up, ye damned fool," hissed another voice. "You just as near went across and told those red devils they're sitting in a trap!"

Margaret covered her lips with her hand. So that was how the men had planned to bluff the Indians out of attacking. She could see that Mr. Ward's shoulders were shaking, as if he were trying not to laugh out loud. Within the public parlor, Captain Coleman had begun speaking again.

"Your words are crooked. Go ahead, tell them that. Two year ago, your kind asked for a truce just as you have asked for today on the pretense of hunting buffalo. And we gave it, but then Harm Simpson was murdered at Brushy Creek and twenty horses run off – so you do understand that trust is in short supply around these parts? 'Sides, we have seen no such herd of buffalo hereabouts as would bring so many hunters down from the high Llano. What assurance do we have that your words are straight, not as crooked as a snake an' lower than it's belly?"

There was a pause within the room, while the second voice put this into the Comanche language, but before the renegade Loflin was even finished, Captain Coleman shouted, "We do no deals, no trade, and agree to no truce with crooked men – your band might not have been the one who broke the last truce, but they who did are your kin, your friends, your kind! Pay heed to my words – these are my words, and listen to them well! You came here tonight with a lie in your heart, intending on robbery and murder – do not shame yourselves by repeating that lie to us! I tell you now and my words are as

115

straight as a lance – we are prepared to meet you on your own terms! Good night to you – our parley is done. You may leave unmolested from this place tonight, under the rules of civilized behavior – but tomorrow morning you might find us not so agreeable to such rules!"

Margaret held her breath as a rumble of guttural discord erupted, accompanied by the clatter of something wooden falling to the floor. The parley was indeed over. The Indians were leaving the parlor, momentarily stayed in the hallway as one of the door sentries unbarred the main door to the outside. The tall white man, clad in a red blanket about his shoulders, was at the back of the group. As Margaret and Mr. Ward watched from the shadows, Captain Coleman followed them into the hall.

With a single gesture, he spun the taller man around to face him, and snarled, "John Loflin, you yellow-bellied son of a whore, I just want to tell you one thing – tomorrow I will make it my especial duty and pleasure to nail your scalp to the trunk of a live-oak tree on Capitol Hill – you savvy me, you white-livered renegade? Now, git – while the getting is good. You won't have another warning."

The tall man in the garb of a Comanche looked down at Captain Coleman; to Margaret's eyes, he looked as if he wished to say something but thought better of it before he followed his Indian comrades out of the door. It was slammed behind them and the sound of the bolts and bar falling into place echoed in the suddenly quiet hallway. Richard Bullock and the four men who had posed as the military commander and senior men of the town emerged from the parlor, just as another handful came from the taproom.

"Well then – did they hear it good and clear?" asked the first of them. Margaret recognized his voice, the stentorian-loud one, who had outlined the supposed trap.

"Any louder, you've been heard clear down at Hornsby's!" answered Captain Coleman, with some asperity. "But the Comanche ain't a subtle people, so I suppose it will pass."

"About as subtle as a cobblestone through a glass window," Mr. Ward murmured to Margaret. "But still – if it served, it served well. We'll know in the morning, for sure."

"Don't let down your guard, gentlemen – we'll stay forted up all night, and into tomorrow if necessary."

Now that the men were done with putting on a play-act for the Comanche, Captain Coleman could allow some of the weariness that he must be feeling to show. Margaret felt as if she had been wrung out like a wet dishcloth, from those hours of fear and tension, but it was not over. The captain continued,

"Draw straws now for mounting sentry duty, and take turns sleeping. Richard, you and the missus – I'll leave billeting to you, being your house and all. Don't anyone let their guard down. Sleep with your weapons loaded and be ready to defend yourselves at any time."

In the china parlor, the women were singing now; they almost sounded cheerful. Margaret could only suppose they had expected the worst, and since the worst had not arrived, perhaps it might not arrive at all. One could only remain for so long in a state of abject terror.

Mrs. Eberly stepped down from her vantage-point upon seeing Margaret, saying, "They went past in a hurry, those Injuns did, just now – don't even think they bothered with a truce flag as they went. They were going as if the very devil was chasing after! What did the Cap'n say to them, that they would take to their heels that way?"

"Not so much what he did say, but what the Comanche thought we could do. The men made them think that many soldiers were already here and two ranger companies coming to our aid within hours," Margaret answered. "They made them believe that we would attack them in the morning, and then he threw them out, saying that their words were crooked and we could not make a truce with liars."

"Oh, he has the nerve, doesn't he?" Mrs. Eberly looked properly appreciative. "Do you think it has worked, Mrs. Vining?"

"We'll know in the morning." Margaret sighed. "We'll stay forted up here until then, he says."

They spent a bitterly uncomfortable and restless night on the floor of the china parlor, Margaret, Hetty, and Mrs. Eberly taking it in turns to keep a watch in the corridor. The Bullocks possessed sufficient quantities of pallets and blankets so that the women and children might have slept well. But with so many children and mothers crammed together for safety in that inner room, every slight noise re-waked any who had managed to sleep. Margaret felt even more wearied in the morning than she had been when she lay down. Just before dawn she did fall into a doze. So having rested a little, it seemed that she was roused again by a distant roll of thunder. Thinking at first she was in her own bed, she felt for the edge of her bed, for her wrapper, and the tinder box that she might light a candle. No, she was in her clothes, lying on the edge of a pallet with Jamie and Peter curled trustfully next to her. It was not thunder, but the sound of someone vigorously pounding on a door at the other end of Bullock's. She sat up, groaning at the ache in her ribs for having slept in a tight corset, and looked for her shoes.

The floor of the parlor was a sea of pallets and blankets spread out over the sleepers. Mrs. Eberly sat bolt upright in a chair by the door, but she had fallen asleep also. Fingers of light crept between cracks in the shutters, through the shooting holes in the corridor. It couldn't be an attack by the Comanche, Margaret told herself – there would be more of a general alarm than someone just pounding on a door. Still, she caught up the loaded musket which she had left leaning against the wall by her head – as Captain Coleman had advised – within easy reach. In the front hallway of Bullock's where the cannon still stood, menacing the front door, one man was already unbarring the door, while two others stood with muskets at the ready. The door swung open, admitting a pearly oblong of light; the sky was masked by clouds and wisps of fog that twined around the trees and between the scattered buildings.

"About damn time," Alois Becker grunted. He also had a musket across his arm and the reins to Bucephalus in his hand, a shadow against the dawn-lightened sky with the darker shadow of the horse behind him. "A man could grow old, waiting for someone to answer a knock at the door. I came for my daughter and the boys. Time to come home."

Captain Coleman emerged from the taproom, still yawning. "Good god, Becker, I was afraid you'd loose your hair this time for sure. An' I ain't real sure it's a good idea, riding around and making a racket like this, let alone heading back to your place."

"I'll do as I see fit," Papa growled. He looked beyond Captain Coleman and the other men to see Margaret. "There you are – come along then, you and Miss Hetty and the brats. Time's wasting and the cows need milking."

"But Papa!" Margaret began, overcome with a mixture of relief and exasperation with her father: Papa was alive, not slaughtered in the doorway of his own house or while he labored in his fields like poor Mr. Fox had been. Irritatingly, he remained as gruff and short-spoken as ever, even while Captain Coleman demanded with considerable heat, "Here then, Becker – how do you know it's safe? There were those red savages all over the place last night at sundown, six-seven hundred of them, near as we could tell, every man jack painted for war and devilment."

"They're gone, now," Papa answered shortly. "Every one – just plenty of tracks heading back up to the Llano. Campfires cold, too – cleared out in the dead of night, near as I can tell."

"You sure 'bout that, Becker?" Captain Coleman's face brightened with sudden hope and relief, as Papa shifted the musket to his other arm. "You certain sure?"

"I just rode up to that hill, didn't I?" Papa growled again. "Scouted all over, didn't see a single god-be-damned live Comanche or have any to-do about making dead ones. They're gone. Hours ago by the look of it."

He looked beyond Captain Coleman, towards the other men, some of them just emerging from the front parlor and the taproom, where they had slept, or nodded over their guard posts, loaded weapons in hand, and to Margaret, and a look of something like panic flashed like lightning over his weather-burnt countenance, and in those blue eyes – the same blue of her own eyes and that of her brothers – a flash that was there and then gone as if it hadn't ever been.

Papa was afraid . . . afraid of something to do with her. She briefly recollected the vile threat that Carl had made to Papa, about what he would tell certain men of Austin if he ever struck her again. It came to her that Papa looked . . . almost apprehensive, as if he had suddenly realized she might have confided in someone about how he had nearly killed her with his bare hands. Forted up at Bullocks' during the interminable afternoon and night just over, such a night of fear and apprehension; in thinking that all was lost and no escape being possible one might confess any kind of personal agony. In a flash of comprehension, Margaret also saw that possibility clearly and wondered – *what if Papa believed she would confirm what Carl said he would say – that Papa had forced her to bed with him?* Margaret's mind shuddered away from that image and action. Papa had never dreamed of doing such a vile deed, she was confident – but he had already once tried to choke the living breath out of her. Just this moment, Papa must have realized that in impulsively coming to Bullock's and demanding that she and the children return this very hour, might confirm Carl's story in the minds of those important men of Austin.

Now she saw clearly what Carl had intended – but a two-edged sword! If Papa were to go on believing in Carl's threat, for her own safety she would be best served by making a small show of apprehension. But this was Papa. Once, long ago, Mama had loved him with the ardor of a young girl, adoring the handsome young man who was the friend of her brothers, the son of Opa Heinrich – and everyone had thought it a good match and Papa a good father, until Mama died. Margaret recalled again, how Mama had always spoken of those days, and of how she had urged Margaret to follow that path, of a woman's duty and artifice, of smoothing the way for a husband, of seeing to his needs and making every excuse for him. *Mama had gone on adoring him to the every last breath of her life.*

The best part of your father was your mother. That is what Race had said to her once, and he was a man with good judgement of people, although it might perhaps have faltered when it came to his own self and of her. One of those things that Margaret knew for certain – she did not wish to be a wife to her husband as Mama had been, supine and adoring. She had no liking, wish, or need to continue worshipping Papa, irrespective of what the commandments ordained, or make any effort to reassure him. The peace of his mind was not a matter of her concern; only the care of her sons, which depended upon her own survival.

"We will come home," Margaret answered, but she made her voice sound hesitant and despised herself in a small part for having done so. "I . . . I will fetch Hetty and Morag, so that we may walk together."

In the meantime, Mr. Ward emerged from the taproom, laughing and knuckling the sleep from his eyes with his one hand. "They're all gone, ye say?" he asked, and Papa nodded. "Every damned one of them?"

Papa nodded again, answering with brusque impatience, "Naught but tracks, the dung from their horses and the ashes of their campfires."

Mr. Ward thumped Captain Coleman on the shoulders with his one hand, exclaiming triumphantly, "Well then, Cap'n, I knew you were a bully hand at poker, but damned if I thought you could get away with bluffing a royal flush with a pair of deuces!" Amid the jubilation and congratulations, Margaret slipped away towards the china parlor, to wake her sons, Hetty, and Morag, to tell them that the Indians were gone and that Opa was come to take them home.

'*Papa is not a bad man,*' she heard her own pleading voice in her ears, as she gathered up her sons and shook Hetty's shoulder. Margaret was already regretting her decision of a moment before to put her sons' lives and her own ahead of Papa's peace of mind. In her memory, her brother answered calmly, '*No? And a pool of water poisoned with alkali is not good to drink from, although it still looks like water. He got us all – you, me, Rudi – on the body of Mama, but he was no more a real father to you and me than a wild mustang is a real father to the foals he sires on any handy mare.*'

I am already regretting having calumniated Papa in thought, seeming to accuse him in his own mind, Margaret considered, as she waked Morag.

"The Indians have gone, and we may go safely home," she said, and Morag sat up from the simple straw pallet, and took the baby to her breast, a look upon her face so innocently grateful that Margaret was shaken once more.

If her brother and Hetty had not overheard the disputation in the front parlor, or if Papa had not suddenly drawn back from his uncontrollable impulse . . . Margaret would have been as dead as any of those in Austin whose bodies had lain in the dead house, until they were washed and clothed for the grave and put away in the earth by their friends and kin. Her sons would have been defenseless against the cruel vagaries of the world, Hetty, Morag and baby Jemima-Mary abandoned to find what way they could, alone. No – she was the captain of women, she would do what she could, and possessing those advantages that she had been given, wielding what power she had in the defense of those which she loved. She would do that, and never feel regret for allowing Papa to live out the rest of his years in fear and apprehension.

Upon consideration, she did feel some regret – that Papa had not been the same tenor of man as his father, Opa Heinrich – that his temper ruled over all else and had alienated this two living children from ever holding him in true filial affection! That fault in Alois Becker had led one child to hate him and the other to secretly fear. Surely Mama was the veriest saint for having cared so much for an unloving and selfish man! *Alas,* Margaret told herself, *I am not anything like the forgiving gentle saint that Mama was – I will hate the people who have wronged and insulted me, I will pick up a musket or whatever weapon I have to hand, and defend mine own with it.*

Chapter 10 – *A Long, Hot Summer*

Some weeks after the great fright given to them all by the Comanche hunting party, Margaret received two letters and sat down in the parlor in the afternoon when the daily work to support her household and family was mostly accomplished – to read, savor, and answer those precious letters. The first was a happy announcement from Margaret Houston from the home that she and General Sam had made for themselves near Liberty on the Trinity River. The General's Margaret had given birth to their first child, a son they had chosen to name Samuel Junior. Baby Sam was thriving, and Margaret Houston had recovered well from the ordeal of childbirth. So often ill and disinclined to live the kind of life that was required of the wife of a man in the public eye, seclusion during her pregnancy had been a welcome relief for her, as she had often written. Such wonderful news! Margaret turned the page, thinking that she would make some baby dresses for her friend from the fine stocks of muslin that she still had in her own clothes-press. According to Margaret Houston, her son was so very much the image of the General that everyone remarked it at once. General Sam must be about over the moon with joy and pride, she thought. Coming so late to fatherhood and family life, at a time when most men of his age would be welcoming grandchildren, he must see this as the most generous of blessings. She recalled how he indulged her boys, had gotten down on the hearthrug and played with them, how he had openly confessed to being envious of Race Vining, for his sons, his home, and his fine horse.

> . . . *I am also sending you several books which I enjoyed very much, including some very fine romances, and also a book of poetry, of which my dear husband very much disapproves. I would send you a copy of Mr. Kennedy's history of Texas, but that it is my favorite and mine only copy, inscribed for me by the author upon the occasion of our meeting. He is a gentleman of very fine manners and superior intellect. I also had occasion to speak with my husband regarding your distress at having had a close acquaintance with the author of that other and most disgraceful history, to which you referred in your last letter. He bids me to convey to you some words of comfort and the assurance that he would – if he thought anything of the gentleman in question and were he still present in Texas – take such action on your behalf so as to render him*

incapable of being welcome in any decent company. As to why he could have written such a carelessly libelous account of events when memories of them are painfully fresh and shared by so many witnesses, my husband suggested that a deep personal animosity towards our nation and citizens by Mr. Hattersley informed the whole of his account. Indeed, he is reputed to have had business interests and investments within Mexico, those enterprises being utterly wrecked by our success in gaining independence. Since Mr. Hattersley's sympathies naturally lie with a lordly tyrant rather than free citizens, my husband believes that he has chosen this means of exacting retribution upon those he blames for the ruin of his own fortunes.

Margaret laid aside the pages of the letter, and found herself nodding in silent agreement. What General Sam had suggested made sense of a sort; deliberate malice, rather than indifferent skills as a historian. That would have sorely disappointed Race Vining to know that a man whom he considered a true and kindred spirit, welcome at their table and sharing so many of the same literary tastes, had in reality been a viper. How very calculating to feign friendship, intending to insult and degrade once removed to a safe distance.

She turned to her other letter, seeing with a certain lightening of her heart that it was addressed in Dr. Williamson's scrawling hand. Poor Doctor Williamson still imprisoned in Perote; a hostage subject to degrading treatment – which his letters to her could not entirely conceal – and the whims of the dictator of Mexico. Some of his fellows had been released, and she hoped that every letter of his which arrived would bear the happy news that he and Danny Fritchie might soon be among them. She slit the seal of it and opened the pages – no, those hopes were dashed.

My very dear Mrs. Vining, it has been put to me that there is a possibility of my release from this place. A formal application for the favor of my liberty, requested by myself and forwarded through the offices of friends whom I have made among the officers of the garrison, would be received at the highest levels and considered with every evidence of favor. After much consideration I have declined with some regret, to make such a request. It pains me to do so, wishing with every hour to breathe the free air and to return to my native land – for such do I consider Texas to be – but I cannot do so and retain any private sense of honor, not while so many of my countrymen continue to be unjustly imprisoned here. My skills as a doctor are essential to my fellow prisoners, for there would otherwise be no care at all for those of us who become sick or injured. My colleague and fellow litigant Dr. Booker was sadly slain by one of our guards some weeks past, leaving no practitioner of the medical arts among us. My sense of duty towards my calling, and care for my fellow prisoners, requires of me that I remain until all of us are allowed to go.

Your last letter with the enclosure was of inestimable value to me, once again reassuring me with regards to your affections. I shall strive in future to be worthy of them.

Margaret frowned at the scribbled words . . . an enclosure with her last letter? She could not think of what he meant by that, unless he referred to the parcel she had sent to Mr. Thompson, with the request that it be conveyed to Dr. Williamson through his good offices, a parcel of as many good things as she contrive to send him; some of his clothes, a warm blanket, some books and the latest newspapers – although, to be frank, the news contained within those pages might be very old by the time he read them. The boys had sent some drawings they had made. The boys were really quite fond of Dr. Williamson, especially Horace. The doctor treated them with the same courtesy and interest as he did with everyone; once he came out of whatever book he was absorbed in. He talked to the boys as if they were adults: in Margaret's judgement he did this because he was unfamiliar with children. The boys found it gratifying to be treated with such respect, so much so that they regarded him nearly in the same heroic light as they did their Uncle Carl. Perhaps that was what Dr. Williamson meant: the boy's drawings had pleased him. She wondered if she should write to him about her fears with regard to her father. Dr. Williamson might have some comforting advice to give her for she had begun to wonder of late if Alois Becker was entirely well, or even sane. Would such confidences add to the burden of his imprisonment? It was not as if there was anything he could do about it from within the walls of Perote. But still, she thought wistfully, it would be a relief to share something of her concern with him. With anyone, actually. Hetty's good sense was a tonic, but Hetty was woman, whose view of the matter and subsequent advice would be that of another woman.

She would indeed relish a confidant regarding her fears for the boys if they remained in Austin; she had the bank draft from Race Vining's family and the friendship of General Sam and his Margaret. Could she return to Gonzales or to any of the established towns and settlements in the east and build a new life and business there? Now and again she had asked herself this very question, and never been able to answer it to her satisfaction. Why should she remain, having the means to go elsewhere in Texas? *I am too stubborn to give up, while others remain,* she thought. *Angelina Eberly stays, and so do Mary and Richard Bullock. They have hopes for the future, even though bats fly in and out of the capitol building and Comanche war parties menace us from the tops of the hills. Yet, Papa would never abandon his house, the hearth, and the apple trees. Papa is stubborn . . . and so am I. I built this house also, putting the earnings of the boardinghouse into it, money that I earned myself. As long as those who also believe and remain . . . I will stay, also.* It was almost a relief to have made some kind of decision. She pulled a fresh sheet of letter-paper out of the writing desk, and opened the ink bottle. Dipping the nib of the pen into it, she addressed the letter to Margaret Houston.

> *Dearest friend ML – Taking your encouragement to heart, I have resolved to begin learning to play the piano . . .*

Austin and those few stubborn citizens remaining continued to be menaced by Indians all during that summer, causing Margaret's resolve to waver now and again, especially in the dark of the night, when something caused her to wake – the distant howling of a prairie wolf, or the drumbeat of horse-hoofs – and she could not sleep again, fearing that such noise presaged another Indian raid. The rattle of the alarm drum or the distant pop of a gunshot – during the day, such noises sent her heart to racing. At those times, she resolved that should matters not improve within a year – if the Legislature did not return to meet in Austin – if the raids from the Comanche and from the Mexicans could not be mitigated or even turned back entirely . . . a year. Perhaps she would wait another year. What were the lives of her sons against such trivial things as a house and a row of apple trees? Margaret raised her eyes from the parlor table where she sat, writing another letter to Doctor Williamson, and looked out upon the trees, the reach of the river shining like quick-silver under the slanting rays of the afternoon sun, and that resolve immediately weakened. She was going every other day to Mary Bullock's china parlor, for piano practice, discovering that she could very well read the complicated musical notes. In the intervals, she studied the scores that Mary had provided to her, thinking that she could hear the clear notes of the piano keys in her own head as she looked at the tad-pole blobs scampering up and down the staves. Mary Bullock had already exclaimed many times that Margaret could elicit music from her own instrument rather better than she herself could do. Now the errant summer breeze that stirred the apple-tree branches had a breath of welcome coolness to it, wandering into the parlor through the tall windows. Out on the porch, Morag was rocking Baby Jemima in her cradle, one foot keeping the cradle moving, while she knitted a pair of socks to send to her husband, the melody of an Irish lullaby sung half under her breath.

Another year, Margaret told herself, another year, and she bent to her letter again, but not before noticing there was someone walking up towards the house from the direction of town, a man on foot with a heavy haversack over his shoulder. She looked again, narrowing her eyes – no, a white man, with a hat on his head and a dark blue round-about jacket over a calico shirt. He looked somewhat familiar, even at a distance, and Margaret rose from the table and went to the front porch for a better look.

"Morag!" she called, careful to keep any scrap of excitement from her voice, in case she would be wrong. "Morag, there's a man coming up from town. I don't recognize him. Could he be a newcomer, looking for a place to stay?"

"Oh, Marm – a new boarder?" Morag set aside her knitting and gave the cradle one more gentle push. "'T would be a blessing now . . . Oh, Mother Mary and Joseph – it's Danny!"

That last came out as a happy shriek; she picked up her skirts in either hand and flew down the steps, across the dooryard, to the open arms of the young man just coming up through the apple trees. The haversack went flying and so did his hat. Danny Fritchie staggered with the joyous impact, his arms wrapped around Morag as if he did not wish to let go, ever. Margaret smiled wistfully; she might once have done so – to embrace and kiss with such exuberance without consideration of propriety, but it was so long since she had been the age that Morag was now. She had become sedate in her affections, even though Race had been often and sometimes long away, in war and peace. Morag's feet were clear of the ground, her petticoat flying, until Danny set her down long enough to retrieve his hat and haversack. The younger boys came from around the side of the house from the vegetable patch, drawn by Morag's cry; they were romping alongside, as happy as puppies set free, and Horace took the haversack from Danny. Now they were walking towards the house again, Danny and Morag each with an arm around the other's waist, as if they could not bear to let go of each other.

"Hetty!" Margaret called into the kitchen, "Morag's Danny has come back. Come and see!" Hetty emerged, wiping her hands on her apron.

"Why so it is," she gasped. "'Tis indeed a miracle for him to be free! There has been nothing in the newspapers, has there, Marm – or anything in the Doctor's letters?"

"Not a word," Margaret answered, racking her memory; there had been no whisper in the newspaper or among the gossip at Bullock's or at Angelina Eberly's of any of the Perote prisoners being set free. And yet here he was, Danny Fritchie, walking up the steps of the house, a grin from ear to ear, his teeth a flash of white in a face burned as dark as any Mexican. He was as thin as a rail, piteously thin, Margaret noticed upon a closer look, and the clothes hung on him as if they had been the gift of a larger man.

"Welcome home, laddy-buck." Hetty embraced him, and held him at arms' length so as to look at him. "Och, and a welcome sight you are!"

"Not half as good as the sight of you, Miss Hetty," Danny answered, his voice roughening with emotion, and Morag exclaimed, in a voice of ecstatic happiness, "Danny – d'ye want to see your daughter, then? Oh, she's a lovely wee darlin' . . . an' I talk of you to her every day so that she might know . . . here she is, Danny-my-darlin'!" and Morag took the baby from her cradle where little Jemima had been looking placidly at the verandah ceiling over her head and waving her little boneless fists at it. She was a blushing-pink pearl of a baby, her little fuzz of hair as ink-dark as Morag's own, and her eyes still the unfocused purple-blue of an infant.

"Say hello to your Da, then," Morag added proudly, as she placed the baby in Danny's arms. He sank onto the bench where Morag had sat as she knitted and rocked the cradle with her foot, with the astonished Jemima in his lap.

It seemed to Margaret that the man and his daughter looked into each other's eyes for one long wondering moment, and then Danny said, "She's a beauty, Meggie . . . I had never in this living world thought that I would ever see her for myself." his voice cracked and broke, as hard as he struggled for composure, but it was as if a dam gave way. He held the baby awkwardly to him and wept in great racking sobs, until Morag took her daughter back.

Margaret whispered to her sons and to Hetty, "We should step inside and leave Danny and Morag alone, since he is so overcome . . . let him have a bit to compose himself." She and Hetty and the boys withdrew into the house, the boys reluctant and clamoring to know more.

"Hush, now," Hetty ordered sternly, and her eyes met Margaret's over the top of their heads. "Himself survived a battle and a killing of his fellows, a long journey, and was held at hard labor in chains in that dreadful place! Give him a little time. He will be hungry, Marm – should I begin fixing supper now?"

127

"Yes," Margaret answered. "And if we can, fix those dishes which Mr. Fritchie would relish. He is altogether too thin for health." Margaret sent the boys to pick fresh vegetables from the garden, and set a tray of fresh bread and cheese for Danny.

"The lad must be hungry after his journey," Hetty whispered. "Hush now. It sounds as if he is better fit to talk. Aye, and what of the poor doctor?"

"I will certainly ask," Margaret answered, "if Danny is willing to speak of those things that he has experienced." She hesitated, recalling how her brother Carl had been so withdrawn upon his return, unwilling to speak of Goliad, of his escape, and how their brother Rudi died under the Mexican's guns. Carl had drawn silence around him, save for that one time when Margaret had convinced him to answer the questions put to him by the newspaperman from the east. The very next day he was gone, the burden of horror too great for him to remain. Perhaps such recollections were easier to bear, under the endless blue sky of the Llano, alone with the whisper of the wind rustling in the curly grass.

Her fears were groundless. Danny smiled openly upon their entrance, his arm still around Morag's shoulders as she leaned into his embrace with Jemima in her lap and Danny contemplating them both with such fondness.

"Aye, she's a little beauty an' no mistake," he was saying, with touching sincerity. "And all this last year . . . I was afraid that I would never lay eyes on her, or you, Meggie – that I would never live to see a field of wildflowers or the Colorado River ever again, nor to sit down at a good meal, or breathe the clean air of freedom. Finally the day came when I could endure no longer. I feared that I would provoke one of the guards into killin' me, or throw myself from the top of the walls rather than live another day in that place. I had to be out."

He looked up at Margaret and Hetty – and it seemed to Margaret that his eyes filled once again. But he conquered that emotion, and continued, "I had to be out of there and away, or something of my soul would die, and without that, I would be a dead man walking. I couldn't bear it. So my friend and I . . . we had a plan to dig a tunnel, which was easy enough, Meggie – and Miss Hetty and Ma'am Vining. It was easy enough, and the very thought of a few hours of freedom – that put heart into us both and those of our friends that we trusted and shared our intentions with. So we did it, and there we were, beyond the walls and the glacis and ditch. I had taken the trouble to rub soot and tallow into my hair to make it look black, and I had learned enough Spanish so that I could pass for a peasant or a working man, at least as far as anyone would take notice. My friend pretended to be deaf and dumb, so that if any asked questions of us, I could answer for both. Sixteen of us escaped in the middle of the night, in the time of no moon. I tell you that it was blissful just to breathe the free air outside those pestilential walls! We would have counted our efforts a success even if we had only gone that far. Freedom – it was a tonic, Miss Hetty, Marm. I don't know how far the others got. I fear that the larger part intended to travel together for protection and comradeship, but several of our fellowship agreed that it would be dangerous, that such a party would attract undue attention from the authorities, once our escape became known. So the boldest of us resolved to go by ones and twos. My companion and I went down to the harbor at Vera Cruz – and there was an American ship at anchor, taking on supplies."

"That was most fortunate," Margaret murmured, and Danny nodded.

"So it was. There was a crowd of sailors and stevedores on the wharf, with a great many rowboats going back and forth between the dockside and the ships at anchor. We made ourselves known to the bosun of one of them, and my heart was in my mouth when we did so." Danny laughed a little as he confessed. "We both had watched him for some time, endeavoring to see if he would be sympathetic to our plight, or would he choose to be strictly neutral. We had a long argument about it. If any had seen us – me arguing with a deaf-mute, the fat would have been in the fire! General Thompson, the American envoy? Although he has been kindly and helpful to us, it's not as though he could do all that much, being a neutral party an' all. And a Yankee ship bein' perhaps more inclined to have Yankee sympathies? We were at least a little afeered that if we made ourselves known as escapees from Perote, that they might just leave us on the dockside, or even call the commander of the presidio and turn us over to them."

"Surely they would not have done so!" Margaret exclaimed, revolted. "You could not think that about the sympathies of your fellow countrymen!"

"Aye, but they're not, are they?" Danny answered. "Fellow countrymen and all! Those anti-Jacksonites, they would not accept Texas as a state because of slavery – an' the abolitionist faction, they were most particularly against it. By withdrawing the promise of statehood, they have left us ever since helpless against the depredations of Santa Anna. Why should we expect any better from the crew of a Yankee ship?"

"Surely they did not refuse succor in the time of your greatest need!" Margaret demanded, and Danny grinned, a wide and happy grin that seemed to split his face from ear to ear again.

"No, they did not – against all our fears and expectations. At our first words in English, they clapped us into their own seafarers' coats and hats, which they took from their own backs, and hustled us into their little boat. They rowed with energy, and took us at once before their ship captain. A very fine and straight-thinking gentleman." Danny Fritchie's voice at once became husky with emotion – emotion soon disciplined. "He immediately entered us in his logbook, as being of his ship's complement. A Yankee, I am sure, from his speech – but absolute in his intention to perjure himself for our safety, and insist that we had been among his company since well before journeying from his last port of call, if any among the authorities at Vera Cruz made inquiry. I do believe," Danny added, "that he deliberately delayed sailing by several days in order to offer a final refuge for any of our fellows who had managed to journey thus far. Indeed, the bosun's mate gave orders to those with shore duties to give immediate preference to anyone claiming to be a Texian who applied to them for aid. I cannot say enough good of Captain Biddle. We were given clothes and such light duties as made his pretense of us being of his crew as would convince anyone watching from a distance . . . duties which did not take us from the refuge of his vessel. But none of our fellow prisoners who had escaped with us came to Vera Cruz, while the good ship *Oriskany* was in port there, so Captain Biddle gave orders to lift anchor. Although," Danny added, "he passed a quiet word to certain other Yankee shipmasters at anchor in Vera Cruz, men whom he trusted, that there might still be some of our comrades searching for a safe refuge. But he had to hoist anchor and make away, lest anyone think it amiss that he remained so long. By good fortune, Captain Biddle's schedule took him to our port of Copano, such as it is. And so he left us, with many good wishes for our safe return . . . and his good crew, all." Danny's eyes were burdened with unshed emotion once again. "They took up a collection for us. They could only give but little, being plain working men, but it was what they had, and greatly treasured by us. I had no wish to linger in Copano or even to stay long in Mina . . ."

"Which they have changed the name of, to Bastrop again." Morag put in, with her eyes as sparkling with joy as the stars.

"Have they?" Danny answered. "Will no' they make up their minds?" he added with a very good essay at the Irish in his speech and Morag laughed. "I longed to see you again, and to see the little one, so I came straightaway. We can go home now, Meggie – a soon as I can ever arrange it."

"Not this very minute, I hope!" Hetty exclaimed, and they all laughed, Margaret thinking how very pleasant it was to be relieved of anxiety on Danny Fritchie's behalf, yet there was one person she held in affection, still imprisoned behind the dark stone walls and earthworks of Perote – and moreover, imprisoned no less by his sense of personal honor towards his fellows.

"What of Doctor Williamson? What do you know of him, and of his condition within the prison?" Margaret asked. "He wrote to us, weeks ago, telling that us that he had been tendered an offer of liberty, but declined as that would leave the remaining prisoners without a doctor. How does he fare – surely, he is not made to wear chains and perform such hard labor as was reported to us in the newspapers. He is not a young man – surely they are not so malicious as to set him to road-making and hauling stones for their walls."

"No," Danny smiled, a tired smile, as if the energy that had driven him though his miraculous escape and carried him over the long journey following was within a whisker of burning out. "We were usually not made to wear chains beyond the first few weeks of captivity, or at fresh labors – I think they did such to break men down, impress upon them the futility of trying to escape. Doctor Williamson was not often made to wear such while we were fellows in misfortune, although he did when first taken prisoner from San Antonio. I think rather that he was held in respect, being an educated man. He did some treating of our guards and their officers, so I think there was some gratitude, also. They were inclined to permit him some small liberties. I think he hardly noticed. You know about O'Doyle and the others who drew black beans at Saltillo?"

"Aye, that we do," Hetty answered, drawing in her breath with a sharp sound. "He was resolved to see that you were freed, y'know."

"That I knew," Danny answered. "I know too that he died bravely. I wish that I had come to know him better. How hard it is to never know of the qualities within until the very end. How many heroes walk among us, their virtues hidden, under an ordinary semblance until some unforeseen chance calls them forth and reveals their true nobility?"

Margaret smiled, answering with a twinge of wistful remembrance, which she did her best to conceal. "That is true indeed. I knew several of our heroes somewhat well when they still appeared to be ordinary men: Colonel Bowie, who was a gentlemanly ruffian and Colonel Travis, too. In his life, before he took charge of the Alamo, I don't believe he ever struck anyone as having any virtues besides being stubborn, arrogant, and exceeding surly in his ordinary dealings. Nothing in his life so well became him as those last few weeks and hours of existence, and his departure from it on the walls of the Alamo fortress. I cannot think of any who knew of him before that time who would have pictured such a noble end. He was a very uncomfortable man, indeed."

"As much as the Old Sir?" Hetty murmured in a low voice. Margaret laughed, saying, "Oh, yes – nearly as uncomfortable as my father. A brooding temper, no judgement at all, and convinced of his own infallibility in such matters, although it is my perception that Colonel Travis was much fairer-spoken than my father." Margaret considered her words. "Extremity is the anvil upon which all are judged in the eyes of others. Colonel Travis and so many of our friends were tested. So was Seamus O'Doyle and Dr. Williamson, I believe – and well-proved their qualities."

Meanwhile, Danny Fritchie stared at her in goggle-eyed disbelief. "You knew them – the men of the Alamo?" he breathed. Margaret sighed a little. Danny and his brother had come to Texas after the victory at San Jacinto, hearing much and knowing little of the temper of men who had lived in that time before, men whom she had known well as a young woman, newly married to her schoolteacher husband. Most who had come to Texas then were men like Alois Becker; men of substance and property – not young hot-heads looking for land and a fight, not necessarily in that order.

"Yes, I did," she answered. "Those that I knew best were our friends and neighbors in Gonzales. Almaron Dickinson was a particular friend, so was Jacob Darst, who went with our ranging company into the Alamo at the height of the siege. They were solid men, of family, honor, and worth, and good neighbors besides. They were called upon to prove themselves, which they did, in full measure . . . but, oh – how they were dearly missed, by those left behind! Think yourself lucky, Mr. Fritchie – you have survived such trials and heroic deeds, and come again to your family. You are fortunate beyond words, to have returned from such an ordeal alive and well."

"Aye," Danny Fritchie answered, and to Margaret it seemed that he answered with new respect, while Hetty murmured, "There ye go again, Marm; ye look like Maeve herself, with her terrible aspect, the judge and queen of us all!"

"Well, I did know them," Margaret answered, defensively. "They were friends of my husband, or husbands and sons of my friends. Nothing about them seemed then to be particularly heroic before the war. They seemed to be quite ordinary. Jacob Darst – his wife sometimes was annoyed with him because he would spend so much time helping neighbors. He would go on a brief errand, so she thought – and return hours later having spent that time helping someone to dig out a stump, or splitting firewood for Mary Millsaps because her husband Isaac was off hunting – and she had only a few sticks of wood left. Almaron Dickinson worked as a blacksmith ordinarily, but he was forever planning strange mechanical devices and drawing pictures on scraps of paper of how they would appear! He and his friend George Kimball had planned to build a hat manufactory in Gonzales. George Kimball died in the Alamo as well. His wife Pru was bearing a child, just as Morag was, only you have lived to see yours and George did not."

Margaret felt tears stinging her eyes. Pru Kimball's child had been born when Pru was a widow of five weeks or so. It was George who had led the Gonzales Ranging Company to the Alamo. She swallowed against that memory of grief for her friends and the life she had once had, as the wife of Gonzales' schoolteacher. She made herself smile fondly at Danny and Morag. "Too sad to think of on this blessed day! Hetty and I, we will make you a supper of all the dishes you like, and the boys will carry your things upstairs to the room that Morag and the baby share. You will wish to return to your own house as soon as you may but you are welcome to stay and recover from the cruelties of imprisonment with us for as long as you please. We all love Morag and little Jemima, so the boys and Hetty will want you to stay as long as you would like."

"So I will, and thank you, Marm," Danny answered with heartfelt fervor. "You have cared for my own dear Meggie and seen to the safeguarding of our family. I would stay out of gratitude for that – but in truth, I do not wish to linger too long. The business that my brothers Nicholas and Richard and I had – I must return to it after having neglected it for so many months. Richard will need my help, of course. He has needed it all these months that I was away, but if you wish to remain here," he stole a sideways look at Morag, who lifted her chin and answered stoutly, "No, Danny – I would return to our home as soon as we may, and you are fit and rested. This is Marm's house, and a bit Hetty's, too, and as fond of it as I am, and a fair refuge it may be – it is not mine. The roof that you built for me I prefer to any other on earth."

"Aye, then," and Danny took Morag's hand in his and kissed her fingers. "We'll go home then as soon as I can manage it."

So young, Margaret thought. They would go to Bastrop, to Danny's house, as a fledgling leaves the nest; young and impetuous and adoring, as careless of the future as she had been when she went from her father's roof to marry the schoolteacher. That was not all heartbreak and tragedy, she reminded herself. She and Race Vining had gotten themselves good years from that time of their marriage; evenings when they had sat reading books, when she had cleaned their tiny house and tended the garden during the day while he taught his classes in the breezeway, made the house fair and comfortable for him. She had loved him past all reasoning, and cherished the memory of that time, when her two oldest sons were babies, all of Texas had seemed a garden and her marriage a fairy-tale come true. But over those happy memories a pall was cast by the more recent events. Race Vining had betrayed her in his deeds long before they ever met. Then he had died, far away in Boston, in the household of his estranged wife and his proud family. He left her to raise her sons alone. Her father was mad, and her brother off and away as Ranger. What was there remaining for her to believe in about man and woman and love?

Chapter 11 – *A Coming Bright Dawn*

As Margaret had expected, Danny Fritchie wasted no time in completing arrangements to return with his family to Bastrop, to this neglected home and the sawmill business which had been left to the care of his surviving brother Richard during his long absence. He procured the use of a light wagon and a team to pull it; he and Morag departed with faces as smiling and happy as those of Margaret's boys were left dolorous. They adored Morag, and Baby Jemima had been as if their own little sister or pet, a tiny being to cherish, to play with and to amuse. Without her, they were bereft, and Peter was especially heartbroken.

"Mama, couldn't you have a baby sister for us?" he asked, in all innocence, on the evening of the day that Morag and Danny and their daughter had departed. Margaret was tucking her son into the bed that he shared with Jamie, in the room that her sons all shared. Margaret felt that question as a stab of ice in her heart. The shutters of the windows stood open to the night breeze and from the larger bed, she knew that Horace and Johnny were listening for her answer. She had longed for a daughter, and never been given one by Race. Now she was nearly thirty and a respectable widow. It wasn't as if potential husbands were not already two for a penny on the far frontier. There were two or three hundred men in Austin or living on farmsteads nearby – most of them single. There were about fifteen girls of marriageable, or nearly marriageable age, and another half-dozen widows, even including the redoubtable and martially disinclined Angelina Eberly among that number.

Now Margaret answered, "I cannot, my dear little duckling; one must be truly married to have babies. Now, if one of you were to court Jemima when she is a young lady and you are proper gentlemen – she would be my daughter. Go to sleep, all of you. Your Opa will want help with the harvest. We will all miss Jemima – until one of you decides to marry her and bring her home to us."

She went downstairs, leaving behind the closed door of the tiny upstairs bedroom a lively discussion between Jamie and Peter over which of them would marry Jemima when they were properly grown – which reminded her of how Mama had talked once of how she came to marry Papa, way back in Chester County, Pennsylvania. Papa had found a red ear of corn at a shucking-bee and claimed a kiss from Mama, and when he asked to court her that was all considered a good thing because their families had been neighbors and friends for years. *Thus are dynasties made,* thought Margaret – *families matching their agreeable children to each other, knowing their qualities and those of their parents, and making their way in the world smooth for the children* – at least in some part. Margaret snuffed out her candle, as she walked through the old parlor, that room next to the kitchen which was part of the old house which her father built when all of this little settlement of which everyone had maintained such ambitious dreams was a humble scattering of cabins and block-houses called Waterloo-on-the-Colorado. She had no need of her candle for she knew it in the dark, every wall and every stick of furniture so placed in it. Her bedroom was that little room that once had housed her mother's loom and weaving-work, a lean-to shed of sawn lumber, a little place which she and Race had claimed for themselves when they had returned after the war.

Margaret undressed in the dark, put on her nightgown, and slid between the bedcovers. This evening there was a breath of coolness in the air, and she was grateful for it. She hated the blistering heat of high summer. One of the reasons she was disinclined to move from Austin was that it truly seemed a little cooler in summers than in the prairie lowlands.

She rolled onto her side and pulled the other pillow closer to her. Truly, she would miss Morag and the baby, as much as Hetty would miss her sister. One more thing that she missed – the company of her husband; how comforting it would have been, to curl into the curve of his arms and listen to his voice in the dark. How reassuring it would have been to share her concerns, share with him something of the burden of responsibilities she felt weighed down by. She missed that, with a dull ache that only came now and again, the memory of laughter and loving care for each other, curled into the shelter of each other, late at night. Race Vining was gone from her, gone from her and buried in Boston. There were certain things that she shared by letter with Doctor Williamson, she thought irreverently, but what would it have been like to share any more than that with him? And she laughed out loud at the very thought of embracing that awkward and absent-minded man, and in bed, no less!

The work of harvest-time, of picking and preserving the apples and the last bounty of the vegetable garden and cornfield consumed her interests to the fullest upon Morag's departure. With the arrival of cooler nights, came time for pig-butchering, a task that Alois Becker performed with skill and grim efficiency: dispatching four yearling pigs with a deft stab, hanging the carcasses from the limb of the nearest oak tree to drain of blood, which Margaret and Hetty collected for blood-sausage – scalding the carcasses, one by one in a huge iron kettle – that and the gutting, which provided the endless lengths of intestine for sausage-casings. Those must be washed clean and put to soak in brine, while Alois cut apart the hams, shoulders, the side meat and set them to brine and then to smoke; there would be bacon, and cured hams, the liver for more sausages, and the heads for head-cheese. The fire in the smokehouse burned night and day, redolent of apple-wood, mesquite and hickory, little puffs of scented smoke appearing from underneath the smokehouse eaves. It was a laborious and occasionally bloody process. Margaret was glad to have no greater part of it than the chopping of those useful scraps of pork flesh and fat, mixing with spices, and the stuffing of endless lengths of sausage – and that was enough of a chore in itself. But such work – over those four yearling pigs! That would provide meals enough; all during butchering time, they had their fill of fresh pork.

Alois traded a surplus to Mr. Bullock and Angelina Eberly, for although Bullock had his own stock of pigs he had long and handsomely owned that Alois Becker had the better of him when it came to smoking hams and sausages. Margaret thought that her father looked briefly pleased at this honest testament to his expertise, when Bullock came with a wagon to harvest the results of his exchange just before Christmas. The Bullock's Inn and Angelina Eberly's house had received a new influx of boarders in anticipation of the next meeting of the Legislature who would, of course, dine on the succulent output of Alois Becker's labor. Margaret was bitterly disappointed that none of this bounty of potential boarders had spilled over to bless her establishment – at least, not so far.

"Aye, well – we should be ready, then!" Hetty affirmed stoutly. "When we're done w' the harvestin' an' the butcherin' an' all, we should turn out the boarders' bedrooms, so that everything shall be fit and ready for new guests. Several fair days should do it – the dusting, and the turning of the mattress-pallets . . . an' Marm, we should see that the ordinary sheets are clean and mended, and that moths have not been makin' a meal of the blankets."

"I suppose that we should," Margaret answered, sighing to think of the work that would make for the two of them. But she and Hetty had standards. Winter after harvest-time was a good time to do that work, even if early spring was held to be the proper time for a good clean-out. "What shall we do with Doctor Williamson's things? I do not like to leave them in the ordinary rooms, especially if we are to begin hosting guests again. I do not like the thought that strangers might make free with his possessions."

"We should put them in the little upstairs room," Hetty answered. When Seamus O'Doyle had done the work on the house to make it fit for renting rooms to boarding gentleman, one of the things that he had done was to complete the loft in Alois Becker's tall blockhouse to make a second story across all the rooms and not just over the parlor. This space was presently divided into three tiny rooms, with dormer windows added for light and space. They were accessed by a steep and angled staircase, which Seamus had also built with clever use of the space and great attention to woodworking: One for her sons, one for Hetty and Morag, which Hetty now held for herself alone, and a third for which Margaret had charged extra. In the last months of his stay, Mr. Hattersley had it for himself. Margaret cringed sometimes to think that much of the penning of his libelous little book had been done there, under her very roof! The room was tiny but completely private, in comparison to the two larger rooms on the ground floor, which had been made from what had been the back verandah – rooms which adjoined, and could accommodate four boarders in each on plain beds made from mesquite poles, and mattresses stuffed with corn-shucks. Plain they might have been – but they had been comfortable enough and spotlessly clean.

"Yes, the little room," Margaret said, with a feeling of fond protectiveness towards Doctor Williamson. Should he come home from Perote as Danny Fritchie had done, tormented and thin, worn down to his very bones from deprivation, and forced labor in captivity, he should have her best room at his disposal! She had begun to hope he would return soon. The newspapers were full of speculation that the Mexican government might soon release the last of the Texians in Perote as a gesture of goodwill. Margaret privately thought very little of such gestures, with the memories of murder and treachery still burning like embers in her heart. She would never hold any good opinion of Lopez de Santa Anna or those creatures who obeyed him – smiling, servile and ever ready to curry favor by murdering Texians.

As soon as the last of the hogs was transformed into hams, sides, and lengths of sausage, she and Hetty began turning out the ordinary linen. When the Legislature should meet again, it must – it must meet in Austin, and she must be ready. She and the boys lugged all of Doctor Williamson's possessions up the narrow twist of staircase, and settled them into the tiny chamber, with the dormer windows that looked one way towards town, and the other way towards rolling hills, that depending on the distance and the time of day, were every shading of color from misty slate to pale lavender.

With the turn of the year, guests began arriving, many previously known to Margaret and welcomed with breathless hope. Her supper table was full of guests once more. She hired young Emma Simpson to help Morag in the afternoons and evenings, to bring dishes from the kitchen and to help in their preparation. They celebrated Christmas and the turning of the year without any incident save a visit from an old acquaintance – or rather, one whom Margaret had only met twice, but whose wife had been one of her companions towards the end of their brutal journey east during the 'runaway scrape.'

On a midweek morning, a light trap rolled up to the house: Margaret heard the wheels of it crunching the river gravel that kept the space before the house from being a muddy swamp. She was dusting the dining room, sweeping breakfast crumbs from the tablecloth, and wondering if would be too soon to remove it for a cleaner one. There was a tiny spot of spilled honey, just where pots of jam, honey. and molasses were clustered, halfway along the table. Margaret clicked her tongue at the carelessness of whoever had spilled it and then wondered if she were beginning to sound too much like Hetty – or even Mama. The cloth was otherwise clean. It would be a trouble to wash the whole thing. She made a mental note to find a salver or perhaps a doily, to put over the place and to stand the jars upon. She had just taken up the dusting cloth and her broom again when she heard the trap.

She went to the dining room window which looked out upon the front of the house; oh, a very fine equipage, drawn by a pair of clean-limbed horses who were commanded by a Negro driver. Good heavens – that must be Mr. Burnett. Liddy Burnett had written to her weeks ago, that her husband had been elected once again to the Legislature. Margaret only knew William Burnett from brief meetings; the first was seeing him among ranks of Sam Houston's ragged army as they marched past the refugee-camp outside of Harrisburg. Liddy Burnett had camped there also, having fled the Burnett's holding on the Brazos River, accompanied by her daughters, their children, and the household slaves. In that wretched encampment filled with exhausted refugees, Mama had died. Liddy Burnett had comforted Margaret and read the burial service for Mama from her *Book of Common Prayer*. The Burnett's Negro driver, Hurst, had built a coffin for Mama from boards scavenged from other wagons.

Margaret had been in two minds about accepting Hurst's labor at Liddy Burnett's direction, for Mama had been against anything to do with or profiting from the labor of a slave. In the end, Margaret offered to pay Hurst with Mama's gold wedding-band, which he accepted after some persuasion. He wanted, Hurst confessed to Margaret, to buy his children free with his wages from hiring-out – a desire that Margaret firmly agreed with, of which Mama would have approved. She had met William Burnett more properly, when he and his two sons-in-law had returned after the victory at San Jacinto, now that they could take their families home again. He was a ruddy and vigorous man of middle years and of a decisive turn of mind. Upon hearing of the distress of two of her friends – Mary Millsaps, and Pru Kimball, left widowed and with children when their husbands had gone with the Gonzales Company to the aid of the doomed Alamo – he and Liddy had offered them hospitality and a refuge at their own home. Mary and Pru, having none of their own to go to, had accepted. From their letters and from Liddy's they had found hospitality there to be a soothing balm for grief and loss.

Margaret set down her broom and dust-cloth and went to the front door, opening it even as William Burnett had raised his hand to knock on it.

"Mrs. Vining!" he exclaimed, sweeping off his hat and bowing over her hand, evidence of pleasure and affection writ clear on his weathered face. At his back, the coachman also removed his hat as soon as he set down a pair of carpet-bags on the top step. Another more familiar face, for this was Hurst, only a little older than he had been – and so elegantly turned out! It amused Margaret to see that both men were growing bald about their heads in the exact same way, the master and man . . . and then she chided herself. There might be a good reason for that. Now that she had thought of it, William Burnett and Hurst did have more of a similarity to each other than could be accounted for than just being of the same age and general build.

"Dear William," Margaret said in answer, "Liddy wrote to me, weeks ago, that you would be visiting Austin – but I did not expect you so promptly. Where are you staying, and for how long? I might offer you hospitality here, you know!"

"I do," and William Burnett kissed her hand. "My wife gave me strict orders that I should consider staying nowhere else but in your establishment – but this is a flying journey to arrange for a place of our own. I would be staying no longer than is necessary to establish some little domestic refuge here . . . a town house, a little establishment of our own. I saw the old French Legation house in passing. Pretty ruinous, but something like that would serve. Liddy entertains houseguests on a pretty extensive level, you know. She would like something like that, of course. So, will you have us, Mrs. Vining? Bullock told me that you were particular, in extending hospitality."

"Of course," Margaret answered, laughing. "No drunkards, no profligates, and only enlightening conversation over the supper-table. No vulgar attentions to the cook and the maids – and to myself, of course. I prefer only upright gentlemen, of earnest disposition, and those whose manners at the table are of the most refined."

"Agreed!" and William Burnett laughed. "You are a lady of the best and purest sort. I only ask – have you a place for Hurst, in addition to myself?"

"I do not at present have a place for separate servant quarters," Margaret answered, although having such was something she ought to consider in expanding the house. "There is a small room in the loft, above the stables – there is no provision for a fireplace in it – but seeing that it is almost summer there is no need for it."

"That will do!" William Burnett answered heartily, although Margaret did notice that he shot a quick look at Hurst before answering as if he wanted to assure himself that Hurst would be agreeable. "Both of us have slept in less comfortable places in our time, haven't we, Hurst?"

"I'll show you to the rooms, then," Margaret answered, when Hurst had made no more than the briefest nod of assent towards his owner. An owner? Margaret thought, to herself; it seemed to her that the two men were making a calculated pretense of that for the benefit of observers. Now and again Liddy Burnett had made a small complaint of how her husband had often indulged Hurst, treated him as a person of more consequence than an ordinary personal slave and attendant should be treated. "And you will probably wish to lock up your horses in our stable at night. My father is around in back – he will show Hurst where to put the horses." At a nod from William Burnett, Hurst clucked gently to the horses; the fancy trap and matched team vanished around the side of the house as Margaret showed Mr. Burnett into one of the bedrooms that would be his – not completely private, for he would share it with another, although Margaret prided herself on the fact that her gentleman guests had single beds, that they would not have to share – and that the two guest bedrooms, which looked out upon the back of the house were relatively large and airy, each with a tall window that looked back onto the garden.

That was another thing that Margaret wished to remedy when she could. Her guest rooms should look the other way, on the vista of the apple trees and the town beyond it, with the cynosure of the view being the height upon which it was hoped that a grand capitol building would rise. Someday Margaret would have that – the house that she and Seamus O'Doyle had dreamed of building, a comfortable, civilized house of well-appointed rooms, fitted with tall windows opening onto shaded galleries, surrounded by apple trees, and gardens. Really, she thought, as she showed William Burnett the dining room, the boarder's parlor and bedrooms, as well as the necessary – she might very well have enough takings from the boarders over the next year or two to begin thinking seriously about it. Tonight, she should take down the copy of the *Builder's Companion* that Seamus O'Doyle had left behind and renew her studies, with an eye towards a decision on how what she wanted in a house might best be accomplished.

Conversation over the supper table that night seemed livelier, more hopeful than it had been in years, Margaret noted. Those new guests, arriving in anticipation of the seat of government returning, brought hope with them, and fresh installments of gossip which had not yet made it into the pages of the newspaper or chewed nearly to death in Bullock's taproom.

"There's talk of another entrepreneur scheme," William Burnett reported. "This one drawing settlers from Europe." He shook his head disparagingly.

From across the table that rangy, red-headed man, John Ford answered in his soft Carolina drawl, "Old news – that Frenchie was given a grant on the Medina two years ago. Haven't noticed too many of his folk bein' right eager to take up an offer." Like William Burnett, John Ford had been elected to the Legislature. His home was in San Augustine where he had practiced both law and medicine, but he also was looking to establish a permanent home in Austin.

"Monsieur D' Castro? No, not the Frenchie. This is being worked up by a society of German nobles; very well-meaning and rich gentlemen by all accounts and by other accounts very well advised. They say even Queen Victoria approves of the scheme, for one of the princes is kin to her. So far they have enlisted ten thousand immigrants from all across Germany." John Ford gave a low whistle of astonishment, and William Burnett continued, "And not just any kind of rabble, either – but farmers and craftsmen. They are having them pay fees to ensure they are a worthy sort."

"Still – worthy or not," John Ford took another bite from the pork cutlet on his plate, adding, "It's a far piece, from there to here, an' a harder road, once here. How much would a tenderfoot know of wilderness an' Indian-fighting, of what conditions would be? An' not one, but ten thousand?"

"I would welcome ten thousand new neighbors." Margaret answered wistfully. "Who would build new homes, make new towns, and import rather more industry. I would not even mind speaking German again, as I did when I was a child. All of my parent's folk were Germans, you know."

"You would get along splendidly, my dear Mrs. Vining, if this society of nobles is able to carry through with their plans," William Burnett assured her, and John Ford added, "I'll say. If they butcher the hogs and keep as good a smokehouse as your Pa does, Mrs. Vining – we'll all get along jes' fine."

That conversation stuck in Margaret's mind – that there might be more of the folk from Opa Heinrich and Oma Katerina's country, coming to settle in Texas. She turned it over in her mind; yes, she would find such very welcome. And if such folk were more like Papa, perhaps he would not be so prone to quarrel . . . or maybe not, since Papa seemed to have quarreled with everyone, all through his life, everyone save Mama. Race Vining had once remarked that Alois Becker could get along best with his neighbors in a place where he had no neighbors. It saddened Margaret to see that her father had retreated from most human contact, like a hibernating bear in a cave. He slept in the corner of the kitchen, frowned with his great shaggy brows at the boys as they did their morning chores, daily growling a few words at her or Hetty.

This was the man whom Mama had loved to her last breath; Margaret wished that she could do something to lessen the shadow of unhappiness that haunted him. She had numerous 'thinks' about this, especially after her father had given in to his furious temper and tried to choke her – before reluctantly concluding that there really wasn't much that she could do. Alois Becker had chosen to imprison himself in a dungeon whose stones were made of anger, mortared together with grief and furious resentment at the fates that took Rudi and Mama from him. He could take no comfort at all in having two children and four grandsons left in this world. Margaret had long since ceased to feel any of her own anger at that. It just was – a thing which existed, as the heights of Mount Bonnell, rising green in the near distance, or as the stump of the huge oak tree that Papa and her brothers had felled in the early days to make the sill-beam for the house. Nothing that she could say or do would ever change the aspect of Mount Bonnell, or the existence of that stump. Still, she thought, as she changed into her nightgown – it might do something for Papa's mood to speak the old language, now and again.

The following morning began as every ordinary morning did – before dawn, with the sky in the east just flushing to apricot and the color of mother-of-pearl. The smell of coffee roasting mingled with the scent of mesquite wood burning in the stove. It was a well-practiced dance: Hetty slicing bacon to crisp in one pan, while collops of ham warmed in the other and sausages sizzled in a third. Margaret busied herself mixing the batter for cornbread, and as soon as that went into the oven she kept a sharp eye on the meats, while Hetty began making the morning biscuits. She would make three batches throughout the day, one for every meal. The night before, she had laid out the necessary ingredients all to hand, and together Margaret and Hetty had set the dining room table for breakfast. One less thing to do during when first efforts in the morning were bent upon getting breakfast to the table piping hot; now Jamie was fetching down the coffee grinder. Johnny and Peter would be bringing in the eggs, while Horace helped Papa with the morning milking. The cream from last night's milking had risen to the top of the milk-pans overnight. In a few minutes Margaret would begin to churn it for fresh butter.

"How many this morning?" she asked Johnny as he came through the door carefully holding a basket of eggs before him.

"Fourteen, Mama," he answered with a yawn. "Peter is bringing the milk for Opa. Opa says he has a headache, and could you make him some willow-bark tea for it?"

"I will," Margaret answered. "Go help Peter – the milkpails will be too heavy for him to carry if they are full."

She thought nothing more than of how to fit another small kettle upon the stove-top to brew the willow-bark tea for Papa's headache, in the middle of the rush to finish breakfast for the boarders and that it presented no more than a minor ruffle to the tenor of hers and Hetty's hurry to put breakfast on the table at the agreed-upon time.

She thought that, until the moment that Johnny cried out from the farmyard. "Mama – come quick! There's something the matter with Opa!"

It was more the sound of panicked fright in her son's voice that brought her instantly to the back door, wiping her hands upon a towel, to see Papa standing stock still in the middle of the farmyard, halfway between the barn and the back door, and Horace with the halters of the milk cows in his hands standing frozen in open stable doorway. It was light enough now, with dawn flushing the eastern sky with brighter colors of apricot and rose, that she could see that her father's face was deeply flushed with color, contorted as if he were feeling nearly unbearable pain. At his feet, milk from the pails that had dropped from his hands spread briefly into a white and swiftly-vanishing puddle. Before she could draw a breath herself to run to her father, he had fallen as a heavy tree topples. He lay like a massive log, at full-length, motionless in the dirt and muck of the farmyard.

"Papa!" Margaret was hardly aware that she had shrieked. His face was against the ground. She pulled at his shoulder, with strength that she didn't know she possessed, until she rolled him to lie on his back. Papa. His face was contorted, his eyes staring up at the dawn-flushed sky. She fell on her knees, taking one of his hands between hers. "Papa, speak to me, Papa – what is the matter? Can you answer me? Papa!" His eyes looked up at the sky, motionless – not a flutter of his eyelids, and Margaret knew instinctively that was not a good sign. Papa's hand in hers; there was no regular beat of a pulse in his wrist when she fumbled to find it. Papa could not be dead. He was as ageless and stubborn as the rocks, as unyielding as the oak stump below the planting of apple trees on the hill where he had first build the house – that house that sheltered her brothers and Mama, to which he clung with so ferocious a will. It just must be that her clumsy fingers could not find the pulse in his wrist. Papa could not be dead, struck down between one moment and the next. There was no pulse to be found, not when she touched his neck, looking for that other and stronger pulse between his grey-shot beard and the open collar of his shirt . . . which, she recalled with a sudden pang, was his oldest and most ragged one, of plain indigo-dyed homespun. Mama's weaving. How many times had Margaret chided him to put on newer garments, he should look like a prosperous man of a prosperous household. Papa had always refused, which she wrote off to his fierce stubborn nature.

There was a hand, taking the place of hers, a knowledgeable one, looking for that pulse which she could not find, yet another hand, helping her to stand. She stood, blinking; it was John Ford, deft and clinical, looking for a pulse with one hand, and finding none, closing Papa's staring eyes. John Ford had been shaving himself; he was shirtless, with his braces hanging loose and a towel around his neck. He still had an open razor in his left hand – hearing her cry, he had reacted instantly. William Burnett had also come at once, but he had been farther along in his morning toilette, for he had on a shirt and neck-cloth half-tied.

"I'm sorry, Miz Vining. He is gone. Gone with God, I would say, swift and sure."

At her side – for it was he who had helped her to stand – William Burnett made the quick gesture of crossing himself, forehead to breast, shoulder to shoulder, in the old-fashioned way that she knew from Hetty and Morag. William and Liddy Burnett followed the high-church English way; there was a logical reason for that, as her husband had once explained to her, but at this moment, she did not recollect any of what he said at the time. Only that Papa was dead, between one moment and the next, with fresh milk spilling into the dirt by his feet, and there was breakfast to be gotten onto the dining room table, and now Peter and Johnny were looking at her with eyes gone wide with disbelief and horror.

"It is Opa," she said to them, barely aware of the words that came from her lips. "I am afraid that he is dead."

There was another face behind those of her sons, a dark Negro face. Hurst had come from the stable, still pulling on that elegant jacket over the shirt and neck-cloth that were the livery of an established and trusted servant. "I may need your services now, Hurst, if I may impose – to build a coffin for my father as you did for my mother, whom he did well love. I believe now that she was the one who loved him best in life and held him to his better nature."

All at once, it was as if all the tears that she had not shed, could not shed for Mama, for Race – and all those other friends for whom she grieved in private such as Seamus O'Doyle – she was overcome with them, for grief and emotions that she could not even put into words, sagging onto William Burnett's shoulder. She could not stand; such was the intensity of them. Papa was gone, and there went one of the underpinnings to her world, and she had not even known it until this moment.

Presently she found herself in the parlor, crying into . . . what was that . . . a dish-towel? The towel that she had in her hands when Johnny called for her; now it was wet entirely, and William Burnett was patting her other hand, and talking in a kind and comforting way. She could not make out the actual words of what he was saying. Since he had two daughters and a wife who loved him excessively, she could only imagine that he was accustomed to sudden storms of this nature. Lucky Liddy Burnett in her fortunate and sensible husband. Suddenly she hiccupped, and the words that he was saying to her came back into focus.

"Hurst brought around the wagon and he and young Ford took your father to that place . . . for proper disposition."

"The dead house." Margaret recovered her voice and mopped at her face with the sodden dishtowel. "I know. There will be no question of what caused his death. It will be rather unusual for Austin, not to blame an untimely end on the Comanche!"

"Do not distress yourself, Mrs. Vining." Mr. Burnett looked a little surprised at her brief levity. "Mr. Ford was in no doubt, being a medical man – and although I am not, I can see the signs of apoplexy. I know your father was of a choleric nature, so it was only to be expected." He patted her hand. "Do you wish me to send the boys to you, now that you are more composed?"

"Where are they – my sons?" Margaret asked, and Mr. Burnett answered easily, "With Miss Hetty; she thought to comfort them with a little breakfast. They did not seem distressed at your loss. Somewhat surprised, I think; but if I am any judge of emotions, they are more subdued than grieving."

"My father was not an easy man," Margaret answered. "Would that he had been! The affection of my sons might have been a comfort to him in his last years, but I am afraid they feared him and looked upon him as a stern, unloving taskmaster."

"I judge that his had been the greater loss." William Burnett stood: he was a man of the world, and one who seemed to grasp that all families were not as amiable as his own appeared to be – and understand that requiring a pretense of grief where none was actually felt was an impossible imposition. "Is there anyone at al, who ought to be notified at once of your father's passing? I am completely at your disposal in your hour of need, Mrs. Vining – Hurst, too. Liddy would insist upon this, if my own sense of honor did not so move me forth."

"My younger brother," Margaret answered. "Carl Becker. He is a sergeant of Rangers in Captain Hays' company in Bexar. I suppose that he should be told, even though he did not hold our father in any greater regard than my sons do. He was a most difficult man, Mr. Burnett. We had another brother, Rudi – who was much loved by all, including my father, perhaps to excess. He died at Goliad. I fear that my father placed the blame for that unfairly and resented Carl for having survived. He said such cruel things to him. I shall be surprised if he has any more grief for Papa than my sons do."

"I will see to sending a messenger to Bexar." Mr. Burnett looked quite pleased at an opportunity to be so instantly of service. He bowed over Margaret's hand – which still held the wadded-up and sopping-wet dishtowel in it, and added with an air of gentle sympathy, "It is still a shock, my dear Mrs. Vining, to loose even the harshest of parents. One might feel quite adrift, I think. Even as such as they were, they remained a rock of certainty, upon which one might always depend. You have my sympathies, Mrs. Vining, and my support, always." And he added, in somewhat of an embarrassed rush, "My own father was also difficult. He had many fine qualities, but he was of such a brutal and autocratic temper that those of his own household – even of his blood – feared him greatly. He was not a gentleman, as those who understand such things would judge them. Our grief at his loss was tempered by relief." On his kindly, middle-aged face was an expression of sorrow and perplexity such as Margaret had never seen, and brought her up short. '*Our fathers plague us, for good or ill,*' she thought. '*William Burnett is a man of near my father's years, yet he is haunted by the memory of a father who was perhaps as cruel to him as Papa was to Carl.*'

"Thank you," Margaret answered finally. "Not least for understanding our peculiar situation."

Chapter 12 – *Returns*

Mr. Burnett's messenger to Carl in Bexar, sent by one of Captain Coleman's volunteers through the good offices of the local alcade, returned to Austin the day before Alois Becker was buried in a ground of Margaret's selecting: just a little way from the stump of the great oak tree on a patch of level ground. The messenger reported that Sergeant Becker was off on a long patrol with the Ranger Company, around the borders of the Comanche-haunted Llano country and perhaps even venturing deep into it. He and his men would likely not return for many months. Margaret had rather expected something of the sort. This absolved her of any responsibility to ask her brother for advice and consent regarding Alois Becker's funeral and the disposition of his property, indeed of any necessity for considering his wishes on the matter. Margaret suspected that her brother would have as little or the same care for the burial of their father as he would in the dispatch of a dead cat or dog into the nearest midden-pit. If he was not present, he would not have to make a pretense of feelings that he did not have, or embarrass her by openly displaying a lack of them.

"I think that he may rest near the apple trees," she had said to Mr. Burnett, and to Mr. Waller and those others who came to pay their respects to a man who, while never being well-liked among his fellow citizens, had something of respect for having been an early settler of the region. "He cared so tenderly for the apple trees – and we may tend his grave easily." '*As no one else is likely to, for the love of him,*' she thought, as she and the boys walked back to the house on that first afternoon when she had talked of a grave for Papa on his own property, and they had gone down to inspect that place, a little below the top of the hill upon which the house sat. '*Mama would have,*' but Mama's grave was under an oak tree near Harrisburg, that branched up in four great limbs. "*The best part of your father – died with your mother,*" Race observed once. All those years since then, the act of living for Alois Becker had been merely existence, a habit; the motion and pretense of living without the heart of it. Margaret wondered, with a twist of unease in her own breast – was all of her life and the manner of her living it since Race had gone from her merely a well-established habit? Was she truly alive and loving, caring for her sons and her household, caring for her town and her friends; not just some peculiar automaton, walking through the days and the necessary tasks out of habit and obligation? That question plagued her, through the hours and days following Alois Becker's passing, although she had some moments of savage amusement upon realizing that she had no need to go into black for her father; she had already been wearing the customary colors of mourning for her husband – as much as these customs could be upheld on the frontier.

'*I am tired of it*,' she thought, as she walked back from the grave where Alois Becker had been put to rest and the earth above mounded up. She would have a fine stone carved, of course, and perhaps a little fencing put around the place to keep the cattle and horses from trampling over where he lay for eternity. '*I am tired of it. I want to go towards living my life in hope. I want to not be afraid. I want to build the house as I want it to be; to live in it as I think fit to live.*' Horace walked at her side, Peter at her other with his hand in hers. The boarders and townsfolk who had attended the brief ceremonies followed behind: Mr. Waller, Richard Bullock and his family, Captain Coleman, Mrs. Simpson and her son and daughter, Angelina Eberly and her family, Mr. Ware, stumping gamely along on his wooden foot.

She and Hetty had laid out the usual spread of cakes, bread and cold meats for the mourners on several tables set out on the porch. There were dozens of saddle horses tied to the rails of the little corral in back, any number of traps and carriages, although most had preferred to walk from their houses nearby. So taken up with the demands of hospitality was she that Margaret had hardly taken notice of the hollow, thudding sound that the clods of earth made against the coffin; they had not the heartrending effect upon her that she had felt upon burying Mama in that lonely grave just outside of Harrisburg.

"So, what will ye do, Mrs. Vining? Will you be hiring anyone to work the land, then?" Angelina Eberly tucked into a platter of vegetable pickles, biscuits and sliced ham, in a shady corner of the porch. Shrewd old storm-crow, Margaret thought, with a mix of annoyance tempered with affection. She must rejoice at the thought of eating food that she had not cooked herself. Margaret was exhausted; she had been receiving the condolences of mourners for much of the afternoon. Now, much as she had expected, the gathering had turned into rather a convivial one, friends gathering with like-minded friends here and there in the parlors or on the porch, enjoying the cool breeze that wafted through the trees and the distant view of the river as the afternoon sun slanted through new leaves and turned the distant Colorado River to quicksilver. Hetty had firmly taken upon herself the duties of keeping the various dishes and platters generously filled, commanding Margaret to play the part of the hostess and move among the guests. Margaret had done so until her feet hurt; so did her hand, from having it so comfortingly pressed and her face ached from having to keep it in the same demure expression. She found it therefore a pleasure to sit in the corner and converse with Mrs. Eberly, whose blunt speech and decided opinions had the merit of being both original and amusing – if now and again more startlingly frank than Margaret usually thought was acceptable at her table.

"There's hardly any of it left to make it worthwhile, save for a hay-field and another of corn. I expect that I shall hire someone to come and plow it in the spring. My father farmed out of habit, I believe – only just enough for household needs. We'll keep the garden and the milk cows, of course. They graze with the Simpson herd, but I will probably sell the draft oxen."

"Aye, and I am not sure that he thought all that much of it himself, any more." Mrs. Eberly shook her black-bonneted head. "Poor man; he got so worn-looking these past two or three years. In his prime, he must have been a handsome, well-set up man."

"He was," Margaret answered, felling a slight twinge of guilt. Carlchen's threat must have weighed very much upon Papa. "More than that – he was magnificent. When I was a child I used to think that Papa looked like the illustration of a king or a god in the old storybooks."

"It's a tragedy, gettin' old," Mrs. Eberly sighed gustily. "But I tell you what, Miz Vining, it's a sight better'n the alternative." Mrs. Eberly still had children, grandchildren, and even step-children living. Margaret supposed that she had the love of those to keep her warm in the evening of life. For Papa, that fire had gone out, years ago.

"He loved my mother so very much," she answered at last, "and my brother Rudi, who fell at Goliad. I fear he was a broken man after those losses. I believe he would have rejoiced in his heavenly reunion with them – which is why I am not myself left desolate with grief. Papa has gone to be with those which he truly loved. I cannot help but think that he would have seen departing from this life as a blessing and relief." Margaret found that belief a considerable irony; since that was what Papa had done throughout much of his life, abandoning herself, her sons, and Carl on the shores of this present world to fend for themselves.

"Aye, you're right, Miz Vining – so it would have been." Mrs. Eberly took another bite out of the biscuit and ham upon her plate. "Maybe it was for the best. He was difficult, and that we all know well. It was to your credit to have been so patient with his ways for these years. But still, where does that leave you, Miz Vining? You cared for him in his declining years; what are you left in his will? Pardon me for speaking so bluntly, but I cannot help noticing that it was your efforts which kept his estate on a level plane and a roof over all of your heads. If your father had a comfortable home in his last years, that was entirely your work and your doing. I would not sit by and see you done out of your rights. What has he left, and what did he leave of it to you? I know that brother of yours is good lad and a brave Ranger, and he would stand to inherit something, I am sure – but where has he been for you, all these years? I won't hear that he has inherited the larger portion, for that will not be fair at all . . . an' pardon me for speaking so blunt an' speaking out of turn, if you'll forgive me, Miz Vining – but it's a man's world, unless we stick up for ourselves and stick together. I am a woman who would see justice done, right and proper!"

"Thank you, Mrs. Eberly," Margaret answered, rather touched by Mrs. Eberly's concern. "You have no need for concern. Papa did not have a will, outlining any share of his property to us . . ."

"Jus' like a man," Mrs. Eberly snorted. "Think he's going to live forever! So, you and your brother share equally. Well, that's only fair, I suppose, less'n he comes back with a new wife an' wants his share in the house! What then, I ask you?"

"I have consulted with Mr. Ford," Margaret answered sedately. "He practices law as well as medicine – and he has advised me. Papa owned several town-lots, as well as this house and the property surrounding. There was also a large sum of currency which Papa had in payment from the State when he sold all the rest. He never spent it – we found it among his things."

Margaret and Hetty, and John Ford had gingerly made inventory of those few personal things which Alois Becker had kept in a small box under his bed in the kitchen. It made a pitiful showing: a small pocket-watch and a silver pen-knife, and a very old Bible in German with a tattered cover. There was a fat wallet of currency – that payment for the land which he had received and hardly spent anything of, two deeds for a pair of town-lots, bought at auction under the oak tree on the day that Austin had been established – which one day might be as valuable as the land upon which the homestead stood. There were also two folded papers, signed by Erastus Smith and an officer whose name Margaret could not call to mind, one testifying to the service of Alois Becker as a scout for the Army during the war, and the other certifying that he had participated with great distinction in the battle at San Jacinto.

"You should be able to apply for a tract of land on the basis of his service," Mr. Ford had remarked upon reading them. Margaret set that thought aside; yes, the widows of the Gonzales men who fell at the Alamo had all been awarded land-tracts, for the faithful service of their husbands. At the very bottom of the box was a small thing of cob-web fine linen, folded small: an elaborately ruffled woman's house-bonnet of the old-fashioned cut, which Margaret had recognized as being Mama's; a ghostly scent of the verbena sachet which Mama had favored still clung to it, although it had mostly taken on the musty-paper odor of the paper currency and the property deeds. Margaret had sat back on her heels on the kitchen floor and thought on how her father had lived as a monk, during those last years of his life. He had his farming tools, the apple trees, two or three ragged shirts, and a hunting coat . . . but so little which was personally his, in the way that Race Vining's books had been his. Papa was buried in the best of his clothes, and Margaret had burned the rest as they were so ragged she wouldn't have given them to a beggar, nor did she wish to cut them into strips to braid a rug from. She did not want Papa to haunt her house any more than he did already.

"Mr. Ford advised that we split the property that Papa left into equal portions," she explained now to Mrs. Eberly. "The town-lots are or would be equal in value to this house. The sum in notes that my father was paid for his land is easily enough apportioned. And I have kept a good account of the cost of improvements that I made to it. I love my brother very dearly, but if he should choose the house over the town-lots, then his portion of Papa's estate would be debited for the cost of improvements that I made to it out of my own earnings. Mr. Ford has drawn up and had witnessed the necessary papers," Margaret added.

Mrs. Eberly set aside her plate, and clapped her hands together. "Mrs. Vining, you have not wasted your time in renting to legislators," she exclaimed. "That is looking after your interests very fairly indeed. I should not have worried so, that you would be done out of your rights and fair share."

"Certainly not," Margaret answered with serene confidence. "It was very kind of you to take such a concern, Mrs. Eberly. If there is a petticoat government in Austin, then you are the uncrowned queen of it, and your rule is gracious and far-seeing! But I have always been good at looking after my family. I believe that we must either see to ourselves and our families, or leave this place. For myself, I had no choice: My husband was invalid, my father mad, and my brother has long chosen to take his place among the ranks of our defenders – from which he may eventually return . . . or not. I wish that I had not needed to acquire and practice such efficiencies, but there you have it. This is where we live. There exist in this world women who must, or perhaps have been made to feel that their duty and obligation to custom obliges them to sit in the parlor with their hands folded, and expect the men of their kin to make their pathway smooth in all respects. I am not among them."

"No," acknowledged Mrs. Eberly, in what seemed to Margaret to be a rather regretful tone of voice. "Would have been nice for us if it were; no bothers, no worries. Everything taken from your shoulders, sitting in the parlor all the morning long, taking calls from visitors. Eh, it would have been restful, wouldn't it?"

"It would have been boring," Margaret answered firmly. Mrs. Eberly laughed and answered, "Miz Vining, there are some days when I would like boring, would like it very much indeed."

"And then you think of how very pleasing it is to arrange your affairs and your household, and the tenor of your day in the manner which best pleases you," Margaret answered. "And I think that I would soon become tired of helpless dependency. It does not do our men any favors to have a helpless seraglio of one inhabitant, hanging uselessly around their necks, week in and week out."

"You never struck me as bein' the helpless type," Mrs. Eberly answered. "Just as well, then."

"I prefer the animating contest of freedom, rather than the tranquility of servitude," Margaret answered. "As would, I believe, any woman of character and education. There is much to be said for being a widow with control of property."

"Aye, well," Mrs. Eberly sighed. "You are very well right – but still, 'tis nice to have a man about the place, sometimes. You know, Mr. Ward has been seriously courting Sue Bean! I hear they're to be married at mid-summer. She's over the moon in love. It *must* be love, then! Poor man, with him short of an arm and a leg as well. I hope she keeps him happy, so I do."

"And away from cannon," Margaret answered very dryly. "He cannot afford loosing another limb."

"Well, two more, but he ought to try and keep hold of that smaller limb that a man has!" Mrs. Eberly chuckled rather knowingly. "That bein' the main bit that keeps a wife happy, after all."

"I'm sure they will be very happy." Margaret thought she made a good pretense of having missed the point of Mrs. Eberly's jest. "Mr. Ward is a very fine and upstanding man. I am certain that he will take care of her and her children."

"Still and all," Mrs. Eberly mused, "he's had his bad times, I am sure – I am equally sure that his experiences must affect him, just as your father's experiences did him. I am not certain I would want to marry a man who bore the burden of such bad fortune, or counsel any daughter of mine to do so."

"If she loves him," Margaret answered, "truly and deeply – then she will not see those pitiably misfortunate scars of the flesh and mind. She will see only his good character, his finer qualities, and make her decision as her heart bids her."

"Oh, she's young, yet." Mrs. Eberly answered. Margaret thought to herself that she was also young – considered next to Mrs. Eberly. Now Mrs. Eberly's keen eyes went past Margaret to a late arrival, a tall and rather slovenly-attired man who had just ridden up to the area before the house. He took off his hat, blinking as he sat upon his horse surveying the gathering. He looked familiar to Margaret in some ways, rough, well-whiskered and clad in the cheap and durable clothes of a workman, and then he ventured tentatively, "Is this my welcome-home party? I did not expect such."

"Well, bless my soul, if it isn't Doctor Williamson!" Mrs. Eberly exclaimed. She added, in a much louder voice, "Say, look well, all ye – it's Doctor Williamson, come home from Perote!" At her words, all within earshot paid attention to the gawky scarecrow of a man, clumsily dismounting from what was obviously a hired nag, who held the reins in his hand and looked around as if he wondered what on earth he should do with them. Indeed, what happened in far Mexico and by what miracle had he arrived here, upon this sorry mount? Gratifyingly, he was soon at the center of a circle of men being warmly congratulated, as everyone exclaimed their relief and questioned him regarding his experiences, slapping his dusty shoulders with approval and enthusiasm of such a hearty sort that it appeared as if he might soon collapse underneath it. Margaret caught the attention of Johnny and Horace, who had been supporting her all this day with all the grave and careful courtesy of their years.

"Go and take the horse from Doctor Williamson, unsaddle the poor beast and let him out into the pasture for a while."

"The doctor looks very ill, Mama," Horace answered. "D'you supposed he was tortured with horrible instruments in Perote and hung about with chains?"

"No, I do not think he was," Margaret said. "He did not write to me complaining of such. The poor man – all he was tortured by was the loss of liberty! I think he was just tired from the journey, for he must have come such a long way! Johnny, if he has brought anything with him take it up to the room. Remember, we have moved his things to the little room upstairs." Before Horace could even move from Margaret's side, Mr. Burnett's man Hurst appeared as if by magic. With efficient courtesy he relieved Dr. Williamson of his horse and the small baggage it carried – mainly Dr. Williamson's sadly battered medical satchel. Margaret came down from the porch and through the crowd of men, which parted for her like her vision of the Red Sea parting before Moses, until she came to the doctor, still looking as baffled as he usually did in social situations.

"I am so very glad that you are free, and come home to us!" she exclaimed, and captured one of his hands in hers. "You must be exhausted after your journey – we would have made a welcome twice as warm as this, if we had even known that you were on your way. Johnny, take the bag from Hurst," she added, as her sons gathered around her, looking at Dr. Williamson with awed respect – and on the part of Peter, no little amount of puzzlement. "We have put those things of yours that you left with us into one of the little rooms upstairs. Do you remember the way, or do you want one of us to show you? There has been so much that has happened, since you went to San Antonio."

"I did not think there would be so much of a crowd," Dr. Williamson answered, peering around, in that baffled manner which suggested that he had misplaced his glasses again. "I . . . I sent a letter to you from Perote, to tell you that we were released . . . I can only think that it must have gone astray. Or that I traveled so rapidly as to outdistance the post."

"No matter; we are overjoyed to see you, and welcome you home," Margaret answered, and Dr. Williamson hesitantly raised her hand to his lips for a brief kiss.

"As much as a home that I have," he said simply. Margaret interpreted his baffled expression. The doctor had never liked small changes within the household, and adjusted to them with reluctance. Now she wondered if it had been right, to move his possessions to the upper and more private room at the top of the house.

"We had not received any letter from you, or indeed any news of the release of the Perote captives," Margaret said. "But you are all the more welcome – this is the day that we have buried my father. He died three days ago of a cerebral stroke."

"Is that a medical diagnosis?" Dr. Williamson inquired; his weathered face bright with sudden interest. "I would not have judged so without I had performed a dissection."

"That was the judgement of Mr. Ford, who was in practice in San Augustine," Margaret answered hastily. How very awkward and how very public that Dr. Williamson returned on the same day as Papa's burial. There had been so much that had happened, over the last two years. Margaret had confided much of her concerns in her letters to him, been frank, humorous, and sometimes needful of reassurance in her letters – and in all the doctor had responded in much the same nature. Now, they were face to face again, not separated by miles and prison walls. Somehow the written words had wrought a connection that was simply not there in face to face conversation. In her mind's eye, she had a picture of him that just did not match his present appearance and presence – and she briefly wondered if he had not created a worshipfully roseate image of her in return. But he was still a trusted friend, a guest under her roof – for she thought of it decidedly as hers, rather than her father's roof – a guest of long-standing, a friend and physician to Race Vining.

"You should rest a little from your long journey," she advised him, "in the room set aside for you, where we placed all the possessions you left with us. Wash, and change into your own clean clothes, then come downstairs and greet your friends." She clasped his hand between hers, overtaken by a sudden feeling of affection and concern. He looked so baffled, so lost. "It is a blessing that you are free and returned to us. Peter, my dear little duckling, will you show Dr. Williamson up to the little room? You remember – the doctor who cared for your Papa?" To her vague distress, her youngest son shook his head – no, he did not recall. Doctor Williamson had been a prisoner in Perote for almost half of his life. "He is our very dear friend," she whispered to her son. "He is tired, and he has had a very long journey. I must stay with the guests who have come to honor your Opa. Show him into the little room, opposite yours and Miss Hetty's, at the top of the stairs. All of his things are there; we made it very pleasant for him."

"Yes, Mama," Peter answered manfully, and turned to Dr. Williamson. "If you would kindly follow me, sir, I will show you to your quarters." Margaret concealed a smile. Peter had been coached by someone well-accustomed to the ways of courtesy and hospitality – most likely Hurst, for she had often observed her youngest son deep in conversation with Mr. Burnett's manservant during the last few days.

"I will see you then, among the guests," Margaret pressed Dr. Williamson's hand between hers once again – intending that slight embrace to be a comfort and encouragement. He still appeared somewhat lost and baffled, above and beyond his usual way. "You are among friends and most welcome," she added, impulsively going upon tip-toes and brushing his bearded cheek with her lips. "And I am glad above all to see you safe. Welcome home!"

With that, Peter led him upstairs, as Hurst led his poor bony livery-stable horse in the other direction. Margaret turned now to the care of her guests – oh, so many of them there were, lingering on a spring afternoon. She was glad of that, for the evidence it gave of Alois Becker being held in the high respect of his fellows, or affection for her as his daughter. But any reason for a gathering; Election Day, a celebration of the victory at San Jacinto, or even just a funeral was embraced eagerly. It had been so when she was a girl in Gonzales. With the keen judgement of a hostess, she sensed that this gathering had been revived, transformed from a wake to a more joyous celebration. She looked into the kitchen, where Hetty was just adding some more wood to the fire. Two pans of biscuits sat on the table, ready for the baking.

"Oh, good," Margaret said, "I was just thinking of more biscuits, and Dr. Williamson likes them so."

"Aye, 'tis a miracle." Hetty shielded her hand with a thick fold of her apron, and closed the firebox door. "And so unexpected, Marm: We had not even made up the bed in the little room! I took up a jug of water and some towels, for Peter said the Doctor wished to wash after his journey, but I was distracted an' all—"

"Oh, dear. I'll see to it, then, Hetty. It will only take a moment." Margaret filled her arms with clean sheets and blankets from the cupboard underneath the stair landing where they kept such things. She made her way up the stairs, thinking that she would only take a few minutes from her guests. Surely Dr. Williamson would have changed into his own clothes and joined the others by now. There was no sound coming from behind the door, which stood half-open so she went in with the linens . . . but he was there, standing before the opened window, as if arrested by the very sight of the sky outside, an open razor in one hand, and half the bristle scraped from his chin.

"I thought you had gone downstairs!" Margaret exclaimed in surprise; surprise which turned almost immediately to concern. She dropped the linens and blanket on the shuck mattress of the bed. "Doctor, are you unwell? Is there something the matter?"

"No . . . that is . . ." he looked at the razor in his hand as if wondering how it came to be there. "I was thinking that it was so very strange to look out of an unbarred window. And that this is not a dream, or Perote was but a nightmare. But it was real."

"It was real," Margaret answered. Danny Fritchie had said much of the same thing, and she thought that Dr. Williamson appeared to be pitiably lost, as if he had well and permanently misplaced his glasses. "And it was a horrible place – but you are free, now."

"Free," he said the word tentatively, as if he did not quite believe. "Free of one set of chains, not another." He had not made a motion to continue shaving, or to change from the rough clothing that he had worn for travel, although he had unbuttoned his collar and cuffs, and draped a towel across his shoulders. Margaret clicked her tongue.

"I cannot imagine what set of chains you mean," she said and began spreading out the sheet, fitting it over the mattress.

"No, you would not," he answered. Margaret's heart was wrung. Danny Fritchie held his baby daughter and wept as though his heart was about to break, remembering the deaths of his friends on the Salado. Carl had looked out at the stars and wrapped silence around him, unable to sleep within walls for years upon his return from Goliad. With his sleeves turned back, she could see the scars of healed sores that encircled Dr. Williamson's wrists like cruel bracelets. Men held their hurts inside; she hoped desperately that those scars were the very least of his. She smoothed a second sheet over the bed, spread out the blanket and turned the sheet back, all while Dr. Williamson made no further motion to complete his toilette. Something ailed the man – Margaret could not think what it might be, save that he might be uncertain about where his things were; those books and extra clothing that he had left behind. She and Hetty and the boys had lugged them all upstairs and arranged them pleasingly in the little room.

"We brushed your good coat, and aired all the other things often," she said, attempting to encourage him. She had guests downstairs, and she had told Hetty she would only be a moment. "Here, I will set them out for you." The little room held a narrow chest of drawers into which she had placed all of his clothing save the coat. The faint scent of verbena rose from the shirt and trousers that she arrayed on the newly-made bed. Margaret loved the odor of verbena – a liking for which she credited to Mama's fondness for it. There was a black neck-cloth in the topmost drawer, and she laid that out as well. He was still looking into the distance, of the aspect of Austin seen over the row of apple-trees, which still held some faint white clouds of bloom among the tender new green leaves.

"You have been very good to me," he said at last. "You wrote to me . . . those letters were welcome. They were . . ."

"You were my husband's friend," she answered firmly. *What was the matter with him*, she wondered, with impatience. She was needed downstairs. His friends and fellow-citizens would be waiting to talk to him, to ask him questions about his experiences in Perote, and for news of those last few held there. "Here are your clothes. I wrote to you because you were our friend and I thought of you with particular fondness for tending my husband, and you were in such desperate need of a confidant."

"I'd have gone mad without your letters and those others from my friends." The expression on his craggy face was one of desolation. She recalled again how her brother could not bear to remain confined within walls.

He and Rudi and the others taken after Coleto Creek had spent a week of imprisonment in the Goliad chapel – so crowded that the fit men and boys had slept on their feet, leaning against the walls and each other for lack of room.

"I'm only happy that my poor scribbles were of comfort to you," Margaret said. "And I would confess that yours were of comfort to me, as well. Sometimes I have felt very alone, even with Hetty and my friends and the boys as my solace. When I was in distress or in confusion – and there were so many times when I was in these last two years – it relieved my heart no end, to have a confidant, someone whom I could pour out my worries." She feared that she might have been too frank, for it seemed that Dr. Williamson was struggling with a powerful emotion which held him speechless. She had already settled the pillow in a clean slip at the head of the bed. Now she came around the foot of the bed to where Dr. Williamson was still standing, irresolute, between the wash-stand with the scrap of mirror-glass hung up over it, and the window, with the razor in his hand. "You are my dear friend, also. Do not doubt that – but you have those friends and men of Austin downstairs waiting for you to come down. Here," she took the straight-razor from his hand, "you are nearly finished – this little bit. Hold still – there." She capably scraped the last of bristle from his cheek, and taking the end of the towel, wiped off the remaining soap, noting almost in passing that his eyes were more grey than blue, and that she needed to reach up a little way, for he was taller than Race had been. "I have put out your clean clothes, Dr. Williamson. Put them on, and come down. Hetty will be taking a batch of fresh biscuits out of the oven. You always liked her biscuits."

"They were always very fine," he answered at last. Margaret touched her fingers to her lips and then brushed his cheek with her fingertips. He was a dear man, but so absent-minded, and she supposed that the confusion of his home-coming – for this was about the only home that he had – must have left him as temporarily at a loss as Danny Fritchie had been. Things had changed, in his absence over the last two years and he was not a man who dealt well with changes.

"There – I have given a distant kiss to you. You are ready to be seen in public, as soon as you put on your clean clothes. Five minutes – that is what I shall tell your friends."

"Friends?" he sounded baffled, uncertain. Margaret concealed a sigh. *What was the matter with him? Honestly, it was as if his experience in Perote had turned his mind to jelly.* Margaret knew that he had a keen mind, if at times a rather eccentric one.

"Yes – you have friends, waiting to welcome you home. They came for Papa's burial, but they have remained to welcome you." She said, in the same kind of encouraging tone that she used to urge her sons when they were small, rather than terrify them into compliance with her wishes with a show of authority; what Hetty called her 'Maeve-face' – the look of an imperious queen whose wishes were not to be casually ignored.

Perhaps she had a bit of the 'Maeve-face' on her at that minute, for Dr. Williamson looked at her, really looked at her as if he understood at long last, and answered, "Then I shall come down. It is the right thing, is it not, Mrs. Vining?"

"Yes, it is," she said, with secret relief that he was going to put on an appearance of amiability. He was so often disinclined to fall in with the demands of what society commanded. Really, this had been so often an embarrassment to her when her table was crowded with boarders and their conversation, and he had propped a medical text against the cruets and read throughout the meal. "Put on those clothes that I have laid out for you. Do you want a manservant to come up and tie your cravat? Mr. Burnett's man, Hurst is an expert. I will send him up, if you require assistance."

"No. I am capable of managing my own cravat," he answered, and Margaret thought to herself that perhaps she ought to send Hurst if Dr. Williamson did not appear within ten minutes.

"Then we shall expect you," she said, fairly sure that she did not say so with her 'Maeve-face'. "You are a man very well-liked in Austin, and so you should have a good welcome home."

Chapter 13 – *Reawakening*

All that summer long, Margaret held to her the feeling that Austin was re-awakening, coming back to life. In June, Mr. Ward married Susan Bean, just as Mrs. Eberly had predicted. The glades of oak-woods below the crown of apple-trees echoed with the sounds of men's voices and the sound of hammering, as houses and offices were built new, or old ones repaired and refurnished.

"I had thought to give it a year," she said to Hetty one morning as they washed the breakfast dishes. "A year, if matters did not improve, if the Legislature and the national offices did not return. It looks as if we might be joined to the United States at last. Margaret, the General's wife, she wrote to me, telling of what her husband had said on the matter. I have always thought that General Houston knows the female heart all too well for he explained it thus; that a woman very much in love with a suitor who did not outwardly seem to care very much for her, would then go flirt publicly with a rival. Not because that rival was one she held in particular affection, but would do so in the hopes of exciting the jealous attention of the one she truly loved, that he might come to realize that he did not want anyone else to take her to wife."

"Aye?" Hetty set another dish to drain. "So Texas is the flirtatious girl, and the United States is the beau she hopes to ask to marry. All this too-ing and fro-ing over the last years has been a romance. Who was the suitor that she flirted with?"

"A political romance," Margaret answered chidingly. "The unwanted suitor was England, of course. Or maybe France; it would have depended on the year and the whims of the Legislature."

"And what is Mexico representing in all o' this?" Hetty brought another dish from the wash pan.

"The near-mad and possessive step-brother," Margaret answered. "Who does not wish anyone else to have her if he cannot – but she has rejected him with force and by the strength of her own will."

"Aye, I've seen weddings like that," Hetty nodded. "Didn't end well, most times; a brawl in the back of the churchyard, at least. An' at worst, a knife in the bridegroom's ribs – the bride's as well, if she were that unlucky." She took another dish from the rinse-water, and frowned thoughtfully. "So, Marm; in the event o' the bridegroom behavin' as a man, and proposing as he should . . . that will mean war with Mexico upon acceptance, will it not?"

"We have been at war with Mexico, whether it be open or not, all these years since San Jacinto," Margaret answered. "I would be relieved to have it done and settled, once and for all. Then we might have something of the peace and security that we had longed and hoped for ever since those days."

"Aye," Hetty nodded soberly. "An' the Young Sir; he would be in it for certain, wouldn't he, Marm?" Margaret wiped the dish with thoughtful care and restored it to the place on the shelves where they kept such items.

"He would, most likely," she answered at last. "But consider, Hetty; my brother, and indeed, all of us – have been in one war or another ever since we first came to this place. Oh, it was peaceful enough at first, and now and again those who made war upon us rested themselves between campaigns, sometimes for as much as a year or two . . . but I think nothing would change for the better without annexation, Hetty. At the very least, we would have no more armies from Mexico, venturing as they will into our lands and towns, taking prisoner whom they wished. And as for the Comanche – the Americans have a regular Army, and trained officers who stand guard, not like our militia, who gather when a great need arises, and then scatter to their own homesteads and businesses once the emergency is past. I do not know how much longer we can keep ourselves free by our own efforts, given the limitations that our government labors under.

"I have listened to the gentleman's conversation, Hetty. They are brave and optimistic. But in my heart I believe that we cannot manage ourselves for much longer as an independent nation. None of the gentlemen would admit, of course, that their own efforts would be proven unequal to the task. But I can read the signs as well as any sensible person may. Our currency is nearly worthless, as beautifully engraved as they are – but each dollar note is worth only three pennies of good American currency! General Sam told the government upon his second inauguration that the treasury is bare. None of the grand plans that President Lamar initiated have been carried out successfully. Indeed, the existence of Austin has hung by a thread for . . . now many years? The army that we can raise is just barely equal to our defense, once an insult is given. Our navy was rented to another rebellious Mexican state! We have no great riches, other than the land, the energy and steadfastness of our people. Our sole hope lies in annexation, and soon." She dried another dish, which Hetty had given to her, and continued. "I just hope that it might all be done with, before my sons are men, Hetty. I hope that they will never have to be soldiers. It is heartache enough that my brother has been one all these years. He was a gentle boy, soft-spoken and kindly. He should not have been tasked with such things as he was burdened with. I think he should have gone to school, which he would have done if my father had not removed my brothers and mother to this place when it was still Waterloo. If war with the Centralists had not come upon us, Carl would have married Harrell's daughter or some other upon whom his liking had fallen, taken up his own holding, and raised apple trees and children. If only a portion of peace had been allotted to us, that peace which was all that we asked but which fate did not grant!"

"Aye, well," Hetty dunked another dish into the pan of rinse-water, and handed it to Margaret. "That's life; which happens when you have made plans. In any case, young Jamie-my-lad, he is called to be a soldier, regardless of whatever expectation we have of annexation. Depend upon it, Marm, he is a young Cuchulain, with the spirit of a warrior bold. Now then, Marm, it was those New Englanders, the Addamses and Henry Clay . . . that was those who blocked us, the first time wasn't it?"

"The Abolitionists, yes – because of the peculiar institution," Margaret answered. "Because it is allowed – although practiced only to a small extant in comparison to those of the United States where it is permitted . . ."

"Ye dinna approve, yoursel', Marm?" Hetty sent her a shrewd look over the dishpans and pile of pots turned upside down to drain. Margaret – convinced that she had never voiced a breath of her true thoughts on the matter to anyone, least of all Hetty – did not hesitate. Hetty was her truest friend and confidant, in this sphere that Margaret had made for herself by her own efforts. Of all still living in this world, she could he honest with Hetty.

"No, I have not, or ever did," Margaret answered. "My mother was most adamant against the practice, and my father . . . that was the one admirable thing in his life, and I am certain he took against it from her example. To own another man or woman, to take the labor as you take the ownership of another human soul . . . my mother considered it was a sin, the worst kind of injustice. So did my late husband. He was from Boston, you remember. We had friends, some of them very dear, who thought nothing of the practice, and my mother held her silence. So did I and so my husband, for we do have to live in the world. Sometimes the only protest we may make is to stand apart in certain things. I would never buy a slave, Hetty."

"Aye, I had wondered," Hetty answered. "For y' might have, y'know. For not very much at all; a girl or two to do the laundry, or as a housemaid."

"No," Margaret did not hesitate a moment. "No, that is one thing that I would never do, following my dear mother's example and my husband's arguments against such. Never would I buy a slave, as I would buy a horse or an ox; I would rather hire any, free or in bondage, black or white or anything in between – but pay honest wages for their labor, and think their hours and lives which I have not paid for to be no particular concern of mine. I have friends who hold slaves, Hetty. I confess that I also do not care for an eternal responsibility, as if for a child that will never grow to adult estate. Nor do I want to live with that poisonous fear of a slave rebellion always in the back of my mind. Those of the gentlemen who have spoken of such . . . it is a thing which haunts their dreams, that some resentment in the slave quarters may one day take fire, and that the colored race will rise against their masters and take retribution for their sufferings. I believe that in their heart of hearts they know that they are in the wrong, and fear judgement – not at the hands of the Almighty, but at the hands of those who have been treated cruelly, or seen their kin and friends served with injustice, an injustice against which there is no appeal. Even if many of my acquaintance are kind to their slaves, and trust them without reservation, and such trust is repaid with unswerving devotion . . . I do not care to walk down that road, Hetty, however tempting it might seem. The road into hell is paved with good intentions."

"Aye, for sure, you have your Maeve-face on again," Hetty answered at last, somewhat taken aback by Margaret's outburst. "I had wondered, now and again. I dinna think you felt so strongly on it, though – having never said ought . . ."

"I should hurt the feelings of many friends, by speaking bluntly," Margaret answered. "As well as harm my own enterprise. There are arguments to be made for abolition, but very few of them would have a good hearing in the boarder's parlor. I can judge the wind, Hetty – and this is my home. Practicality constrains me from making my opinions known openly, but in my actions and in the way I conduct my business I will not be constrained. Perhaps, without anything being said at all, this house might serve as a shining beacon of how an establishment may be run without the taint of the peculiar institution. I might demonstrate that the payment of good wages for honest labor serves as an example and reproach to those who would depend upon slaved labor."

"There was no need to fair snap my head off," Hetty replied, bending her head over the dishpan once more. "Mother Mary and Joseph, I only asked. Still, there might be summat to what you say. I'd not like to live, worryin' about some black de'il, thinkin' of how aisy it would be t' cut me own throat . . . an' here it is; nigras is the only ones that we Irish may look down upon, when a' is said an' done."

"No slaves then, Hetty." Margaret patted Hetty's shoulder. "Not in this household, not this enterprise – no one for you to look down upon, I fear."

"I might still hold the Indians in scorn, Marm?" Hetty asked, and Margaret began to laugh.

"If you must," she answered, when she had recovered her composure. "I will have need to hire, soon – but black or white, free or slave, I shall pay wages. You and Emma cannot do all the work yourselves. I am thinking that I should take that portion of my father's inheritance soon and expand the house as I have always desired. The talk among the boarders is that Austin should be the capitol of the state, as it has been the nation. We would still have legislators and men of business needing comfortable lodgings. If annexation would spell the end of our fears of raids from the Comanche, it may be that Austin would regain the standing that it had when President Lamar first established it. Think of it, Hetty – there would be stores, and schools and libraries . . . more than poor Mr. Burke's reading room . . . churches and the theater, all those adornments of civilization. Mr. Bullock may expand his inn and Dr. Williamson his medical practice. There would be even more gentlemen of good repute wishing to board with us. I would like that, and I would like to expand the house!"

"Aye, like the house of the Emain Macha, the House of the Spears as they called it in the old tales . . . but doesn't he seem to be as odd a body? Dr. Williamson, I mean."

"He always has been odd," Margaret answered, but could not keep the worry entirely out of her voice. It was true that Dr. Williamson was eccentric, and most often seemed entirely unscathed by social assurance, but Margaret had long since become used to that lack in him. Still, there was that much of a change in his manner that she was worried. He was a grown man, of course; well into middle age and sufficiently exposed to the fortunes and misfortunes of life that the cruelty of capture and imprisonment in Perote should not have scarred him as terribly as Goliad had marked her brother. Carl had been like a ghost, silent and unable to bear sleeping indoors – he still could barely endure confinement within walls, and Papa's harshness towards him had eventually driven him away from his roof . . . or the roof as it had been then. At least Dr. Williamson had not witnessed the brutal murder of most of his comrades in one fell moment.

There was one matter which Margaret kept from Hetty as she finished drying the dishes, putting them into their accustomed place. That very morning, as soon as Dr. Williamson had taken up his doctor's bag and walked to town on a round of calls upon patients, Margaret had gone upstairs to his room for the daily housekeeping; re-making the bed, sweeping and dusting, emptying the chamber-pot, and putting away such garments as were laid about, or consigning them to the laundry for further attention. The tiny room at the top of the house was left in the usual small disarray expected of an absentminded man. Margaret had opened the windows a little wider to admit that small stirring of the summer air which offered the promise of alleviating some of the heat that built up into that room under the roof-shingles as the day wore on.

She shook out the blankets and the sheet, plumped up the single pillow, and smoothed the bedclothes flat. For a wonder, Dr. Williamson had not left his nightshirt in a crumpled ball on the floor, instead leaving it carelessly hung from the bedpost. Margaret also shook it out, considered taking it for the laundry – no. She and Hetty would do the usual laundry on the traditional day for it. Dusting – no, not that much necessary, although she swept the cloth over the little table that Mr. Hattersley had used as a writing-desk. Apparently Dr. Williamson did also, for it was piled with paper scraps, several medical publications, an ink-bottle and several pens . . . which had splattered ink on the rough-cut sheet of blotting-paper they were left upon. Oh – the doctor would probably not like it, that she had straightened out his desk! Most of her boarders did not like to have their personal papers tampered with, even when it came to housekeeping – but still, this was Dr. Williamson, who would very likely never even notice.

Margaret arranged the books and publications in a neat stack, the paper scraps in another, and then she noticed yet another paper, half-underneath the blotting paper with just a corner showing. She drew it out – a much folded scrap, half a sheet of letter-paper, and worn along those edges as though it had been folded small to keep in a breast-pocket, but taken out often. To her surprise, she recognized her own careful handwriting, and Shakespeare's 116th love sonnet that she had once copied out for her sons as a penmanship exercise. At once she recalled how she had lost the first copy, lost among the pages of letters that she had been writing to Margaret Houston and to the doctor. Papa had opened the front door, and an errant breeze had sent all the pages flying. Margaret bit her lower lip, recalling . . . yes, she must have gathered up this scrap with the pages of the letter to Dr. Williamson, and accidentally included it.

Now she remembered, with a sinking feeling of horror and embarrassment how he had mentioned . . . what had he said? It had puzzled her mightily at the time. *Your last letter with the enclosure was of inestimable value to me, once again reassuring me with regards to your affections. I shall strive in future to be worthy of them* . . . This must have been the enclosure that he meant – obviously, for he had treasured it all this time, carried it folded small.

That day of his return, he must have been trying to say something to her in his awkward way, something that he could not quite bring himself to say, even in letters. Margaret reviewed in her mind that strange exchange between them when she had come upstairs to make up the bed upon his return from Perote on the day of Papa's funeral. He had almost seemed as if he were expecting her to . . . oh, dear. The realization broke on her like a thunderclap from one of these sudden Texas storms, sweeping in from over the horizon between one breath and the next. The doctor had thought of her all during his time in Perote as if they were sweethearts, and she had considered him to be no more than a friend . . . in fact, she had treated him as casually as if he were any of the other boarders, or her brother, and all that time, he had been waiting for something more. Her cheeks felt hot with blushing for her own carelessness. She carefully replaced the much-folded scrap – the edges of paper and the folds in which it had been kept fraying with much use – under the edge of the blotting paper, and considered what now must she do. This notion that Doctor Williamson was in love with her was a deeply unsettling one. It was always in the back of her mind that certain of her gentleman boarders had sometimes entertained romantic thoughts of her, and now and again one of them might be excessively gallant in their attentions. She prided herself in serenely parrying such tentative displays of affection, and in doing so with such gentle but firm consideration that none of the gentlemen ever thought the worst of her upon being discouraged by not seeing them reciprocated. But none of them were anything like Doctor Williamson, so kind, and yet so unskilled at this kind of social flirtation. He was completely innocent of this, Margaret thought, with renewed exasperation – kind, but yet so bumbling. He had been completely open – as open as he could ever bring himself to be, and yet she had not seen it, not considered that he also might have been in love – but everything she had said in reply to him on the day of his return from Perote, every gesture and word – all of which she had thought of as being kind, instead were cruel, lacerating an innocent heart. She was sure of her own; that Dr. Williamson was someone she considered as a dear and good friend, as was Seamus O'Doyle, or John Ford, or even William Burnett.

As she finished tidying his room, she was considering how she might – or even if she ought to – respond to him. She could not possibly be in love with him, in any case. He was as erudite as Race had been, but in a single-minded way, focused on his medical practice, and nowhere near as appealing in his person, with his rough-hewn face and straggling hair the color of frost-killed weeds. No, not the least a man to catch a woman's eye or hold her interest . . . although his eyes were gray-blue and sometimes innocently childlike. It would drive her mad to be responsible for him, to guide his uncertain footsteps through society, such as it was, to intercede with all as Mama had with Papa's quarrelsome nature, to keep a watchful eye always. Margaret did not need that. She had already had one husband, and her heart was nearly healed from his breaking of it. Margaret would risk no further damage to it from love – or to her boys.

And she had no need to marry a provider. Neither had Angelina Eberly or Nancy Simpson, for weren't they all women of property and certain years, capable of providing all that was needful for their families?

In the end, she decided, as she went on with the morning housekeeping, perhaps she should do nothing more than she had already. Soon enough, a man would tire of unrequited affections and transfer them elsewhere. If her unwitting enclosure of a sonnet from Shakespeare in her letter to the doctor had taken root and grown in his imagination as love on her part . . . perhaps refusing it water and nourishment might cause it to wither unspoken. She put aside those thoughts and went downstairs to perform the same housekeeping to the two rooms of the boarder's quarters. But even after her conversation with Hetty, regarding the oddity that was Dr. Williamson, her thoughts concerning him continued to roil in her mind, especially at odd moments when she caught sight of him, or when he spoke to her during meals at the boarder's table. She tried to put those thoughts and questions aside, as she would have swept a crumb from the tablecloth . . . but still, they took root again and came up like weeds despite all of her efforts to uproot them entire.

Several weeks passed, while the summer heat continued to bake the shingled roofs of Waterloo, the roofs that Papa had built and that Seamus O'Doyle had extended. Margaret had begun to map out in her mind – too soon to commit those dreams to paper, and hire carpenters to make them into reality – the extension of the house that she had dreamed of for these many years. She envisioned a new building, two stories tall, extending out from the front of the original house. There would be four rooms on the ground floor, on either side of a central hallway with a stair in it; on the ground floor, the hallway would be as wide and generous as to serve as another room, just as the house that Seamus O'Doyle had designed for the Frenchman. On the upper story, six rooms – and across the front, a pair of galleries under a wide gable, overlooking Austin and the apple trees: such a building would take up much of the forecourt to Papa's house, building over entirely the garden that Mama had cherished with the rose bushes. But all of that could be replanted, and Margaret's heart lifted to think of the rooms of her dreams actually being within her grasp: airy, tall-ceilinged rooms, with long windows, opening onto a gallery. And if she designed it carefully, there would be space for a wing on either side, for more rooms adjoining . . . Margaret fell asleep every evening with the *Builder's Companion* falling open on the sheet over her lap and her mind afire with possibilities.

Upon a late afternoon in July, when the summer sun still burned as bright as brass in the afternoon skies, and the boys had gone from their lessons to cool off with a swim in the deepest pool of Shoal Creek with their friends, Margaret took a large basket and walked down towards town. She intended to stop at Bullock's to see if the stagecoach had brought mail for any in her household, and on her return to pick enough grapes from the wild vines growing among the tangled woods along Shoal Creek. The boys had said the day before that the grapes were ripe, hanging in gold-green and royally purple-colored bunches just upstream from the place which they and the other boys of Austin favored as a swimming hole. Margaret was glad to hear of this, for unlike many other grape-tangles, this one bore particularly sweet-tasting fruit.

There was no mail, for the stage had not arrived, but to counter this momentary disappointment, she met Mrs. Eberly, Mary Bullock, and pretty little Miss Sinks just coming away from the same fruitless errand, and she told them of the grapes hanging in generous swags from the lower branches in such numbers as Margaret's single basket would likely make no appreciable dent in the bounty.

"Then we shall come also," Julia Sinks offered. "It will doubtless be cooler by the creek than in town."

"And Frank will come with us as protection," Mary Bullock added, and Margaret cautioned, "And you should bring gloves as well, for the grapes are extraordinarily harsh on our hands . . . did you know that one might save and dry the grape-skins from making jelly, and in winter make a very pleasant tea by steeping in water with a little sugar?"

"I did not know that," Julia Sinks answered. "How very little goes to waste in a well-run kitchen!"

Mrs. Eberly, Mary Bullock, and Margaret's eyes met in amused commiseration, and Mary Bullock said, "Dear Julia, you would be amazed at the use to which every scrap is put!" and the three older women began regaling Julia Sinks with tales of ever-more extraordinary thrift, as they walked along Pecan Street towards a path which led along the banks of Shoal Creek where it twisted it's way between steep and well-wooded banks towards the great silver-green sweep of the Colorado River. Now and again a breath of light breeze, cooled by the water and the green shade. fanned their cheeks and briefly lifted the brim of Margaret's wide-brimmed hat.

"You see," Margaret said at last, "our households are also our businesses. A thing saved for another purpose, or repaired – or re-woven as my mother used to do with those blankets of Mexican wool – that is money in the purse. In the days when we first came to Texas, all that we had brought with us had to be made to last, because to replace anything would be beyond our purse, were it even possible at all. There was a pottery pitcher," Margaret continued, "a fine salt-glazed pitcher of grey with a blue figure of flowers and birds. My mother was very fond of it, as it was quite large, but some time after I had married Mr. Vining the handle of it broke – and it was too heavy a pitcher to use without a handle. My father took it to old Mr. Sowell, who was the blacksmith in Gonzales, and had him beat out two narrow iron bands, to go around the neck and base of the pitcher, and attach an iron handle. We have it still in the household; neither Hetty nor I are able to set aside habits of thrift so early begun. Someday I might be able to buy two or five or more salt-glazed grey pitchers with blue decorations on them . . . or I might not, and in the meantime, the pitcher with the iron handle is still a useful thing."

By that point in their converse, the path which they followed had dipped close to the creek bank above the deep pool which the boys favored for swimming. They could hear their happy shouts and splashes faintly, at the short distance, for the high banks muffled sound. Margaret noted with some sympathy that Frank Bullock looked enviously in that direction, although he said never a word as they approached the particular tangle where the wild grapes grew thickest and sweetest. He hitched the old musket higher on his shoulder and stood a little apart from the women as they donned their gloves, or shielded their hands with a fold of apron, and began pulling bunches of dark amethyst grapes from among the pale green leaves.

Margaret was careful with the clusters that she selected – none withered or moldy, and she took care to avoid those with hovering wasps. Within moments, she and Mrs. Eberly had moved to the other side of the thicket housing the tangle, although they could still hear Mary and Julia speaking softly as they worked in similar fashion.

"Grape jelly on Hetty's hot biscuits," Margaret said, looking at her basket with satisfaction. "I can near taste them already. My mother always held to her family tradition; seven sweet dishes and seven sours at every meal. Jams and sweet preserves, fruit in syrup, pies and apple butter, pickles of every vegetable, and chow-chow and green tomato relish . . . aside from all else, of course."

"With that at your table, no wonder you have so many gentlemen guests." Mrs. Eberly answered. It pleased Margaret that Mrs. Eberly sounded envious. "And them returning, also! I don't think there's as many a fine table as yours in all of Texas." She added with an air of transparent calculation," If it ever comes to it, I would offer you an' Miss Moylan a partnership – we could be in business together, you to see to the vittles side of it, me to the housekeeping."

"No," Margaret laughed, and flashed a smile at Mrs. Eberly through a screen of grape leaves. "The competition between us is bracing . . . besides, there is room enough in Austin for us all, when the Legislature returns."

"Aye, they will," Mrs. Eberly added another cluster of grapes to her own basket. "So this matter of annexation; d'ye think something will come of it this time?"

"I believe so," Margaret answered. "Mr. Polk is campaigning on a platform of promising to add Texas to the United States, if I may credit what I read in the newspapers. Perhaps the time is right at long last. Otherwise, we may remain independent and make our alliances where we may. With England, if it comes to that. We might seek the shelter of being a British protectorate, which would secure us against invasion from Mexico again."

"Never!" Mrs. Eberly answered with considerable indignation. "Curtsey to some la-de-da-milord? Our folk fought against them twice for independence! Does General Sam think we would allow them to rule over us again?"

"We would still rule ourselves, as we have done these last eight years since San Jacinto." Margaret answered. "But if we cannot be annexed to the United States, being a Crown Colony would be next best; at least, a better situation than rule by Mexico again. I believe – and I am certain you share this conviction, Mrs. Eberly – any condition would be preferable to being under the rule of the butcher of Zacatecas and Goliad, who gave the orders to decimate our men at Saltillo in that vile lottery. I would not like it, but I would prefer the condescension of lords and princes to the brutality of those who showed their true colors over the bodies of my brother and of poor Mr. O'Doyle. And I do trust in the judgement of General Sam, after all."

"He burned San Felipe," Mrs. Eberly answered, and Margaret could hear the edge of bitter resentment in her voice. "Burned us out, root and branch – the inn that my first husband and I had built; I walked away with my children and nothing but what we could carry."

"We all did, Mrs. Eberly," Margaret said gently. That night when she and Mama had packed Papa's wagon and gone away from that little house in Gonzales which she had so loved – the house and school which had been hers and her husbands', where she had been happiest of all in her life – that night was still painfully vivid in her memory and dreams. She and Mama, Maggie Darst, and young Davy, had looked back, after midnight, as they staggered along the road east, following the Army. They saw the sky branded with orange, the glow of the flames that burned Gonzales and consumed their dreams of prosperity. In his wisdom and in their defense, General Sam had dictated the strategy of Fabius – to burn and spoil all before the advancing army of Lopez de Santa Anna, to fall back, and fall back again, leaving only desolation before the armies of Mexico. It was a hard and bitter decision, but if General Sam had ever quailed from it no one would ever know – save perhaps the Savior and judge of all. Or maybe Margaret Lea would know; if General Sam had ever confessed anything to anyone of his private thoughts of those contentious days, it would have been to her. Margaret was convinced that General Sam was one of those who reposed trust and affection in womankind, with special affection always towards Margaret Lea as his wife, who against so many expectations had made him happy. But Margaret was a friend to both the General and his lady. Thanks to her husband's tutelage, she understood and accepted the strategy that General Sam had ordered in that tragic spring of 1836.

"Aye, it was a long time ago, was it not?" Mrs. Eberly deftly cut another bunch of grapes from the thicket before her. "Or so it seems, although by the count of years, not many since then. Oh, my. We have wandered, Mrs. Vining."

"Not far," Margaret answered. Mrs. Eberly was a little ahead of her, as the two women took and cut bunches of wild grapes, letting them fall into baskets that Margaret had brought and that Mary Bullock had provided from the Inn, when the diversion of harvesting grapes had come upon them. The grape bunches were heavy with juice, a dusky bloom upon their skins. Another week – even another two or three days would have been too late, for they would have begun to spoil and molder, as the birds, wasps and wild creatures would have gotten to them. A movement caught her eye; a flash of brilliant red, too large to be a bird, as Mrs. Eberly peered down into the creek below, mere steps from the top of the earthen bank that fell down into Shoal Creek.

The bank on the side where Margaret and the others gathered grapes were very steep, a small precipice, tumbling straight down to the water below. On the other side of Shoal Creek, the bank was gently sloped and adorned with flowering shrubs, shaded generously with the limbs of oak and cypress. At the water's edge, a number of flattened boulders made a set of stair steps from the grassy bank to the water's edge. Against that background of green, something moved, a flash of red again – like the red of the blankets that the Comanche favored, something too tall to be an animal, to large to be a bird like a cardinal male. Margaret stifled a gasp; it was a man, an Indian, she was certain at her first glimpse, and remembered how she and Hetty, with Morag and the children had run frantically for the shelter of Bullock's Inn.

"There is someone down there," she said with icy calm to Mrs. Eberly. "On the bank of the creek, opposite."

"Oh, aye?" Mrs. Eberly answered, equally calm. "One of the men or even one of the boys, going for a swim, I daresay. It's hot enough today – I wish I could go for a swim myself. The gentlemen will have their ways, I reckon."

"It might be an Indian," Margaret whispered. "Although there have been none seen so close, during the hours of daylight . . . they come and go as they please, after dark and under the full moon."

"There's always young Frankie with his musket." Mrs. Eberly whispered in reassurance. "Me, I'd rather know for sure, before raising an alarm." She set down her basket, and stole quietly towards where she might have a better view of the creek below, screened by the thicket and grape-tangle, and Margaret followed suit. "It's only one that I can see . . . oh, my. I do not think it is one o' them Comanche. I cannot tell for sure, w'out his clothes – but I think it may be one o' ours."

Margaret looked over Mrs. Eberly's stout black-clad shoulders. Yes, indeed it was a white man, standing on the largest of the stones below and opposite, a naked man who had just finished piling his boots and clothing into a neat pile on a higher stone, poised as if to relish the thought of plunging into the cool, deep waters of Shoal Creek. He was a tall and sinewy gangle; mostly pale on his body, burnt brown on his face and arms, too light for an Indian and with altogether too much hair on his person to be one of the Comanche, who aside from what was on their heads were otherwise as hairless as snakes. Standing on that rocky bank, his clothing and boots set aside in that tidy pile; for a startled moment Margaret thought how he looked like an ancient statue of a sprite or a faun from her husband's books of art and history. Here was a solitary wild creature of the woods, relishing the freedom and aloneness of it – the woods and water, the touch of sunlight on bare skin. Margaret suddenly realized that it was indelicate of her to be watching this; not the nudity, but that she was invading a private moment of contentment, an experience of pure happiness.

"I believe it is Dr. Williamson," she breathed, as the naked figure below stepped from the rock and into the water, where he sank immediately for a moment until his head surfaced from the cool green depths, and he swam with powerful but ungainly strokes across the length of the creek and then back.

"Aye?" Mrs. Eberly whispered, "I wouldna have recognized him without his glasses. Still and all – we both being widows, it's nothing we'd not have ever seen before."

Much relieved, Angelina Eberly and Margaret withdrew soundlessly from the edge of the creek, and the thin scrim of green which would have hidden them from below. As they did so, Mrs. Eberly added with a chuckle which just missed being lewd, "Who would have thought it, to look at him – he is set up as a stallion and not a gelding after all!"

Chapter 14 – *From a Far Land Returned*

Late in the year, as the weather turned to cool, from the breathless heat of summer, Carl returned from wherever and whatever he had been doing at the bidding of his Ranger commander in Bexar. He did not come around to the back of the house to the old farmyard, but presented himself at the new front door, looking around at the work being done with a studiedly veiled expression. The walls of the new expansion were up and finished on the outside and in the upstairs, but the workmen that Margaret had hired were still plastering and painting in the downstairs, and installing glazed windows and doors. There was a new public parlor and dining room, an office, and a private family parlor which had incorporated the old dining room and parlor made by walling in the original porch. These four rooms were on either side of a generous stair-hall which could be made to serve as yet another reception room. Up on the second story, there were suites of bed-chambers on either side of the upper stair-hall, and space left for a corridor to new wings, one on either side of the new building. She had taken one of those rooms for herself, and allocated another for Hetty. In the old part of the house, Hetty's old room and that which her sons had shared were made into a single room by demolishing the partition between, and a passageway made to connect the upper floor hallway to the older part of the house. The little bedchamber off the parlor, which Margaret and Race had shared, having once been Maria Becker's weaving room, was now merely another small private room to rent to boarders.

Upon hearing someone calling her name from the front of the house, Margaret armed herself with Seamus O'Doyle's *American Builder's Companion* and sallied forth from the kitchen. She had been relentless in harrying the carpenters and workmen. She came out through the new building with the book under her arm, expecting that she would have to explain matters once again. Really, it was just as if men did not give a woman credit for sense and education when it came to planning a house. It quite vexed Margaret, though she was tactfully not open in expressing her feelings on this matter . . . not to the workmen that she depended upon to complete every detail of the new house in the exacting manner that she made no bones about expecting.

The new door had not yet been hung, so she looked out upon the new gallery at her brother who stood with his back turned to her, seeming to look at the view beyond the apple trees, now heavy with fruit. He was riding a new horse, Margaret noticed almost at once, upon seeing it hitched carelessly to a bit of scaffolding left in the front, where the upper-floor exterior of the house had been whitewashed. The new horse was a long-legged and elegantly formed grey creature, with powerful haunches, and a mane and tail so dark they looked almost black.

Hearing her step upon the unfinished wood floor, Carl turned and half-smiled, "H'lo, M'grete. I wondered for a time if I had come to the right place."

She flung her arms about him, wondering why she felt like crying and laughing at one and the same time. When had he become so tall, taller than Papa, as solid as an oak tree, and a very rock for capability? She remembered how Opa Heinrich, long ago in Pennsylvania, had assured her (with a mischievous smile hidden in his beard) that if she lifted her baby brother every day, when she and he were grown, she would still be able to lift him! Unexpectedly, she felt a sense of immense comfort, as if she leaned against a sturdy support, and her eyes threatened to overflow with the tears that she had not shed in all the days since Papa was buried and Carl away in the Llano.

Now she sniffled, and wiped them away with the back of her hand. "We missed you," she began, straightening herself from his light embrace, just as he said, "I didn't hear about Papa until mid-summer, M'grete. I'd have come if I could have – but for you, not him. Not sure what help I would have been, though."

"I had the help of our friends." Margaret tried to keep the reproachful tone from her voice. "They were very kind. We buried him below the orchard. Papa would have preferred that, I thought. He told me many times, that he did not wish ever to leave this place. You should pay your respects to him, little brother."

"Why?" Carl shrugged, unembarrassed. "I had none for him in life, why does death make a difference?"

"He was still our father," Margaret insisted, although without much conviction. Her brother grunted and answered, "I'll not pretend to feel any grief." He shot her a very shrewd look, after casting a quick glance around the new façade of the house. "You seem to have overcome yours, as well."

"It's been months," Margaret answered, with some indignation. Carl was in a little way correct. She had grieved for Alois Becker – for Papa, who had once been young and handsome, beloved of Mama, an indulgent and selectively provident father – but increasingly had found it relatively easy to bear his loss. Cross, murderously quarrelsome, cruel with his words and indifferent to all but his own pain, it had required much of her reserve of tact and familial affection to maintain some semblance of a proper family life. She had not realized how much of a burden his ill-temper had become until relieved of it upon his death, although she would not have confessed so to anyone, least of all to Carl. "I had always wanted to expand the house, should the business of a boardinghouse recover to justify it. And it has. I used my half of what Papa left. He died without a will, you should know – we are his only heirs. Rightfully, his properties are split between us, half to you and half to me. There's this house and two town lots which will be of equal value in time."

"I don't care," Carl shrugged. "You keep it all; it's nothing to me, and you have the boys to raise." He looked down at her, his eyes as calm and blue as the sky overhead. "I don't want to owe Papa a single thing – not a stick or a stone or a twenty-dollar bill. T'wouldn't be fitting. It was Rudi who mattered to him, when all was said and done. You put up with him all this time. You keep it, M'grete. You've earned it fair and square."

"But if you settle down, how would you live, what would you use to establish yourself with?" Margaret was genuinely shocked. That would not be right or fair; Carlchen was Alois Becker's only son; no matter how little they had thought of each other, or said in public what little they thought of each other. It was not right for her to benefit at Carl's expense.

"I dunno, M'grete," her brother smiled at her, the same sweet and open smile from when he was a child. "My enlistment's nearly up. I guess I'll sort it out when I next talk to Jack. I'm supposed to meet him in Washington-on-the-Brazos. He sent word that he has an errand for me. We've been paid in certificates for land – the Rangers are. Sam Maverick says I can apply for more, on account of having fought at Bexar and been with Fannin. Don't worry about me, I've got all I need for now. More; I got two good horses."

"You live out of your saddlebags." Margaret thought that her heart might break, for saying those words. Papa had come to Texas to get an inheritance of land for them all – for Rudi, first of course – but for them all, to possess and pass down to his children more acres than could be counted by an ambitious farmer from Chester County in Pennsylvania. "You are a vagabond, a wandering soldier, always on the road, sleeping under a hedge or even just the open sky. That's no way to live, no way at all. When are you going to settle down, little brother?"

"I dunno – when it suits me to," Carl answered mildly. Margaret sighed.

"Well then," she answered, "if that is what you truly want, then come and stay with us for a while until you have to speak to that Jack person. Recollect what it is to have a home. Take your horse around to the stable. I have changed nothing about that part of the house, it is as it ever was."

"Don't mean nothing to me if you had." Carl went to untie his saddle-horse from the scaffolding. Margaret followed him; she rather admired the look of her brother's mount. Aside from the color, he had much the same elegant and well-muscled form as Bucephalus. There must be as much thoroughbred in him as there was in Bucephalus. As Carl untied the reins, she reached out to pat the grey horses' long muzzle. Just as her fingers brushed that velvety nose, the grey horse tossed his head and her brother snatched her wrist away. Those wicked long teeth snapped closed on the place where her fingers had been, a split-of-a-second before.

"He don't like strangers much," Carl observed.

"I can see that," Margaret answered. "You didn't buy him for his good temper, did you?"

"Didn't buy him," Carl reached up and tweaked the horse's ear. "Hellion, behave! I got him after the Salado fight. He was an escaped Mex cavalry horse. I think I killed his owner, so he has a bit of a grudge, still." He swung up easily into Hellion's saddle. Margaret could only think that the gray horse was well-named at that, and her brother had obviously spent so much time in the saddle that a mere walk around the side of the house to the stable was an imposition.

"Quite understandably." Margaret's tone was as dry as the dust on the little road coming up the hill towards the house. "Warn the boys about him, Carlchen. I have two doctors living under the roof at present, but I would want to avoid unnecessary medical expenses. Come to the kitchen when you have put your hell-horse out to pasture, and Hetty and I will fix you something to eat."

"Apple pie?" he asked over his shoulder. "I'm always ready for apple pie, M'grete."

"Don't I know it!" Margaret answered. "Give whatever things you have to Hetty, and we'll sort out a bed for you." She wondered how long he would stay this time, now that there was no need for Carl and Papa to step around each other like dogs bristling for a fight – and only then did she realize they had spoken to each other in English, as if the language they had spoken together as children was a thing which had died with Papa.

Once in the kitchen, she told Hetty that Carl was back, and Hetty beamed. "It's about time, isn't it, Marm? Did he say aught about staying, this time? An' he knew about the Old Sir's passing, did he not?"

"Yes," Margaret rummaged through the pie safe – yes, of course there were several apple pies in it, made from fresh fruit newly harvested, the tender crust breaking sweetly over the high mountains of cinnamon-scented fruit within. "He did not say how long he would stay. He must meet with his captain, but he didn't say when . . . but his enlistment is nearly up. I so hope that he will come home for good."

"I'll light a candle and ask for that from Mother Mary," Hetty assured her, and in a little while Carl walked quietly in with a coat and pair of saddlebags over one shoulder and a long carbine over the other. Jamie and Peter followed after, in wide-eyed wonder and worship.

"Take your uncle's things up to your room," Margaret told them. She had already cut a slab of pie for him. "And you – sit and eat. And between bites, tell us how long you are staying and if not for long, then when you will return."

"Two weeks," Carl answered, with his mouth already full. "Then . . . whatever Jack has for me to do; I dunno when I'd be back. All depends. They say that General Sam is angling for an offer of annexation again." He swallowed, and nodded thanks to Hetty for the bowl of savory ham and cabbage soup that she had put on the table next to the pie. Margaret sliced bread from a whole loaf, still warm from the oven and with a crust that crackled like crisp brown paper, and set it next to the plate. "I expect it will have something to do with that. The Mexes won't take it well," he added seriously.

"That's what Marm and I were thinking." Hetty turned from the stove to take down clean plates from the dresser, to set the table for the midday meal for the boarders. The new dining room had been first finished, as Margaret had dictated to the workmen. "An' what were you doing all this time, then?"

"Chasing Comanche, mostly," he answered around another mouthful, and Hetty riposted, "Then did you catch any?"

"Some," he said. At his back Margaret sent a quick frown and a shake of the head towards Hetty. When her brother became exceedingly terse in his answers, it meant that he did not want to talk about the subject at all.

Or at least, not to the womenfolk; that evening in the old parlor next to the kitchen, with a cozy fire burning in the limestone fireplace that had warmed both rooms in the old days, he spoke of these matters to John Ford, to William Burnett and some of the other gentleman boarders, of what he had been doing all summer in the Staked Plain and the tenuous borderlands between the Nueces and the Rio Grande. A bloody business, it turned out, told in Carl's quiet and passionless voice – stories of sudden brutal attacks by the Comanche, of bloody murder and excruciating torture, of sickening things done to the innocent and defenseless, of hot pursuit, and cold retaliation. Margaret listened in the kitchen as she moved silently about, laying out the preparations for tomorrow's breakfast. She was absolutely horrified to discover Peter and Jamie in their nightshirts, sitting on the lower stairs, just out of sight, and listening with breathless interest – although Peter's eyes were huge, in his pale face.

"Go upstairs to bed at once!" Margaret commanded, in a furious whisper, and they obeyed in a flurry of pattering feet and nightshirt hems. She looked into the parlor and said, "Gentleman, I pray that you change your topic of conversation to one that is less unsettling . . . the boys have been listening."

"No better way to learn what they may face as men," John Ford answered, as the gentlemen rose from their chairs, all save Dr. Williamson, who sat in the corner reading by the light of the single lamp.

William Burnett ventured with the air of a peacemaker, "I will agree with our hostess in this matter . . . there may be damage done to tender souls, learning of such cruelties too young." He also looked as revolted as Margaret felt, upon hearing her brother's soft-voiced accounts. No doubt William Burnett was relieved at an excuse to not hear any more. Margaret was certain in her heart that what her brother had witnessed or done over his interminable service as a Ranger was probably much more horrific than he would ever speak about – to anyone, let alone the gentleman of her boarder's parlor.

Mr. Burnett continued, "Shall we talk about the German princeling that has newly-arrived in Galveston? He is the head of a noble society, wanting to settle thousands of German émigrés in Texas."

"I shall believe that when I actually see a shipload of them arrive!" John Ford answered, and added feelingly, "poor bastards . . . sorry, Marm Vining. Unless they know what they are getting into it will not be easy for them."

"It's only him, so far," Mr. Burnett allowed, in a voice which mingled relish and relief, in the darkened parlor where the firelight and the light of the single lamp brushed edges of gold and cinnabar on the edges of the shelves and furniture, the picture-frames and the faces of the men sitting there. "With a princely retinue, including a troop of soldiers, a private chef, and an expert huntsman."

Carl drawled, "I had heard there was a Frenchy with a grant south of Bexar – is that the one? Everyone seemed to think he was a sensible man."

"No, this one is a real prince," Mr. Burnett began to say, but Carl stifled a yawn and said, "Sorry – I'm all-in. Good night, all." He rose awkwardly and looked around for the way. In the old days, he and the boys had slept in a loft over the old parlor and a simple ladder let upwards to it. Margaret whispered, "Just follow the stairs – we put your things into the boys' room. There is already a cot made up for you there."

As her brother followed her quiet-voiced direction, he looked at her with a faint sideways smile, and asked, "M'grete, are you going to build this house any bigger? I swear, soon I shall need one of the Tonk scouts to track a way from one end to the other."

"I have a business to run and the comfort of my guests to see to," she answered briskly.

The hour was already late – the parlor clock chimed sweetly as Margaret set about her customary last duty of the day, that of seeing that the doors were locked against the night, the kitchen fire banked, and her sons settled in their beds for the night. They were already fast asleep when she opened the door at the top of the landing. The flickering light of her candle danced in the draft from the opened window like a mad thing, and she shielded it with her hand. Even her brother – and she was obscurely pleased to note this – was asleep. He would have opened the window before going to bed, not being able to endure a completely closed room. At least he could bear sleeping indoors again. When he had first returned after Goliad as a boy of sixteen and a bit, he had taken a blanket and slept in the woods or under the apple trees more often than not.

Margaret took the candle, and retired to her own room. Although she had taken possession of one of the new rooms upstairs, it did not seem as comfortable to her as the little room off the parlor that had been hers and Races' for the years that they lived in Waterloo-that-was, and then hers alone. It was not as familiar to her in the dark as the little room had been, just big enough for their bed, the clothes-press, and the cradle for Peter when he was a baby. She was still not sure that she really cared to sleep in the larger room, although it would certainly be more comfortable in the summer, with larger windows open to what cool breezes there were. It lacked something of the cozy feel of a familiar nest. With winter coming on, Margaret considered moving back downstairs. Again, she fell asleep over the *Builder's Companion*, with her mind running over thoughts of the farther extensions that she would build – comfortable and luxuriously spacious rooms, to take in even more boarders . . . and perhaps even suitable quarters for attendants and bondservants, like Hurst. Better quarters than that room in the stable . . .

She was not aware that she had fallen asleep until wakened abruptly and suddenly by a scream, the voice of a child. Another scream – it was Peter, terrified and incoherent, and she went from the bed, casting aside the *Builder's Companion*, not even pausing to snatch up her wrapper or even a shawl. This was her son, her youngest and her baby, even though he was almost five years old, above the age of what her husband had considered the age of reason – that was her child and he was frantic with fear. She flung open the door to the room where the boys slept to see them all sitting up, as wide-eyed as a nest of owls in their beds, and her brother, barefoot but otherwise clothed and with his knife in hand, that long knife which had ever been his companion in his journeys into the Llano, standing between them and the doorway. The room was dimly lit by a sliver of moon, which cast a faint pale shadow on the floor, and gleamed along the edge of Carl's great knife as if it were made of silver.

"He had a bad dream," Carl said, letting his hand with the knife in it drop to his side. "Make him stop screaming, M'grete. I can't stand the sound of screaming!"

The boys and her brother seemed dazed with sleep, all but Peter, who was a half-seen shadow sitting up in bed sobbing with the horror of what he had dreamed. Margaret was incensed. Her boys had never had bad dreams . . . well, Johnny had and often when he was smaller, especially after the burning of Gonzalez. But Peter was a bold boy, nearly as fearless as Jamie – whose insouciance and lack of fear occasionally gave her nightmares on that account.

Margaret snatched her youngest son to her breast, and turned on her brother, demanding indignantly, "Now, look what you have done! Peter has had nightmares from your stories of the Comanche! We have lived here all these years, and the Comanche have raided and killed within town boundaries, but he has never once had bad dreams about it until now!"

"I am sorry, M'grete." Carl sounded nearly as woebegone as Peter did, whose sobs were now slightly muffled by the folds of Margaret's nightgown. Carl fumbled for the belt that held the sheaths for his knife and the pair of repeating pistols, which Margaret saw in the dimness that he had hung from a peg in the wall above the cot, within easy reach of his hands in the dark. "I did not know the boys were listening. I would never have said anything, otherwise. Those were things that I . . . well, I thought I should make folk understand, you see. Some of them are important men, in the Legislature. They should understand clear what we are up against on the frontier and in the Llano country. They live in settled lands. It's been years since Plum Creek, even more years since those in the eastern settlements needed to worry about the Comanche. There are new people come to Texas, who never would know unless we tell them. I thought they should hear what the Rangers guard them against, all unknowing. They sleep safe in their beds of a night, go about their business in the morning with never a care. They have been safe so long they take it as a natural thing, as sunshine in the day, and fund us with a pittance, year to year. Your boarding gentlemen, M'grete – I wanted to make them understand, since they are important men. And as John Ford said – your boys should know of such dangers ..."

"Aye, well – and so they do!" Margaret held Peter close to her. "Hush, hush, my dear little duckling: So, little brother – now you have scared my son out of his next year's growth. Don't talk of these things again – unless and until you are certain that my boys are out of hearing. Promise me."

"I will." Carl still sounded distressed, even more than Peter, whose sobs were now dying away. Margaret relented. "I understand," she said, "that you have seen things that no civilized person should see, and perhaps have done or witnessed things that no man of honor should wish to do and keep silence ... and I know very well that we are all kept safe by the efforts of such men as your Ranger friends, for which we are grateful beyond what words can say, but my sons are innocents!"

In the darkness, Jamie – who shared a bed with Peter crawled closer across the bed, and piped up, "Mama – I'll protect Peter, just see if I will!"

"I'm certain you would, Jamie-duckling ... but you are children still. Go to sleep, and let Uncle Carl and the men see to protecting us from Indians."

"They're not children for long, M'grete," Carl said, very softly, a breath above a whisper, "and children their age, Mex and Texian alike, die at Comanche hands all the time, or else they are taken."

"I know that!" Margaret hissed between her teeth. "But I want to protect my sons from that knowledge, at least for a time! Is that too much to ask?"

There was a step in the hallway, and a wavering halo of candlelight casting a golden shadow on Hetty's pale red hair, raveling down her back, and on the heavy plaid shawl that she had drawn around herself.

Looking in from the doorway, Hetty took in the situation in a single glance. "Oh, a nightmare was it?" she asked, the very tone of her voice implying that such things were trifling things, and almost to be expected. "Never mind – that happens, after eating spicy food too close to bedtime or listening to stories about boggarts and banshees and all. D'you wish me to tell a good story t'ye, Peter – something of kindly magic, as Morag used to tell, or will ye be going to sleep again like a good boy?"

"I should take him to my room for the rest of the night," Margaret said, but the child in her lap knuckled the tears from his eyes and said very clearly, "No, Mama. It was just a horrid dream. It was a dream and I woke up."

"Will you sleep now?" Margaret asked anxiously. Over Hetty's shoulder appeared another figure, bearing another candle, the craggy countenance and straggling hair of Dr. Williamson, puzzled and kindly all at once.

"Has someone been taken ill?" he inquired, with his usual expression of bafflement. "I am at your service, of course," he added, with something of a start at noting Margaret's presence – and Margaret perceived embarrassment in his expression. She was in her nightgown, having thought of nothing else but that one of her sons was in distress. Almost immediately, Hetty set her candle on the window-ledge and caught up a blanket from the foot of the bed to wrap around Margaret's shoulders.

"No, no," Hetty answered, her very presence – and presence of mind – being a reassurance to Margaret. "Maybe a drop of laudanum, in a cup of hot milk will serve . . . it's very soothing, hot milk. Dinna ye fret, Marm . . . I will go downstairs this instant, and heat up a pot of milk, for I think the boys will all want some. Now then," Hetty flapped her hand at Horace and Johnny, who were both sitting up in their bed. "Go back to sleep, all of yez and if ye canna, then I will be up with it directly."

"Laudanum sometimes brings on curious dreams," Dr. Williamson warned, as he made to follow Hetty, who replied, "Aye, and so does sage tea . . . but nobbut as frightening as the dreams that send one screaming like a banshee." The sound of their voices faded down the stairway, in the direction of the kitchen.

"Mama?" That was Peter's voice, from about the vicinity of her collarbone, and Margaret's fears for her son were somewhat relieved, for his voice sounded very much more like his normal and confidant self. "I will go to back to sleep. I am not a baby any more, Mama, that you would need to sit with me all night. I just had a bad dream. Next time I will know that it is a dream, and I will make myself wake up. It is true, you can make yourself wake up from a bad dream – isn't it, Uncle Carl?"

"Most times, yes," Carl answered, heavily. From that, Margaret knew that there were certain dreams that her brother would never be able to wake up from. But, regardless – morning would come. Life would go on. She believed that such dreams would fade through repetition, through the intercession of life, with it's homely concerns.

That had been her own experience, but it had always troubled Margaret that there seemed to be nothing she could do for her brother to bring him peace of mind, a way of getting on with the world as it was, something to bring him back to a civilized and settled life, rewarded with all of the small domestic joys and triumphs that an ordinary life offered. Even General Sam, after a life lived on the highest pinnacles of adventure and war had found a treasure-store of domesticity in a life shared with Margaret Lea. Margaret did not want to see her brother dead in some nameless and unknown affray on the frontier, hastily buried in an unmarked grave in the desert country between the Nueces and the Grand River or, worse yet, to know that he had been tortured to an agonizing death at the hands of the Comanche. The longer that he continued in that life, the more certain the odds of that fate; such a certainty saddened Margaret unutterably.

She cuddled her son to her, thinking of how big he had grown, this youngest of her children – mourning momentarily the fact that he for sure, and Jamie almost certainly, would have no memory of their father – who, no matter how he had treated Margaret in respect of his Boston marriage, had been a loving father to those sons of his born in Texas. A father would have been good for her sons, showing them the ways and manners of a gentleman, done for them what she could not. Mothers had other lessons for sons, to teach them sweetness and sympathy for those in need, to define for them all by example of what a good woman should be, to educate them in letters and courtesy. A father would teach them a different sort of chivalry, the harsher arts; to stand for themselves unflinchingly, to wield the weapons of war and set them down when they were no longer needed or required. Alois Becker had been a bad model of a man for her sons.

Now she said, smoothing back Peter's tumbled fair hair, as straight and pale as sun-bleached straw. "Then lie down again and go to sleep, my dear little ducking. I will sit with you, until Hetty comes with a cup of hot milk. Then you will drink it and go back to sleep like a good boy."

"Yes, Mama," Peter answered. Margaret was reassured, for he sounded content and confident. Sons grew and went from their mother's loving hands, into the world of men. A wise mother would allow this, for a man tied to maternal leading-strings was a crippled thing, incapable of fulfilling the hopes invested in him. Still, her boys were so young that this was a wrenching prospect for Margaret, and she often regretted that she had not been blessed with a daughter. Margaret had begun to have an instinct about certain matters, and one of them was that she would have no more children. Her monthly courses had become erratic and sometimes scanty . . . and she did not mind very much, for it was less trouble to take care of, if the change that ordinarily came to older women had come to her. These matters were disposed of at the whim of a higher power.

She sat with Peter in her lap, and Jamie curled next to her, waiting for Hetty's return with the hot milk as she had promised. Horace and Johnny had already curled up in their bed, and Carl lay on his pallet, with his eyes looking up towards the underside of the shingles that covered the roof. She recollected that when she first came into her son's sleeping-chamber, responding to

Peter's screams, Carl – even half-asleep, had leapt to a position defending the doorway, with his knife in hand. A true Ranger, defending the innocent unthinkingly and without hesitation; the town of Austin needed that sure defense – and so did Texas, Margaret knew. So her brother had served for many a year – did not this long service permit any end, to pass on that burden and obligation to another?

Waiting for Hetty, she looked about, seeing the enlarged room with critical eyes. This room was a simple one, the attic of a crude cabin. Margaret made a mental note that when the day came for the building of another addition, she would make better and more commodious rooms for her family.

Presently she heard Hetty's steps upon the stair, and she said to her son, "Here is your hot milk, dear little duckling. Drink it down, and go to sleep. Remember, you will know a bad dream now, and be able to wake yourself from it."

Hetty bustled in, with a tray full of tin and pottery mugs. "Now, they're not too hot for ye, now? It's good milk, from yesterday's milking – drink it down, and go to sleep. You too, young Sir, it's in me mind that you need a good night's sleeping as well. There's only a wee drop of Dr. Williamson's good syrup in it. Will do ye good, nonetheless." Hetty put one of the mugs into Peter's hands, and stood over Peter and Margaret both, as Peter obediently drank it down. "That's a good boy," Hetty said, as she took back the empty mug. "And I have one for yerself, Ma'am. No, dinna put on your Maeve-face w'me – ye'll go to your room an' drink it all down. The doctor says it will be good for ye. This one is f'yeself, young sir."

Hetty handed another mug to Carl, who took it, and looked into it with a straight and expressionless face. "No, there's barely a drap o' laudanum innit, take it an' drink. This is Marm's house; we're safe enough that you may sleep until ye're tired of sleeping. Drink it down, now there's a good lad. Now," Hetty fixed Margaret with a severe look, and gestured towards the door with the tray which held one last full mug of milk upon it. "Go to your own chamber, Marm. We have ourselves work tomorrow, enough that we canna be awake to all hours."

Margaret obeyed – it was less trouble than protesting to Hetty. Peter and Jamie had pulled the covers to their ears; Margaret thought that Jamie might already have dozed off. Carl drained his cup in two or three gulps – obviously agreeing with Margaret that it was easier than to argue with Hetty. He lay down on his pallet, but Margaret noted as she closed door that Hetty's candle caught a gleam from eyes that were still open. Hetty chivvied her to her own room, where she gratefully slid her cold, bare feet under the covers that she had thrown back at Peter's first scream.

"You're not going to stand over me, waiting for me to drink this?" Margaret asked, as Hetty handed her the warm mug.

"Aye," Hetty answered. "Dinna fret, there's only the tiniest drop in it. The Doctor, he measured carefully." She looked immensely thoughtful, a slight frown of concentration wrinkling her freckled countenance. Margaret sensed that Hetty had something on her mind, something faintly troubling to her.

"What is it, Hetty? Is there something going on?"

"I canna be certain," Hetty answered slowly. "But I have begun to think . . . that maybe Doctor Williamson is in love w'ye. His eyes follow ye, as Danny Fritchie's did when he first courted Morag. Has he ever said aught about such feelings, Marm?"

"No, not . . . directly," Margaret answered warily. "I know that . . . now and again, I am admired by some of the gentlemen boarders. But their attentions are respectful, and I do not encourage them. What makes you believe that the doctor has particular feelings towards me?"

"It is just a sense that I have." Hetty shrugged. "Are ye going to look at that milk the rest of the night, Marm? I know that he does – because I see things, also – knowing that I love you as a sister, Marm."

"I know, Hetty." Margaret obediently drank from the milk, tasting the faint bitter tang of the medicine in it masked with a bit of honey. "And we have had so much reason to be grateful to you. I don't know how the boys and I would have managed without you, all this time."

"Aye, you would have," Hetty answered comfortably. "Queen Maeve herself could nae have managed any better. Good night, Marm."

"Good night, Hetty." Margaret answered, and until the drop of laudanum syrup pulled her down into dreamless sleep, she wondered if Hetty was right.

Chapter 15 – *Servants and Masters*

Carl departed for Washington on the Brazos some ten days later, having helped the boys harvest the late-season hay. Margaret watched him covertly as he worked at this and other chores such as chopping firewood. As far as she could recall, this was the first time he had willingly picked up any of the work of a farm since the day he had left Papa's roof. He had preferred hunting the open fields and the woods whenever he had returned before. Now Margaret saw clearly that it was not a disinclination for that kind of work; he had preferred that refuge rather than have anything to do with Papa. The boys frankly adored their uncle, and Margaret thought wistfully of how good it would be for them if he returned to Austin for good once this last errand for the Rangers was done. But on a clear late summer morning, with the leaves of the sycamore trees below just beginning to be touched with gold and a faint mist rising from the river and from Shoal Creek, Carl saddled up that leggy, bad-tempered horse of his in the stable yard, flung a rolled-up blanket and a pair of saddlebags over the back of the saddle, and a long holster for his rifle from the horn, and still looked vaguely surprised when Margaret and Hetty and the boys emerged from the house.

"You cannot leave from here without a proper farewell," Margaret chided him. "You may insist that it is not – but this is your home, and the boys and I are your family, until the day when you have your own. Hetty has baked you a pan of biscuits, there are apples and cured sausage, and even some sweets." She handed him a small haversack bulging with good things. "Come home as soon as you may, little brother. We'll be waiting for you, until then."

"I'll bring one of the Tonks to scout the house for me," Carl leaned down to kiss Margaret's cheek, to shake hands gravely with the older boys and ruffle Jamie and Peter's fair heads. "By Christmas mebbe, if I've nothing better to do."

"You had best," Margaret answered sternly. "Or I will send Mr. Burnett's Hurst to track you down and bring you back. We'll see you at Christmas, little brother – the only excuse you would have for not coming home would be another Mexican invasion. The next president will be sworn in at that time, and there will be festivities and parties enough for all. Goodbye – and keep yourself safe. If you can, teach that horse of yours some good manners," she added, as Hellion snapped irritably at nothing in particular.

"He's perfectly well-mannered," her brother answered, as he untied the reins from the post where he had tied them. "As long as you are in the saddle, and have him firm in check. Bye, M'grete." Without another word, he was gone, with the speed of a hawk launching into the sky, and Margaret stifled a sigh. Why did he seem so eager to be away, now that the new part of the house was finished, in a mad scramble of plaster trugs and rolls of canvas expertly painted in pleasing tints and panels and applied to the walls, the new glass windows and tall louvered doors allowing light and air in equal measure into her spacious and airy rooms? It lifted her soul, every time she came out into the new hallway, the gleaming expanse of golden-varnished cypress planks that made the floor, the staircase to the upper floor curving down into it, and the walls of pale yellow, which held the afternoon sunshine like a cup of honey dispensing sweetness by the drop. At some time, when she saw what she liked, she would adorn those walls with pictures, and the floors with finer rugs than those of braided or hooked rags, but for now, the very space, color, and light were adornment enough.

"Aye, there he goes." Hetty looked at the settling dust in the stable yard. "I know ye hope that he might remain, Marm, but that's a fool's dream. This is your house and it was the Old Sir's before that. It will never be his. If he settles down, he will want his own place, something untainted, something without memories attached. I think the Young Sir is haunted by memories, memories of an ill-kind attached to this place. Which is a pity – and a heartfelt one at that, for others of us have nothing but memories of the best kind, of love and welcome, of kindliness within these walls . . . or of these walls as far as ye should build them, Marm."

"I fear so, Hetty," Margaret answered as they returned to the kitchen where they had been engaged in the morning washing-up, after breakfast for the boarders was done. "My mother and father, my brothers – lived very happily here, or so my mother told me in letters, over and over again. Once they all had a deep fondness for this place – my father to the end of his days, not wishing me to change very much. You are quite right – for Carl, that fondness is tainted. I do not blame him for being reluctant to return; all that is unchanged is a stab at the heart in reminding him of how it was. And that which I have changed since then, reminds him that he has made himself a stranger and that years have passed. Men!" Margaret added. "I despair sometimes, Hetty! One cannot live with one such as my father was or endure long without them."

"Unless one takes the holy vows," Hetty agreed, "and then ye have the bishop and the priest who hears confessions. Still, Marm," and she shot a very shrewd look towards Margaret, "did ye ever think o' marrying again?"

189

"No," Margaret sighed. "Although there was an old black witch-woman that my brothers and I met on the day that I turned twelve years old. She looked at my hand and told me that I would have two husbands and a large house."

"Two out of three," Hetty answered. "No bad at all for a gypsy fortune-teller . . . what else did she tell ye?"

"Some things that turned out to be true," Margaret answered. "So I had confidence in her gifts of prophecy – or at least I did when I was a girl. She told me that I would meet the man who would be my first husband on the thirty-first day from my birthday. And so I did – not realizing it at the time, of course; that was the first day of school for us, upon arrival in San Felipe – I was sure that it would be some callow schoolboy, but it turned out to be my schoolmaster instead." Margaret felt a deep melancholy, upon remembering that first day of school in what was the capital city of Mr. Austin's colony, all those years ago when Race Vining was hale and handsome, a fit man for a schoolgirl to fall in love with almost at the first moment of her beholding him.

Yes, she had been a schoolgirl. He had taught her many things, above the pleasures and delights of marriage. She was – as once he had told her – his master-working as a teacher. Under his guidance, she had become a lady of culture and education, of polished manners and confident in the ways of society – a society well beyond the simple demands of the frontier. She had held her own with everyone she encountered ever since in her profession of being a boardinghouse keeper.

That had been his gift to her, his wife of the heart. Of his wife in law, all he had done for her was to father a daughter upon her body and return to her house to die. Margaret hoped, with an unladylike and mordant turn of mind, that Race had not discommoded his legal wife too much at the end of his life. She considered the demands of nursing an invalid – no, Annabel Saltinstall Vining had probably diverted much of the burden of that onto servants. The Vinings and the Saltinstalls of Boston were ancient families as things in America went, full of past glories and honors, not burdened very much with present involvement in matters of state, or of children. Of those who bore the surname of Vining, she was certain that her sons were the only ones to bear it into the next generation. The Vinings of Boston; Race Vinings' older brothers had been childless or the fathers of daughters. She was lost in that grim contemplation, until Hetty broke into her reverie over the dishpan.

"An' what else did the gypsy witch tell ye, Marm – anything else of your husband that was to be?"

"She said I would marry first for love, and then friendship. "Margaret answered hastily. "I would have ten years and one of happiness with him who came first, which came true and also that I would have many friends and some of them powerful men, but that very few would truly know my heart."

"Well, I know yer heart," Hetty answered, "since I've been yer friend, all these years since Morag and I came to Austin. Ye should marry again, as the ald witch prophesied, no matter how much or little ye credited what she told ye . . ." and she looked at Margaret very knowingly, over the dishpan, and her voice roughened with sympathy. "Ye're a woman for a man, an' young still. I've seen the way that Doctor Williamson looks after ye, with his heart in his eyes, the way Danny would look after Morag before he worked up enough nerve to speak fer hisself. Ye could do worse than encourage him, Marm – and I'll say so only this once and then niver again. Gi' him a kind look an' a kiss, an' he'd be at yer feet, swearing devotion everlasting. The lads need a father, otherwise they will look to anyone who shows them a bit o'kindness an' respect – sometimes that will no' be fitting. That Hurst – Mr. Burnett's man? He an' young Peter are as thick as thieves, but he's hardly a proper gennelman, is he?"

"Not a proper gentleman," Margaret answered swiftly, "but he is one of nature's own, and of a noble character that I can see as such would not be a better example for my son. I am not in haste to marry, even with your encouraging me to set my cap at Dr. Williamson. He's a dear friend, and that is all."

"Aye, that's good," Hetty replied, and Margaret wondered at Hetty's expression of grim practicality – really, it was almost as if Hetty had a fear for her marrying. "So, aye," Hetty continued after a moment, as she continued to dunk the cleaned dishes into a pan of rinse-water, from which they went to Margaret's dish-towel swathed hands, and then into the cupboard. "What else did she say, that made ye so recall her words? Did she also make a prophecy for your brothers, then?"

"She said that water would be Carlchen's savior, and we should have no fear of it on his behalf. He ran to the river and jumped in – that was how he saved himself at Goliad. Of my brother Rudi, all she would say was that she saw dark smoke around him, like a bonfire." Margaret shuddered, and seeing this, Hetty crossed herself hastily with a suds-covered hand. "They burned the bodies of those slain there, or left them to lie in the open until General Rusk came to gather them up, months later. I have never liked to think on that, Hetty. Rudi was . . . so intensely alive, so charming and vital, that to think of him dead and his remnant treated by his murderers as carelessly as a piece of

191

trash! I am nauseated to recall such, even now. I should have named one of the younger boys after him, but I could not endure how the mere saying of his dear name would have reminded me at every repetition of his piteous end, the waste of his life – all for the pride and convenience of a Mexican autocrat, insensately angry that all would not instantly obey his commands."

Margaret stared out of the one kitchen window remaining, which looked out onto the garden and what had become the stable yard. There Hurst was curry-combing Bucephalus, attended by Peter, perched on the topmost rail around the small pen next to the stable. She had already sold the last pair of Papa's oxen – she had no need or time enough to oversee the farm work as Papa had; there was barely enough land left to be profitable in growing corn or wheat, over and above the needs of the household. She could afford to hire a local man to plow the corn plot or the vegetable garden for less cost in care, trouble and silage than it would to keep a well-trained ox-team standing idle most of the year. *Papa had such a good hand with oxen*, Margaret thought. His repute with training them had stood above all others – under his hand, as tame and gentle as kittens, although much more biddable to commands than kittens were. Two yoke of his had conveyed Margaret and her family from Gonzales all the way to near Harrisburg during the war, under the inexpert command of Margaret herself and a mere boy of fourteen, and never given cause for unease.

"I would sell Bucephalus, too," Margaret ventured aloud, "save that my husband so prized him. Horace and Johnny ride him now and again, and sometimes Dr. Williamson will borrow him for an afternoon, if he has a call at a farmstead at some distance from here. I would buy a mule team and a trap though – for the use of the household if I thought the boys could care for them properly. I will probably have to hire a man to do chores soon."

"And two more girls, to make the beds, sweep the rooms, and do the laundry," Hetty answered. "We ha'e hired out the laundry to Marm Eberly, which is a load from our backs, but I still dinna think they do as well with it as they would have if I had the judging o' the finished."

"You are set upon perfection in all things," Margaret smiled at Hetty, still efficiently rinsing dishes, who answered, "Aye well – honest work is worth the doing of it, is it not? And as well as you may do it, for an offering and gift to the Lord Above – you are contented in your work always, for the ambition and confidence of always having done your best. And sometimes, you might even make a living from it. Perfection is a habit, Marm – as well as a discipline – and those that have the wit to appreciate it? They do so, and pay good coin!"

"So they do!" Margaret answered, for she had just this week filled up the remaining empty rooms with gentlemen boarders and with Liddy Burnett, who had lately arrived to join her husband in Austin, since their residence there was nearly finished.

Her reunion with Liddy was somewhat strained. It had been nearly eight years since they had parted, and aside from having been stranded in the same refugee party, they had little in common of age, experience, and outlook upon life. Liddy Burnett as a correspondent and living in Margaret's memory as having been a stalwart comrade in time of trouble was somewhat more comfortable than Liddy Burnett in physical presence. It appeared to gall the present Liddy that Margaret had actual duties to perform with her own hands throughout most of the hours of a working day – that she must weigh in and perform such duties as cooking, butter-churning, making the beds, and dusting, making pickles and jams and pies throughout the mornings. The only routine of Margaret's daily life of which Liddy approved wholeheartedly was that Margaret gathered her sons into the family parlor of an afternoon – when the boys were done with such chores as had been assigned – and she gave them lessons there for some hours. However, even that approval was measured out sparingly, for Liddy had invited herself into the private parlor almost at once upon arrival, commenting censoriously on the lack of proper board-schools for Horace and Johnny, and the fact that Margaret spent the mornings attending to the needs of her household.

"I feel that my husband's example and library have left me better able to oversee the education of our children," Margaret had answered mildly, after turning over in her mind several less tactful answers. "Until we have more proper schools, that is." *Dear Liddy – I am not one of your daughters. Do not presume to dictate how I am to live my life or conduct my household.*

"You should not have to work at such base occupations," Liddy had answered, not the least bit mollified. "Margaret – you a lady, and should not have to work alongside your . . ." and here, Liddy's nostrils had flared, just the slightest bit, "hired girls. What would folk think – that you must work as hard as a nigra slave?"

"I do not care what folk think, as long as they are content with my hospitality," Margaret had answered. Later she wished that she had been able to riposte with Hetty's remark about honest work being an offering and a gift. Now, she wiped the plates and mused, "You are correct – another two or three girls, and a man to do the outside work, the heavy carrying and lifting, perhaps to look after the horses . . . the girls – that will be no problem, we will hire them as we always had, from daughters of folk that we know – A good and reliable man, not a conformed sot, and not apt to go haring off into the wilderness in pursuit of some mad rumor."

Margaret turned over the names of all those she knew who might be able to perform such duties, or recommend such to her, and came up as empty as a bucket drawn up from a dry well. All those whom she knew as reliable and responsible men were those who already had profitable or somewhat promising businesses of their own, to which they rightfully gave the largest portion of their attention. Of those being footloose and fancy-free? She knew nothing– such were not among her boarders or acquaintance. Oh, if Carl would only return from the Rangers for good and all! That would resolve both her immediate problem, and perhaps mend that hurt in his soul which had taken him away from a civilized live for way too long.

She supposed that she had mentioned something of her need to hire a good and reliable man in passing to one of the boarders, although she could never afterwards recall precisely whom, or what she had said. On a weekday morning in early autumn, just as Liddy and William Burnett prepared to take possession of their new house, William Burnett politely rapped on the doorjamb of the enlarged parlor, which Margaret used as her office and as a schoolroom for her sons. The Burnett's new house was built high on a hill, near to the crumbling house built by Seamus O'Doyle for the then-French Consul – he who had engaged in a long feud with Richard Bullock and become a laughing-stock all across Texas. Now she looked up from a book of sonnets which had been one especially beloved by her husband, and smiled at William Burnett.

"I thought you and Liddy were already gone to your own house!" Margaret exclaimed, upon seeing Mr. Burnett still standing irresolute in the doorway. "Come in, come in! Liddy was telling me that three cart-loads of your furniture and household fittings had just arrived from your country place, and that she would be all week in unpacking and deciding where they would best go in the new house."

"It's a lot of work, to setting up housekeeping," Mr. Burnett agreed, seating himself in the chair opposite. "And Liddy – she is a master of it, no less than you are yourself, dear Mrs. Vining."

"Thank you for thinking so," Margaret returned sedately, and waited for William Burnett to come to the point. "I shall be very sorry to have you and Liddy going to your own establishment. You are friends, no less than guests – pray do not be strangers once you have removed from my roof to your own. The boys will be heartbroken at loosing the company of Hurst."

"Would they?" Unexpectedly, Mr. Burnett's face lightened, as if he had just seen a short cut to that which he really wanted to talk about. Margaret sighed inwardly; there were often so many circumlocutions in polite converse. Her husband had often amused himself to the point of laughter in explaining them to her, as if he had been brought to see how ridiculous they were by her very own mystification. Alois Becker had often and painfully been blunt in his converse, but no one had ever accused him of wasting time in social niceties. Margaret reflected that perhaps in this instance her own blood and early habits were only lightly veneered over by Race Vining's tutelage. Now William Burnett continued, "I am glad to hear that. Hurst is as fine a nigra as any I ever owned. Honest, responsible, and trustworthy – I tell you, Mrs. Vining, I'd trust him, over and above just about every white man I know. In the spring of 1836, I handed him my best shotgun and told him to see to taking Liddy and the girls and the children as far east as they could go – over the Sabine to Liddy's folk in Alabama if need be. I gave him charge of two teams of my finest Kentucky mules, and he took the sturdiest wagon, and I never had a moment of doubt that he would do the best that he could, while I was away with the Army."

"I remember," Margaret said softly. "I met them first upon the road, as they were burying little Jeffy – I think. Miss Elizabeth's son. Later, when we met up again near Harrisburg, Hurst built a coffin for my mother from boards taken from the wagons in our encampment. He dug the grave for her, and I have always been grateful for his work and consideration."

Margaret left unmentioned that she had paid Hurst with Mama's wedding-ring, even though Libby Burnett had directed him, in a most imperious manner, to perform those necessary duties.

"Aye," and Mr. Burnett's eyes filled briefly. "Poor little lad. When I recollect those days, and think on how many brave men that we lost; over and above I think of Jeffy. That journey in the rain, the cold and hardship; all that killed that dear little angel and your mother, too – as sure as those damned Mexes killed our lads at the Alamo, or at Goliad! Just three years old Jeffy was; mayhap he wouldn't have lived to any great age at all. He had the fits sometimes, but Lizzie thought that he was growing out of them. I have always been certain . . . ah, but I am going on too long, Mrs. Vining. I came to you to talk about Hurst; not about Jeffy or your mother, God rest them both."

"About Hurst?" Margaret asked in as soft and unhurried a tone as she could manage; William Burnett recovered something of his usual countenance of bluff confidence.

"M'dear Livvy has never trusted Hurst in the same degree as I have always done. He was from my family's place and we were raised together. She says that he takes too many unsuitable liberties with me, because of that association." William Burnett's expression took on something of that faint look of embarrassment which Margaret had noted whenever mention of the peculiar institution touched upon familial intimacies. Now she recalled Liddy writing, in one of her letters, *'Every woman among one's closest neighbors always knows, precisely and to the ultimate degree – who has fathered the paler-complexioned children, tumbling about every slave quarters but those of our own establishment – sometimes this humiliation is intolerable. Men live with their wives and their concubines, while their lawful wives may make no protest, save amongst ourselves. And yet we endure – for what? I no longer know, since economy and custom persevere!'*

Livvy had been more frank in her letters during the years of their correspondence than she had ever been in person. Margaret wondered sometimes, if there were matters best confided in letters, yet shied away from face to face. Such things as she had put on paper and sent to Dr. Williamson that she had never dared say in person! Margaret had long noted that Hurst and William Burnett had a marked likeness to each other in face and build, the likeness of kin, of brothers or cousins. Of the same close blood, she concluded sadly: one man free and the master, being gotten legitimately in the marriage bed, the other under circumstances which she – and very likely Liddy Burnett – shuddered to contemplate. The other was condemned by custom to servitude by the admixture of darker blood – from a mother held in chattel slavery. William Burnett doubtlessly knew the exact degree and provenance of that mixture. Such was the bond of kin between him and Hurst, tragic and unspeakable. Yet, they were as fond and protective of each other as brothers commonly were expected to be. Liddy suspected and resented – such an awful tangle! Margaret remembered what she had told Hetty; not wishing to own slaves, risking that terrible anger of a resentful bondservant as a poisonous fog under her roof.

"You were saying," Margaret urged him gently, for William Burnett seemed to be momentarily lost among his thoughts and his affection for his . . . whatever Hurst was to him besides his chattel. Mr. Burnett started, and recovered his thoughts. "Y'see, Hurst came to me to ask a favor . . . no secrets in the slave quarters. Never has been, never will; anything you wish to find out about a family, their nigras will always know. He said he had heard that you wished to hire a man, to work about the place now that your father is gone to his rest. I'll make no secret of it; Hurst has never gotten on with Liddy or my dear wife with him. I'm going on in years m'self, and it's come to me more and more that I should give Hurst his freedom before I take my own eternal reward. I'd put it in my will, but Liddy would never stand for that. She keeps all my papers, y'see. She'd know, and if I were not there . . . an' Hurst, a sturdy an' well-trained nigra like him? He's worth at least sixteen hundred dollars on the block, even as old as he is, she would say; may as well take the money that he'd be worth and burn it in the fireplace. Liddy has a better head for accounts than I do. Too trustful, that's what she'd say to me. Funny thing," William Burnett laughed wryly. "It's what Hurst himself has told me, many a time." Margaret thought she might have to encourage him again in his wanderings, but fortunately Mr. Burnett recalled the purpose of his errand just as she was about to loose all patience.

"So, the brass tacks of it is; Hurst – and I have agreed – that is, if you would agree, he should like to hire out to you, for wages, and that he would buy his freedom from us – from Liddy and me, out of them. It's a thing that he has set upon – he's enterprising as all get-out and no mistake. He bought out the older of his two children, just from saving every cent that he could – got the little pickaninny an education and an apprenticeship in a good trade as a free nigra, and he's on a good way to buying out the younger, too. Don't know how he manages it, but he does. Comes from . . ." and Mr. Burnett looked slightly embarrassed, as he coughed and rearranged the subject. "Anyway – Hurst, he'd be of good use to you and your establishment. The arrangement would be that you would pay wages to him directly. Liddy says that you need a good coachman and all-around man of work. Anything you could put to him, he can do. He can even cook, after a sort, although I don't think Miss Hetty could be replaced in that regard within your establishment. And he likes this situation." Mr. Burnett actually looked as if he would be pleading. "I have seen that your boys hold him in affection."

"The boys are very fond of him," Margaret ventured, already aware that Peter and Jamie were looking up from their assignments with a sudden air of intense interest. They had become unaccountably devoted to Hurst; Peter in particular had such an expression on his face – no, the boys thought the world of Hurst. She may as well have him in her employ, since she could not command her brother.

"Very well," she said at last. "I will hire Hurst, under the conditions that you have outlined. He is an upright man, even given his condition, and that you think the world of him is an excellent reference in my eyes. But I should like to speak with him, face to face, and privately if you would allow that."

She had thought that perhaps William Burnett would be apprehensive in being excluded from any conversation that she would have with his bondsman, even if she were chaperoned by her four sons, now busily making an elaborate pretense of attention to their lessons.

"No, that will be splendid," he answered with hearty relief. "He is waiting just outside in the hall – it won't take a moment." He gathered himself up from the chair with an expression of intense relief already on his ruddy countenance.

'No wonder,' Margaret thought, *'that William Burnett was among the worst poker-players of all the gentlemen renting rooms in her establishment. He could no more keep his thoughts from his face than the sun could keep lightening the sky immediately upon rising. There was no more transparently obvious representative to the Legislature in Austin – I hope they keep him far from anything that requires discretion and certain devious habits of mind. Otherwise, we may yet be lost.'*

In the space of a moment, Hurst was already in the small parlor, standing before her, turning his hat in his hand, and obviously dressed in the best that he had – castoffs from his master Margaret saw at once. She recognized them from the laundry, and from the care she took in daily arranging the boarder's quarters. She briefly gestured towards the chair which William Burnett had yielded, and Hurst shook his head.

"I'd best be standing, Miz Vining, it ain't proper."

"Oh, do sit down, Hurst," she said impatiently. "I would like not to have a crick in my neck from looking up at you . . . and I would like to speak with you as easily as I spoke to Mr. Burnett. This is my own house, and my own parlor. I will be the judge of what is proper within it. And I say that I would prefer that we converse eye to eye. Now then," she added as he reluctantly yielded, sitting on the very edge of the chair. "I have always thought of you with affection and respect. You performed a service for my family – and I have been grateful to you ever since. Mr. Burnett tells me that you would like to hire out for wages, so that you may purchase freedom for your youngest boy, and for yourself. Is that true?"

"It surely is, Miz Vining," he answered. "I have saved up near-nuff for Wash . . . Wash, that's his name, after Washington. Oncet I see Wash with his freedom papers, an' settled in a good trade . . . then I buy myself."

"What of your wife, the mother of your boys," Margaret spoke before she thought. "Have you already bought her freedom, then?"

"No, ma'am," Hurst answered, and she thought she detected a thin trace of sorrow and resentment in his stolid middle aged to ageless dark countenance. "She . . . Ab'gail that jumped over the broom w'me . . . Ol' Miz Bennett gave her as a weddin' gift to her niece, back in Alabam. Ten year ago, or so that was. Ab'gail, she was high-yeller, an' could do fine sewing, an' being a mother, she could mind the childer. Miz Bennett's niece had a sore need for a good house nigra."

"I see," Margaret answered, though she honestly could not and was thoroughly appalled. A woman, torn away from her children and her husband-in-custom, sent as a wedding gift to a faraway place to be the handmaid of a woman too spoilt and inept to do her own sewing and mind her own children? Surely slavery was an abomination. Mama was right to have been quietly against it all these years. Those of hers and Race's friends, who owned slaves, usually owned only a few, half a dozen at most. From what Margaret had observed they would no more have considered breaking up their slaves' families than they would have their own. Margaret was horrified in the confines of her own mind. She would not have thought Libby Burnett capable of such subtle and unthinking cruelty, not the woman who had been so kind, had read the service of burial for Mama out of her own prayer book, and corresponded so long and so frankly with her for years after their first meeting. The Libby that Margaret thought she knew was too fine and considerate a woman to have been so heartless.

'*Ah,*' the interior Margaret whispered inexorably; '*those finer feelings are limited to humans of the same color. Those of a darker hue merit the same level of feeling that I would feel towards the animals in the barn, to Papa's oxen – which I sold without a moment's consideration of their beast-feelings; I would not sell Bucephalus, since I have a sentimental fondness for him – so is this the same manner which slave-owners feel about their human cattle? Of the wickedness of the peculiar institution, perhaps the coarsening of human kindness amongst those who practice it is the subtler of the damage wrought!*'

"Did you ever have a thought to buying her – your wife – from Mrs. Bennett's niece? I am sure it could be arranged."

"She wasn't my wife no longer," Hurst answered, stolidly. "Miz Bennett's niece, she had her husband give Ab'gail to his foreman. She has since had three childer by him, and sent word that she is contented to be where she is."

"I am sorry to hear of a loss such as this," Margaret was shocked out of all intent to be tactful. "Then you are hired, at the wages of fifteen dollars for the month, and you may keep any such small payments that the boarding gentlemen wish to give you for additional service and errands. Based on our previous acquaintance, and of how useful you have been in these last few months, I have a good opinion of your character, Hurst. My plans for the next expansion of my establishment shall include more suitable rooms than beggarly quarters in the stable-loft."

"Thank you, Miz Vining," Hurst answered, a brief glint of humor showing in his eyes. "Climbing up that ol' ladder, that does get to me, now and again, 'specially after a day of work."

"This will happen," Margaret answered firmly. "For I have plans to make my home a show place – but if you can endure the loft for a little longer . . . now, one more matter. Boys," she raised her voice a little, and gathered up their attention, though she was fairly sure all of the boys' ears were turned towards her, despite the pretense they made of attending to their schoolwork. As soon as their eyes were fixed upon her, she continued, "From now on, Mr. Bennett's Hurst will be working here at our house, doing the kind of work that Opa did; seeing to the outside, to repairs and chores, taking care of the horses. Mr. – er," she was diverted. "What shall we address you as, then?"

"At Marse Bennett's home place, the folk there call me Daddy," Hurst answered. "'Specially the younger ones."

"Very well – boys, Daddy Hurst will be working for me now, just as Hetty does. Just as Hetty commands respect in my household, so will Daddy Hurst in equal measure. When you have chores in the garden, or to do with caring for old Bucephalus and Daddy Hurst asks you to do this and such, you will do as he asks. We should never become so proud as to think that we are above doing the work of living that needs to be done to keep us fed, and clothed, with a roof over our head."

"Or the mattress stuffed with cornshucks." Young Horace said wisely, and Johnny smiled; they both remembered that momentous day when their father had first began to cough up blood from his crippled lungs and Margaret had decided unilaterally that she would be the one who would direct their fortunes from now on, with the city of Austin busy a-building in the valley below Alois Becker's tall log blockhouse.

"Miz Vining," Hurst rose from the chair, from that edge of it upon which he had been uneasily perched, "I am mos' grateful to be in your employment. I will . . . " he paused, and Margaret fancied that he had been coached and rehearsed by Mr. Bennett as his words did not reflect any of the patios of the slave quarters, "endeavor to give every satisfaction and honor to your household, to the bes' of my humble abilities."

"Never humble," Margaret corrected. "You work for me now, Hurst. I am not humble. I am a Vining and a Becker before that. This house is never humble."

Chapter 16 – *Princes and Palatinates*

In early September Margaret received a letter from Carl, sent from Washington-on-the-Brazos. This missive was written on fine paper and in her younger brother's erratic handwriting, informing her that he had taken service with that German princeling – the Prince of Solms and Braunfels – who had appeared in midsummer to see to the settling of a fabulously large number of immigrants from Germany onto an entrepreneur grant.

"There are such tales about him – the Prince, not the Young Sir," Hetty marveled, when Margaret showed her the letter as they were remaking beds in the boarder's rooms. Margaret had kept the letter in the pocket of her apron ever since it had come in the post to Bullock's. "Such as I could no' believe at first, but they were told to me by folk not inclined to tell stories, not like poor Seamus – aye, what a tale he could have woven of this! The man arriving with a' his servants, an' a proper party o' sworn men, making no less than a royal procession! Did ye ever think we would see the loike?"

"I think that I may have seen or heard – at one or two removes – of just about every oddity that could exist in Texas, or elsewhere," Margaret answered.

Hetty squinted at the letter, and after a careful study, remarked. "Aye, in a letter, the young Sir says about as much as he does when he is present in the flesh." She handed the single sheet of paper back to Margaret, and the two of them resumed deftly re-plumping feather pillows and straightening sheets and blankets, working from either side of the bed with the practiced skill and efficiency of women long-accustomed to working in partnership. "So, Marm, what d'ye make of it all?"

"I cannot think that Carl would take employment with such as this Prince seems to be without some deeper purpose. No," Margaret added, as she folded the letter away. "I am almost certain that his Captain prevailed upon him for that very reason. This Prince Solms is a disquieting person. What does he want in Texas, aside from so-many-acres to settle his folk upon? What purpose might he have, even if he is honest and fair, and in the same earnest as M'sieu de Castro? There are many powers abroad in the world, Hetty, all working for their own purposes. There are so many entrepreneurs who have come here and taken up a settlement grant, yet how many have actually brought enough settlers to meet their contract?"

"No' so many," Hetty answered. Hers and Morag's parents had come to settle a grant on the Nueces a few years after Alois Becker had brought his family to San Felipe and then to Gonzales. That grant had done better than most, but mostly resulted in stranding a handful of poor and hopeful Irish settlers in a mismanaged and comparatively undefended colony. San Patricio, it was called. Most of the sensible and ambitious had abandoned it within a few years, including Hetty's brother, who upon their parent's deaths from a purulent fever, had taken his sisters north into the wooded uplands and established a tavern at Beeson's Crossing.

"Of those who have successfully settled a grant in Texas, and brought in sufficient settlers to account their venture a success; how many are there?" Margaret ventured, as they moved on to the next bedroom, full of beds left askew and items of clothing scattered every-which-where. Margaret carried a broom and pan, and Hetty a basket for laundry dirtied beyond re-use. "And how many have made a profit upon such a scheme?"

Hetty shook her head. "Only three or four o' the first, counting Mr. Austin and Colonel DeWitt among them, o'course. As for a profit? In respect and affection, a full measure an' o'erflowing; but a profit on the black-ink side of the ledger, from those who made an honest attempt? No, none a'tall, that I may bring to mind." She sighed very deeply. "More had hopes, o'course. Remember that French fellow, who fought w' Richard Bullock over his pigs? He represented his government in settling a French colony, an' even General Sam thought well of it. But it's God's ain truth that many more o' them entrepreneuring gentlemen are blackguards seein' a foine chance to skin the unwary – there is one of them born ivry minute who has hopes! This German princeling may ha'e deeper pockets than most, and might yet bring over a fair number to settle his grant . . . but the word is among the gossips that his consortium o'gentlemen was prevailed to purchase an existing grant an' that would be why the Young Sir would be keeping a weather eye upon it all."

"The grant that Prince Solms' company has purchased?" Margaret asked. She had not heard any of this gossip. Perhaps there was a disadvantage to insisting on elevating conversation at her table. "Have you heard anything of where it is located? M. de Castro contracted for a fair grant south of Bexar – closer to the edge of the unsettled lands than I or my brother – would surely have advised . . . but still, a fair plot of land, on the Medina River. If they organize, protect themselves from the raiding Comanche as we did in the early days in Gonzales – they might very well make a success of it."

Hetty was already shaking her head, "Nae, the princeling and his friends with deep moneybags . . . so I have heard tell, from Mr. Ford no less – it was a grant from another set of scoundrels with a contract – a grant away out between the Llano and San Saba Rivers, extending as far west as . . . aweel, who knows?"

Margaret was so appalled upon hearing this that she sat down upon the edge of the unmade bed, the letter in her hand. "Prince Solms couldn't possibly be serious!" she exclaimed and Hetty nodded.

"A right pig in a poke, Marm!" she answered. "Ye know, there's some as ought not to be allowed out w'out a keeper, and it sounds like his high-and-mightiness might be one o'em."

Margaret said, and could not keep the wondering disbelief from her voice, "A grant and a settlement between the Llano and the San Saba; the Spanish had a fort and a mission, some seventy years ago. So the stories had it which my husband's friends from Bexar told us. James Bowie led a party of men there, near ten years ago, looking for the silver mines that were supposed to be out that way. There weren't any, of course. My husband often said to me that the Spanish were mad for searching out gold and silver mines; having found so many in Mexico they were convinced that they must be thick upon the ground everywhere else in their possessions. But there were none that any could find, at least not in Texas. That grant, if you heard aright, Hetty, and I am sure that you did; that grant of land would put them leagues into the Comanche hunting grounds. Has Prince Solms or any with his consortium ever laid eyes on those lands, or even set foot in Texas before this? The man must be a complete fool; does he pay heed to any sensible advice?"

Hetty shook her head, "I'm beginning to think not. Perhaps it is a good thing that Captain Hays saw fit to send the Young Sir w' the Prince on a long scout."

"We can always hope that nothing much will come of it all, if they are all such fools," Margaret said, "although I confess, I would like to be able to speak German now and again, as we did when I was a girl."

"You may yet get a chance, Marm. It was in the newspapers that came into Bullock's today, there was already a ship made port in Galveston Harbor, packed full of settlers for the Prince's grant and to hear them tell it in the taproom, there were three or four more ready to set sail from Germany within weeks." Hetty looked rather pleased. "It would be a grand thing for the Young Sir, though – being useful to the Prince and to all these poor folk, new to the country. Me Mam, I remember, she cried and cried for days when she first saw where we were going to live. If she could have, she would have gone straight back to Wexford, or even to New Orleans."

"My mother might have considered doing just that," Margaret said, "but Papa had already decided upon his land. Through some confusion over it,

Papa fought with Mr. Austin, and removed to Colonel DeWitts' and then to here. But Mama would never have said a word against his wishes. When I was a child, I thought of Texas as a veritable Garden of Eden, full of marvels and wonders. There was nowhere else that I would rather live, although I sometimes wished that my father had been more able to get along with his fellows. He might have been a man of greater consequence, thereby."

Margaret wiped a duster across the dressing table which sat in one of the new rooms, a room with a view over the apple trees to where the capitol of their Texas would soon arise, from a shambles of wood–plank shanties and rough log-built cabins. There would yet be a city there, as Bo Lamar had envisioned when he and Race had sat on the porch and envisioned a civilized, genteel place, with all the virtues and offices of a settled city. They were almost halfway to it, with the Legislature soon to meet again, and to swear in Dr. Jones as the new president at the turn of the year.

"Poor Papa," she said, almost as if to herself, "He had many fine qualities, Hetty – indeed, he did. Resolution, iron perseverance in time of trouble, skill with an ox-team and with propagating appletrees – and he had the wit to see what Texas would be . . . but so many flaws are laid to his account! Hot temper, unforgiving judgement, no clear-eyed ability to work with those with whom he did not agree to the glory of a higher purpose – so many virtues and yet so many faults, bound up in the person of a single soul! It was as if my mother was the other half to him, as if in her own person she tempered those faults. Do you believe that a marriage is like that, Hetty? A mingling from two persons of strengths and faults, each shoring up the weaknesses and faults of the other with their own virtues, as if fitting together in one loving whole?"

"I have not been married, or even wish to be, so I canna say." Hetty returned. "There may be something to what ye say; that it's two people, who must make a team of it, once yoked in harness; one may have a talent that the other may lack. In marrying, they may come to an agreement, but it must be amiable, or they will live at logger-heads wi'each other. Marm," and Hetty looked at her, very earnestly, "if ye e'er consider marriage again, make sure that it is an agreement ye come to – that ye both can live w'your strengths an' still be amenable an' comfortable to his own, what'ere they might be, and he can endure as a man an' humbly admit to yours. No' all that many as would marry under those conditions, an' that is a fact!"

"I do not think that I will marry again," Margaret answered, although that was counter to the old black witch's prophecy – that prophecy which she had put so much of her private belief upon!

Hetty only shrugged, saying, "Ye're a woman for a man, Marm. Ye might have the pick o'enny o'the gentry of Austin, an' even all of Texas, when the Legislature meets."

"I would rather marry an amiable friend, Hetty," Margaret answered. "I have not the luxury of an unbroken heart, merely one which has been carefully pieced back together and mended. The stress of tempestuous romance may be too great for it to bear. I have the boys to think of, after all. I do not need to marry for security."

"Aye." Hetty bundled up the dirty sheets taken from the bed which they had just remade. "You have many amiable gentlemen admirers, Marm. Just close your eyes and pick one, an' spare everyone else the suspense of wondering!"

"Henrietta Brigit Moylan," Margaret began in mock-indignation – oddly enough, it was as if she were twelve years old again and she and her school-fellow Edwina Brackett were teasing each other in whispers, while the attention of the young schoolmaster of San Felipe was safely distracted. "You should be struck down for being so forward and unladylike!"

"Aye well, I'm not a lady," Hetty answered sturdily. And she and Margaret went to sort out the next room.

Some weeks later, she received a second letter from her brother, as ill-spelled as the first, and her heart sank as she read the address; from Bexar – her brother had returned to the Rangers. The long scout with Prince Solms' enterprise was done, although Margaret was left in the dark about whatever conclusion her brother had reached regarding the viability of the Prince's Adelsverein project, either privately or officially in his capacity as Colonel Hay's emissary. From what Hetty had gleaned from gossip and relayed to Margaret, it seemed as if the whole project was headed straight for disaster, as a ship driven by the wind onto a rock-ribbed shore. Margaret set it aside, as she had other and more immediate matters to concern her attention.

The Legislature was going to meet in Austin once again, to the undisguised relief of all. Although Dr. Anson Jones – General Sam's political protégée – looked to be likely elected as the next president of Texas, there was no doubt at all that the Legislature and all of the offices of government would return. General Sam had given way with good grace, faced with the stubbornness of the good bourgeoisie of Austin. Perhaps were many in Texas who had decided in their own hearts – that a fair established capital city in the heart of Texas could not be abandoned, not without some embarrassment. It also appeared as if – under General Sam's canny guidance – the long-hoped-for annexation by the United States would come to pass. Margaret already had a fair gathering of paid guests, and promise of more in December, when the Legislature began gathering. She welcomed with great relief the turn of the year, when it was cool enough at night for a good warming fire in the boarder's parlor, when the last of the leaves on the apple trees dropped, leaving their bare and shapely branches etched against a blue sky, and the sycamores and cypress trees flamed gold and bronze and then dropped their own leaves in vivid pools of color upon the ground underneath. The last of the harvested apples were packed in sawdust in barrels, hopefully to remain fairly fresh and wholesome through the winter, and the dried apple quarters cut from the strings they had been threaded upon and packed away in boxes.

After a lifetime in Texas, Margaret relished autumn over every other season – for the relief of the summer heat, and for the beauty and bounty of the harvest season. In the absence of Alois Becker, her household butchered only one hog to fill the smokehouse and meet their own needs for a time. Daddy Hurst oversaw that effort with his usual tough capability. Margaret had once told him that he was a jack of all trades and a master of none, at which he had chuckled wryly at the vision of himself – 'dis ol' Nigra' was how he put it – as a master of anything. He was not quite the expert that Alois Becker had been, at hog-butchery or even overseeing the little left of the Becker's farming interests, but then very few were. Margaret felt that Daddy Hurst's efforts in those respects were well and above just about what anyone else might have been able to perform – and to her, quite satisfactory. She liked Hurst, for his pawky wit and the character of rough and gentlemanly honor that she sensed about him. She hoped that the Burnetts did not miss his capabilities in their establishment, although she was fairly sure that William did, much more than Liddy.

She was searching out the last of the potatoes in the garden on that Sunday afternoon, hoping there would be enough for the boarder's supper, and thinking about laundry on the following morning – the family laundry only, which she and Hetty would do. They had already begun sending the boardinghouse laundry in baskets to Mrs. Eberly's, as she and Hetty had decided between them that it was cheaper to send it to Angelina Eberly's establishment rather than hire another girl or two to see to it themselves. Very soon it would be time to start Sunday dinner; Margaret straightened with a groan from tumbling the potato hill with a short shovel, looking for fresh potatoes. She would have had the boys to assist her, but she could see Horace and Johnny walking through that lower pasture – which once had been Papa's cornfield – in search of their two milk cows. The cows undoubtedly had been grazing all through the lazy afternoon with others of their kind, notably Mrs. Simpson's small herd, favoring those places along Shoal Creek, a little way from the scattering of houses.

She shaded her eyes. There were her two boys, with Emma and Tommy Simpson; time for the afternoon milking, and to retrieve the cows from wherever they had wandered in search of good browse and shade, switching their tails lazily against the plague of late-season flies. Presently, with the milking done, Emma would come up to the sprawling house on top of the rise above the river and the eccentric sprawl of Austin, ready to put on a spotlessly clean white apron and help with serving the supper dishes. Margaret liked to think of how her house moved, apparently by clockwork, all in its appointed place at the correct time and season. Having everything properly organized made it seem effortless and graceful to the outsider. Margaret thought sometimes with interior amusement that it must be like seeing a duck or some other water-bird, gliding serenely across the still water, without having a glimpse of that frantic paddling underneath the surface which powered that seemingly effortless movement.

The boys would do the afternoon milking when they returned with the cows, Margaret thought – and she would continue digging for potatoes; really, it was not difficult deciding which she preferred to do, on a cool November afternoon. Hunting for potatoes in the rich earth was something like hunting for buried treasure. Presently, she would scrub her hands and fingernails clean, dress herself in her best black dress, and preside over the dining table. She decided long since, that no matter how much of a gentle lady she was and how her husband had trained her to be; she would never forget that she was the daughter of a stubborn and hardworking Dutch farmer. Peter and Jamie were helping Hurst, as he split wood for the evening fires, collecting chips and twigs for kindling as they scattered from the wood-block, or from underneath the cross-cut saw frame. She approved of this, although she sensed that many of her boarders did not. Her sons should not forget what it was like to work with one's hands, the better that they should appreciate the leisure and education which such labors had enabled them to possess.

It had long been Margaret's belief that folk like the Vinings of her husband's blood and family had been so long-established that they thought of a high position in society as only their right and due, something that fell upon them as simply as the morning sunshine did. They were thus accustomed to look with ready scorn on labor and those who performed it, never considering those ancestors who had made such a position possible several generations back. Margaret did not doubt for an instant that the original Vining must have had to do much the same work as her father had. Arriving on a strange shore, unpeopled save for hostile Indians, nothing but the rich soil and the urgency of providing for a family? Those early Vinings did what they needed to in those days – and since those days, they had taken such pride in having been first-arrived in a distant colony. How dared they dare look scornfully upon her, once their blood had run thin and they forgot the ways of their ancestors? Her sons should never fall into that trap, Margaret felt instinctively: they should never forget how to do things, even should Austin become as civilized and rarified a place as Boston.

She unearthed enough potatoes to half-fill the bushel-basket, taking a great deal of satisfaction in doing so. There would be enough for tomorrow's supper as well . . . she hefted the basket and carried them into the house, thinking that she ought to go in and put on her large apron to help Hetty in the kitchen until the boys returned with the cows for the afternoon milking. Where were the boys? They were taking a long time with the cows, and Margaret lingered on the back steps for a moment, savoring the cool late-afternoon breeze and the sight of the sun dropping low enough in the west to turn reaches of the Colorado to pure rippling silver. Faintly born upon the breeze were voices – shouts and cries, but at so far a distance that she could not be certain – they could be the voices of birds as they settled to their evening roosts in trees on the slopes of Mount Bonnell. She went to put the basket of potatoes in the kitchen, but her steps were arrested as she stepped over the threshold – was that not the voice of a child, calling faintly for "Mama?" She set down the basket just inside the kitchen and hastened outside, listening intently. Suddenly the afternoon seemed overtaken by a brooding quiet, and Margaret's heart sank, unaccountably. She knew in her bones that something was happening. At the woodpile Hurst set aside his ax upon seeing the expression on her face.

"Miz Vining, is dey somting de matter?"

"I am not sure, Hurst," she answered slowly. "Send the boys inside. There is a feeling in the air that I do not like. Suddenly everything is quiet, as if there is a storm brewing. " Even as Hurst shooed Peter and Jamie inside, first one of their milk cows and then the other appeared, trotting heavily and reluctantly into the farmyard, urged along by a breathless and pale Johnny. Margaret ran towards her son, her heart in her mouth,

"You shouldn't make the cows run, Johnny-love, it will spoil the milk," she said to him, looking at his face, which was flushed with the exertion of running – but his eyes were frightened. He couldn't speak for breathlessness, and she added, "Catch your breath, and tell me calmly, what is the meaning of all this?"

"Injuns!" he gasped. "Injuns – in the meadow by Shoal Creek. We saw them . . . they took . . ."

"Where is your brother?" Margaret demanded, her heart in her mouth for sudden apprehension. Horace, serious and responsible, clever and the image of his father, the love of her life – where was he? Taken? By whom? She knew the answer before Johnny caught his breath, still breathing so hard that he could scarcely form words between the effort of drawing air into his lungs.

"Comanche, Mama . . . they took Tommy and Emma from beside the creek. Horace is coming with Mrs. Simpson – she saw . . ." and then Johnny couldn't speak, and Margaret held her son to her and commanded Hurst, who was standing over them both.

"Ride to town and tell them to sound an alarm!" she commanded. "Take Bucephalus or any of the horses, just go and as fast as you may!" At that moment Horace stumbled into the farmyard, leading Mrs. Simpson by an arm around her waist. Her neighbor was distraught, hatless, and her hair tumbling out of the neat bun she ordinarily pinned it into, hanging like witch-locks around her face. Margaret's immediate sense of elated relief was countered by the desolate expression upon her neighbor's face, and the shocked horror upon her son's countenance.

"They took the children!" Mrs. Simpson exclaimed, and collapsed into Margaret's arms, "They took them – those horrible savages – and they are gone . . ." her words dissolved into a welter of wailing grief, so that she could hardly speak for it. Horace explained gravely, "We saw them from a short distance, Mama."

He was pale, yet his cheeks burned in bright spots from exertion. "Johnny and I went past the Simpson place, after the cows and Mrs. Simpson waved at us from the verandah. She said she had the takings from a bee-tree to share with you and while she was telling us, and fetching out a crock of honey, she told Tommy and Emma to go on ahead towards the meadow by Shoal Creek to bring in the cows, and likely that was where ours were. So we went after, and I told Mrs. Simpson that I would take the crock when we returned that way with our cows and we saw them, Mama – a little ahead of us, as we crossed the hilltop and looked down at the creekside below. Tommy and Emma were walking a little apart. And the cows, we could see the cows, you know how they bunch together when something distresses them – our cows and the Simpsons' and some others – and suddenly the birds, they burst out of the bushes, as if there was something like to frighten them. I took Johnny's hand as he was about to call to Tommy and Emma and I said, 'No, keep quiet – I think we should go back. I don't like the feel of this, there's something all wrong,' and just as I said this . . ."

Clinging to Margaret's hand like it was something to keep her from drowning, Mrs. Simpson cried out, as if she were in the depths of an agonizing childbirth. "They took them – they took my children, they are gone – oh, send for the men, for the ranger company to follow as soon and as fast as they may . . . Emma is of such an age . . . " Mrs. Simpson dissolved into such agonies of grief and concern that she could no longer speak coherently.

Margaret patted her hands, pleading for calm. "They will go at once. See, Hurst has already taken my husband's old horse without even bothering to saddle him! The men of the town will come, they will follow and get back your daughter and son."

She went on soothing Mrs. Simpson, who was so far gone in hysterical grief that her mouth twisted like the face of a tragic mask in one Race's old books. It was in the back of Margaret's mind that this might ultimately be a fruitless effort. What words could there be to comfort a woman upon the sudden and frightful loss of her children? The only time she had seen such emotions in her life before, was during the war for independence, when Erastus Smith – General Sam's chief of scouts and spies and a kindly, fatherly man – had taken it on himself to tell her parents that Rudi and Carl were dead in the mass executions at Goliad. Mama had been in just the same agony of grief, horrible to see and heart-rending to hear.

Hetty stood with a half-peeled potato on one hand and a kitchen knife in the other saying with resolute calm over the top of their heads, "I have told such gentlemen as are here at this time, what has happened. They will be ready in a moment. Lad, tell us sure, then; what did you see?"

"They came out of the brush," Johnny answered, his lip trembling. Johnny was sensitive and had been fearful as a child. He had outgrown the fear, but not the tender sensitivity. He was nearly the age of Tommy Simpson, a frequent playfellow. And Emma, who came to the house every afternoon, to help serve supper? Margaret's household would take this hard, very hard indeed.

Johnny continued, "On their horses, some of them and others with bows in their hands – and one of them – one of them on horseback, he leaned down and snatched Tommy by the neck of his shirt, and drew him up across the front of his saddle. Another took Emma, just reached down to take her around the waist, but she was fighting something fearful, screaming and kicking. I thought she might get away, as she is 'most grownup."

"I thought – as she was fighting so hard, she would win free very soon," Horace said miserably. "But they all went off in a terrible rush towards the peak of Mount Bonnell. There were many of them, I could see their blankets and feathers as they rode – they were all brave in war-paint. I didn't know that we could do anything, Mama, save run back to Mrs. Simpson's. When we told her, she wanted to go to where the cows were – where the Indians had taken Emma and Tommy and follow after them. I knew that wouldn't do any good. The Indians were already gone. We went a little way after them. The cows had scattered in fright, but ours came to us. I told Johnny to drive them home while I made Mrs. Simpson come with us to raise the alarm. So we did, Mama – and I think we did right, but . . ." Her oldest son hesitated. "Mama, I should have called out to Emma and Tommy, knowing that there was something wrong. I should have warned them, they are our friends. I should have done something. Even if that warning was too late and did no good – I knew there was something odd, when the birds burst from the trees and all was so quiet."

"You did nothing wrong," Margaret chose her words carefully. "God, who orders these earthly things – knows all hearts, and all ends. Chance and discretion saved you and Johnny. If you had not hung back and kept silent, who then would have raised a prompt alarm? I would have not been concerned for another half hour, at least. By that time, the Indians would have been miles from here."

She saw immediately that Horace was reassured by her words; his very expression was of resolve and determination. The rattle of the alarm drum rose from the direction of town, even as she heard the hoofbeats of a horse, ridden at a fast trot up the hill towards the front of the house. "Help me bring Mrs. Simpson to the family parlor," she murmured to Hetty. She turned, half-supporting the distraught Mrs. Simpson, as Captain Coleman rode into the stable yard, breathless and with his hunting coat hastily thrown on.

"I've got the word, and the boys are turning out. They'll be here in a minute or two, Mrs. Vining. We'll need your lad to go with us to show us where the children were taken. It'll save time, if we know where to start tracking. Although," and Captain Coleman's face was momentarily downcast, "we have only a few hours more of daylight in which to follow them with any assurance of success."

"As soon as Hurst returns with Bucephalus," Horace answered evenly.

Mrs. Simpson clutched at Captain Coleman's coat-sleeve, as Hetty began leading her inside the house. "Find my children!" she begged, "Find them, and bring them back – Tommy is only twelve and Emma . . . she's at the age when they would degrade her with the most unspeakably vile abuse!"

"We'll find them, and return them to you," Captain Coleman answered steadily. "You have my word upon it – we will do our best." Margaret noted that there was little confidence in his expression. Those were comforting words to a woman in an agony of distress for the fate of her children. The Indians had already half-an hour's lead on the men of Austin's ranging volunteers. On fast horses they would be miles away, even before Captain Coleman's volunteers gathered up their weapons, saddled their horses, and rode in hot pursuit.

There was another horse coming up the hill now, the sleek and long-legged form of Bucephalus with Hurst clinging gamely to his back, as nimbly as an Indian himself. Horace straightened himself and squared his young shoulders, an oddly adult expression of determination on his face. He called across the yard.

"Hurst – would you saddle Bucephalus now, and prepare him for me to ride with Captain Coleman and the others? I must go to show the exact place where Emma and Tommy were taken and the direction that the Indians went up Mount Bonnell. And," Horace added, in a tone of voice that resonated with decision. "Mama, I will ride with them as long as I am needed. Bucephalus is old, but he is still fast. I will be thirteen, this very month, Mama. I am old enough to ride with the men, as far as they will go."

Margaret felt as if she had been struck at the heart. She wanted to forbid this, instantly, instinctively; but Horace had asked it, with such sober consideration and resolve. He was a year older than Tommy, a year younger than Emma – and he had spent so much of his life at hazard! Ever since she and Race had come to Waterloo-that-was, on the very edge of the frontier, his life and existence as the son of his father, educated and bookish, had been imperiled by the constant threat of raids by the Comanche. Death or captivity, one or the other; Margaret could not forget how Horace and Johnny had stepped up and loaded for her and Mrs. Eberly when the Comanche raiding party had come to town and been bluffed away by Captain Coleman's brazen pretense of military superiority. Her husband had wished so much that his sons be educated and cultured. He and Margaret hoped that Austin would be a city of advantages and refinement before the boys were very much older. That very hope had kept them here for so long; Race's failing health not permitting them to start again elsewhere.

She recalled the words she had said to Maggie Darst at the camping place at the McClure's on Pecan Creek, on that day after Gonzales had been burned at General Sam's order. Young Davy Darst had gone to General Sam to ask to be enlisted in his tiny, desperate army, although he was only fourteen. *"Our boy-children are not torn from our arms,"* she had told his frantic mother, on that occasion." *They go willingly, wishing to be counted as men. And to be a man, a gentle perfect knight . . . that is a commendable thing to be, and that is what our sons long to become! How can they not, when there are so many splendid examples around them, to emulate and follow?"*

Horace was old enough to be taken by the Comanche, on the cusp of being kept alive as a useful captive or killed by them, thinking him to be of the age of a fighting warrior. Well then; old enough to be the fighter and defender of his family, of his family's land and holdings, old enough to take a musket, a carbine in hand.

Margaret looked at her son and answered with a resolve in her voice that masked her true feelings, "Then take your Opa's shotgun with you and the Mexican dragoon pistol that he had from San Jacinto. I will have Hetty pack some hardtack and cheese and dried jerky for you. You may be many days on the trail. Take your warm coat, and I will see that Hurst will saddle Bucephalus with a good blanket. Gather your things now, and Hurst will see to your being ready to go with the company."

Margaret prided herself on how resolute and fearless she sounded at that moment, a woman of Spartan resolve, although inside she felt as if she would howl just as poor Mrs. Simpson was now wailing in the parlor. When the men assembled in the farmyard, breathless and frantic, having been torn at a moments notice for their workaday business, Horace was among them, a slight but confident figure. It relieved Margaret immeasurably that a watchful Hurst rode among them too, mounted on one of William Burnett's fine Kentucky mules, although Margaret could not decide if Hurst was nominating himself to the volunteer company to better keep a watchful and guardian eye on her son or on William Burnett.

Chapter 17 – *Lost Children*

It was as Margaret had feared all afternoon and evening, long after sunset, even though she hung lanterns from the edge of the verandah and listened with every fiber of her being, as she and the younger boys and Dr. Williamson ate a lonely supper, attended by Hetty in the almost-empty dining room. The other boarders had gone with the searchers. Dr. Williamson alone remained, as he had been asked to attend a patient in town whose condition did not amend until nearly sundown. He had no horse, being accustomed to ride Bucephalus on those occasions when he had need of one. He looked at Margaret with an expression of deep concern on his face, so much that Margaret was moved to reassure him regarding her own state of mind. Dr. Williamson was so good and trusty a friend and she hoped to relieve something of the distress for her that he so obviously felt.

"My son is with Captain Caldwell and some brave and trusty men of the town – I am certain they will not allow harm to come to him."

The distress on his face eased a trifle, and Margaret thought again of how good a friend he had been to Race and herself all these years – and of her words to Hetty about preferring to marry a friend, rather than risk her own heart, her peace of mind and the welfare of her sons, in marrying in a mood of irrational passion, as so many women seemed to think appropriate – either that, or in a cold-blooded assessment of a man as potentially a good and stable provider. The doctor was a good and kindly man. In his letters from Perote and in hers to him, they had shared so many confidences. Margaret was assured that the doctor deserved so much more that what life had so far allotted to him. Perhaps she should marry someone such as he was, but her mind quailed from that thought; that she would marry for cold calculation, after she had known passionate love and the melding of two kindred souls. A marriage for friendship would seem like a diet of dry bread and water, compared to a rich feast. As fond as she was of the doctor, she was repelled at the thought of treating him so.

Upon being assured of her own relative peace of mind, Dr. Williamson took himself off to tend the next-most distressful female in the household. He very kindly fixed a heavy sedative draught for Mrs. Simpson, and she lay sleeping in her clothes in one of the guest bedrooms, for Margaret did not think it advisable that she should go to her own home . . . not alone on this dangerous evening, most certainly not to spend the night in a house where every object should remind her of that sudden and shattering loss. Should

Emma and Tommy be found and restored to their mother, the volunteers would bring them to Margaret's house. But as more time passed – the more quarter-hours that dragged past, measured by the ticking hands of the tall clock in the hallway – the more it became sadly clear to Margaret that Emma and Tommy Simpson were gone beyond rescue. It was already full dark, the silvery orb of the moon just swinging above the dark shapes of the trees outside. She and Hetty were washing up the last of the supper dishes when they heard the sounds of horses in the farmyard, the jingling of tack and spurs that signaled the riders were not Indians. She unbarred and opened the door to see her son and Hurst, under the faint light of a lantern hung from a bracket by the back door. William Burnett sat still on his horse at the edge of that pale circle of gold painted by the lights of her house and the glory of the autumn stars in the sky with Orion swinging low, the stars of his sword-belt as clear as any other.

"They haven't found them," William Burnett confessed wearily, "although we saw them from a distance . . . and God help us, the children, we think. But we lost the trail over the top of Mount Bonnell – not for lack of daylight, but for all the stones and gravel at the peak. Captain Caldwell and the rest have camped at the place where they lost the trail in hopes of continuing at first light from that place. Hurst and I were sent to bear that message, and to see your son safely home, although – to young Master Vining's credit – he did wish to continue. But he is not a trained soldier, and having already done his duty . . . everyone thought it best. I don't know how I shall have the fortitude to break this to Mrs. Simpson."

"She is sleeping. Dr. Williamson was kind enough to fix something for her so that she could sleep. Come in and have a bite of supper." Margaret offered, and William Burnett demurred, saying that his Liddy would have already made arrangements for his late meal. Margaret could not help but notice that he looked immensely relieved upon being spared the duty of bringing such indeterminate and disheartening news to Mrs. Simpson. Poor man; William Burnett was kindly intended, but Mrs. Simpson was not a stoic. Margaret knew already that she would take bad news so very ill that any man not absolutely heroic in his toleration of feminine vapors would take to his heels or at least seize on any reason to withdraw gracefully from having to perform such a duty.

After seeing to poor, faithful Bucephalus, Horace and Hurst fell gratefully upon those leftovers served up to them at opposite ends of the kitchen table, relating the details of their fruitless search between ravenous bites.

The company had gone immediately to the place where Horace and Johnny had seen the cows browsing on that gentle autumn afternoon, in the meadow by Shoal Creek, as Horace and Hurst related the account of events disjointed between consumption of supper. At the place where the cows had been pastured, where Emma and Tommy were abruptly stolen away, the earth was torn up by the hoofs of a dozen and more unshod horses; the damp soil revealed many prints of moccasin-shod feet. They found Tommy's straw hat where it had fallen into the midst of a grape-tangle, and one of Emma's shoes . . . and distressingly, part of the torn sleeve of the dress she had been wearing, some distance farther up along the clear trail to the top of Mount Bonnell. They had even fleetingly seen the war-party, heading with breathless speed up to the summit, and had redoubled their frantic efforts. Horace insisted that he had seen a flash of Emma's blue calico dress, and the tumble of her light brown hair; Margaret thought that might have been a hopeful exaggeration, but Hurst averred that he and all the others of the pursing force had seen the same. And then the clear trail dissolved into the tumbled gravel and stones at the summit, just as the sun dropped below the horizon. Where it continued among the timbered slopes of the other side, was any man's guess in the dark.

"Captain Caldwell said that he would camp with the men at the top and follow in the morning," Horace explained. "He thought he could pick up the trail down the opposite slope as soon as it was proper light after sunrise and carry on. He said I had been a help, leading them to the exact spot, but . . ." he looked down at his plate and said, "I thought we'd be able to catch up to them, Mama. I thought we'd get Emma and Tommy back." His expression was desolate, and the tone of his voice just as so. "We followed them so fast, Mama. I was certain of it."

"But they were faster still," Margaret answered. "That is not to any lack of yours, or of our men – it is just that they have at least three-quarters of an hour lead, and if they travel in darkness, that will put them ahead of all but the fastest riders and the best trackers."

"What will happen to Tommy and Emmy, if we don't find them soon?" Horace asked, and Margaret saw the flash in Hurst's eyes. No, the Negro serving man knew what happened to children – and men and women alike, taken by a Comanche raiding party. But it was not his place to answer, at Margaret's kitchen table. That was for her to say.

"I don't know," she answered carefully at last. "But I can promise you this – there will be no stone unturned to get them back. Captain Caldwell will take up this with the government, and with the Indian agents – and those at the trading posts, known for doing business with the Indians. Those children taken – we will get back. This is the capital city of Texas; what does it say against the honor of this state, that children or any other going about their business of a day might be taken suddenly captive without any answer from our government? This is an insult against Texas, and we are a proud people. We do not brook insults of this kind, Horace. Always remember that."

"Yes, Mama," her son answered meekly, and Hurst did not say a word. Margaret thought from the way that Hetty rolled her eyes as she poured cream off the top of the milk pans set out after the afternoon milking – that the expression on her own countenance must have been what Hetty called her "Maeve-face," imperious and queenly.

When Carl appeared at her house late in December Margaret asked him the same question that her son had asked. As usual, Carl appeared without a word of warning or anything other than turning that ill-tempered grey horse of his into the pasture and dropping his coat and saddlebags in the kitchen, where Margaret and Hetty were baking cakes and gingerbread for the Christmas celebrations. Margaret asked it privately, in a moment when Hetty was out in the smokehouse fetching in the succulently smoked ham for the supper which Margaret would serve on Christmas Day, along with a well-roasted stuffed turkey and a braised beef-brisket.

"The children of our neighbor, Mrs. Simpson. were taken last month by a Comanche or Waco raiding party." She said abruptly, as her brother ate as if he had not had a good meal for six months. "Sit up straight, Carlchen – and use your fork. You eat with the manners of a starving refugee. Captain Caldwell and the others followed the trail, up over Mount Bonnell – but they lost it over a patch of gravel and rock and could not recover it, no matter how much they searched."

"Prolly lost it, through mucking up the trail with their own tracks." Carl answered indistinctly. Margaret commanded again, "Don't speak with your mouth full, Carlchen. Horace saw the children taken. Through good fortune and chance, he and Johnny were a little distance behind when Emma and Tommy were captured."

"Oh?" her brother looked up at her over a forkful of sausages and potato. "Emma – is that the girl who was waiting on the table, the last time I was here? Pretty girl, greenish eyes and light-brown hair, the color of cypress leaves in the fall?"

"Yes – that was her," Margaret answered sadly. "Search as they could for the children, and they searched for days, some of them, as the time away from their business allowed; there was never any trail or clue found, save one of her shoes and a piece of her dress and her brother's hat. Their mother asked again and again, most piteously, what would become of them."

"I will tell you straight, then," her brother answered, following upon a swallow of what was in his mouth. "They will be whores or slaves, if they survived over a day or so. If they see promise in the boy – a warrior, if they do not think he is too old. They like 'em to be young and easy molded to their ways. Otherwise, just as I have said; Sold to the high bidder, if the price is right and they have gotten all the use from them that they want. I expect," he added, as he took an ostentatious forkful from his plate, "that may not be what you wanted to hear, or tell to her mother."

"Emma was fighting them," Margaret said, feeling sick at the bottom of her stomach. "She was resisting, and fighting, even as they took her."

"Good," Carl answered. "They may have killed her straightaway. All for the best, considering what they commonly do to captives."

Margaret thought back to those days right after the capture of Emma and Tommy. Captain Caldwell and the other volunteers had returned after a long day of fruitlessly searching the tumbled thickets and heights on the far side of Mount Bonnell for a clear trail, or any trace of the children – any more scraps of their clothing, a line of broken branches, the marks of unshod hooves scouring the ground – and found none. Tommy and Emma had vanished with their captors into thin air. Mrs. Simpson had listened to their halting accounts and their painfully-expressed regrets with a face of stone, spurning even Margaret's sympathy. She had thanked Margaret for her hospitality, Dr. Williamson for his care, and the men of Austin for their determination, in as cold a voice as ever masked depths of pain deeper than the deepest well, and walked back to her empty house, even spurning offers from Margaret and Mrs. Eberly to accompany her. Margaret would have gone with her anyway, but for Angelina Eberly catching her elbow.

"No, dearie. Leave her be – she's not a woman for sympathy now. She's too proud to weep for herself in front of everyone."

"She shouldn't be alone!" Margaret protested, seeing Mrs. Simpson's straight, calico-clad back, her head (hatless, since she had rushed away from her house on the day the children were taken, thinking nothing of custom or sheltering her complexion from the sun) vanishing down the hill towards the lonely dog-trot cabin. She could hear the distant miserable lowing of the cows, which had not been milked that day or the day before. Now Tommy and Emma would not be there to help her with that chore. It broke Margaret's heart a little, to think of that; a woman suddenly bereft, and the misery of spurning offered help.

Angelina Eberly patted Margaret's hand. "Don't you fret, Miz Vining. I'll go along myself in a little while, and mebbe send one o' my girls to help. It will take time, for her to recover herself. Them first days of it is the worst, as I expect you should know. It don't much get better with time, but you do get so as to be able to face folk and bear up. We'll do what we can for her. Lands' sake, I don't know where I'd get milk for butter for the guests if it weren't for her! Give her a bit, Miz Vining, she'll come round, and I think for sure Dr. Jones and the government, they'll put out the word. We'll get them back."

"Our President in petticoats," Margaret had said then, somewhat comforted by Mrs. Eberly's robust good sense. "Whose rule is wise, generous, and just!" At that, the Widow Eberly had patted her hand again and laughed, even though the fear was in both of their minds that Mrs. Simpson would not long tolerate the solitude in that house which had been the home for her children and the keystone of her enterprise in Austin.

Their fears were soon proved to have a basis. Within a week, Mrs. Simpson sold some of her cows and used the money to hire men to drive the rest to Bastrop, where her oldest boy was working for her brother. She made no bones about leaving Austin as soon as she could. Margaret had been right about her not being able to endure living in a house in a place which constantly reminded her of the loss of her youngest children, around every turn, and upon every glance at the hills, and the meadows where Tommy and Emma had seen to pasturing the cows.

Mrs. Simpson packed up a few things from her house into a trunk and rode away on a freight-wagon taking a load of cypress logs to the sawmill, with the trunk sitting on top of the logs, and herself on the wagon seat, not looking back at Austin, her friends who had come to bid her farewell, or to the eminence of Mount Bonnell . . . that height where Tommy and Emma had last been seen alive.

Now Margaret wondered, as she and Hetty bustled about in the kitchen which was the basis for her own enterprise, and not for the first time, about what her brother had experienced in all those years of being a Ranger and a soldier, those things which had put such a hard and defensive shell upon him. After one of her serious 'thinks' on this topic, she realized perhaps such a shell was essential to the survival of the happy and gentle-souled little boy he had once been.

"You should think about marrying, Carlchen," she said abruptly. "Marrying and settling down, with your own family. You're of an age to consider it. Most men your age already have done so. Unless they are confirmed and dedicated bachelors, more in love with the lure of adventure and the company of their own kind."

"No," he shook his head and swallowed another mouthful. "I'm not one of those fellers – I like girls fine."

"Do you have one, in particular, Carlchen?" she asked, hardly daring and almost apprehensive of the answer, for he looked at once cheerful and then melancholy, as he lifted another fork of sausage and potatoes from the plate. "Tell me about her, if you will. Do you love her, and are you and she of a mind to marry?"

"High-bred Mex, in Bexar," he answered indistinctly. "No, I don't love her. I like her fine though. She turns heads all over Bexar – and she ain't a whore, M'grete." Suddenly he looked quite embarrassed. "She's already married to a connection of the Veramendi. Older 'n her, o'course. Don Erasimo – a rich man w' a big house in Bexar and a grand *rancho* in the de Leon grant, an' of the – what he called '*limpieza de sangre.'* He took up w' me because I talked the old language. German – he wanted to speak it himself again, mebbe teach it to Dona Inez. They're friends to me, both in a way. It's odd enough, Jack said. He jokes about it; says I am the ladies' pet. But he has met Dona Inez, so I cannot think what he means to imply about her in saying that."

"I am not quite sure I want to hear any more," Margaret answered after a moment. "But if she is honestly and happily married, you should not be paying her particular attentions, Carlchen. You might be tempting her from her marriage vows, no matter how indulgent a husband might be towards an innocent friendship."

Her brother mumbled something that sounded suspiciously like, 'not all that innocent,' which Margaret strenuously pretended not to have heard. "Nonetheless," she continued, "When you have found a girl that you seriously intend to court, you should let me know of it. Mama left a small thing of hers, in trust to me for a woman who would be your wife – a family heirloom and not to be disposed upon some light-o-love," she added severely, and for a brief moment he looked as chided as he had when he was a small boy, a boy easily lifted into her arms.

"Yes, M'grete," he said, consciously mimicking a small child, with such an exaggerated air of meekness that they both laughed and Margaret continued, "A nice girl, Carlchen – of whom Mama would have approved, who would make you happy. Now, I meant to ask you, what came of this business with the Prince of Solms and Braunfels, with his entrepreneur scheme to bring folk from the old country to Texas?"

Her brother shook his head, as he began lifting more forkfuls of sausage and potato towards his mouth. He was careful, though, to chew and swallow between answers. "Nothing came of it, M'grete. So I reported to Jack. The prince was a fool – the worst kind of fool, the kind with money and powerful friends, living in a fool's little world, where all is pleasant and agreeable, an' no one says aught to counter what everyone in it believes and says, so everyone goes on believing it. He'll strand a lot of other poor innocent fools in the way of a Comanche raiding party and Jack says of course it will then be all our fault, for not protecting them poor greenhorns in their settlement – all the way out between the San Saba and the Llano, assuming they get that far. Don't know what else we could have done, except hope and pray someone with a bigger ration of sense will replace him. He's seen to buying a tract of land in the uplands north of Bexar to start a settlement on. Pretty place – they call it the Fountains, little bitty branch runs out from it to the Guadalupe. Don Erasimo was chortling about that when I talked to him last week in Bexar. The Veramendis skint him good an' proper on the sale. Wonder the Prince had his shirt and trousers left, let alone any money, after they got through with him." Carl looked at her very earnestly. "D'ye know, the Prince has to have two valets help him on with his trousers of a morning? I saw it, myself. Dunno how many Bexar lawyers it took for them to skin them off him! More than two, I reckon. Any roads, it seems that he has three or four chartered ships at Galveston, arrived with his settlers. If they have any sense, they'll walk away from the Verein the minute they set foot in Texas. Mebbe to Mr. Castro, on his grant on the Medina – he's a man with sense. Sense enough to ask for help, when he realizes that he needs it."

"Anyway," he continued, after scraping his plate clean, "I'm done with the Prince of Solms and whatever, and all his works. Jack asked me to stick by him just long enough to find out what he's about, and if he has any chance at all. My word to Jack is that if that Adelsverein enterprise succeeds, it will be in spite of him. Besides, the word is there'll be trouble with Mexico in the spring, with all this annexation talk. That's more my business than being that fool's bear-leader. This time – since the war-talk is in all earnest – most likely it is true. Tell you what, M'grete," and her little brother looked at her, his eyes the sunny blue of the skies and a look of quiet but eager satisfaction in them. "I'd like to be shed of those Mex bandit raids over our border once and for all. I'd like to see them in their gold-braid uniforms settled, all humble and meek, never daring to set a toe over the Nueces again. I'd like to see Santa Anna an' General Cos an' the rest of them – every Mex who ever set foot in Texas with warlike intent – up before a wall in front of a firing squad for what they did to ours at Saltillo and Goliad, and ever' place else."

"Have a care, Carlchen," Margaret answered crisply. "Not every 'Mex' – as you say – in our Texas was a Centralist creature. What of Don de Leon, of Senator de Zavala, of Juan Seguin, and your Don Erasimo, and poor Esteban Menchaca? They fought for our nation, served gloriously, and some of them died just as gloriously."

"Mebbe," he said, and Margaret realized with a pang that once again, she and her brother had been speaking English to each other, as if the old language was a quaint old habit which they had long outgrown with the passing of Papa. "I feel bad about Juan Seguin – he was one of ours, tried and true, an' a true friend to General Sam 'til all that new trash drove him out of San Antonio. "

"He and his horsemen guarded us all the way," Margaret said, deep in remembering of the tall and courtly man who had been Race Vining's good friend and commanded the company of Bexar horsemen who had covered the retreat of Sam Houston's army – and the helpless train of women who had followed in their wake – all the way into East Texas. There had been many new settlers come to Texas and San Antonio in the half-dozen years after San Jacinto, many of them ignorant of the honorable service done by men such as Juan Seguin in the brief and bitter war against Santa Anna and his Centralists. To them it was an old fight, hardly worth consideration, and stalwart settlers of Mexican blood, long established in Tejas – such as the de Leons and Juan Seguin – were hastily and brutally lumped in with those who had sided with Santa Anna.

Margaret was pulled back from her recollections of those days in Gonzales, when she and her husband had extended hospitality to Juan and his cousins, the Menchaca brothers, by the voice of her brother saying, "They say that Colonel Seguin came back to San Antonio with Woll's army as a scout and guide. That didn't win him any new friends."

"He was forced into it, I am certain," Margaret answered with assurance. Her husband's dear friend could not, would not have turned traitor otherwise to his friends of the Federalist cause, his comrades in war, many of whose bodies had been burned in huge pyres along the Alameda, the road to the Powderhouse Hill, after the fall of the Alamo. Upon his return to San Antonio after the victory at San Jacinto, it was Juan Seguin who had gathered up all the cold ashes and bones, in accordance with a vow that he had taken. There was a marble tomb in the San Fernando church containing such remains as he had been able to find – the very church from whose tower and by Santa Anna's order, the dreaded 'no quarter' banner had been flown. It was an ugly, dark little church, so her husband had often told her, but the stumpy bell-tower was the tallest height anywhere around. "His enmity towards Santa Anna and the Centralist faction was everlasting – but the demands and suspicions of the new Texians left him nowhere else to go, other than over the border to his kindred, only to have himself and his family held hostage by the vile dictator, Santa Anna. I believe in my soul, Carlchen – that there is a special place in Hell for those who force others to betray their true friends."

Under her gaze, her younger brother shrugged and looked towards his plate, which was now near to empty. "I'd like some more sausage and potato and egg, M'Grete."

"Do you never have a good meal, in all those times you are away from this roof?" Margaret demanded as she gestured towards the hovering Hetty, who immediately put the smallest of the heavy iron pans onto the stovetop again.

"It never tastes as good," Carl answered. Hetty beamed and Margaret said, "And that is another reason to see to settling down with a roof of your own, Carlchen – so that you may have a good meal more often than every six months or so! What about Papa's town-lots? You could build a house on one of them and take up a trade!"

"I dunno at what," her brother answered. "An' I said before, I don't want anything of his, not now or ever. I don't like towns 'r settled places, M'grete. Too . . . to crowded. Noisy. I have land certificates – I'll call them in when I have a good mind to."

"And when will that be?" Margaret demanded, trying to keep a note of weary cynicism from her voice, and her brother smiled at her, as sunny and placid as ever.

"After we settle the Mexes again. They'll be madder 'n wet hens when Texas joins the United States, depend on it. Jack an' me, we'll go with the Rangers, as always."

"There'll be something else after that," Margaret said. A kind of bleak weariness fell upon her. "Some other great emergency for the Rangers to ride for. You'll go on, and on, and on. There will always be some excuse. And then you'll be taken captive or killed in some meaningless, endless skirmish, and buried in an unmarked grave and I will only know my brother is dead if I chance to read of it in the newspapers, months afterwards."

"Maybe," Carl scraped the plate with his fingers, and licked from them the last crumbs of bacon fat, and egg, and bits of crunchy fried potato. "Sooner that than be killed on my own doorstep by the Comanche, minding my own business." He looked at her with bland expression, which overlaid a world of bitter experience and added, "Or have my children stolen away from me. No one should have to bear that, M'grete. Which is why I do what I do, and Jack and the others. I do not mind the Comanche living as they will out in the Llano, but that they see such as your friend Miz Simpson as persons that they make free upon, to rob and slaughter at will, for mischief or gain, without retribution? No." and her brother's face hardened, into that determined and soldier-like mask which she had noted once before – the day that he had pulled their father's hands from around her throat. "We will not bear that, M'grete. If they will not cease from raiding into our settlements, they will have exacted upon them every kind of retribution that we can bring to bear. That is our sworn duty; blood for blood, eye for eye."

"Have a care that you are not eventually rendered eyeless, little brother," Margaret answered at last. "I think you have been too long about this appointed duty. Be careful that you do not become what you have fought so long against."

She thought, from the slight flinch of his countenance, that her verbal shot might well have hit home. He and their brother Rudi had never been reflective, given as she was to sit and consider matters seriously and thoroughly, unraveling them as a woman does with a hank of yarn full of tangles, although Carl had sometimes seemed to evince more of this introspection than Rudi. Of people, and their thoughts, and the way they did what they might be moved to do – of all these things, Margaret was accustomed to consider. Sometimes she thought that she could read a person as well as she could one of her husband's books. It was all so very easy, once you sat down and carefully considered it all; what you knew of a person, from what they said, and of actions observed, drawn from that deep well of knowledge. People were simple and obvious creatures; once you had at least some month's acquaintance of them, their habits and their thinking, as revealed in casual bits of conversation – why then, their characters and method of thinking were laid very plain. Margaret thought that might account for her success as a boarding-house keeper. Of course, she must admit plainly and to herself, this skill had sometimes failed her as in the case of Mr. Hattersley. And her misjudgment of Mr. Hattersley paled next to the catastrophic betrayal of her trust in her husband. There had been such warning signs as she should have been able to clearly see, but she had been so besotted with love and adoration for him, certain in her own mind that the bonds of love and marriage between them were both original and everlasting.

The intelligence that Race Vining had married in Boston, to another woman whom he had long held in affection, had a child with her, long before he had ever come to Texas, and wooed and married her – that came as a shattering blow to Margaret. In one awful hour, her trust in her husband had been utterly destroyed, after ten years of a loving marriage. Worse than that – her trust in her own judgement of character had been shaken to the point of doubting the veracity of any man claiming to hold her in affection. If she had not been able to trust the husband of her own heart, the father of her children, whom could she trust? She was no more than a silly girl, easily seduced and abandoned. Better to wear widow's weeds, and run a boardinghouse, than to allow another man close enough to entrust her heart and the welfare of her sons to his care.

Still, she recollected how she had exchanged such affectionate letters with Dr. Williamson during his imprisonment in Perote – how pleased that he had appeared, upon returning to her household. She considered again, as she had before, if she should encourage Dr. Williamson to propose marriage to her, even though she was certain she did not love him. As her brother said of his light of affections in Bexar; she did not love him, but she liked him fine. And Margaret admitted with a sigh – no one here in Austin would envy her in the least for possessing the affections of a man as graceless and awkward as the Doctor.

Chapter 18 – *Very Welcome Guests*

It seemed to Margaret most particularly, that Christmas – the tenth Christmastide that her family had celebrated since coming to Waterloo – was one of the merriest and most joyous of all. Austin was reviving again, with the promise of being the capital of the state upon annexation – even if that might bring on another war with Mexico. Angelina Eberly, the Bullocks, and all of her neighbors who had hung on through the bitter times felt vindicated and relieved, having lived through the worst days. They could now see the line of bright sunshine under the edge of the dark cloud passing overhead. A war with Mexico was a threat they had been living under since Margaret's oldest son was an infant.

"Today's troubles are enough for today," Margaret said to Hetty as they set the table for Christmas dinner. This time, the dining room table, with all the leaves in it, augmented by a number of wide planks set on saw-horses – she had decreed to be set out in the wide central hallway. "And it is Christmas Day, so we can put off thinking about troubles for a while!"

Margaret intended to celebrate the season in the grand style of her dreams: the table itself and added planks were covered with fine white cloths, and surrounded by every single chair in the house, even those brought down from the guest and family bedrooms. The white-covered expanse of the table top was plainly ornamented by cut greenery, gilded pinecones, and garlands of the mountain laurel berries. Carl and her sons had brought out the tables and boards, brought down the chairs from the upstairs rooms unaided, for Daddy Hurst had asked – somewhat apprehensively – for leave to spend the holiday in the Burnett's household with his son and friends in the Burnetts' servant's quarters. Margaret gave permission, hiding her annoyance that Hurst would not be there to assist at a time when she would need him. But one of her new boarders, a colleague of Dr. Williamson's, a Dr. Harper, gave permission for his own slave and personal attendant to be available to Margaret for such heavy work outside as she thought fit to pay him for. Mose was a huge sullen mountain of a lad, quite dark of complexion, and Margaret thought sometimes that he was not terribly intelligent and she certainly would not have trusted him as well as she trusted Daddy Hurst, but Mose ably filled in with the outside chores, bringing in wood, and taking care of her guests' horses. Margaret even saw him smile once or twice, when she had offered him some small courtesy and words of thanks such as she was accustomed to tendering towards Daddy Hurst, so she was somewhat reassured. Still, Dr.

Harper's Mose was not someone she would have willingly hired. In his person and mien, he provided ample demonstration of how slaveholders might have cause for secretly fearing their human cattle.

"Oh, 'tis grand, Marm!" Hetty said at last as they stood back, admiring their handiwork. "Mam would hae been proud – them at the castle couldn't have done any better!"

"Well, it could, if we had more silver and gold plate." Margaret replied, pleased at once by Hetty's enthusiasm, and slightly deprecating. The table-dressings that she had; candlestick holders, tazzas filled with fruit – oranges, nuts, and pineapples, and vases filled with greenery, winter-berries and wax flowers . . . all those adornments themselves were mostly of plain frontier make. The largest candelabra and several of the smaller were of Mexican silver and gleamed as brightly as they could, from Hetty rubbing and polishing away every scrap of tarnish with fine wood-ash. For this occasion, they were filled with candles of fine pure beeswax, which would burn clean and without any smoke, scenting the room with the faintest odor of honey – rather than the cheap tallow candles which burnt sullenly and melted into pools of rancid-smelling beef fat.

With the return of some slight portion of prosperity, Margaret had considered what would make the best return on an investment of a portion of her profits, considering that she must make at least as good an appearance of refinement and luxury as did the Bullocks and Angelina Eberly. She bought some fine pieces of New Orleans-made furniture for the best guest bedrooms, thirty full settings and a number of serving dishes of good English china, and the same of delicately-engraved Irish crystal glasses and decanters, for use at her table for fine suppers such as this one. She paid the import duty on it all, almost without flinching. Of ordinary glass tumblers she had a plenty, the good and the best – all gleaming and clean, the plain plate forks, knives, and spoons all polished to as near a degree as the silver. Under candlelight, it would be a sublime sight – and one that Margaret was sure would not be soon forgotten in Austin. Among her guests tonight would be Dr. Anson Jones, now elected president of Texas, and at a last minute – General Sam himself. He had appeared in Austin that very afternoon, in a trap driven by a smiling Negro bondsman, the General's rugged yet magnetically charming countenance beaming at her over an armful of parcels.

"My dear Mrs. Vining!" he greeted her, as she answered an energetic knock upon the front door, only remembering at the last minute that Hetty had commanded her not to answer the door herself but allow herself or one of the hired girls to do so. "Like the Greeks, I come bearing gifts, but at the command of my dearest Maggie Lea to deliver them personally!"

"General!" Margaret's heart lifted. That was the emotion that he aroused among his friends and even of those who counted most often as his political enemies. Few could resist the pull of his regard on their hearts – he whom nearly all resident in Texas had owed their continuing existence there to his perspicuity and courage. "You are welcome indeed, with or without gifts. Is Margaret with you? I had so long wished to see her again!"

"No, alas – she is not – her health and disinclination to travel kept her from accompanying me. This time in earnest and to her distress – for she dearly wished also to see you again and the improvements you have made to your household. I am charged to give a full report to her upon my return, just as I am charged with conveying her best wishes and affection, along with her gifts! This largest is from her to you, Mrs. Vining – she took great care with it, and made me promise to give it into the hands of no one but yourself upon arrival!"

"You are welcome in any case." Margaret said again. "And as a friend, at least as much as a guest. The children had their first sight of our Christmas tree last night and opened such gifts as we had for them – but they will be glad of another installment."

"A Christmas tree?" General Sam's face lit up in boyish delight. "You celebrate the season in the latest style, Mrs. Vining!"

"It was the custom among my family," Margaret answered, and she took several of the parcels from the General, including the large, folio-shaped one, which she could tell was a book of some sort – feeling as she did when in his company, divided in her respect for him as one of the great men of Texas, for his consideration and affection as a dear friend . . . but his decision to call the meeting of the Legislature to a place other than Austin had done great harm to her friends here. Many folk such as Angelina Eberly were still angry over how the General had ruthlessly commanded that all be laid waste in the wake of his army's retreat in the bitter year of the rebellion against Mexico.

Even so, Margaret was contented with having General Sam and his wife as the friends of her household, to remember her husband and her father to General Sam and – should the occasion ever require it – to recommend the service of her brother and her sons to him. Had General Sam not claimed that he forgot nothing – neither a name of a man or a service done, nor the face of an admirable woman? Now she took some more of the parcels from his arms, cheerfully putting aside Hetty's strictures, and led General Sam into the boarders' parlor, where she had the Christmas tree set up to be a delight for all, not merely for the happiness of her children. It was the afternoon Christmas Day, so the parlor was star-scattered with some of her boarders: Dr. Williamson and his friend, Dr. Harper, Mr. Ford, and some others – all of whom immediately leapt to their feet, either in respect to herself or respect to her guest.

"It is wonderful!" General Sam exclaimed, in unabashed delight.

"It is supposed – when the candles are lit – to seem like a young fir tree, with the light of stars seen at a clear midnight through its branches," Margaret explained. "It was the custom of my family, long before it became a fashion among the English royalty. The children have always taken such pleasure from it that we have carried on. Mr. Ernst at Industry has taken a large quantity of German glass ornaments through his establishment. For courtesy, he has sent me some, since they have so recently become fashionable. I would like that my sons become fond of the custom of their ancestors." Margaret added wistfully, "so I do what I can to make such a practice popular!"

"And so you have done!" General Sam exclaimed, with the heartiest of approval. "I rejoice to see that your household prospers, Mrs. Vining. It is a good omen, that our queen city here upon the Colorado contains such brave and optimistic citizens within it!"

"No thanks to you, sir!" Margaret thought she heard a cynical and sotto-voice comment at her back, and hoped that General Sam had not also heard.

"The gentlemen will gather here in the guest-parlor, before supper is served." Margaret raised her voice slightly. "I think that there are many among them – both those boarding regularly, and those coming for supper tonight – who will wish to pay their respects to you . . . among them my own sons, whom I believe you will remember."

"I do, indeed." The General's countenance was alight as that of an eager boy himself. "They must now be well-grown! I should like to meet them once again, especially that bold clever lad . . . Jamie, was it?"

"My brother is also present in my household this season," Margaret said. "Sergeant Carl Becker. You might know him by repute, if not in person – as he was one of those few who escaped the killing of our prisoners at Goliad. He has served since then as a Ranger, first with Colonel Smith, and then with Captain Hays in Bexar. I will tell him to bring the boys to you . . . I must withdraw at this moment to oversee supper."

"The work of a smooth-running household is never done," General Sam smiled at her with complete sympathy. "Especially when hospitality is involved; bachelors never know what subtle work is involved! Do not exert yourself to take special care of me, Mrs. Vining – although if you have a room free for tonight, I would appreciate it. I came straight here instead of to Mrs. Eberlys' as is my usual custom."

"I do so have a room available," Margaret answered, her heart lifting at the unworthy sense of triumphing over Mrs. Eberly – old storm-crow! "The finest is at your disposal, General, and newly-furnished as well. There is a view from the windows of the whole city of Austin, the river and the hills, laid out below this house – which aspect I hope will make your heart fonder of it! I will have Mose bring your luggage up to it . . . the first room at the top of the stairs, the one with a tall four-post bed in it."

Margaret felt quite pleased that she had kept that particular room aside. It was good and well that General Sam should have the use of it, and new-fitted out with so many pieces of elegant furniture from New Orleans, too! She laid all the parcels under the Christmas tree, save for the folio-book-shaped one which she took with her, and excused herself from the parlor. The gentlemen all acknowledged her departure with something of a distracted air. Margaret slipped into the little family parlor, which had become her office and schoolroom for her sons – her own private place on the ground floor, and looked at the present from Margaret Lea with a sense of expectant joy that she had not felt since she was a child herself. A Christmas present, for herself, sent by a very good friend who well-knew her interests and enthusiasms, a friend who had taken the trouble to obtain something special, a friend who would consider and select something . . . perhaps not lavish, or rare, but something what would appeal very personally to Margaret. She removed the wrappings around the book, slowly, to prolong the delicious sense of suspense and excitement. It was, as Margaret had expected – a folio-sized and richly clothbound book – but bound along the short side . . . a thick book of music, of transcriptions for piano – some written for a single instrument, and others arranged – of certain grand orchestral works by Mozart.

Margaret opened it, relishing the feel of heavy paper and the sight of stave after stave after stave of music, those black tadpole-shaped notes in disciplined companies, scampering up and down the lines. Oh, she could hear it in her head, and longed more than anything in the world to go at once to Mary Bullock's china parlor and open her present and play the music, to see if it would sound as rich in the real world as it did in her imagination. How very kind of Maggie Lea to choose something so rare and personal. Mary Bullock would be green with envy! Margaret laid the folio on the parlor table, as it was almost too large to fit onto the bookshelves without turning it sideways, and went to search out her brother and her sons. She thought they had withdrawn from all the household fuss into the pasture below the house which had once been Alois Becker's cornfield – which now appeared to be serving as an out-of-doors classroom. There was a tall stake with a fluttering bit of cloth tied to the top of it, in the middle of the field. Her brother sat in the saddle of his ill-tempered grey Hell-horse, with Peter in front of him, while Johnny and Jamie lined up like birds on a branch on the topmost rail of the zig-zag pole fence which had enclosed the field – all watching Horace ride across towards the stake, at a gallop on old Bucephalus, with one of Carl's Paterson pistols in his free hand. Margaret grasped at once what was going on: Horace was attempting to hit the stake with a shot from horseback at a dead gallop. Jamie was already clamoring to have a chance at it, as Horace lowered the pistol and fired several times, until he was well past the flagged-stake – having missed it at all attempts.

Margaret watched from above, half-hidden in the sketchy shelter of the apple trees, feeling a lump in her throat for sentiment. This is what Race might have done with his sons if he had lived and been in good health. He might have taught the proper manly arts that the boys would have found necessary to learn, in that Texas which had turned from a garden of paradise into the field of war that many portions of it had since proved to be. Even if keen marksmanship from the saddle of a galloping horse was not one of the traditional skills that her husband had been schooled in – fencing was about the most elegant of the martial arts that Race Vining had been taught – he would have approved. To ensure peace one must practice for war, he had been fond of reminding Margaret and Maggie Darst, when Maggie fumed about the hours taken up by regular militia drill of the Gonzales Volunteers. A reputation for having practiced assiduously for war and being passably skilled in its execution, he had then usually added, was no finer guarantee of being left alone to live in peace. Certainly that strategy had worked very well upon the Comanche. After the great fight at Plum Creek, when the Penataka raiding band had fallen upon the settlements and burned Linnville to the ground some years ago, the southern Comanche division had not dared to ride into the Texian settlements again. And Captain Coleman's audacious bluff, in the face of a Comanche war party in the year that Morag had birthed a daughter for Danny Fritchie . . . that had ensured a semblance of peace for a good long while.

Now Horace was riding back towards Carl: Margaret could read the abashed and embarrassed expression upon his face from that distance, but could not hear the words that her brother said. Few and of some reassurance, she guessed, from the manner in which Horace's face lightened as Carl took from him the Paterson pistol and handed him another one. A skill was something which required practice, and her brother looked to be an excellent teacher, patient and ever-encouraging. The Hell-horse snapped irritably at old Bucephalus' flank as Horace wheeled him around. Margaret was struck with a familiar ache in her heart, seeing her son leaning forward in the saddle over that sleek black neck extended in a full gallop, the clean and bright-shod hoofs flashing and drumming across the pasture. Horace was nearly grown to his height, lean and wiry as his father had been, and Bucephalus might be old, but he lived to run: how often had Margaret watched her husband race Bucephalus and never be beaten? The five shots that Horace fired in quick succession at the stake came to her as a distant popping sound, and she saw that at least two of them had hit home, the stake rocking too and fro, as the cloth banner attached to the top fluttered like a victory flag. Now Horace wheeled Bucephalus and whooped like an Indian in triumph, as he rode him in a tight circle three times around the post, exuberantly waving the Paterson over his head, while Johnny and Jamie cheered from their perch on the topmost fence rail, and Carl called, "Good shooting, hoss – that's prime! Now, I'll show you how it's really done!"

It looked to Margaret, watching from above, as if Carl fiddled briefly with the revolver in hand, taking something from out of one of his breast-pockets – whatever task he had to do was done in a moment – and in another moment, Horace on Bucephalus were side by side with Carl and the Hell-horse. In the bare wink of an eye, Carl had lifted Peter – mostly by one arm, and Margaret involuntarily gasped to see this casual disposition of her dearest little son – and transferred him to the front of Horace's saddle, upon Bucephalus. For a suspended moment, she and the boys below all watched, as Carl finished fiddling with the single Paterson. In the blink of an eye, he dug his heels into the flanks of his Hell-horse, who responded with an explosive leap into a dead run towards the flagged stake. In another blink, Carl looked to have thrown himself out of the saddle entirely – no, that was not so, there was one leg thrown over the saddle still and a hand on the pommel, hardly to be seen over the side of the Hell-horse, who had accelerated from a fast trot into a full gallop – and just as the horse exploded into that gallop, stretching to tear up the distance, there came the flash of a pistol-shot from under his neck . . . Margaret blinked, for the Hell-horse did not even hesitate in his stride. Another, and yet another, as the flagged stake shivered and splintered, until nothing was left but a bare nub and the flag upon it fell to the earth, and there was her brother, wheeling around at the bottom of the pasture as he appeared – most magically upright in the saddle again – laughing as he looked towards the boys.

"That's how it's done by Jack Hays' Rangers!" he called to them exuberantly, grinning from ear to ear. He had lost his hat in that run – it lay on the grass near the splintered stake. He dug his spurred heels into the horse's iron-gray flanks, and the beast obeyed, another explosion of speed – and as the horse passed by the stake and his fallen hat upon the stubbled earth, Carl leaned down from the saddle again and deftly scooped up his hat from the ground. The boys, especially Horace and Jamie, were loud in their admiration of this feat – and indeed, as Margaret came down from between the apple trees towards where Johnny and Jamie were sitting on the topmost fence rail, Jamie was loudly insisting that he wanted to try it.

"Not until you're a mite bigger, hoss," Carl answered, smiling down upon them all, blue eyes as clear as the sky behind his head, looking as carefree and as happy as if he were one of the boys himself. "And with your mama's permission, of course."

"Mama, might I try?" Jamie shrilled, as Margaret came close, and Peter echoed his older brother, begging her to allow him to do such feats of horse-and-marksmanship as their uncle had just demonstrated.

"Not until you are Horace's age," Margaret answered firmly, "and that under-the-horse's neck shooting trick – I'd forbid him to do that, save that I am sure that he and the other older boys will be trying it once out of sight. I came to fetch you all – General Sam has come calling just now – he is in the boarders' parlor asking after you all."

"Is he?" Jamie's face was alight with hero-worship. "Does he truly remember us from when he came to call after you heard that Papa was dead?"

"Of course," Margaret answered. "General Sam forgets nothing – especially not the name and family of one of his loyal soldiers . . . which your Papa was. And," she shot a severe look at her brother, who seemed hardly impressed at all, "he would know of you by repute, little brother. You should make yourself known to him personally, if you are not already."

"I've met the General," Carl answered. "Now and again, some of the boys and I – meaning Jack's boys – we've had a fine old time drinking the local thirst-parlors dry in Huntsville and Washington on the Brazos. He might remember me, even from three sheets in the wind."

"Carlchen," Margaret put on her most severe expression. "The General is married now, to a very respectable Christian lady – you are not to encourage him to stray from the path of domesticity."

Her brother roared with frank laughter. "M'grete," he answered finally, still deeply amused, "I don't think there's anyone could put the General off from what he wanted to do – no matter if it was to go on a spree or sit in your parlor passing the tea-cups and reading the newspapers from the East. General Sam will do as he wishes and there isn't a man in Texas who has a better right to do as he thinks best."

"Do not lead him astray!" Margaret ordered once again, and her brother laughed and told Horace to come and help him put up the horses, and the younger boys to go make themselves fit for the parlor to renew acquaintance with the great General Sam.

Later, Margaret accounted the afternoon as a completely satisfactory success: she lingered in the doorway of the parlor, as her sons – hastily washed and combed, thrust into cleaner shirts and coats – entered bashfully into the parlor, led by Jamie and Horace, to be noticed in courtesy by all the boarders present and welcomed most warmly by General Sam, who did not seem to think a week had passed since he saw them last, not almost four years ago. His rugged countenance beamed as warmly at them as if he was – if not their own father, at least an uncle or similar kinsman, and Margaret withdrew to her kitchen offices, and the bustle of activity in the kitchen, where Hetty oversaw the efforts of the girls whom Margaret had hired to help serve on this momentous occasion. Most of them were very young, the daughters of her neighbors. Hetty guarded them as she had with Morag, with stern and rough-spoken affection, and a heart as malleable as warm butter. Morag saw that the girls had their hair and fingernails as clean as they might be, dressed in their best dark dresses, covered up with spotless and starched white aprons, as they went to serve supper, to answer the front door and see visitors to the parlor. Hetty had most of them so terrified into respectfulness that many of the girls – even if they knew Margaret rather well – would hardly venture a word in her presence.

"It's how it must be, Marm," Hetty explained, some six years ago, when Margaret had seen the need for a boardinghouse appealing to the best among the gentlemen of the Legislature. "Ye're the queen of the household – her ladyship, all fair and terrible, and above the ordinary. I can see to the ordinary, but you must seem to float above it all."

"I am sure you are right, Hetty," Margaret had answered on that occasion, not quite seeing how it must be – when she worked side by side with Hetty and Morag for all these years.

Hetty had just looked at her, with a look of exasperation veiled in affection and answered, "It's the way o' the gentry, Marm. Ye wish to have a household of gentry, to have a grand establishment, to cater to the best of all that we have here. Th' way that Himself wished to have, although he was a gentleman never to say so to your face, so it was. Th' way of a fine household," Hetty explained, "is like one of those fine steam-paddle ships. The stokers work away below decks, shovelin' in the wood or coal or whatever – and the wheel turns, and there the ship moves, fine an' clean an' white above the water, an' the captain in a good cloth coat on the wheel-deck. It's the way of it, Marm – you must seem to be fine and above it all, above the way of th' work o' the way of makin' the ship move . . . no, no, Marm – y'see, y' are shaking y' head at the silliness of it. But it is the way o' the gentry. Himself was trained up in t' way of the gentry, for a' that he came out here and proved himself a brave man, an' pretended to himself – an' perhaps to you, that he didn't mind a' the work that ye had to do. Only, Marm – be the captain, in a fine clean coat!"

"I will," Margaret had assured her, and since her household now prospered so very well, she concluded that Hetty was doubtless correct in this.

That night she presided at the head of the long dining table, and surveyed the table, crowded elbow to elbow with her many important guests, and the succession of dishes arriving from the kitchen, with a sense of contented triumph. This is what she had wanted – had possessed something of in the heady days when Austin was first building and gentlemen boarders had crowded to her table . . . although it was a much smaller table then, set in a narrow room cobbled from the verandah of her father's simple log house. It had contented her then, to earn a living and provide for her family through her own enterprise, to bring amusing company under her father's roof to divert her invalid husband with talk of books and politics, and the finer matters of the mind. During the fallow years, after the departure of her husband, and the slow withering of President Lamar's new capital city, she had sometimes doubted that she would ever sit at the head of such a table again. Now, her faith in herself, hers and Hetty's hard work had been recovered, rewarded abundantly, pressed down and overflowing.

She smiled and chatted with those guests closest to her, all the while watchful of the service of Hetty and the girls, listening to the boisterous conversation at the other end of the table. It sounded as if the General was having an excellent evening as well, although Margaret wished that his dear Maggie Lea had felt well enough to accompany him on this visit. The General had reformed himself in many ways upon marriage, but his reputation for drinking remained. A little way down the table, Margaret noted that Carl and John Ford were talking, their heads bent together. Louisa Ford met Margaret's eye and smiled a rather indulgent smile. "Men will be men," she formed the words silently, and Margaret laughed a little to herself. Pretty Julia Sinks was sitting next to her young husband, both of them rather wide-eyed at the majesty and ornament of Margaret's table on this Christmas Day. Mrs. Eberly – who had left her own establishment to the care of her older children on this momentous day, at Margaret's pleading – was simultaneously tucking into a full plate of victuals and looking around with a considering eye. *Shrewd old storm-crow*, Margaret thought to herself, with fond exasperation – *she is already thinking again of asking Hetty and me to form a partnership with her. And no doubt enjoying food that she has not cooked or overseen the preparation of herself: dear Angelina – for all of your vast age and experience, Hetty and I could still teach you lessons in keeping an establishment of the gentry.*

"I'd trouble you for the recipe for that red cabbage." Mrs. Eberly raised her voice, to be heard from halfway down the table, "and the biscuits, too."

Margaret smiled. "It was one of my husband's favorite dishes," she answered. "Since my own dear mother first cooked it for him when we were courting; I will write it down for you and send it to you, for it is very plain – and I am sure you will find it simple in preparation. But I must keep the recipe for Hetty's biscuits to myself, for that is her own secret in preparation."

"One doesn't meddle in the magic, if one should want the magic to continue!" From down the table, General Sam smiled at her, his voice a commanding rumble, clearly to be heard. He raised his glass. "To magic, gentlemen, the magic of a well-run house, and to the skills of our hostess tonight!" Margaret had also splurged on the provision of wine – in honor of hers' and Carl's ancestral homeland, a very nice pale Rhenish. In her very best new glass goblets, it gleamed as liquid gold under the light of wax tapers; all the gentlemen drank deep and cheered, and Margaret felt as if she had reached a kind of pinnacle of ambition. She had her boys, her friends – Hetty, General Sam, Doctor Williamson, even the old storm-crow, Angelina Eberly. The house was as fine and comfortable as her labors and that of Hetty could make it. Austin would rebuild now, as a state capital, if not the capital of the Republic, and it would fulfill every dream that President Lamar and folk such as the Bullocks and Race Vining had ever had of it. And Margaret – she would be a part of it; the political hostess without peer and above reproach.

She went to her own chamber that evening, exhausted and triumphant, having performed her usual late-night round; Hetty and the girls had seen to the mountain of washing-up, the boys were settled in their beds, and the doors to the outside were all latched and locked. Margaret could not leave off from that long-established habit. There were boarders in the public parlor still, and she hesitated for a moment, wondering if she should tap on the door and bid them goodnight. No, it was late; and although their voices were somewhat raised in loud merriment, she heard her brother's among them. Her boarders were gentlemen, and in any case, her brother was there – and if she could not look to her brother to maintain the good name and gentility of her house, then who indeed could she look to? Margaret withdrew to her own room – put off her dress and outer garments, and luxuriated in the warmth of the fire that Mose had laid and started to burn in the fireplace – and too, in the warmth of the jug of hot water that she had carried upstairs to wash herself in, before drawing on her nightgown and slipping underneath the covers. Her last thought before she dropped into comfortable sleep was that although this room was very pleasantly large, it did not content her as much as she thought it would when she laid out the plans for the grand extension. She would prefer a room with windows which looked out upon the apple trees; something on the ground floor, adjacent to the oldest part of the house, perhaps. She fell asleep, considering it, although once or twice it seemed that her dreams were disturbed by the sound of someone chopping firewood.

Chapter 19 – *The Last of the Lone Star*

In the morning, Margaret rose at the usual hour, when the sky had just begun to pale in the east and it was yet too early for the rooster to begin setting up a ruckus in the chicken pen. She had a house full of guests, even though most of them had not spent the night. One of the last things that Hetty had done before retiring for the night was to have Mose move the dining table back into the room where it normally resided and return the household chairs to their usual places. Margaret viewed the now-empty hall with a sigh for the temporary glory that it had housed on the previous day. Now to see to breakfast for those guests who remained.

That breakfast should be every bit as good as the supper on Christmas night – for Margaret would not allow any diminution of her hospitality. She tied on her kitchen apron and walked into the kitchen, where she halted just inside the door, arrested by the expressions on the faces of the three within. Hetty bristled with unspoken irritation, even as she paused in rolling out the dough for the first batch of breakfast biscuits. Mose – who stood by the stove with an empty metal hot-water canister in each of his huge hands – had a nervous and apprehensive expression on his dark and usually uncommunicative face. Carl sat at the end of the kitchen table, interrupted in the act of wolfing down a plate of bacon, sausage, and hash made from the leftovers of last night's feast. He looked nearly as nervous as Mose, and his expression – especially as Margaret appeared in the doorway – appeared to be as guilty as a small child caught in the midst of some awful mischief, mischief for which he was certain to be punished.

Margaret took in each countenance in a lighting-flash, apprehended that something had happened in her household, and demanded, "What is the matter, then?"

Mose answered, in his thick and barely articulate mumble. "I took de hot watter to de gennelmun rooms, mam . . . an' de Gen'ral, he still 'sleep, mam . . . but he don' chop down de bedpos', mam."

"What?" Margaret demanded, and Mose only looked more stolid. "He chop down de bedpos', mam. Gen'ral Sam," as Carl said, with an air of someone trying to placate an unappeasable fury. "He took an ax to the bedposts, M'grete. He . . . got a little merry last night, I guess – after you had gone to bed. Some of the others . . . well, there was bottles bein' passed. I didn't think he would take to your best bedstead, though."

Hetty looked from Margaret's face to that of her brother, and the hapless Mose, and murmured, "Mother Mary save him, she's got her Maeve face on, for certain."

"There wasn't anything I could do, M'grete," Carl temporized, even as Mose returned to filling the canisters from the hot-water reservoir at the side of the vast cook stove. "He's the General. I did not think you would object to the men getting a little merry on Christmas. You had wine with dinner, after all, M'grete."

"I do not object to the drinking of alcohol under my roof," Margaret answered, in a voice tight with suppressed fury. "I object when men drink of it to excess. And I object most strenuously to barbarous conduct after they have drunk to excess. Little Brother, Mose. You may bring up the hot water later – for a now, each of you fetch a bucket of cold from the spring-house, please. Then all of you come with me."

"I just put the biscuits in..." Hetty began to protest, but Margaret cut her off with a few curt words, as Mose and Carl obeyed. "This will not take a moment."

The heels of Margaret shoes made a brisk tattoo on the floor, echoing in the hall as she swept imperiously up the staircase, in her fury outdistancing all of her acolytes. At the top of the stairs, the door to the best guest room stood slightly ajar: Mose had not closed it entirely on his departure. Margaret waited for the two men to climb the stairs, Hetty puffing in their wake. She took a deep breath, Mose's words having prepared her for the worst. Well, now she knew why she had dreamed of someone chopping wood during the night. She opened the door all the way; oh, no. The room smelt faintly of stale drink, underlaid with odor of sweat and male toiletries. The slave man's words and her own imagination had not prepared her for what she now saw. General Sam lay snoring in the middle of the bed, on top of the counterpane with his boots and coat cast carelessly aside on the floor amid splinters and roughly-hacked chunks of cherry-wood. All four of the tall and gracefully carved bedposts were roughly hewn down, almost level with the head and footboard. Margaret felt sickened by the intensity of her anger: her best bed, purchased at such a cost, from the earnings of hers and Hetty's labor – a beautifully-wrought and cherished thing, deliberately mutilated. Behind her, Hetty gasped, horrified alike. They had both taken such pride in the new furniture, in the look of their best guest room. Now, Margaret was certain she would never look at it again in quite the same way, now that it had been so desecrated.

"Carlchen," she said, and her voice shook. "And Mose. I want you to waken the General with the cold water. And once he is awake, assist him in resuming his clothing. Assemble his luggage, too. Carlchen, you will see him conveyed to Mrs. Eberly's without delay." Carl hesitated, and Mose looked between them, and to the ruined bed with General Sam snoring in deep sleep.

"B'foa breakfast?" Mose ventured, and Margaret snapped. "Yes. The water, Carlchen – it is how one rouses drunks, is it not?" Shrugging, Carl carried his bucket to one side of the bed, Mose to the other. They hoisted the buckets to chest-level, poised to pour them out onto the sleeping General Sam, while Margaret watched, hawk-eyed. "Now!"

Carl emptied the bucket, Mose doing so a split-second later. Margaret turned on her heel, as General Sam bolted upright with a bellow. The very satisfactory sounds of sputtering and curses followed her down the stairs, Hetty fairly running in order to keep up. Margaret thought that Hetty once or twice started speak, but thought better of it. The two girls who assisted with the kitchen and the table were in the kitchen when they returned – no, they did not dare to speak either, once they had glimpsed her face.

Having seen breakfast preparations completed, Margaret withdrew to the private sitting room, simmering with such anger that she did not entirely trust herself not to give way to an unladylike fit of temper in the presence of her guests or the kitchen help. Her pride with last night's triumph had turned to ashes – ashes, dust, and chips of wood, scattered on the floor of her best guest room. Presently, Hetty tapped respectfully on the doorjamb and put her head into the room.

"Marm . . . are you not going to take breakfast, as usual?"

"I think not, Hetty. I am not . . . in a cordial mood this morning."

"I should think not," Hetty shook her head. "Aye, well. Your Maeve-face, Marm, is something that would curdle the digestion of an innocent man, so it's for the best, not presiding over the table this morning . . . though I will say that if the Young Sir was right wi' regard to th' gentlemen bein' merry last night, some of them may have a curdled digestion this morning anyway. I'll bring a tray for you."

"Thank you, Hetty," Margaret said, not for the first time grateful for Hetty's friendship and support. What a lonely prospect this enterprise of hers would have been, without Hetty, her friend and good right arm these years past!

Presently, Hetty brought her a tray, beautifully set with a plate of food; biscuits with a dab of preserves, another of fresh butter, and a little dish of honey, some scrambled egg, and a pat of sausage, spiced and fried to crispy goodness. Margaret ate all of it, although she was not particularly hungry. If she did not clean the plate, then Hetty would notice and feel something of hurt, although every bit of it was as flavorful and expertly cooked, as Margaret had always required. As she was buttering the last biscuit-half, she heard the rumble of a deep male voice, speaking from somewhere beyond the turns in the corridor that enlarging Alois Becker's simple log blockhouse had made inevitable. It sounded like General Sam's voice. Margaret chewed and swallowed that last bite of biscuit, just as Hetty and her brother appeared in the doorway. Both of them appeared rather apprehensive.

"Th' General, he wishes a word w'ye, Marm." Hetty was twisting her hand in a damp dishtowel. Obviously, she had been interrupted in sorting out the influx of dirty dishes, mid-breakfast.

Carl had nothing in his hands, yet he looked equally as unsettled, as he ventured, "M'grete, I think he wishes to tender an apology . . . "

"As well he might," Margaret answered crisply. "For he is a great man, of which better conduct might have been expected and his wife is a dear friend, who will be most cruelly disappointed to hear of his abuse of the hospitality of my house. Say to the General that I am most disappointed. Say to him that I am so distressed with anger that I do not trust myself to be courteous with regard to this incident. I fear that anything I might say with regard to this unfortunate occurrence will spell ruin to our friendship, a mutual friendship and regard which I have treasured for many years – so I will not receive him. Leave him to tender his apology to me through you. Assure him that at some time in the future, I will welcome him to my house again, but not at present. And if you would remind him," Margaret added, as Hetty and Carl exchanged looks of apprehension, "of a piece of advice which he once rendered to me, regarding silence giving no purchase to gossiping tongues – I will be most grateful."

"Yes, Marm," Hetty answered, although she did not look happy at having to bear such a stern message to the General.

Carl hesitated for a moment, as the door closed behind Hetty. "I'm real sorry about the bed, M'grete," he ventured at last. "I don't reckon there is any way to fix it back."

"No," Margaret answered. She had not thought about what she would do about the bed. "If you would, Carlchen – take the bed apart, and put the pieces in the barn. Hurst is a fair carpenter; I will ask him what he might be able to do upon his return. I am certain that General Sam is ready to depart now."

With that, Carl nodded, and left the little parlor. Margaret contemplated the remains of her breakfast, wondering how it could be that every man whom she loved, cared for, or respected had let her down in one way or another, beginning with her husband and the wife that he had left in Boston. Papa, ridden and haunted by his foul temper. Carl, away in the Llano, leaving all the business of life for her to see to. Seamus O'Doyle had left, and so had the Englishman, Mr. Hattersley – he who had only come to Texas to write his vile little book, feigning friendship all the while. And now General Sam had smashed the best bed. Were there no men in her life worthy of her deepest trust at all?

Although Margaret vowed to herself and to Hetty that she would say no word of the matter of the wrecked bed, it was too delicious a morsel for the gossips to allow it to remain untouched, even while preparations went forward in the weeks after Christmas for the formal annexation to the United States. During that time, Margaret and General Sam encountered each other, making nothing more than a show of careful courtesy. Only Mrs. Eberly dared ask Margaret outright for the particulars, to which Margaret responded, "For the respect in which I hold the General and the friendship I have with Mrs. Houston, I do not care to discuss it."

In January, Carl received a message from Bexar and departed. Margaret could not contain her disappointment: he had never remained so long before, nearly two months, and she had begun to believe that perhaps her brother might yet be looking kindly upon settling down. But no – not if the failure of Mr. Slidell's mission to Mexico was any indication, and in far California, American settlers were restive against the Mexican government of that place.

"Looks like it will be heating up again," Carl explained laconically, as Margaret filled his haversack with bread and cured sausage, and as many of last seasons' apples as she could fit. The last of the harvest had been stored in barrels of sawdust in the coldest corner of the barn, and still retained much of their freshness. "Jack has been called to recruit a body to serve as scouts with the American Army. They say Gen'ral Taylor is ordered to the Nueces. His men won't know it the way the Rangers do, and that's for sure." He smiled, with an expression of deep contentment in his eyes. "Looks like we'll make ol' Santy Anna behave himself for good and all, this time."

"Be careful," Margaret said, aware of a feeling of helplessness; how many more times would her brother court death in the Llano, or in the Nueces borderlands and escape unscathed?

"I always am, M'grete," he answered. Margaret and the boys watched him go, from the deep gallery at the front of the house. He waved once from the bottom of the hill, before spurring his big grey horse into a trot on the road that led to the south.

On a bright late-winter day, blessed with a fair sky and pure white clouds floating in it, Margaret, her sons, Hetty, and all of her household gathered on the hillside below the white-washed capitol building. They stood with hundreds of their neighbors and citizens gathered from across Texas for the formal ceremony to mark Annexation, men in their best jackets and top-hats, and so many ladies, their mantles and the ribbons of their bonnets fluttering. All had put on the very best of the garments they possessed to mark this momentous day.

"It has seemed so long-promised, that I cannot believe this day has come," Margaret remarked. "Like a woman's wedding day, at long last!" She and Hetty laughed, recalling how Margaret had likened the endless negotiations regarding annexing Texas to the United States to a flirtatious girl.

"Aye, but without the rejected suitor at the back of the church," Hetty replied, comfortably.

"The rejected suitor is all the way the other side of the Nueces and the Rio Grande," Margaret observed, "and with a regular Army to ensure that he stays there!"

She did not like to say any more on that subject, not to spoil her sons' pleasure in the day. There was the President, Dr. Jones, with General Sam and a whole host of important men on a platform erected in front of the capitol building porch, which made a splendid stage for what was to follow. The flag – the three fields of red, blue, and white, with a single five-pointed white star on the blue field snapped in the brisk wind. The staff from which it flew stood close to the porch which was adorned with tri-colored bunting. Margaret's eyes rested briefly upon General Sam, who looked as happy as a bridegroom himself. No, he had long wanted Annexation, had schemed and negotiated for it for at least half of the eventful decade just past. Delivery was at hand, after ten years of intrigue, war and threats of war on two fronts. Margaret recollected other words of the witch-woman on the banks of the Sabine – the day of her twelfth birthday, when Alois Becker and his family first arrived in Texas.

"He in a big rush to be a Mexican ... don't he know dat America gwine follow him, no matter?" The old witch had chuckled in rich amusement. For a long time Margaret had wondered how she had known such things about the future. The last but one of her predictions was about to come true: America had followed them, at long last. The future of Austin was secure as well,

which was of no little relief to Margaret and Angelina Eberly: it would be the capital of the state government, and the Legislature would continue to meet at the accustomed interval.

What with all the comings and goings over the last year, Margaret's enterprise had done well. As she stood among the crowd, with Peter's hand in hers and Horace offering his elbow with all the hesitant gallantry of a young gentleman of fifteen, her thoughts began to wander; perhaps this summer would be a good time to add another wing to the house. A sawn-plank structure could be built with great rapidity, as she had seen . . . and she would certainly be able to fill the rooms. Why, she and Hetty had to turn away prospective boarders, after filling all the rooms with three and four gentleman guests to a room, which was not the kind of gracious hospitality that Margaret wished her house to be known for. And when had Horace grown so tall – the top of his head was above the level of her shoulder?

Her wandering mind was suddenly concentrated – it seemed that the speeches were over, and the attention of the crowd was suddenly riveted as Dr. Jones stepped forward to the foot of the flagpole. He unwound the lines, stretched them out and began to lower away – the proud single-star flag.

In a loud voice, Dr. Jones declaimed, "The final act in this great drama is now performed – the Republic of Texas is no more!" A gasp swept the crowd, a murmuring almost of grief, and Margaret felt tears sting her eyelids. She had not expected this: that she and everyone would be so moved by the ending of their brief and desperate republic, born from the ashes of the fires of rebellion, the ashes of fires which had burned the body of her brother outside the Goliad citadel, the fires from the pyres set on the Alameda in Bexar to burn those fallen in the defense of the Alamo. Ten years of war on two fronts, against a resentful, treacherous Mexico and the avaricious and brutal Comanche, ten years of steering an uncertain course in a leaking vessel between Scylla and Charybdis, seeking recognition from the great nations, and safety for her citizens, by their own efforts keep in tenuous safety and freedom . . . and now to arrive in that promised safe harbor.

As the flag came down, it was General Sam, the architect of it all, who stepped forward – perhaps on an impulse, and perhaps it had all been planned – and gathered the folds of it into his arms, as if it were something that he cherished and wished no risk of harm. Margaret and her sons stood very close; she could see that General Sam was deeply moved. He was a terribly sentimental man, Margaret knew – one of those who felt no shame in revealing strong emotion. He had held Sue Dickinson's hand, and wept as she told of what had happened in Bexar, on the evening that Gonzales burned and

Margaret and her family and friends began their long retreat to the east. Now someone stepped forward with a new flag, many-striped in the same colors, with a constellation of twenty stars arrayed on the blue field, a flag which unfurled and snapped in the bright wind, the sound of it sounding so very loud in the murmuring silence.

"Mama, will we still be Texians, when we are Americans?" Horace asked in a low voice, and at her other side, her youngest piped up, "I'd rather be a Texian!"

"Yes, we will," Margaret answered, feeling as of her throat were to close on her voice. "We will always remember what it is to be Texians; that we were here and held our own for ten long years."

She hosted a gala at-home that night, at which Dr. Jones and the General did make brief appearances, for there were many celebrations going on in Austin; a chance to celebrate before picking up one last burden. It now appeared that war was inevitable with Mexico, yet again – but at least this time, they would not be fighting it alone. This cheered Margaret immensely, but did not in the least relieve her apprehensions regarding her brother.

Almost as soon as the celebrations were done, she set about planning the new addition: a long wing of six rooms on the ground floor with a corridor between, and four larger rooms above, the ground floor to be surrounded on three sides by a deep porch. All the ground-floor rooms would have tall French-style glass windows, some of them opening as doors onto the porch. The roof overhead would provide shade on the hottest summer days, the windows would admit the slightest passing breeze, and the best of them a view of the apple trees and the town below. This work provided a welcome distraction: for when she was thinking of the best disposition of fireplaces within the rooms, the efficient draft of chimneys, and where to procure good hardware for the doors and glass for the many windows, she was not worrying about Carl, or such of her other friends and acquaintances when the fighting began in earnest, in mid-summer.

John Ford's wife became ill at about that time, although she had been in uncertain health for many months. It wrung Margaret's heart to witness John Ford's concern for his wife, and his increasing distress as his medical arts proved fruitless to arrest Louisa's decline. Another reason for Margaret to spend her time buried in the plans and the unfolding of the new wing of the house – a diversion from cares and worry, while soldiers and statesmen came and went. So the nervous summer of 1846 passed, broken only by a brief coda to the heartbreak of Mrs. Simpson and her lost children. On a mid-afternoon in early summer, a small party of horsemen came to the back of the house, where now besides the smokehouse and the spring-house, there was a newly-enlarged stable, a new summer kitchen, and three little cabins to house the Negro attendants of her guests. At first Margaret thought the horsemen were more workmen arrived, to begin shingling the roof of the new wing, which had already arisen in skeletal timber form to that side of the house which overlooked the river, and which Margaret had decreed would have the best views and the best chances of catching the lightest breath of a breeze on a hot summer day.

Hetty came rustling to fetch Margaret from the private parlor and schoolroom, where her sons were having their daily lessons.

"Marm," Hetty whispered, "It's young Mr. Simpson – from Bastrop, with his little brother, him who was taken nearly two year ago. They have a party of men with them, now . . . to follow the trail along of where himself and Emma were taken."

"Oh, my God!" Margaret immediately dropped her pen – she was writing a letter to Margaret Houston. She and the boys both sprang up from the tasks at hand.

Horace insisted firmly, "Mama, I will go with them!" and Jamie exclaimed, "Oh, Mama – was Tommy with the Indians all this time?" while Hetty added, "I asked after the girl. They wi'not say. I'd say from their faces . . ." Hetty looked at Johnny and Peter's faces and bit back what she was about to say at first, adding only, "I dinna think there'll be hope, Marm."

"I fear not," Margaret replied softly so that only Hetty could hear, as her family emerged from the breezeway between the back of the house and the summer kitchen. Yes, there was Captain Coleman, a handful of other volunteers from Austin, and a thin young man with an angry face who must be the oldest Simpson. He had not come to live in Austin with his mother and younger siblings, but worked in Bastrop in an enterprise set up by Mrs. Simpson's brother . . . and there was Tommy. Margaret could have wept – for he looked immeasurably older, older than the year and a half since he and Emma had been taken by an Indian raiding party, older by far than Johnny, who was his age. Thin as a rail and burnt as darkly brown as any of the Comanche, as brown as the white renegade who had come with the raiding party on the day that Captain Coleman's bluff had sent them packing. Tommy's hair had grown long, and harshly sun-streaked. Now he sat in the saddle of one of those spry little mustang ponies, looking at nothing more than his hands, as Margaret exclaimed, "Oh, Tommy – we are so glad to see you safe and back with us again! Your mother was devastated with grief, and now she must be happy beyond measure. What of Emma, was she also ransomed as well?"

Tommy looked at his hands without speaking. His older brother answered for him. "Emma was killed almost at once, Miz Vining, so them red devils could make a get-away."

"I'm so sorry," Margaret answered, although she was not in truth surprised.

"I tole her," Tommy whispered, "I tole her not to fight them, she didn't ought to make sich a noise, mebbe they'd treat her fair. But one of them, he took her away with him into a thicket over beyond Mount Bonnell an' came back at once w' her hair hangin' on his saddle. He showed it to me, an' he laughed an' laughed . . ."

"Hearing of this is a terrible grief to all of us," Margaret said. "With no news of her, we did have some small shreds of hope. But now, alas . . . Do you want Horace and Daddy Hurst to go with you? My son wishes to and Daddy will want to, if you can wait for a moment." There was little need to wait, for Tommy nodded silently, and Horace had already gone to fetch Daddy Hurst from the stables. In a moment, they had Bucephalus saddled, and Daddy riding on one of the draft mules which Margaret had purchased to pull a light wagon for errands. In a few minutes the party vanished silently among the green shadows of the woods at the foot of Mount Bonnell.

Some hours later, Daddy Hurst returned alone. "They done found her, Miz Vining – jus' where the boy said. They ast me to fetch up the coffin they done have made. Eighteen months, pert-near nothing but bones. They knew it wuz her by the scraps o' her dress."

The next morning, Margaret saw a small wagon, heading out from Austin on the river road towards Bastrop, a wagon with the coffin on the back of it. It was too far away to see which of the brothers was driving, and which was riding the paint pony. But there was no doubt about who was in the back of that wagon – the last remains of a pretty girl with hair the color of cypress leaves in the fall, a pretty and feisty girl who fought against her captors to the very last ounce of strength.

The war with Mexico ground on, all summer long. Now and again Margaret had a brief and usually unsatisfactory message from her brother who was, as Hetty had observed, as uncommunicative in writing as he was in person. Margaret and her household took universal satisfaction in the fact that this time the fighting was all on Mexican soil. Only the town of Mier had ever before felt the wrath of an army invading from the North. Now it looked as if Mexico was about to become sated on that banquet, as General Taylor's army, and the Texian Rangers under Carl's old comrade Colonel Hays besieged Monterrey.

"Let them have a taste of what they have served to us all too often!" Margaret exclaimed one night at the supper table. "And see if they relish that dish any better! Do you know," she added thoughtfully, "although my brother has served with Colonel Hays since – I believe it has been ten years – I have never met him in person!"

"He must be the only important man in Texas who has never dined at your table," John Ford chuckled – which Margaret was glad to see, since Louisa Ford was still quite unwell, and her husband was so terribly worried about her. At least, dining at the table of an old friend was an opportunity for him to set his troubles and worries aside for a little. "When he next presents himself in Austin, Ma'am, I will do my best to see that he has an invitation – and bring him myself, if there is no other way to persuade him!"

"Do, please – my brother is so completely innocent of social graces that he would never think to invite Colonel Hays himself," Margaret replied, and everyone at the table laughed. Margaret was very pleased: her table was one of the most sought-after in Austin, and the dining room was set in splendor almost every night.

* * *

With the news of the fall of Monterrey came the longed for end of the summer's heat, and the new wing was complete. Margaret so liked the look and the comfortable aspect of the new wing that she moved her own articles of furniture and possessions into the room nearest the existing house, that had a view from the long windows which pleased her enormously. No, this was much better than the upstairs room, and it was more convenient to her office-parlor and the kitchen – the very heart of her enterprise. Now that autumn had arrived, Margaret rejoiced in the cool breezes and relief from the discomfort of sweat-dampened linen against her skin. Fastidious to the core, she had come to hate the smell of clothing and sheets which became ringed with pale yellow stains over the blistering days and stifling heat of summer. One of her private sources of happiness for having done so well with taking in boarders was being able to hire laundresses, so she and Hetty did not need to labor long days over the washtub and scrubbing board.

With autumn came the turning of leaves, and an early rain, which came dribbling out of sullen grey clouds that lingered for days. Now it became necessary to close the windows in the evening to keep out the chill, no matter how Margaret had relished and welcomed the first breaths of winter. Why did not the weather remain at a comfortable median for more than a few weeks in the spring and in the fall, Margaret wondered – neither too hot or too cold?

"Takes me back to Wexford, it does, Marm," Hetty said, half vexed and half longing, "Weeks would go by, with niver a sight of the sun, and our Mam would say if it went on any longer, we would be after growing moss on us. And it's fair cold of a night, Marm – I think it is time to allow a fire in the boarders' parlor of an evening."

"We should order another wagon-load of wood," Margaret answered, "in addition to what we already have cured and split for fires. I like the smell of a wood-fire of an evening, Hetty. I daresay the boarders will relish it also."

"Nothing takes me home than the smell o' peat burning." Hetty replied, "Our Mam would tell us that our hearth-fire had been burning since before her Mam was born." She sighed nostalgically, and Margaret said, "If there were a peat-bog in this country, I would send Daddy Hurst to cut some for you, Hetty – just to remind you of Wexford. But there isn't – so we make do with what we have."

"Oh, but I don't miss it that much, Marm," Hetty answered. "The soot it made inside our cot was dreadful . . ." She tilted her head, listening to the sound of rain, thrumming on the verandah roof outside of Margaret's little parlor. A fringe of rainwater fell off the veranda edge, and the rain itself veiled the distant view of Papa's apple trees all in gray. "It's coming down proper, now, Marm. To be sure I pity any Christian out in the weather tonight!"

Chapter 20 - *A Vow Taken*

The rain fell all that day and into the night: Margaret woke up several times, alternately wakened and soothed again by the sound. On one of these awakenings, she recollected drowsily how the river would be running high in a couple of days, up and over the knobby knees of the cypress trees on its banks. And the streets of Austin would be awash with mud . . . she made a mental note to see that the maids took special care. Perhaps she should speak to the boarders about cleaning their boots at the doorway. Margaret turned over in her bed and was nearly to sleep again, when a distant grumble of thunder jolted her awake. No, that was not thunder; she sat up in bed. Someone outside was launching heavy blows on the front door downstairs, as frantically as if the house were afire or a Comanche raiding party were chasing him.

"In the house!" a man's voice, shouting. "Open up!" The blows on the door seemed to shake the whole front of the house. Much more of this, Margaret feared they would burst the door from the hinges and latch. She fumbled for her wrapper and shawl. Her hair fell down her back, half-unraveled from a loose night-braid into a spill of silver-gilt.

"Mama?" Horace's sleepy voice came from the top of the stairs. "What is it, Mama?"

"I don't know," she answered, "Go back to bed – it's probably a friend of one of our gentlemen who forgot the time of night and thought it a proper hour to pay a call." It was pitch dark in her room, only a few embers glowed in the bedroom fireplace, like rubies all but buried in ashes, but she knew her own house by touch and habit. She took a paper spill from a little brass box on the mantelpiece and touched it to the brightest of the coals. When the spill flamed up, burning brightly, she lit the oil lamp with it, and hurried towards the main hallway, holding the lamp ahead of herself. As she passed by the door to the family parlor, the tall-case clock beside it chimed the hour – one o'clock of a wet and dreary midnight.

Another lamp cast a mellow golden glow, moving among the leaping shadows – Hetty, coming from the direction of her bedroom, also holding a lamp. Now the pounding at the door seemed ever more violent, and the voices on the other side of it heard more clearly.

"Who is there!" Margaret called, with her hand on the latch, "What do you want?"

"Open up! We've got a sick man here!" shouted one of those outside, and Margaret could hear Daddy Hurst' voice outside, remonstrating with them. He must have heard the racket and come around from his little cabin. She fumbled at the latch with one hand, wondering why anyone would be dragging a sick man out in this rain and cold rather than just fetching Dr. Williamson to attend their friend.

"They're looking for a doctor," she said with relief to Hetty. "Fetch Dr. Williamson – or Dr. Harper, if he has returned from his patient, before they waken the whole household." The front door swung open, admitting a gust of cold wind and rain. The flame in the lamp she held flickered, than sprang up again, feebly illuminating the scene on her doorstep. Two – no, three men stood there, with an indignant Daddy Hurst beside them holding up a tin lantern. The light cast tiny slivers of reflection on their wet clothing, on the cover of the wagon beyond. A team of horses stood in harness, their heads hanging miserably, but all was otherwise in darkness as a fresh wind stirred the nearly-bare apple tree branches and shredded off a few more leaves.

"You Miz Vining?" one of the men asked. He was ragged and hatless like his fellows, with a beard so thick and hair so long that in the dark hardly any of his face could be seen. He smelt powerfully of unwashed flesh, of horses and wet clothing: Margaret assumed at once that they were all three derelicts, drunkards. Some saloonkeeper in town, exasperated out of all patience with them, had chosen to play a crude jest by sending them to her house; she who rented rooms to legislators and men of quality – and ever since she had thrown out General Sam for chopping apart her best bed renown for her lack of toleration for drunkards.

"I am, sir," Margaret demanded. "What is the meaning of this, at this hour of the morning?

"The adjutant tole us to bring him," the ragged man answered, "as long as we were going this away home. Tole us he'd have the skin off our . . . beg pardon, ma'am, but ol' Bigfoot Wallace, he ain't a feller t'say no to. So we came straight here, soonest we crossed the river. 'Miz Vining, the boardinghouse,' they done tole us. Them trees yonder, them are apple trees, sure 'nuff, just like the Colonel said." He cast a quick look at his fellows, "We found 'er, Cole! Hooo-whee, and I cain't wait no longer to get wetter on the inside than I am on the out!"

"I cain't be no wetter on the outside," the man addressed as Cole answered, "but I'll surely look to getting wetter on my own inside!" Now Margaret saw they were holding up the third, wrapped in a Mexican horse-blanket, and drooping as if his very bones had turned as pliant as boiled leather. Like them, he was also the picture of derelict humanity, and appeared to be completely insensible. His head lolled to one side; that much she could see, in the dark.

"Who is he?" Margaret demanded, indignant that anyone would think to send such a person to her – so sick that if the other two had not been holding onto him, he would have fallen across the doorstep.

"Dunno, Ma'am," the first man answered, obstinately repeating, "they tole us to take him here – an' ma'am, I think you better send for a doctor."

"He took a wound at Monterrey," the man called Cole volunteered. "And he ain't been real pert since. He got the ague too, real bad. Say, ma'am, we done our part."

Behind her in the hallway, she heard Dr. Williamson, "I don't know why they didn't bring him directly to me, Miss Hetty, but I may attest as a doctor that my patients and their friends often do strange things."

At once, the first man said with relief, "Hey, Cole – there's the sawbones. Let's go, I got me a powerful hankerin' to get my whistle whetted." Without a further word, they let go their grip on the man between. As their support was removed he folded up on the doorstep like a bag of old clothes. His face turned towards the light as he fell. In horrified disbelief, Margaret recognized Carl, unshaven, sick and filthy. *Why had she not known him at once, even in the dark, and in his condition – been so quick to assume that this was some awful and embarrassing prank?*

She had not seen his face clear until that moment. Meanwhile at her elbow, Dr. Williamson was kneeling, all professional and patient curiosity, saying, "Hurst – if you will, help me bring him inside and close the door against the cold. This is not the best place for me to make a proper examination. Mrs. Vining, is there something the matter?" He was as unruffled as if this occurrence on her very doorstep was nothing more than a balky child and an over-attentive mother.

Margaret knelt at Carl's side, taking his head onto her lap and saying, "It is my brother, Doctor Williamson – The last I knew he was with in Mexico with the Rangers. I did not know him at first – Doctor, I must know what ails him!" She knew that her voice was rising; she was on the verge of making a frantic display of herself. This was Carl; she had always looked upon him as the first of her own children, whom she had cared for lovingly when she was barely more than a child herself. Carl had never been ill, baby and child – escaping the dreadful plagues which heartlessly snuffed small lives like someone quenching the faint flame of a candle. Now he shook so violently that his teeth fair rattled in his head.

"Rudi . . . is that the soldiers coming for us?" he mumbled in German. His eyes were half-open, but unseeing. His hands clutched the blanket around his shoulders as if it were the one thing keeping him from freezing to death. Dr. Williamson firmly took a corner of it in his hands and tugged it back. Underneath, Carl was naked save for a pair of ragged trousers that looked as if they had been used to clean chimneys with, and a mass of equally filthy dressing and bandages wound around his left shoulder, arm, and upper body. The bandages at his shoulder were the darkest; stained black in the dim lamplight with what Margaret knew must be blood.

Doctor Williamson looked upon what lay underneath the blanket, and then put it back, saying in tones of utter and commanding calm, "Hurst, if you will be so kind, waken Dr. Harper and that boy of his. Tell them I am in need of their assistance, this instant. Mrs. Vining, pray compose yourself; I must have a place to use as a surgery? A room both warm and well-lighted, with a sturdy table; perhaps your kitchen?"

"Yes, of cours.," Margaret gathered her thoughts, mentally steadying herself. "Hetty, see to it. Take what Dr. Williamson requires to the kitchen and bring me also some clean blankets."

"And if you would ensure that there is plenty of boiling water," Dr. Williamson added, getting to his feet. "It has been reported that cleanliness is most efficacious in preventing adverse outcomes following surgery . . . although it appears in this case that unsanitary conditions have done their best to no avail."

Margaret blinked – was that a small witticism? It was comforting to her, that Dr. Williamson was entirely calm. Someone tapped on the outside door again. Before anyone could reply, the man Cole opened it and put his head around the jamb, saying, "Sorry, Ma'am. We durn-near forgot his traps. Y'all take care of him – he's one of Jack Hays' boys!" He dropped his burden just inside the doorway; a saddle with a pair of saddlebags attached to it, and a rough bundle, and drew the door closed, before Margaret could think of anything to say in response. At that moment, Hetty came with an armload of blankets. Unbidden, she spread two of them over Carl, even as he lay on the floor.

"You should also prepare a sickroom," Dr. Williamson continued unruffled. "A room airy and warm, free of dust and mephitic odors. Convalescence is aided by quiet and restful surroundings."

"Of course." Margaret was steadied at once; rooms, comfortable rooms; that was her business and stock in trade. If the task of nursing her brother back to health could be broken into a series of small tasks, taken one at a time

– she could accomplish each one as it was presented to her. "Hetty, the room across from mine in the new wing; make up the bed with clean sheets and start a fire in the fireplace to take the chill off."

Hetty stood, her place taken by a yawning Dr. Harper hastily tucking the tails of his shirt into his trousers. He was followed as always by Mose, who carried his doctor's bag and attended upon him sometimes as a valet and mostly as his orderly and assistant.

The two doctors held a quiet colloquy over Margaret's head, as she settled the additional blankets around Carl, and breathed, "Oh, little brother – where have you been, all this time – and what happened to you in Mexico?" There was no answer, only the thready whisper: *"Rudi, are the soldiers coming for us?"*

When the men carried him towards the kitchen, Margaret followed with her lamp. At the door, Dr. Williamson said over his shoulder, "Mrs. Vining, there is no need for you to attend on this. Rough surgery is no place for a woman."

"I have seen uglier things than sickness and half-healed wounds, as you well know," Margaret replied. Dr. Williamson shook his head. "Perhaps – but when wounds so grievously affect a person close and dear to you, I would rather that my hands remain steady, and my judgement and comments to Dr. Harper remain unclouded by consideration for your possible distress. You do understand, Mrs. Vining?"

Margaret realized that for the first time in . . . how long it had been, that a man had evidenced a real concern for her state of mind, and more sincerely than that which superficial custom commanded. Her eyes swam with sudden tears: so often had Dr. Williamson been unobtrusively kind to her? His letters from Perote, his care after the Simpson children were stolen by the Indians . . . she had thought they had become closer friends through the letters they had exchanged while he was imprisoned in that awful place. She had rejoiced when he was freed and returned to Texas, joy tempered with embarrassment over how he had seemed – from the accidental inclusion of a love-sonnet in one of her letters – to have thought of her as a sweetheart. Since his return, he had seemed to accept that there was nothing between them but the kindly concern of friends. Even given that regard, Margaret now realized how she had never really taken particular note of his qualities. He had been one of the boarders: sober, gentlemanly, never demanding – a source of amusement, for his terrible absentmindedness and unvarying habit of bringing a book or some abstruse medical journal to the table, propping it against the cruets and reading throughout the meal in lieu of conversation with the other boarders.

She still blushed to think of how she and Mrs. Eberly had accidentally observed him from the grape-tangle on the bank above the deep swimming hole in Shoal Creek. Only the fact that he could barely see without his glasses had saved everyone hideous embarrassment.

"I shall withdraw to assist Hetty in preparing a room," Margaret answered bravely. "It is kind of you to consider my feelings."

His countenance brightened. "Dr. Harper and I will need some more lamps. And towels as well as new, clean dressings and bandages. We shall do our best for him. Take that as my – our heartfelt assurance, Mar – Mrs. Vining. Do not fear for your brother. He is young and otherwise fit and strong."

"I trust, Doctor – that whatever you must do for him will be completed by sunrise," Hetty put in, her voice tart and reassuringly confident as she reappeared at Margaret's elbow. "It is my kitchen that you will be taking over and at that time, we will need to begin with preparations for breakfast, unless that you think it fitting that your fellows should all be starvin' come that time."

"We are inspired by anticipation of your biscuits, Miss Hetty." Dr. Williamson answered, with a gallant half-bow, and Margaret thought to herself, *Oh my, he does have a sense of the ridiculous, after all.* She relayed the doctor's instructions to Hetty as regards more lamps and towels, and took an armful of sheets and pillows to the room which she thought might serve best in her brother's convalescence. She met Daddy Hurst at the doorway. He also had his arms full.

"Miz Margaret, I thought I should bring Mr. Carl's traps and things to his room," Daddy shook his head. "He shore do travel light, don't he?"

"I don't think my brother ever put much value on material possessions," Margaret answered. "Put them on the chair and see if Doctor Williamson needs further assistance." Margaret found it oddly soothing, making up the bed and settling fresh covers on the pillows. She took such pride in her establishment, of providing shelter and such comforts, and now Carl stood in such dire need of them. What manner of care had he, since being wounded? The man Cole said only that he had taken a wound at Monterrey; Margaret counted back. Monterrey had fallen weeks ago, although it had taken almost that long a time for the news to arrive. She turned back the bedcovers, and considered what other care could be taken; if he was suffering from the cold, shivering from the ague – a hot-water bottle might prove comforting. She went as far as the kitchen doorway, now brilliantly lit by nearly every lamp in the house. Carl lay supine on the kitchen table, pinned into place there by

Mose holding his legs and Dr. Harper gripping him by the arms. The light winked on a bright steel scalpel in Dr. Williamson's hand.

Margaret had only to hear Dr. Harper asking, in tones of revulsion, "My god – look! Are those maggots?"

"Oh, yes," Dr. Williamson replied, utterly serene and unsurprised. "They have a certain efficacy when it comes to cleaning a wound of this type. Otherwise the putrefying flesh would poison the patient's system."

Margaret swallowed against the up-rush of nausea in the back of her throat and fled. In the room intended as the sickroom she sought for something else to do; her eyes fell on the meager pile of her Carl's belongings. Yes, she would sort through them – put them into place, hang any clothing up to dry before the fire, now crackling merrily away. That would pass the time well enough, although as she lifted the first item, she realized it might not take much time at all. His heavy buckskin leather hunting coat, trimmed with strips of leather fringe as was the Indian custom . . . a haversack with some dirty calico kerchiefs, a bullet-mold, and a long-handled ladle obviously used to melt lead. A few more rough lumps of lead weighted the bottom of the haversack, a handful of finished shot, and an odd little assortment of tools and picks on a ring. A pair of knives – a small one with a long blade and a polished wooden hilt and that huge hunting knife with a hilt of cow-horn polished and scored to provide a good hand-grip and the recurve blade that Mr. Bowie had made so popular in Texas as to attach his own name to that style. That pair of holstered long-barreled Paterson Colt revolvers, the holsters attached to a stout leather belt, which he had once shown to her and to Mrs. Eberly.

She placed the contents of the haversack in the bottom drawer of the dresser, and opened the saddlebags, wondering if her brother had any other clothing with him at all. It appeared that he had traveled to the war in Mexico with little in the way of extra clothes: a pair of worn moccasins with the Indian-pattern quill ornament half fallen off, two pair of socks, several rather cleaner kerchiefs, and a single shirt comprised his entire wardrobe. The other saddlebag held a small book, a broken length of silver chain, a pocket-watch with a cracked crystal face, and a heavy ring of Mexican silver. She opened the book; it was in Spanish. The inscription in the front indicated that it belonged originally to someone in Monterrey; war loot, then.

She shook out the shirt, recognizing it as one she had made and presented to him at Christmas, now quite faded from the original color, although neatly mended. It was clean, no need to have it laundered. Margaret began re-folding the shirt – and then took a second look. It had been mended by a careful and expert seamstress, tears and worst-worn places reinforced with neat calico patches. The stitches were tiny, not of the sort made by most men, who could barely thread a needle. So, in the eight months or so that he had been away – Carl had found a woman, or perhaps a girl. Margaret didn't think that it was his light-of-love Dona-whatever-her name was in Bexar. He didn't love her, she remembered him saying, but he liked her fine. Margaret didn't believe that a high-born married Mexican lady of Bexar would be fond enough of Carl as to mend his shirt with her own hands. In the interim her brother must have found another lover, one who thought enough of him to do his mending, and he cared enough for her to keep her handiwork by him. It had been Margaret's experience that men otherwise shed outworn garments as carelessly as a snake sheds an old skin. She sat in the rocking chair next to the freshly-made bed, considering this new matter until Dr. Williamson appeared in the doorway, fastidiously drying his hands on a towel.

"We are finished with our examinations, Mrs. Vining." He seemed almost cheerful. "I think I may bear some good news . . . although your brother's wounds were deep and considerable, they appear to be healing cleanly. I cannot detect any impairment of his breathing through his injuries; Dr. Harper concurs with my judgement that any such as may develop may be due to a fever of the lungs. And that is what I fear is affecting him most – the rigors of the journey, as well as the ague. Our forces in Mexico have been most particularly affected by it, did you know? Fortunately, quinine-bark affords a remedy of sorts. I will make up a quantity of a suitable tincture, which you must see that our patient accepts. Dr. Harper is applying fresh dressings, this moment. Mose and Hurst will bring him along directly." Dr. Williamson looked as pleased with his good news as a young boy bringing a pretty fairing to a girl that he liked, or a knight bringing the prize of the tournament to his lady.

"Thank you – for your efforts. Thank you both." Margaret felt as if she might weep from sheer gratitude and relief. Dr. Williamson looked at the towel in his hands if not quite sure how he came to be holding it.

"It was our pleasure to be of service in this," he said earnestly. "To you, and to one of our heroes of Monterrey. I have the utmost respect for you, Mar – er, Mrs. Vining . . . and to be able to do this small service."

"It is not a small service," Margaret answered, her heart overflowing with such a multitude of emotions. "It is no small service at all, but a very great one, and for someone whom I love very dearly. I am more grateful to you, Doctor, than I can say." She rose from the chair; on an impulse that she could not identify, she was moved to embrace him, to reach her arms up to his shoulders – she meant to kiss his cheek, lightly frosted with stubble, but that very moment, he turned his head towards hers and the kiss fell on his lips. Fell and met gratefully, and returned with tenderness, as his arms went around her. For a moment the world swam; she would have fallen, but for the quiet strength of him, a tree to lean against as her knees wobbled.

"My most dear Margaret," he whispered, only those words. The world swam again, the golden lamplight seemed to pulse like a heart beating – no, it was not the lamp, it was his heart against hers, under his shirt-front and vest as she leaned her head on his shoulder. A faint scent of camphor rose from the cloth . . . *Oh*, she thought – *it has been so long since Race held me thus, so long that I have nearly forgotten what it was like to rest upon a man's strength, to be tenderly kissed and caressed.* She lifted her head, and this time as he kissed her, she sensed the tiny spark of desire that threatened to burst into full flame. *How could this have come about,* she thought in a small corner of her mind – *this is the doctor, who was Race's friend. He has lived in our house for years, how has it come to this, these feelings from nowhere?*

A shuffle of footsteps in the hallway brought them to their senses as efficiently as a dash of ice water; she hastily stepped back, as his arms dropped from around her. She did not dare look at his face, lest some slight expression reveal the tumult within.

Dr. Harper appeared in the doorway; he had not removed his surgical apron – and now that the excitement of performing surgery was finished, he was half-stifling a yawn. Mose followed him, his great ox-like strength making an easy burden of carrying Carl in his arms as if he weighed no more than one of her sons. Margaret hastily turned back the bedcovers.

"We dared not use ether because of the necessity for light," Dr. Harper said, as Mose laid Carl on the bed. The filthy bandages and the unspeakable trousers had been replaced by clean dressings and a striped nightshirt of Dr. Williamson's which Margaret recognized from the laundry. "A few drops of syrup of opium were sufficient, but I fear this fellow has a hard head, as they took a good long time to have the required stupefying effect." He yawned again, as Mose and Margaret replaced the bedcovers over her brother. He lay quietly now. With purple shadows under his eyes, and a growth of beard on his chin he looked more like Papa then ever. "He will sleep sound. You need not fear lest he vomit from the after-effects of ether," Dr. Harper added.

"I will sit by him for a while," Margaret declared, for she was still shaken from that brief moment with the doctor. Her worry over Carl was too intense to allow sleep to come easily, and it was nearly dawn.

Dr. Williamson was looking at her with his usual look of kindly concern. "You should not exhaust yourself, then, Mrs. Vining – it would do no good for your brother and your children to make yourself ill through over-work caring for an invalid."

"I have done so before without injury to my own health," she answered, wondering if had been her imagination that Dr. Williamson had called her his most dear Margaret. "And it is nearly the time I would be rising anyway. But thank you all, gentlemen – and Mose, for your care of my brother. I am more grateful than I may say."

"Anything to ensure Miss Hetty's biscuits at breakfast," Dr. Harper answered jauntily. "And indeed, anyone for whom you care, Mrs. Vining, is someone whom we perforce must care for as well."

He stifled a yawn again, converting a gesture of covering his mouth to a mock tipping of his non-existent hat, and withdrew, trailed by the stoic Mose, and Dr. Williamson, who did look anxiously after her. Margaret thought he might have spoken to her again but for Hetty bustling in with a kettle full of steaming water in her hand, shielded by a towel, and some more towels and a pair of metal hot-water bottles under her other arm.

"There now," she said briskly. "The fire is well alight, Marm – nothin' better for the ague an' shivers than a hot-water bottle. Oh, the poor laddie . . . such a look of the Old Sir he has now, does he not? I shall look in on him now and again, after breakfast is on th' table. Now you, Marm . . ." she shot an especially severe look at Margaret, "ye should rest, y'know, whin ye can. I am sure that the Young Sir will not come to any harm . . . for he is home again, and under a good roof!" She bustled about, filling the bottles and wrapping them in towels, and while she and Margaret were seeing to this, Dr. Williamson had vanished. Margaret was so tired and wandering in her mind by this time that she hardly took notice, and in any case was fair convinced that she had dreamed the whole interlude of their embrace. She sank into the rocking chair, with her warm shawl about her, and the easy breathing of her brother in the bed to reassure her; nothing of that dreadful catch and wheeze in his breath, nothing to recall the times that she had sat by the bedside of Race in the depths of that sickness which eventually killed him. Horace Templeton Vining had died far away in Boston – for which she still felt regret. In a note painfully written on his deathbed, he had said that she was the wife of his heart, not that woman in Boston who was his unloved wife-in-law. The discovery of his bigamy had stabbed her to the heart, but he had promised to make amends by divorcing his Boston wife. His long absence in the East on this errand had half way convinced Margaret that he had chosen to remain there, forgetting that promise. She would not know until months later that his shocked and horrified family had kept him from writing to her and procuring the divorce . . . it was all so long ago, Margaret thought – five years. In that time she had become independent, made a good living for herself and her sons, for Hetty and Morag. She would see that Carl was restored to health, even help him towards finding a little worldly happiness . . . but she was so very tired. The rocking chair was comfortable enough. She leaned back in it, wrapped the shawl around her, and slept for some hours, while the wind threw rain against the windows

For the next week, Margaret's world revolved around the sickroom where Carl lay delirious, shivering from the ague, or flushed with a fever that only Dr. Williamson's tincture of quinine could relieve. He was not sensible during that time, although his speech occasionally sounded rational. It struck Margaret as curious that for a man of very few words when in his right mind, he was downright voluble when out of it. He spoke in German and English – sometimes Spanish as well, to Jack Hays, or to other people whose names Margaret did not recognize; sometimes it was just ordinary talk, but more often he was calling out desperate commands in the thick of a fight long over. Once, he looked at Margaret with an expression of horror on his face, saying, "She's going for the child . . . and I don't think she can swim a lick!" Once or twice, heartbreakingly, he talked to Rudi and Mama. Several times, Margaret thought he was talking to herself – but in his fevered wanderings, he was talking to woman with a name rather like her own. In all that time, he never talked to Papa. Margaret was inexpressibly saddened by this; it was as if Papa had ceased existing for Carl even in delirium. Which was a supreme irony, for in looking at his face, Margaret could clearly see Papa in him, see the mature resemblance. Rudi, whom Papa loved so dearly, had never lived long enough for Margaret to note such a likeness. Now Carl, whom Papa had scorned, was his image – although not in temperament. Papa and Carl could not have been less alike.

Dr. Williamson faithfully attended on Carl morning and evening, as his first and last patient of the day. Within that first week, Margaret grew accustomed to being the doctor's assistant at those times when he opened up the bandages to check on the healing of the wounds, which within days had almost ceased to drain, while edges of the flesh granulated very satisfactorily. After some days of this, she got over feeling sick when the doctor expressed his satisfaction by pointing out to her every stitch of surgery and every degree of evidence in healing of those jagged slashes across Carl's shoulder and arm.

"It will all heal very nicely," Dr. Williamson assured her, "but he will be left with scars to show for it. Still – a very lucky man to have escaped without much infection. If anything came close to killing him, it was the ague and the journey home."

Margaret was busying herself gathering up the used and soiled lint and bandages. It seemed to her also that her brother was truly sleeping. He had not thrashed around in the bed or called out for some hours. During those moments when he came closest to lucidity, she had been able to get him to drink water or beef-tea and Dr. Williams' quinine-bark concoction.

"I begin to hope that the fevers are finally broken," she said. Dr. Williams nodded. On an impulse, she added, "Come and sit with us in the family parlor for a few moments before supper."

"Might I?" The doctor looked shyly pleased at the invitation, and Margaret wondered what had possessed her to offer it. The family parlor was her own, where Horace, Johnny, and Jamie had their lessons, where she mended their clothes, and kept her husband's library of books, and the little desk with her own account books neatly lined up. It was her private refuge, and not often shared with any but friends. But when she considered it, that way – Dr. Williamson was a friend – the one who had been with her establishment almost from the very first day, even before Hetty. Seamus O'Doyle was dead at Saltillo, Mr. Hattersley gone back to England ages since, little Morag and Danny Fritchie and baby Jemima gone home to Bastrop. Papa and Race were in their graves; only she and the boys would recall how they had begun making mattresses from ticking to stuff them with corn-shucks on the day that Margaret had resolved to make a living for them all.

"Of course," Margaret answered. "You are welcome to come and sit with us at any time," she added, "especially if you are tired of the noise in the boarders' parlor."

"I thank you, Mrs. Vining – that is very kind of you." Margaret thought he might have said more, but seemed to think better of it.

Dr. Williamson sat with them in the parlor that evening; he read the latest newspaper, but otherwise seemed to make himself an inconspicuous and rather restful presence. Margaret began to wonder if she truly had imagined that moment in the sickroom where he had kissed her, calling her his most dear Margaret. She had just about concluded that she had indeed imagined it, although sometimes she fancied that his eyes fell upon her with a certain amount of wistful affection, just as Hetty had once claimed. There was also the dream she had one night, a most peculiar dream in which that odd moment in the sickroom on the night of Carl's return had not only happened, but continued to an imagining of her and the doctor, with naked limbs entangled, embracing in her bed, a dream that – in the way of dreams – somehow merged with her memories of her husband doing just that, and she woke just then, feeling that flush of acute pleasure which had most always attended upon such intimacies. She lay awake for some minutes, staring at the ceiling overhead and wondering how that memory had crept into her dreaming mind. Of course, she had seen the doctor naked – just for that flash of a moment when she and Mrs. Eberly had seen him swimming in the waters of Shoal Creek, below where they had been harvesting grapes from a thicket on the bank above; he was a tall awkward gangle of bones and sinewy muscle, not anything like Race, who had been lean as a greyhound yet well-formed. Margaret blushed still to recall Mrs. Eberly chuckling and observing, "Who would have thought it, to look at him – he is set up as a stallion and not a gelding after all!"

Chapter 21 – *The Gift of Loving Friendship*

The darkness came early on these early winter days, and the warmth of the cozy family parlor was most welcome. She could look across the room at the heads of her sons, bent over their school studies around the oval table, while Peter played with his favorite toy horse and wagon on the hearth rug. This was the room that she was fondest of; in every way it was as fine as one of those rooms in the airy and modern house that Seamus O'Doyle had built for the Frenchman. Nonetheless, she was happy enough, on those evenings; comforting to look across the room and see Dr. Williamson. His very presence was comfort and reassurance. After another few days she fancied that she could see improvement in her brother's condition. The spasms of shivering, the violent fevers seemed to ease, and he spoke less often. She did not therefore spend so many late evening hours attending the sickroom, but slept more often in her own bed – but with an ear attuned to any odd noises from there in the night.

She woke at near midnight on the thirteenth day after Carl's return, hearing the musical chiming from the clock in the boarder's parlor striking the three-quarter hour – but that was not what had startled her into wakefulness. A voice? A footstep on the floor the room opposite, or the sound of someone falling? She sat up in bed at once, her heart in her very throat for thinking that Carl had attempted to get out of bed and fallen from weakness upon the floor. She lit a candle with shaking fingers, not bothering to put on a wrap or a shawl over her nightgown. What if he had broken open the just-healing wound once again? The house was dark, save for her candle, and a thread of light showing under the closed door of Carl's room. She opened the door without knocking, and was abashed to discover Dr. Williamson leaning over the bed with his stethoscope in his hands. He was in his shirt-sleeves, and stocking feet and appeared quite rumpled, as if he had been sleeping in his clothes.

"Mrs. Vining! I am sorry – I did not mean to wake you!" he exclaimed.

"Is there something the matter with my brother?" she demanded, almost in the same instant, for the Carl lay motionless and silent under the covers.

"No," he answered hastily, "No, nothing wrong – in fact, most extraordinarily promising, for I believe the wound-fever as at last broken." He blinked at her – oh, the dear man was entirely lost without his spectacles. Margaret was sure that she or Hetty would find them somewhere about the house in the morning. "I . . . I thought I should check on my patient, one last time before I retired for the night. Observe – laudable perspiration."

"Let me see." Margaret hastened to the bedside, her heart still in her throat. She brushed her fingers across her sleeping brother's forehead; yes, the doctor was correct. His flesh was slightly damp, and if not precisely cool to the touch, then no warmer than a healthy child or man deep in healing sleep. *Oh, she thought, I shall have to get that awful beard off of him, I don't care for seeing nothing more of a man's face than a wad of hair and it makes him look too much like Papa – which I know Carl would hate.* Aloud, she exclaimed, "You are right – the fever has broken, at last!" She felt tears prickling her eyelids, and sternly blinked them back. "Thank God – I have been in such mortal fear for him – not just these past weeks, but for every day that I knew his company was on a campaign against the Indians, or on the border. He is my only living relative now – and more precious to me than any other, save my children."

"Then he is dear to me also, knowing the regard in which you hold him," the doctor answered with such passionate intensity that Margaret blinked. "For you have become very dear to me also, these past few years. I did not dare to speak of my affections . . . knowing of your devotion to your late husband. He was my friend, inasmuch as I have friends . . . but I confess that I was deeply envious of him, envious for his possession of the finest jewel of womanhood that I know of."

"Oh, my dear doctor," Margaret did not know whether to laugh or cry. "I am not a jewel, only an ordinary woman! Merely one who wishes to secure a portion of joy and happiness for my family and those whom I am accustomed to think of as my family! I am no paragon, there are thousands like me, each of us tending to our families, and garden that we are allotted. I value your affections, truly I do. I think of you as a very dear friend – and not only for your care of my brother, but for all that you have done for my husband from the very day that we met. If there is a jewel among us, then it would be you, for all that you have done for us, in humble care and devotion."

"I am? I do?" Dr. Williamson seemed honestly baffled by her words. Out of sheer exasperation, Margaret set aside the candle that she held, and embraced him, feeling the warmth of him under the thin shirt, his ribs and the pitiful thinness of the flesh that overlay them. Perote had made a tragic mark upon him, even as much as Goliad and Monterrey had left an indelible mark upon her brother. What could she do that might erase and heal those brutal scars and memories? In the next moment, he bent down to her and kissed her; he was one of those men whom she loved and wished to keep safe, to shelter in her fierce affection, a man who had been an unobtrusive friend for all these years, and so she returned that kiss.

It seemed to Margaret that now a curious fire ran over her flesh. That tiny spark of desire that she had sensed upon that first peculiar embrace now took fire and flamed up, so swift and overwhelming. She gave over to it entirely, surrendering in that brief moment. Dreams and reality merged – had she swooned again, or was this something that she had dreamed, the feeling of a man's chest against hers, strength and gentleness – her soft and yielding breast against his hardness and that particularly male aspect urgently questing for entry.

Now she was in her own bed, without any memory of how she had gotten there, or how she had come to be divested of her nightgown and the doctor of his clothing – only that she was there. The doctor was there also – breathing above her in the darkness, moving inexorably within her, his gentle kisses sending her flesh aflame and turning her bones to water . . . *I ought not to be doing this . . . it is wrong*, she thought with that small part of her mind. *I dreamed of something like this – how is this become real, I have known him forever, and now it has suddenly come to this, that he is giving me the pleasure that only a husband ought to give, pleasure in such measure that I can barely encompass it . . . is he the one that I am to marry for friendship, as the witch foretold?*

"Dearest Margaret," he whispered, and she pulled him closer to her, as he shuddered in that ultimate convulsion. It seemed as if he was without words for a moment, and Margaret wrapped her arms even more tightly around his shoulders. The weight of him pressed her deeper into the mattress; she could not have escaped, being thus captured, nor did she want to. "I have often thought of this . . . this madness. Forgive me. I did not think to take advantage of you in this manner," he confessed at last, and Margaret answered, her voice sounding faint in her own ears, "I would not have allowed this to happen did I not desire it also. If this is madness, then I share it equally."

"I . . . I should leave, then." He made as if to lift himself from the bed, and Margaret found that gesture unbearable, the thought of his departure unthinkable.

"No," she whispered with sudden frantic energy. "No. Stay with me, Henry. If you found a spring of water after many days in the desert . . . wouldn't you drink until you are no longer thirsty?" *And I am indeed mad,* Margaret thought, *to let such longings possesses me – to let him possess me – and I do not care!*

"Truly?" he sounded as if he had been allowed a glimpse of paradise, disbelieving and joyous, all at once. Margaret cupped his face in her one hand, as they lay side by side; in the faint light from the fire, dying amidst its embers in the fireplace, he looked so very young, almost boyish.

"Yes – truly, my very dear doctor," Margaret answered, and the words came to her as a confession. "I find that I am in such need of affections, such as my husband and I once engaged in. It is very wanton of me, I know . . . but having become accustomed to them . . . to endure without is difficult at times, although not quite as difficult as it is to be without a husband, to be totally in responsibilities, alone without a companionable helpmate! I do wish that you would remain. Your presence in the family parlor and your care have been so very comforting to us."

"It was what I promised him, dearest Margaret." His hand reached out again, straying across her breast and shoulder, to toy with the spread of her hair which had come entirely unbraided.

"Promised whom?" Margaret settled herself against the length of his body, her cheek laid next to his shoulder, and one arm laid around his waist, thinking with one corner of her practical, housewifely mind that he was still too dreadfully thin and perhaps she and Hetty could contrive something of special nourishment for him as well as for Carl.

"What I promised to Mr. Vining, upon his departure from Galveston – I would guard and protect you and the children in his absence in Boston." He hesitated for a moment before continuing. "He vouchsafed to me the purpose of his errand, you see. I was . . . horrified. I . . . had tried for days to discourage him from it, knowing as I did that his health was not equal to the journey. And when finally he confessed to me . . . I agreed. For your sake, such peril would be well-risked. I had long . . . held the greatest respect for you, you see."

"I do see," Margaret was deeply shaken, moved near to tears. All this time, Henry Williamson had known of Race Vining's bigamous marriage, had taken a solemn promise to look after her and the boys – been faithful to it, never revealing a word of this to her! "And so you remained, save for those two dreadful years in Perote. I confess that sometimes I did wonder why you stayed – even returned here from prison, when you could have made a life and a home for yourself elsewhere. I did not even begin to guess that it was for reasons as noble as this."

"I had promised," he answered with utter simplicity. "And, you see . . . I am not the kind of man to court and marry. I have never quite known what to say to people in conversation. Most usually it is the wrong thing. The practice of medicine is the life I know. To live in your house these past few years . . . is the most contentment that fortune has ever blessed me with, and more than I could have ever looked for."

"I don't know about what a man would do in your situation, when it came to courting," Margaret answered, "but for yourself, you suit me very well just as you are." And she sat up a little against the tumbled pillows and kissed him again.

Henry Williamson remained all night in her bed, until long after the dawn pinkened the sky outside; there were moments in the hours of darkness when he made as if to go, and others when she regretfully suggested that he ought to, but each time the kisses intended to be a farewell turned from languorous to passionate. The tender parting embrace was reversed, as they clung to each other every more tightly; each time Margaret thought that satiety had been reached, that the embers of utter contentment had died down to a steady glow, the fires leaped up again. But when she heard the faint distant sounds of Hetty shuffling her iron pots on the patent-stove – that was when she knew that they both must rise. How curious, how her perceptions could change within a bare few hours, she thought. In the cold hours of daylight, her lips felt bruised from those kisses, joyously and passionately given or taken, and those particular female parts ached also – as pulpy as a wind-fallen apple, although she was unsure if that was because it had been so long since she had bedded with her husband, or because of Henry Williamson's own vigor in paying marital attentions. Curiously, she did not feel the least bit tired for having had so little sleep; she felt refreshed, her energy renewed, and not the least bit guilty for having indulged her own impulses. Such indulgence rewarded and made happy a man who had been so devoted, deserved so very much – and yet had asked for so very little. In a little while, she must sit at the head of the breakfast table and pretend that nothing the least untoward had happened during the night.

"It is time," she said, pushing back the bedcovers and shivering slightly at the touch of cool air on her bare flesh. Henry Williamson was already sitting on the edge of the bed, looking blankly towards the floor.

"I think I left my clothes there," he said. "And my glasses . . . have you seen them?"

"You had left them somewhere else last night," Margaret answered, as she began weaving her hair into the usual loose braid. "Hetty or I will look for them today. Where did you leave my nightgown?"

"Somewhere," he answered, and he turned around to peer at her. "You know Margaret – you are more beautiful at this moment than I have ever seen you. We should consider getting married."

"I think we should," Margaret agreed sedately. It seemed so very logical, and right, as if they had agreed upon it without speaking – but as the birds flew, turning in the sky in unison with each other. "Anyone seeing us this moment would think we were anyway. But I would first like some time to acquaint the boys with the idea. And I should like my brother to be convalescent – at least, enough that I may talk to him about this." She found her wrapper lying across the blanket-chest at the foot of her bed . . . and crumpled on the floor by the trunk she found Henry's shirt and trousers. "Here," she gathered them up, "Your clothes – if you put them on, you may slip across the hallway and make a pretense of attending my brother before breakfast. We left him sleeping soundly last night, the fever having broken."

"Oh yes." His face brightened. "I had not thought of that – I think of one thing at a time, to the exclusion of all others. Useful when it comes to medicine, I think." He had already gotten into his clothes while she hastily remade the bed, and poured water into the basin from the ewer on the washstand. She kissed him lightly as he made to depart, and noticed with a touch of fond exasperation that he barely noticed.

At mid-morning and after helping Hetty and the girls clear away the breakfast dishes, she took her accustomed place in the rocking chair drawn up to the bedside, mending a ripped tablecloth by reweaving the broken threads with careful stitches, while she waited for her brother to wake. Sunshine spilled into the room, and cast moving leaf-shadows on the floor. Carl's fever was well and truly broken and Margaret was certain that he had slept that last night soundly, peacefully. She thought that his eyes were moving, under closed lids; she ceased rocking, and laid her hand on his forehead.

"Open your eyes, little brother. I know you're awake." She commanded with stern fondness. He obeyed, and to her relief there was awareness in his gaze, and some little curiosity as those sky-colored eyes roved around the room.

"How did you know I was awake?" His voice was hoarse, scratchy.

"I've been watching, and I know you very well, little brother." Margaret answered. Another long pause, while he continued reconnoitering the room.

"How long . . ." He began to cough; Margaret brought a cup of Dr. Williamson's tincture to his lips. He drank a little, and asked. "Have I been here for very long?"

"Your friends dropped you on my doorstep like a load of dirty laundry two weeks since," Margaret answered, with some asperity. "They said you took that wound in the fighting before Monterrey. This is the first time you have been sensible. Doctor Williamson has been attending you every morning and evening."

"Very dedicated of him," Carl observed, and Margaret had to smile. *Little brother, he cares for you because he is a good doctor – and also because he loves me to distraction.* Aloud, she said only, "He's one of my boarders. Nothing is too good for our heroes of Monterrey, although I suppose I shall have to discount his rent in courtesy. Shall I help you to sit up? You should, if you feel strong enough." *I may as well discount his rent, for I will marry him – his missing spectacles and his absent mind and all.*

"I've enough of looking at the ceiling, Margaret."

"Very well, then." Margaret helped him lift his head and shoulders, deftly sliding a couple of pillows, before letting him sink down onto them. "Let me know when you've had enough."

"This is new. You have built on another wing?"

"Yes, six rooms downstairs, three up. They had just begun building it when you were here last. I had meant to rent these three, but they have such a pleasant aspect, I have kept them for the family. You should come home more often."

"Home," he observed in wry tones. "It's that place that when they dump you on the doorstep like dirty laundry, they have to take you in."

"So true," Margaret agreed. She took up her tablecloth from the sewing table beside her. "As it is, you turn up every couple of months with your clothing in rags and fit only to be burnt and a beard like a wild man, saying very little of where you have been and what you have been doing, save that it was at Jack Hays' bidding. This last time, I thought you were working for that Prince Fancy-Trousers. Oh my, the stories that went around about him – at least the ones the boarders would tell me." The sewing reminded her of his carefully mended shirt, and her relief that his fever had abated led her to tease him, just the tiniest bit. "At least this time you found someone to mend your clothes for you. You should tell me about her, little brother."

"Her? Why would you think that, Margaret?" he returned, in a very bland voice. The beard hid much of his face, so she could not read his expression.

"I unpacked your saddlebags and for a marvel found a shirt in it which wasn't in rags. In fact, it was mended very neatly and folded up with great care. I have met men who can tell one end of the needle from the other, and even make stitches with it, under extreme duress, but never as neatly or as small as a woman does. I was not born last night. You either have a pet mouse whom you have taught to sew, or you have met a woman in the last year who thinks well enough of you to do your mending. Who is she, Carl?"

"She thinks well of me because I pulled her niece out of the river," Carl answered morosely. "It's a long story."

"You should tell it to me, then," Margaret set aside her mending. The beard irked her – it was not her brother's face, but that of Papa. It did not suit him. "I have an idea. You shall tell me about her as I shave off those dreadful whiskers — really, you look so much a stranger with them that I can't bear it. Don't laugh, little brother, I used to barber Mr. Vining all the time when he was too weakened. We used to have some of our nicest talks, then."

"Well. of course, you were the one holding the razor," Carl answered with amusement.

"Don't be provoking. You'll feel much better without all that awful bristle. It makes you look too much like Papa, anyway." What a good idea, she thought – Race had always felt revived by her care in barbering him. She had noted the same with the boarders upon returning from the care of a good barber, and concluded that to a man, a good shave did the same as a new bonnet did for most women.

But as she went to fetch a bowl of warm water from the kitchen, Carl muttered, "I'd sooner live in hell with my back broke than go around looking like him."

Margaret felt her throat tighten. *Oh, Papa, you never had the slightest idea of what you did to Carl, did you?* She gathered the towels, and the necessary articles from Horace's room, reasoning that he was several years from having a serious need of them, and why should he begrudge the use of them to his uncle? She also gathered her thoughts – she had taken much comfort from this ritual when Race had been so very ill. Now she perched on the edge of the bed, saying, "I think I will clip off the worst of it first. Tell me about this girl. You rescued a child? Of course — all the sentimental novels have something like this. What is she like?"

"A very spirited filly," Carl answered as if he were thinking carefully. "She's tall with good lines, and totally fearless. Looking at her was like looking into a whole corral of horses, seeing just that one and knowing that is the one you want, no matter the asking price."

Margaret looked at him with fondness and no little exasperation; no doubt that was the way that Henry Williamson looked upon her – the knowing and the absolute certainty of wanting – but hapless as he was with words he had still put it better than that.

"Oh dear. Never tell her that, little brother. A horse, indeed; not the most romantic thought. You should think of something more gallant."

"I can't. She's like a fine thoroughbred that I want for my own, and that's all. Pa always did say I was a dullard compared to Rudi."

"Oh?" Margaret thought she had enough of men and their thinking. They always claimed that women were sentimental, emotional – but that was nothing as to the simmering anger stored up by men. "So he did. And did you take it so to yourself, thinking it was true? Papa loved Rudi, over and above you and me; live with that, little brother. Should what he thought and said stab you so to the heart?"

"We loved Rudi too, Margaret. He was the best of brothers."

"He was that, indeed." Margaret answered, and her throat closed in grief, remembering Rudi – so impulsive and adventurous. And Papa had made him into a perfect martyr-saint, disdaining the son he had never had much use for. Poor Carl – imperfect, but very much alive – only because of Rudi's last gesture, standing between his brother and the mouths of the executioner's muskets. Margaret wondered if that was what had made Papa angriest of all with Carl. "What I have always remembered most was how he loved pranks and practical jokes, and making people laugh. There wasn't a shred of malice in him, either. Even the people he pranked were always laughing, afterwards. Hot towel, little brother. Hold still and think about what you are going to tell me about this girl of yours. Who is her family, and where did you meet them?" She swathed a hot, damp towel on his lower face, and from behind it, he answered indistinctly.

The story came out in fits and starts. Before Carl and the Rangers went to the war in Mexico, he had met a girl – a German girl, whose family had come to settle Prince Solms' grant. They had gone to a new settlement in the western hills, and Carl had not seen her since then. Margaret listened, as she swabbed lather onto his face, thinking that perhaps she had been too hasty in wanting to shave off that awful beard. He was tiring, and his eyes had bruised shadows under them. Perhaps she should not press his reserve so hard. It might only be fair to share her own concerns.

She took up the straight razor, and commanded, "Hold still or you'll get a mouthful of soap. Perhaps I should tell you some of my own thoughts now. Listen and hold still, you should not talk during this next part."

"You have a very sharp razor within an inch of my throat. That ensures my complete attention, Margaret." *Good*, Margaret thought; *he looked amused.*

She settled herself more comfortably on the bed. "Well, I am considering marriage again — to Doctor Williamson. He has asked me so,

271

several times, and I am inclined to accept. I do not need to marry, but I enjoy his company and think I would relish more of it. And also the boys like him. Really, little brother, I should cut your hair, as well. Remind me on this. Anyway, I am considering his proposal with all care. Do not think I would neglect securing my own interests and those of the boys. I have not rented rooms to lawyers and legislators for nothing! I think if I appealed to certain of my boarders, I could get a bill passed for my exclusive benefit!" As she talked, Margaret worked away with the razor, turning his face this way or that with her other hand, and thinking of all the things that she might not say; of Race and his Boston wife, of Dr. Williamson's promise to him, and of how they had already spend most of a night together. Her brother listened with quiet attention, regardless of the razor. She finished, saying, "It is not as if the boys need a fatherly example, as you would be if you visited more often. But I like him, and relish his presence without being particularly set upon it. So, tell me now. What do you think?"

"I should have to meet him, while in my right mind, of course," her brother answered, as she rinsed the razor. "Other than that, just be certain of your own interests, in letting him control your property."

"I have already seen to that," Margaret answered. Really – did her brother think herself to be helpless, at the mercy of every charming scoundrel? After all, she had run the boardinghouse for nearly ten years now, in good times and in bad, with Hetty's assistance. "Now, hold still, this is the tricky part . . . there. I am finished. You can talk to me and tell me true. You met this party of folk from the Old Country. Who are they and how did her niece get into the river?" She rinsed off the razor and looked carefully at his face – very pale about the mouth and cheeks without the beard; it would have looked even odder except that the weathering on the upper part of his face had also faded while he had been ill.

"Steinmetz. Christian Friedrich Steinmetz," Carl answered. "He makes clocks, but he farms a little on the side. He had a wife but she died on the boat coming over; he now has two sons, a son-in-law, and three pretty daughters."

"Sounds like one of Mama's old fairy tales." Margaret dabbled away a bit of foam with a towel. *How much further did she dare question her brother about this girl? If she pried too much, he would not say anything at all. Where was the girl now? Had he written to her while he was in the war in Mexico?* Margaret thought not. "I suppose it is the youngest and prettiest that you have charmed," she ventured, and Carl began to laugh, a hearty laugh that turned into a fit of painful coughing.

"The youngest and prettiest is all of two years old," he gasped, when he could speak again. "Oh damn, it hurts when I do that! The middle daughter is the married one. She has a little girl – the one I pulled out of the river."

"So, you have set your heart on the oldest daughter ... hold still again." Margaret made neat work of the last bit of stubble on his cheek. "Lift up your chin, now, I am nearly finished. How does she regard you, little brother?"

"I don't know." He sank back onto the pillow. Without the beard he looked pale, pale and ill. "They were very kindly folk. They made much ado about loaning me dry clothes. She brought my own back to me and we talked for a little." No doubt about the way that he said "she." This was no calf-love for Jacob Harrell's daughter in Waterloo-that-was, when her brother had been a boy, before he and Rudi had been swept up in the war-fever of the rebellion against Mexico ... or anything of his fondness for the noble Dona Inez of Bexar, she of the rich husband and of the pure Spanish blood. Now Carlchen was a man, and yearning for this girl – and if he had not been so very ill, Margaret was certain that nothing would have brought him to speak of the clockmakers' daughter from the Old Country. Quiet as a boy, now he was practically a sphinx. "It was ... very agreeable, passing the time with them; as I remember it being when Mama and Rudi were alive."

In a flash of illumination, Margaret realized that it was not only the clock-maker's daughter whom her brother admired. Was she the one he spoke of in his fever, the one who couldn't swim, but who still tried to rescue the child? Bravery; he would like that, of course, but perhaps he also wanted the company of her family as well, all those sisters and brothers and a clever, kindly father, who did not – Margaret was willing to wager – play favorites among his sons. And such company was an improvement over men like Cole, who had dumped him on her doorstep ... or those high-bred ladies of Bexar.

"What were you planning to do, then?" Margaret asked. "I think I should take away the extra pillows and let you lie down again to rest."

"I wasn't thinking so far ahead," Carl answered. "And I'm too tired to think about it now."

"I shouldn't have had you sit up for so long," Margaret said remorsefully as she tidied up the towels and the bowl of water. "Now that you are home, perhaps you can send a message to them. No doubt they think of you fondly."

Even as she spoke, Carl had drifted into sleep again; that quiet and healing sleep, not the troubled tossing and turning. Margaret resettled the quilt around him, thinking that he appeared just now as she had always thought of him – hardly older than Horace when he left Alois Becker's farmstead for good at the height of the summer after the war; sixteen, gawky and not quite filled out. Margaret emptied the basin into the slops jar and gathered up the damp towels. She looked down at her brother, thinking, *He is too shy to tell me your name, clockmaker's daughter from the Old Country. But treat him with kindness; that is all I ask of you. Just because my little brother will not show his hurts, doesn't mean he doesn't feel them.*

Chapter 22 – *The Wife to Be*

"Hetty," Margaret ventured as she and Hetty washed up the dishes from the midday meal on the day that Carl had wakened from the troubled delirium which had claimed him since his most recent and unexpected return. "I believe that I shall marry Dr. Williamson. He has already asked me, and I have agreed."

"Aye?" Hetty sounded unmoved – to Margaret's vague chagrin, since she had thought that Hetty would at least be taken somewhat by surprise. "About time . . . since he has only been looking afther ye wi' eyes like a lovelorn calf since . . . aye, two or three years now, iver since he came back from Perote? An' ye said yourself, he's a man w' a good trade, amiable – if somewhat absent in mind, most of the day. But not from your bed last night, I might make fair to mention."

"Henrietta Bridget Moylan!" Margaret fair blushed to the roots of her hair – how would Hetty know anything of what had happened between herself and the doctor that previous night? Hetty had gone to her own chamber long since, and Margaret was certain that Henry Williamson had slipped quietly from her room without anyone being the wiser. "Whatever would lead you to think there was something improper between us?"

Hetty chuckled, not the least discomfited. "When I went into the dining room at cock-crow this morning to see that the girls had laid the breakfast table proper, I found Doctor Williamson's eye-glasses on the sideboard. So, I took them up to his room, thinking that he might be awake and wanting them, but when I tapped at the door, he was no' within, an' his bed had not been slept in. I left them on the dressing-table, thinking it was none of my business, only t' see, as I came down again, a glimpse of him coming from your room. Aye, an' it might hae been that he was telling you something of the Young Sir's condition. O'course, that's what I'd say to enny who saw the same," she added slyly, "but th' Doctor, he did have a look of a cat who's been at the cream."

"There's not a secret that I can keep from you for very long," Margaret admitted, laughing and still pink with embarrassment. "But yes. We were in my room together. It was something that happened so suddenly. I realized how very fond that I am of him, Hetty. He is a good and worthy man, and all this time I did not see those noble qualities in him! I knew very well that he felt tenderly towards me . . . but so also do many of the gentlemen, and I have always taken great care in turning such affections gently aside. I thought to myself for all this time that he has rented a room, he is an old friend . . . and we have been easy and comfortable in that friendship, such as I had with so many other honorable men of my acquaintance. I did not think that I should ever fall in love with such as General Sam, or Mr. Burnett, or Mr. Ford. I did not think that I could ever love anyone, after my husband."

"Aye," Hetty answered sturdily, beginning to roll out the dough for the breakfast biscuits. She did not seem in the least shocked at Margaret's confessions, which Margaret found to be vaguely comforting. Like Angelina Eberly, Hetty was one of those women who – having experienced much and observed more – had thereby moved far beyond being startled by anything at all of the human condition. "Once burned, Marm – twice wary, as our Mam used to say. Mr. Vining," and now Hetty seemed to search carefully for words, as she deftly wielded the rolling pin this way and that on the mass of biscuit dough, "the master – he left ye burned badly, Marm, did he not?" She cast a shrewd glance in Margaret's direction, and Margaret thought how she might like to tell Hetty of Race Vining's ultimate betrayal. No – remembering General Sam's advice. *Scandal dies, deprived of nourishment, if no one speaks of it.* And that two may keep a secret, if one of them is dead, and the others who know of the matter are far away in Boston and equally motivated to keep silence.

"He left me uncertain of my own judgement in those matters of the heart," Margaret finally answered. "And unwilling to place myself – and my sons and my property – in the power of anyone other than myself; my affections had been . . . not misplaced, Hetty. My husband had many noble qualities, and I loved him so very dearly! But he had faults also – and to my cost, that love that I bore for him led me to overlook them. Since I could not then see his faults, how could I how observe and judge any man fairly . . . since I could then put my sons and myself at risk?"

"The Doctor, now – he is a foine man," Hetty said. If she suspected Margaret's silence on certain matters, she gave no evidence of it. "Whatever his faults may be, I am certain, Marm – we know every one of them. That he leaves his nightshirt on the floor, forgets his spectacles everywhere an' canna live on his own w'out such as we to look after him? We know all, in ivry detail. In marryin' him, ye are no' buyin' a pig in a poke. All ye know of him? That is what ye shall have – an' that ye love him ennyway? I dinna think ye have gone wrong, Marm. He may be a difficult man, Marm – but now ye know where all those difficulties lie."

"So I do," Margaret answered, recalling the old black witch's prophecy: that she would marry once for love and once for friendship. *But love will grow from friendship, having deep and sturdy roots.* "I have come to love him very much, and I think will love him even more; as a woman and not the child I was when I first decided that I should marry Mr. Vining."

"So." Hetty sent her another sideways glance, as Margaret began to break eggs into a bowl – for the first batch of scrambled eggs for the boarders' table. "How do yer menfolk think of this? The Young Sir and the boys? They might have much to think and to say about this, for sure, Marm – it is a disruption to the way of yer household. "

"My brother does not have any objection," Margaret answered. "Save that he expressed a wish to converse with the Doctor when in his right mind – I told him of this as I shaved off that dreadful beard that he had grown in Mexico."

"He is your wee brother," Hetty said. "I think, Marm – he will not raise any objection. It is the boys – they might feel that ye will be displacing them from your affection . . . or even that you discount their father."

"I know," Margaret answered. This was one of the things she had pondered all morning, after Carl had gone back to sleep; how to tell the boys – although she was sure that Peter, having no memory of his father, would readily accept Henry Williamson as a member of the family. "It's not as if anything would really change as far as they are concerned," she mused aloud. "He already lives under my roof, eats at my table, sits with us in the private parlor of an evening, tutors Horace and Johnny . . . everything that a father might do, short of withdrawing to the same room as I at bedtime. I expect that I will only have to tell them that, and hope for the best."

Now that she had considered what to say to her sons, Margaret began to feel some nervous apprehension, such as she had not felt since she was a child herself. When to tell them? Very soon, she thought. This was the day that she walked down to Bullock's Inn, for her piano practice in Mary Bullock's china parlor, and she began the hour with her mind fairly distracted, even as her fingers caressed the ivory keys, coaxing music from them. She lost herself for a while in that music – for this was something which demanded all of her attention – and at least felt somewhat calmer as she bade Mary goodbye and returned to her own house. The wind stirred the leafless branches over her head, and those last few bronze leaves still clinging to the mighty oak trees, as she rehearsed again what she would say to them, before beginning their afternoon lessons. It was a chill day, the sky scoured clean and blue by the winds out of the north, and she pulled her warm mantle closer about her. The house looked even more inviting than usual: the seat of her realm, a small castle crowning the hill and surrounded by the tonsure of the orchard.

"Boys, I have something important to tell you," she ventured, when the four of them had settled around the table, slates and books at hand.

Before she could say another word, Jamie piped up, "When are you going to marry Doctor Will, Mama?" and they all looked at her with cheerful expectancy.

"Very soon, I think." Margaret answered, as the knot of tension at the back of her neck, and between her shoulders lessened with such alacrity that she felt quite limp with relief. They already knew, and they were not unhappy – in fact, the boys seemed quite pleased on the matter. "But . . . how did you know?"

"Doctor Will asked us, straight out." Horace answered. "This morning, as he went out to do his calls and we were doing our chores; he told us that he loved you very much, and wanted to know if we would mind if he courted you. He said that nothing much would change – he has always liked things just as they are, with the house and all. He would continue giving us lessons, just as he always has. And Daddy Hurst, when he brought around Bucephalus for Doctor Will, he heard what we were saying, and he told us that since Eve in the Bible was made from a rib of Adam, it meant that a man and a woman were supposed to be a part of each other. Did he ask you, Mama – and did you say yes?"

"You talked with Hurst?" Margaret was torn between amusement and a sense of embarrassment – did everyone know her private business? Hetty always insisted that Peter and Hurst were as thick as thieves, and that it wasn't a suitable friendship. Peter nodded, and Jamie said, "Daddy Hurst – he thought it was a grand idea. An' we like Doctor Will. It would be nice to have a papa again, too," he added wistfully, as Peter demanded, "When are you going to marry him, then, Mama?"

"I had not thought so far ahead," Margaret had not, but the more that she considered it – Christmas would be a good time. There would be parties and celebrations, gatherings of friends – and family. "Perhaps Christmas would be a good time. Yes – Christmas. Perhaps your uncle will be better by then."

She was still in the private parlor with the boys when Doctor Williamson returned from his round of calls – for a wonder, having today remembered his hat, coat, medical bag and the ever-patient Bucephalus. Margaret looked up at a step in the doorway, and saw that he lingered in the doorway, as if he were still uncertain of his welcome – either that, or he wished to relish the scene of domestic comfort and tranquility.

At any rate, she sprang from her seat, exclaiming, "You are early, my dear doctor – we have only just finished lessons!" She swiftly embraced him, kissed his cheek in a wifely fashion, thinking all the time of how comforting it was to do so – and likewise comfortable. Henry Williamson was as dear and familiar as a well-worn garment. He returned the kiss, putting his arms about her lightly – a hesitant embrace but made with growing confidence, ignoring with commendable assurance the mock-gagging sound that Jamie made.

"Ugh – they're kissing!" Jamie whispered, and Doctor Williamson observed calmly, "Yes, James – I will always kiss your mother, upon returning after an absence of some hours. If you are in some gastric distress, I might administer a dose of bismuth. I have brought the latest newspapers from Houston and San Augustine – the stage brought them to Bullocks' this afternoon."

"Oh, good – is there news of the war in Mexico?" Margaret asked – still thinking how comforting, how reassuring it was to be embraced so and be kissed as if it were only the customary courtesy of a fond couple towards each other.

"There is," her soon-to-be husband answered, and Margaret brushed her lips against his cheek once more, saying, "Then share it with the boys . . . I should see if Carl is still sleeping. We had such a long talk this morning, as he was in his right mind once again. I could not stand the sight of that awful beard, so I barbered him, but I fear the effort was all too much for him."

"It was not, dearest Margaret," Doctor Williamson answered. "I looked in on him just now and conducted an examination, since he is awake again. I believe he is on the road to recovery – although his appetite is not yet recovered, I think that a light meal, a little nourishing broth . . ."

"Thank you, my dear Doctor," Margaret exclaimed, and briefly kissed him just one more time. "Share the newspapers with the boys – I will return in a few moments, as soon as I have seen to Carl."

The dying light of afternoon filled the sickroom with an amber glow. There was no need for a lamp to be lit: Carl was already asleep – the quiet healing sleep. Margaret did not disturb him but tiptoed out of the room, feeling an almost unutterable sense of happiness and contentment, such as she had not felt in years. Carl would recover and she would be wed to her dear friend; perhaps of her own happiness some portion would be gifted to her brother.

From that moment, the days passed, flowing tranquilly as the river, the business of her household turning as the gears of a well-ordered clock, while

Carl rested, and slept, to wake again to take a few bites of Hetty's nourishing invalid dishes. Margaret and Henry spent tranquil evenings in the family parlor with the boys, although he did not come to her bedroom again, in unspoken agreement that it would not be fitting until the proper time. A week passed, then another; Carl was awake for a little longer each day, able to sit up in bed for a longer time and entertain visits from the boys, who of course were overflowing with questions about the war in Mexico.

"And so what is your opinion of my suitor?" Margaret asked one evening, as she brought in a folding tray with a little dish of chopped beef and vegetables, and some of Hetty's biscuits, already buttered. She set the tray at the side of the bed, and piled up some pillows so that her brother could sit up against them. "Now that you have made his acquaintance in your right mind, of course." She placed the tray on his lap; now she would keep him company for a while, watching like a hawk for signs of a returning appetite. It seemed that he ate for the first time with an interest in what she had put in front of him.

"He seems well-intentioned, but passing absent-minded." Carl replied, lifting a bite of well-cooked beef to his mouth. Hetty had purposefully cut everything rather small. Margaret smiled fondly.

"Oh, he has no mind for anything but medicine. He comes to dinner reading some foreign medical journal and props it against the cruets. We are all quite used to him returning from a day of house-calls and forgetting where he has left his coat, or his hat, or even his horse."

"Then you should accept his suit if you wish it and if it would make you happy." Carl set down his fork. "He's too absent-minded to even remember that you have property, let alone where he left his own traps. Might I have a little more, Margaret?"

"You are hungry?" Margaret exclaimed – the dish of beef was entirely clean. "That is a good sign, indeed. Yes, of course. Let me get some more from the kitchen." She took the plate from the tray on his knees. As she did, Carl added very simply, "Her name is Margaretha."

"Oh," said Margaret thoughtfully. She stood for a minute, in the pool of lamplight. So, that was the name of his German girl who had mended his shirt; whose family had been kind to him. She was overtaken with the certainty that if her brother had any chance of happiness and family life, than it would be with his Margaretha, and resolved that she would do what she could to ensure that outcome. And of course – she could do that. Anyone who was anyone in Texas came to eat at her table, sooner or later. She ventured, "If you please, I shall talk to some of my friends and see how we might find out where to find her family. But only if you would like."

"Yes . . . if you can. Thank you, Margaret."

On an impulse, she bent and dropped a kiss on his forehead – as if he were the age of Peter – and replied, "Don't mention it, little brother."

Margaret reviewed all that her brother had said of the German girl and her family: Margaretha of the family Steinmetz, from near Ulm in the old country. There might have been many German settlers come at once, and an awful to-do about bringing them up from the coast, where many of them had been left to shift for themselves on a bleak and desolate shore, and then with settling them all – and there had been much sickness and many dead among them during all this time. Many of those who survived, so she had heard, had gone to a new settlement perched on the edge of the hills by a little branch of the Guadalupe River, a town named for the Prince of Solms and Braunfels; that one whom Carl had called a fool with money and friends. That new settlement was in a place which once had been called 'the Fountains', from the springs which rose up and fed a little river that ran into Guadalupe. Yes, she would write to the man who had taken his place, as the factor for the Verein, Mr. Meusebach. Surely he would know the whereabouts and fortunes of the Steinmetz family of Ulm; she would sit down and write a letter to him, the very next day.

She had to wait until two days before Christmas for an answer and by that time she was half-distracted by the plans for Christmas dinner . . . and her own wedding, for which she said over and over that she did not wish to have much of a fuss made. She would wear a new dress, in the pale lavender color of half-mourning, at Hetty's and Mrs. Eberly's insistence. One of her boarders, a Mr. Cartwright from Nacogdoches, was a Justice of the Peace, and he readily agreed to do the honors. Carl, while still terribly pale and uncertain on his feet, was able by then to rise from the sickbed, dress and totter as far as the private parlor to spend some hours in the afternoons and early evening with the family. Margaret, assured repeatedly by her brother and her husband-to-be of his relative fitness, finally allowed herself to leave the house and walk down to Bullocks to see if the mail coach had arrived. For some reason, Carl, Henry, and the boys seems eager for her to do this. Hetty enlightened her, as she put on her bonnet and mantle.

"They say they've a bitty wee Christmas surprise for you," she whispered. "So ye should stay away . . . oh, an hour at least. And go from the front of the house, Marm, also."

"And I am supposed to pay no notion to the freight wagon, then?" Margaret asked, with a pleasurable feeling of anticipation. "Well, then – I suppose I am to be gifted with some furniture, and they want it to be a surprise. An hour then."

"At least, Marm . . . I believe it may take them that long."

Margaret left by purpose from the front door, managing by heroic effort to keep from looking into the stable-yard. Whatever it was – a single large crate, by the looks of it – which several draymen, Daddy Hurst, and Dr. Harper's slave Mose, and Henry Williamson were struggling to lower from the wagon and it seemed to be very heavy.

There was a single letter for her, among all the letters for her household; Margaret broke the seal upon it as soon as she had left Bullocks, reading it as she walked – for it was very short, confirming what she had already begun to suspect and written by a man in haste to deal with other things. It seemed that the family Steinmetz had departed New Braunfels nearly eight months ago, for that new Verein settlement farther west on the Pedernales River, where – to the best knowledge of the harried Mr. Meusebach, they had since remained. He regretted, he added in a terse postscript, that he had no more information. The new settlement was called Fredrichsburg. Margaret folded up the note and put it in the pocket of her dress skirt – she would find a time to tell her brother privately.

She must have been gone long enough, since the dray was gone, with its driver. She didn't see anything of the crate, and was reminded of how Alois Becker would have used every plank of it to build something useful.

"Is it safe for me now?" she asked of Hetty, as she walked into the kitchen.

"'Tis now," Hetty replied, wiping her floury hands on her apron. Most unaccustomed, for she was in the middle of preparing the supper biscuits, she took off her apron and hung it over the back of the kitchen rocking chair. "They are waiting for you in the little parlor." The private parlor was adorned for Christmas with a tall cut pine tree decorated with candles and garlands of bright red mountain-laurel seeds, drilled through and strung together, and a number of fragile blown-glass ornaments. All throughout the house, in the public rooms and the private alike, garlands of evergreens and brave red ribbons adorned the walls and fireplaces.

The door to the parlor was open but a crack: as she came down the hallway towards it, Margaret heard the scuffling of feet and Peter's voice exclaiming, "Mama's here!" and such sounds of excitement couldn't be muffled by a number of young boys. "She's coming!"

She waited, Hetty at her back, for the noise within to diminish before she tapped on the door. "May I come in now?" she called, and there was Henry, smiling almost like a boy himself, who opened the parlor door, answering, "Yes, my dear Margaret – you may see your present now." He kissed her cheek, as he had always promised to do following upon any absence from each other. Margaret brushed his lips with hers, thinking again how comforting and comfortable Henry Williamson was. "Merry Christmas, dear wife!"

Margaret was struck to silence, nearly for the first time in her life. There in her study and family parlor, the table, chairs and bookcases had been hastily rearranged to accommodate a new piece of furniture, a gleaming confection of polished wood, of ivory and ebony-wood keys; a small and elegant parlor pianoforte. Her precious folio of piano transcriptions was set invitingly open on the little stand which held the music to be played. There was even a bench of the same wood and design, with gracefully turned legs, sitting before the keys. Was this her gift – truly, it was the most beautiful and lavish present that anyone had ever thought of giving to her, the one thing that she most desired, yet wistfully acknowledged that such a frivolous, luxurious thing was so far beyond her practical nature as to be impossible. At last, she whispered, "Henry . . . it's beautiful. Is it really mine?"

"It is," Henry answered. "On one condition – that you play it for us every day." He looked as pleased with her happy reaction as if he himself had been given the gift that he had most wanted for years. In a way he was, Margaret reflected; the next day she would marry him, making to him the gift of herself and her love, things which he had longed for silently and hopelessly for so long. "Play it for us now," he added, as Margaret embraced him once again, thinking that she was blessed beyond words, having once again been given the gift of the love of a worthy man. A passing awkward man, but worthy in so many ways!

In all the excitement over the piano, she found a moment to give Carl the letter from Mr. Meusebach. He had taken refuge on the day bed where Race Vining had so often lain as an invalid, and Margaret felt a qualm – had he over-taxed his convalescent strength in helping Henry and the boys with the piano? She took it from her dress pocket and pressed it into his hand.

"If you are too tired, you should go back to your room," she said, appraising his color. "This is from a Mr. Meusebach, whom I think you already know. Your Margaretha and her family have gone farther into the west, to a new settlement on the Pedernales. He says nothing more. This letter is all I know – read it, and then let me know what you wish to do with this knowledge."

She pressed the letter into his hand and left him to do as he wished with it, and the knowledge that it contained. The piano called to her now – it was hers; she could play on it every day and for as long as she pleased, without inconveniencing Mary Bullock, and for the amusement of her sons and husband-to-be.

She played some simple tunes and some of the music from the cherished folio which had been Margaret Lea's gift. Because of the season, Margaret fell into playing the first bars of *Joseph Lieber, Joseph mein*. She began to sing the dear familiar words, a song that she and Mama and Rudi had sung, and Papa also – for he had been amiable enough and possessed of a fine deep tenor voice, in that time before when she and her brothers had been children and Mama had tamed his ill-nature. There was a movement; at her side, Carl took a place on the piano bench, and joined her in the song, as Henry, and the boys hushed to better hear them:

> *"Joseph, lieber Joseph mein,*
> *Hilf mir wiegen mein Kindelein!*
> *Will es wiegen und singen ein:*
> *Nun schlaf in Ruh, Die Äuglein zu,*
> *O Jesus!"*

"That's a beautiful song, my dear," Henry looked up from his medical journal, as Carl and Margaret sang the final verse. "I have never heard you sing it before . . . is it new?"

"We used to sing it when we were children," Margaret answered. "Oh we knew so many songs, songs that I almost never sing myself, now. The boys were never very interested in learning the old songs. Their father didn't speak German, and all their friends spoke English."

"You haven't taught them songs like this? Like *Tannenbaum*?" Carl asked, almost incredulously. Margaret recalled how they had always sung, at Mama's urging; she, and Rudi, Mama and Papa. When they were a family, when Mama and Rudi were alive and Papa still a man capable of being in reasonable comity with the world and his children, it seemed that they had never stopped singing. Margaret looked down at the keys, her fingers moving on them – such a lovely tone this piano had, even if it was a bit janglely for having been transported to her parlor from – wherever the doctor had purchased it.

"Oh, little brother, it is one of those things that one lets go, almost without thinking of it," she answered softly, over the music. "It's not like you spent much time singing old songs at Christmas, once you left home. I don't know how you could expect anything different of me. Things do not stay the same, as much as we would wish them to."

"I know that," Carl answered. Margaret spared a glance at him – he did not look well. She should chase him back to his room, for he must be fit enough tomorrow to stand up as a witness at her second wedding.

"She would know all the old songs, little brother. That one you spoke to me of, when you first came home." Carl's face became very still, while Margaret wondered if she should have mentioned it at all. She lowered her voice and asked gently in the language of their mutual childhood, which she now had so little occasion to speak. "Your Margaretha – you have never sent word to her, or a letter? We know from the letter today – they had gone with a large party to Mr. Meusebach's new settlement on the Pedernales. Have you taken any thought to what you should say or do, now?"

"No." Carl answered softly.

"Why not, then?" Margaret asked, although she already knew why. Her brother had been so much alone, in the endless reaches of the Llano country – the wind whispering in the short grass and the sky a vault of blue over his head – that he had no skill with humankind any more, unless it was with the Indians that he fought, and his disreputable Ranger comrades . . . men like Cole, men like those who had dispatched him sick and injured on an endless ride in a jolting Dearborn wagon, all that way from Monterrey, to be dumped at her doorway like so much trash. Carl was so long in answering that she began to think he would not, that he would quietly leave the parlor with her question unanswered.

"There has been so much sickness among them," He answered finally, under cover of the gentle, random chords that she drew from the keyboard. "At the coast and in the Comal settlement. She might also be married by now. Either way, I would rather not know for sure. Just go on thinking her alive and free. This is so – as long as I do not know for sure otherwise."

"You are an idiot, little brother," Margaret said at last, stern and compassionate. What men believed until faced with evidence to the contrary was almost limitless. Carl was not an exception to that rule. As long as he believed, and saw nothing to contradict those beliefs, he would go on doing so.

Now he said, with a rueful and sideways glance. "So Papa always said. But it's how I wish to let it lie. I will do something when I am better fit. Just not now."

Margaret shook her head, and her hands caressed the ivory keys, "Don't leave it wait too long, then." And perhaps he had a point, for he could barely stand, worn to thread-paper thinness by wounds and illness; hardly in a good state for winning a woman's affections unless she had an unaccountable fondness for nursing sick and feeble things. In Margaret's experience, unless love was well-established beforehand, such light affections wouldn't last past the first wound-dressing or the emptying of a pan of vomit.

In the morning, she married Henry Williamson, standing up before Mr. Cartwright and her household, along with many of her friends. It was a brief ceremony, quite perfunctory, and she was thinking all through it that it was merely a set of words and ritual. She and Henry had already been married for a long time – he to her, from the time that he promised Race to look after her and the boys, she to him for a somewhat shorter period. And that she could make a comfortable home for her brother, at long last – and that best of all, Henry Williamson had not the slightest wish to interfere with the running of her household, whatsoever. She considered all that afternoon, while she received congratulations and good wishes from all of their friends, what sort of gift she would make to him, something which would please him as much as the piano had pleased her.

That night the two of them lay, tangled affectionately together – as at last they could, being blessed by law and custom, although as Margaret considered it, they had long been married in their true minds. Christmas Eve had passed pleasantly, lit by the candles on the tree in the small parlor, and the happiness and good cheer in the larger. Hetty, Carl, and Daddy Hurst had each solemnly promised that none of the gentlemen boarders – or any other residents of Austin – would have an opportunity to make a rude chaivari under the windows of the wedded couple's house.

Now Margaret nestled into the curve of his arms, laying her head against his chest and feeling the beat of his heart against hers – that faithful and loving heart so finally rewarded, and ventured, "I have considered my present for you, my dearest old doctor – that you should have a surgery of your own where your patients might come, and you can minister to them – even to doing all that you were doing when we first met and your office was your satchel and two boards over a pair of barrels under a canvas roof. Would you like that?"

"It depends," he replied, and Margaret shivered with delight as his fingers absently caressed the long curve of her back, as of he were inventorying every bone, rib and muscle. "What are you planning this time? Another addition to the house?"

"A small one," she answered as he made a small unhappy moan of protest; dear old doctor. "No, I know that you do not like disruption to your routine – but this would be a minor matter. A small addition, another wing of the house . . . a matter of merely two rooms below and two above, connected by a corridor . . . no, you would relish it, dear love – an office and surgery, and a place for your patients to come – a door to the outside, so that they need not trouble to come through the house . . . " and she elaborated on the new addition, constructed and arranged for his particular needs, with several shelves for his books, and a desk of his own, where he could do his own business . . . until he stopped her mouth with a kiss and whispered,

"It sounds perfection indeed, dearest Margaret. And now?"

"What then? I will talk to the carpenters tomorrow . . . oh, not tomorrow, since it is Christmas. The day after, I think."

"Margaret . . . " and he kissed her again, very tenderly, and she felt that the particular male part of him had begun to rouse. "I am in the mood again for marital congress . . . "

"My dear doctor!" Margaret tightened her arms about him. "We do have so much lost time to make up for then, do we not?"

"Two years alone in Perote!" Henry whispered into her ear, and she laughed and drew him into herself, wondering once more how she had been so very blessed.

Winter passed, the peace of Margaret's household hardly touched upon by war waging in faraway Mexico. The only sadness which came Margaret's way to dim her utter and complete happiness was the death of Louisa Ford. As dearly John Ford loved her and exercised all of his medical talents on her behalf, she died shortly before Carl's return home, leaving her husband distraught – and often enough to come to Margaret's house and eat a distracted supper. The management of the newspaper, and the lively political wrangling which ensued from editing a frontier newspaper had lost savor for him, as Margaret suspected the practice of medicine and law had also lost savor in sequence. John Ford's restless intellect mastered them for a diversion and then cast them aside as a child bored with a once-new toy. He and Carl talked much about their adventures as Rangers, and of what Carl had experienced in Mexico, in low voices at the end of the table and in the boarders' parlor after supper.

Margaret observed, thinking with resignation that Carl would go back to the Rangers yet again once he was healed, and perhaps take John Ford with him . . . but as the weeks and months passed, Carl remained – and she began to hope that perhaps he might be taking the first steps toward settling down. She also began to hope that once he was truly fit and well – and he was not strong for many months – that he might decide to settle at long last into a trade of some sort, or onto property that he had for service as a Ranger and for having served at Goliad in the war.

That dream came crashing down, the afternoon that she came into the parlor to administer her son's lessons, and Peter, all agog with excitement – exclaimed, "Mama! Colonel Jack Hayes himself came to look for Uncle Carl today! They went off together, an' Uncle Carl said to say that he would be going with him but that I should tell you that he would be back for supper."

"Oh, dear," Margaret exclaimed. Oh, for the dream that her brother would settle down. Well, it was a nice one, but here Jack Hayes appeared again, like a bad and tempting sprite snapping his fingers and her brother would obey. Margaret's heart was cold yet resigned within her. This last time, Carl had barely survived. She was not well-inclined to welcome her brother's dearest friend upon their return a number of hours later.

Carl was riding a leggy brown horse, a brown horse with three white socks and a white blaze upon his nose, which had come from who-knows-where, but Margaret was far more taken with interest in the man who accompanied him – a small and slight man, with a boyish face, barely hazed with a beard. They came up the front stairs and into the hallway, laughing like brothers – and slightly inebriated, Margaret noted with some disapproval.

"M'grete," Carl said expansively, "I'd like to present . . ." he hiccupped slightly, "M'friend Jack Hays. Jack – this is m'sister, M'grete. Mrs. Williamson. Everyone comes to her table, eventually."

"Mrs. Williamson," Jack bowed gracefully over her hand. He spoke in a light and husky Tennessee drawl but his speech was gentle, educated. Margaret had long experience in sizing up men – and had the uncomfortable feeling that this Jack Hays was just about equally accomplished in that. "I am purely devastated, ma'am, at my bad fortune until this very moment. Dutch has often claimed before this, that everyone who is anyone in Texas has dined at your table. I have no excuse for not having done so until now – save that my duties elsewhere have kept me from that pleasure."

"You are welcome then, Colonel Hays," Margaret answered. "I may consider my standing as a hostess unimpaired, now that you have graced us with your presence." Jack Hays colored like Horace did when teased and Carl hooted with laughter.

"No reason to make a fuss over him, M'grete," He slapped Jack on the shoulder, at which the redoubtable Colonel Hays staggered slightly and returned the favor. "Any ol' bit of food will do for us, M'grete."

"My table is famous because we do not serve 'any ol' bit of food," Margaret answered, in the quelling tone of voice she used for Peter and Jamie when they were most obstreperous. "Tonight we will have a venison roast, with game bird pie, baked squash and baked custard or apple pie for afters. With seven sweet preserves and seven sours."

"Ma'am Williamson, I am forevermore in your debt!" Jack Hays bowed again extravagantly over her hand, exclaiming, "I'm sure an' certain that I have never set down at such a rich-laid table in all the time I have been in Texas!"

It proved to be a very merry meal indeed; her establishment was full of Jack Hay's friends and acquaintances; even those who did not know him had heard of his many exploits. He was becomingly modest about them all, and deftly turned most inquiries into accounts of the service and heroics of other men. But he said nothing of what he had come to Austin for, nor did Carl.

Late that evening, Margaret tapped gently on the door of Carl's room.

"Come in," came the quiet answer from within, and Margaret opened the door. Her heart sank: he was cleaning and loading those long patent revolvers which had lain unused in a dresser drawer for much of the winter, save for one day when he had felt well enough to venture down to the lower pasture and practice with them. He had nearly put himself into a relapse from exhaustion. Now the extra barrels and all the tools were spread out on a square of flannel in the middle of the bed; the knives and his long carbine lay next to them, with the meager contents of his saddlebags. His buckskin trail coat hung from the bedpost.

"You're away again?" Margaret observed, gratified that her voice was perfectly calm, unsurprised.

"Early in the morning, yes."

"You were planning to say goodbye to us, this time?"

"Of course." He sounded vaguely offended.

Margaret sighed. "Jack Hays snaps his fingers and you come running. At least linger tomorrow long enough for a good breakfast."

"I have to get an early start. I've a need to catch up to a party who may have left from the Fountains already."

"So it will be an early breakfast. You need not steal away from my house like a thief. And I'll pack some supplies for you also."

"I'm traveling light . . ." He looked up from his polishing, as Margaret sat herself down on the edge of the bed opposite him and surveyed the assortment spread across the counterpane. ". . . and not taking much."

"You have room for an extra shirt," Margaret observed; yes, the mended shirt which had come home with him from the war. "By this I see you have room for a little hope in your heart, little brother. Good for you." She had half-expected this, since Carl had chosen to remain so long. It seemed that he had come to a decision at last, and now she took a small bottle out of her apron pocket, rolling the shirt around it. "I put a portion of opodeldoc liniment in a small bottle. The Doctor advises its use when your shoulder aches. He says you have complained of it once or twice. Where are you bound this time, or is that something you may not say?"

"I may," Carl answered. "John Meusebach is going into the Llano country to make peace with the Comanche and buy a little time for his settlers. Jack is sending me as—a sort of bodyguard, I guess—and to keep an eye on things."

"A spy, in other words," Margaret said. Her brother shrugged obliquely.

"It wouldn't be for the first time. Meusebach is supposed to be going to the new colony on the Pedernales first and gathering his party. Then he intends journeying to San Saba to meet the Comanche chiefs at a large encampment there."

Be careful then," Margaret commanded, proud that she kept her composure: he was going away yet again. How many times more could he gamble with his life? He finished reassembling the pistol, and slid it into the waiting holster.

"I always am, Margaret."

"One more thing; your friends went to that settlement, did they not? I believe it is now called Friedrichsburg. Will you search for her there?" She did not have to specify who she meant – the clockmaker's daughter, Margaretha – who was as brave and fine as a high-spirited horse, and for whom Carl had yearned for months.

"I might." Margaret sighed, mildly exasperated: now he had gone back to being as much a sphinx as ever.

When he did not elaborate, she continued, "Should you find her and discover that things with her are as you wish – and if they work out as you seem to hope, you must let me know."

"Why is that? Do you need to approve of her first?"

"That might not be a bad idea," Margaret answered. "But no, there is a gift I have for her, a little brooch of Mama's. She intended it to be for your wife whenever you married, but died thinking you and Rudi were both killed at Goliad. She gave it to me then, to hold for my boys. She meant it for you, though, and you shall have it. Just let me know."

His head bent over his work, and she could barely hear his answer. "I will, Margaret. Thank you."

"Good night then." She stood up and went to the door, but as she slipped out she whispered, "It would have made Mama so happy to know you lived. Take care, little brother, until you return again. Don't wait until you are near-killed next time."

"I won't," he promised as she eased the door closed.

In the dark morning, well before dawn, he appeared silently in the kitchen, dressed for the trail. Margaret and Hetty were already at breakfast preparations for the boarders – they plied him with food, which he wolfed silently in his customary manner as if not expecting another good meal for weeks. When Margaret followed him to the door, she saw that the leggy brown horse with three white socks and the blaze on his nose was already saddled, and tied to the porch post waiting for him. The winter fog had come up from the river; all was grey and quiet, save for the sound of condensation dripping off the branches and the edge of the roof.

"When will we see you again, little brother?" she whispered, as she embraced him one last time, again vaguely astounded that he was now as tall as herself, taller than Henry, and all the lumps of things in the pockets of his trail-coat pressed against her breast and her arms.

"After this scout, I think." he answered slowly. "I'm not going back to the Rangers, M'grete. I'm done – my last enlistment's up. I told Jack yesterday, this last is just a favor to him, because it gave me a reason to search her out; Margaretha. And if she's free and will have me, then I'll reckon I'll settle down just like you wanted."

"Good," Margaret took his face between her hands and looked at him very seriously. "It's about time, Carlchen. There are plenty of good lands around Austin . . . and a chance to take up a trade."

"No," he shook his head, and his eyes were as distant as they always were when he talked about the Llano and the unpeopled country. "I think . . . to the west. Not here. It's too settled. I wouldn't be able to breathe."

"See what your Margaretha will have to say about that!" Margaret said. At that, he laughed, kissed her cheek, and went to his horse. Margaret could hear the sounds of horse hooves tap-tapping along the road for quite a time. Just as Carl vanished into the fog, away towards the river and the road to the south, he turned and waved to her, standing on the porch.

"Take care, Carlchen, until you come back to us," Margaret whispered to herself. For nearly the first time in ten years, she was certain that he would.

Coda: The Apple Tree Branch in Bloom

"Open the curtains, Little One," Margaret asked Horrie. Her voice was husky, and not strong. "I want to see the apple trees. Are they blooming yet?"

"A little bit," four-and-a-half year old Horrie answered. "On the southern side of the house mostly." Obediently he scrambled down from where he had been lying on top of the counterpane, curled close with his head against Margaret's shoulder, listening to her tell stories – stories to him which seemed to come from antiquity, of mighty and god-like heroes, of deeds and adventures, and all the better because some of them were kin, and Gran'mere had known them all. He trotted across the room and pulled the heavy curtains aside, which Mama had drawn when she last visited Gran'mere's room, in spite of Gran'mere protesting that she didn't want to be shut away. Behind him, on the tall bed . . . which had oddly-shortened posts at each corner, and about which Gran'mere had said there was a story but one she would get to presently . . . Gran'mere sighed.

"So many stories, Little One. I may not have time to tell them all. Some you must seek out yourself when you are a little older." Her eyes moved restlessly towards the window. "I wish that I could see my city . . . I always thought of it as my city, Little One. Your Opa Becker, he was here before it was a city, and much of the land it was built on was formerly his."

Horrie screwed up his serious little face. He came and wriggled his way onto the bed again, there being a tall chair next to it which Horrie had made use of for this purpose. He curled up next to her as he had been. "You're not too tired to tell me another story, are you, Gran'mere?"

"I'm afraid I am, dear Little One. Perhaps you should ask me questions, so that I may rest my voice."

"I think I remember Carlchen," he ventured presently. "Your little brother, Gran'mere, but he was not as old as you. He looked like the picture in your cabinet of curiosities."

"No, dear Little One: that was his son Dolph, who was his very image. Dolph was named for Rudi . . . I was glad that Carlchen's son was named thus. He came to visit a year ago. I thought he would stay with us, but he went to join with Colonel John Ford's cavalry company instead."

"What did happen to your brother, Gran'mere?" Horrie looked as if he had tucked away that information in as tidy a fashion as he put away his grandfather's precious books. "Did he ever come back?"

"He did," Margaret answered, and her voice sounded fainter, huskier. "Several times; once with his wife and their children; when your father and mother were married, he was there, with us. With our family. He had a measure of happiness allotted to him, Little One, for a good many years – I was very glad of that, for he deserved such joy so very much, more than any other man that I knew, save General Sam and one other. Your Gran'pere . . . your father and his brothers always called him Doctor-Papa . . . he had a similar measure of happiness as well, measured out, pressed down and overflowing."

"But what happened to him?" Horrie persisted. Gran'mere looked so very sad now, and there were tears trickling out of the corners of her eyes.

"The war happened to him," she answered, in a voice of inexpressible sorrow. "Just as it happened to your Gran'pere – at least I could come and minister to him, among all the sick in that wretched camp. For your father and your uncles Johnny and Jamie? There was nothing I could do for them, Little One. They fell in battle, your father first, and then your uncles. Carrying the standard, for a minute or two – oh, my boys! Such a useless, pointless task! Of all of them, only Jamie ought to have been a soldier, but there you are . . . every man thinks meanly of himself for not having been one. I wish that I could see your uncle Peter one more time, but I fear that I shall not."

"Has the war happened to him, too?" Horrie asked, with sudden urgent concern, as he sought out a corner of the crisply clean sheet and carefully blotted Margaret's tears with it.

"He was alive, the last that we had heard," Margaret answered, her voice now sounding even more faint, as if it were more a labor for her to speak, and her grandson's voice was filled with anxiety.

"Gran'mere, do you want me to fetch Miz Hetty?"

"No," Margaret smiled, a faint and reassuring smile. "No, Little One. I would have you open the door to the veranda . . . leave it open. I crave the fresh air. I do not care if it is cold, it will not matter. One more task . . . Go around to the side of the orchard that is in bloom and break me off a little branch with blossoms on it. Bring it to me, so I may see the apple trees in bloom!" Her voice seemed to strengthen as she spoke, commanding one last time, and Horrie obeyed, sliding down from the bed, trotting across the room, which was on the ground floor of Gran'mere's house, a room in the wing where the back windows and verandah looked away from town, into the thin woods with the river beyond and below. Horrie loved his Gran'mere, and obeyed without question, for although she very rarely issued orders – his mother was more for demanding instant obedience – that which she requested seemed most sensible, and comprehensible. He ran out from the opened glassed door, leaving it open while a crisp spring breeze blew into the room.

Gran'mere's house was very large, and the apple trees that were starting to bloom were all the way to the other side. Horrie took the shortest route, running around the back – past the porch which led into the winter kitchen, thumping across the covered arbor that thrust a finger out to the summer kitchen, past the ramble of little cabins that housed Daddy Hurst and the other darkies, the springhouse and the smokehouse, the stable yard with the barn beyond, the neglected vegetable garden, with Daddy Hurst looking moodily over the fence which kept stray cattle and pigs out of it.

"Marse Horace, where you be goin' in such a hurry?" Daddy called to Horace, and Horrie skidded to a breathless halt.

"Gran'mere, she wants me to fetch a branch of apple tree with the blossoms upon it. She said she wishes to see them in bloom, one more time."

"Then, we better do as Miz Margaret says." Daddy Hurst, who was older than anyone Horrie knew, even older than Gran'mere, straightened from leaning against the fence, with a look on his aged African face that Horrie couldn't fathom. But he went with Horrie to the edge of the orchard, where there was a rotting oak stump, and a little space with a slab of carved stone and a little iron fence about it. Daddy Hurst reached up to a tall branch, one that Horrie could not have reached on his own, and carefully broke off a branch upon which the blossoms were clustered the thickest. "You bes' take that to Miz Margaret, you hear?" he said to Horrie, but Horrie was already away, running as fast as he could with the apple branch, towards the room where he had left the tall French door open, where his dearest Gran'mere lay on a tall bed with strangely carved bedposts.

Horrie came in through the opened door, the chill breeze at his back, seeing that his mother and Miss Hetty were already standing by the bed, on either side – bringing the apple branch as Gran'mere had asked.

"Oh, Horrie – close the door!" Mama snapped, her voice even more cross than usual, and Horrie looked in bewilderment towards Hetty, who had Gran'mere's slack hand in hers and a look of devastated grief on her face.

"Gran'mere wanted to see the apple blossoms," Horrie ventured uncertainly. "She sent me for a branch of it, so that she could see . . ." Mama and Miz Hetty, they were looking at him with a strange expression. And Gran'mere, her eyes were half open, and unseeing.

"She . . . is gone." Miz Hetty whispered. "That may be the last thing she asked for. I'll put it in her hands, just as she asked . . ." Mama opened her mouth to say something, but Miz Hetty gave her such a look that she closed it again at once, as Miz Hetty continued, regardless of the tears streaming down her face. "She was so very ill – she could have gone at any time. Queen Maeve, so terrible proud . . ."

"Gran'mere can't be gone." Horrie gave the branch of apple-blossom to Hetty, who gently folded Gran'mere's hand around the stem and laid it on her breast. "She still had stories to tell me."

"Aye, and so she may have," Miz Hetty answered, as she gently patted Horrie's cheek. "Such a grand lady! But she can tell them no more, and so you must search them out for yourself."

Becker – Vining Family

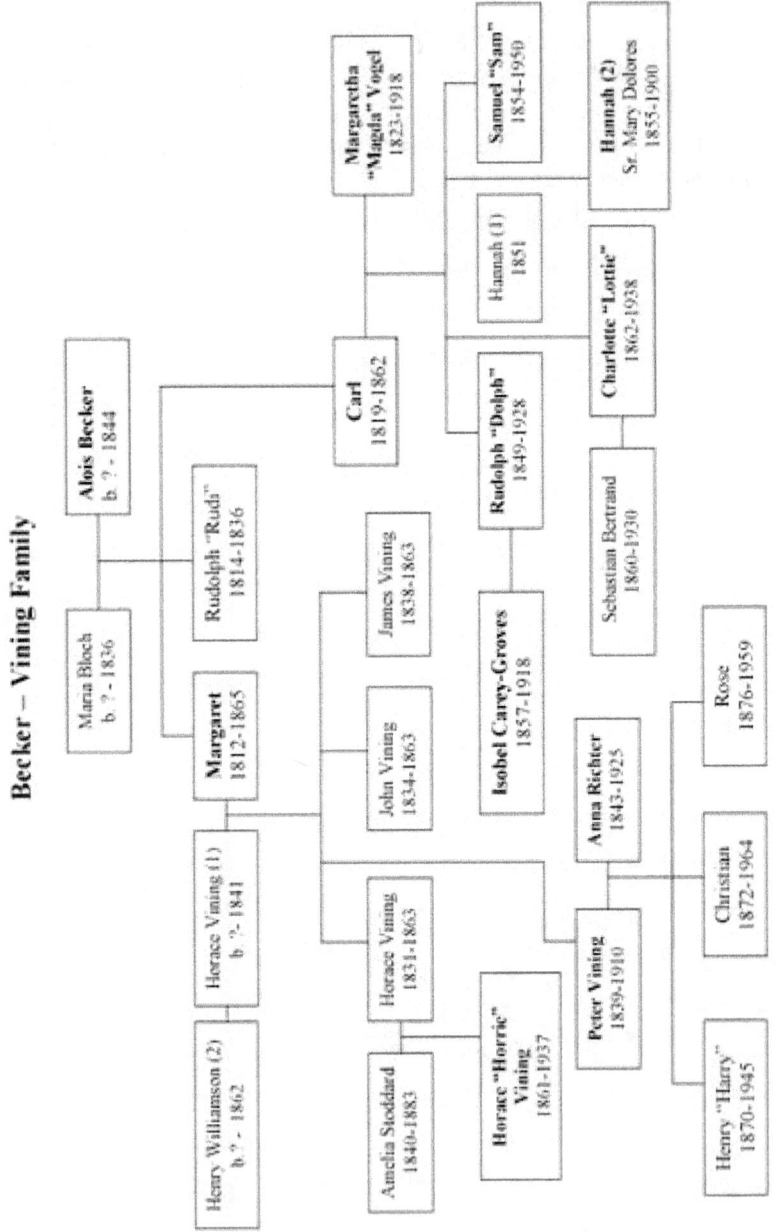

Notes: The Pig War, the Archives War, Woll's Invasion, and Other Notable Incidents

Like love, the course of true republic never did run smooth. So it turned out for the infant Republic of Texas. While such characters as Margaret Becker Vining Williamson, her brothers, family, household and husbands are entirely created – many of those others named as friends and neighbors are not; Angelina Eberly, Thomas Ward, Captain Coleman, the Bullock and Simpson families are historic characters, although not so well known to history as Sam Houston and Jack Hays. Many of the incidents such as Captain Coleman's bluff, and the kidnapping of the Simpson children occurred, although sometimes not quite in the way that I outlined.

Austin – formerly known as Waterloo – had a perilous existence, just as related. For accounts of incidents in those early days, I have drawn on an account by Jeffrey Kerr; *The Republic of Austin.* The Pig War – the extended dispute between the French Legate and the owner of Bullock's inn really did happen, more or less as outlined, and is thought by some historians to have contributed to the failure of a French-led entrepreneur scheme to bring thousands of settlers to Texas – just as the Adelsverein entrepreneurs did with German settlers at a slightly later date and with a little more success. The Comte de Saligny, or the "no-count" as he was scornfully called by many of the residents of Austin, departed Texas in considerable of a huff. However, the French Legation still exists, although it was not built by Seamus O'Doyle – who is fictional character. It was mostly likely designed and constructed by Thomas Ward, who (in addition to having been an early mayor of Austin and the unfortunate resident cannon expert), had also trained as an engineer and worked as a builder. Today it is the only residential building remaining in Austin from that era. It is now a museum, maintained by the Daughters of the Republic of Texas, after having been a private home for more than a hundred years.

The incident of General Sam chopping down the bedposts is one of those things which did happen, but elsewhere and likely before or in the early days of his marriage to Margaret Lea, who took a very dim view of such antics. She was half his age when they married and everyone – her family and his friends alike, confidently expected their marriage to last no more than six months. To the astonishment of all, it turned out to be a long, loving and successful one. She eventually prevailed upon him to stop drinking entirely, they wrote to each other every single day that they were apart, and Sam Houston died with her name on his lips.

A site of outstanding natural beauty, Austin was nonetheless at the very edge of the Texas frontier. Sam Houston's unhappiness with having the center of government at such a distance from the more settled portions of Texas was open: he did indeed try to have the public records of the Republic moved from Austin, over the strenuous objections of the residents. In the dead of night on December 29th, 1842, a party of men acting under Houston's direction arrived, with orders to remove the archives – in secret and without shedding any blood. Unfortunately, they were rather noisy about loading the wagons. Angelina Eberly woke, looked out of a window and immediately realized what was going on. She ran outside, and fired off the six-pound cannon that the residents kept loaded with grapeshot in case of an Indian attack. The shot alerted the vigilance committee – and supposedly punched a hole in the side of the General Land Office Building. The men fled with three wagons full of documents, pursued within hours by the volunteers of the vigilance committee, who caught up with them the next day. The archives were returned. Sam Houston had specified no bloodshed; the following year, he was admonished by the Legislature for trying to relocate the capitol.

The Legislature did return to Austin in 1845. Following upon annexation by the United States, the state capital would remain there, as it has ever since. Curiously, Angelina Eberly – who had fired the shot that ensured it would do so – eventually moved her hotel business to Indianola, the Queen City of the Gulf coast. She did not marry again, and ran a profitable and well-frequented hotel there, until her death in 1860.

Sam Houston did have a very real basis for concern, with regard to Austin as the capitol city. The enmity of Antonio Lopez de Santa Anna against the runaway province of Texas proved to be unrelenting. A low-grade boarder war simmered away for all the decade that the Republic of Texas existed. In March of 1842 a brief raid by General Rafael Vasquez and some 400 soldiers made a lightening-fast dash over the Rio Grande, while another 150 soldiers struck at Goliad and Refugio. They met little resistance – and departed at speed before Texan forces could assemble and retaliate. That was followed in September by General Adrian Woll's organized incursion – which, as described in this book, resulted in the capture of the District Court. Every Anglo-Texian man in San Antonio was taken as prisoners of war into Mexico.

This included the judge, district attorney, assistant district attorney, court clerk, court interpreter, every member of the San Antonio Bar save one, and a handful of litigants and residents; a total of fifty-five. Once in Mexico, some of them, like Samuel Maverick, were paroled and permitted to leave as a personal favor to the US Consul in Mexico City. Others, like the fictional Daniel Fritchie escaped, but most of the San Antonio prisoners were kept for two years at hard labor in Perote Prison, as described, until an armistice was signed between Mexico and Texas in March of 1844. Austin was a mere eighty miles farther into the interior of Texas than San Antonio; what would satisfy the autocratic Santa Anna more, than to capture the Legislature of Texas, while in session?

Woll's brief occupation of Bexar ended with pitched fight on the banks of Salado Creek to the north of town, between elements of his force, lured out to fight in the open against the assembled militia volunteers from across Texas. There is a monument by the side of Holbrook Road commemorating this. Another stone at the side of the Austin Highway by the bridge crossing Salado Creek, commemorating the massacre the Dawson Company from Bastrop and the upper Colorado. Only fifteen of Dawson's men would survive; they, like the other prisoners were taken to Perote.

The raid set off a series of repercussions, the most immediate being the launching of the Somervell punitive expedition, and the wholly volunteer Mier expedition into Mexico. The Black Bean Draw took place at Saltillo, Mexico, following an abortive escape attempt by the Mier expedition prisoners. A furious Santa Anna declared that all the prisoners should be executed, but was eventually convinced to execute only one in ten. Seventeen black beans and 159 white were placed in a pottery jar and covered with a light cloth. The 179 prisoners were made to reach into the jar, draw a bean, and then hand it to the Mexican officer in charge of deciding which prisoners would be executed. In reality it was one James Cocke, who remarked upon drawing a black bean, "They only rob me of forty years," and it was he who gave away his clothes, not Seamus O'Doyle. It was actually another Texian, Ewan Cameron, who opened his coat and shouted, "Fuerza!" (Fire) at the firing squad. Cameron had drawn a white bean, but was executed anyway, being particularly hated by the guards. One might easily begin to comprehend, upon reading such accounts, why the Texians of the time entertained such abiding hatred for Lopez de Santa Anna.

Finally, the character of Mr. Hattersley – the historian with the poisoned pen – is based upon the pamphleteer and lawyer Nicholas Doran Maillard. Historically, Doran Maillard chose the town of Richmond as his residence during the early 1840s. By then, Richmond had existed as a town for about twenty years, incorporating many elements and refinements such as a newspaper, the *Richmond Telescope*. The charming and cultured Mr. Maillard was heartily welcomed by the residents of Richmond – he was very popular for his ability in mixing drinks, for one, and he also served a stint as editor of the *Telescope*. He told everyone that he was writing a book, and made friends everywhere. Richmond was then home to a number of prominent figures in early Texas, to include Jane Long, the wife of an early adventurer, Sam Houston's chief scout, Erastus 'Deaf' Smith, and Sam Houston's arch-rival, Mirabeau Lamar. Mr. Maillard gave every evidence of enjoying his time in Richmond, and appeared to leave with reluctance after six months, pleading the death of a relative, back in England. So the publication of his history of Texas came as a considerable shock to the good and trusting citizens of Richmond and elsewhere.

The title of – and the quotes from Adolphus Hattersley's book – are taken directly from Doran Maillard. It is speculated that his so-called history was intended to discourage the British government from recognizing Texas. Thomas Cutrer, in *The English Texans* theorizes that Maillard might also have had a monetary motivation. The government of Mexico was deeply in debt to various English banking houses and bond-holders, for loans made before 1836 which had been secured by Texas lands. Those bankers were under the threat of Mexico defaulting on ten million pounds worth of loans. If Mexico did not control of those Texas acres, English bankers would have to eat the loss. One has the impression from Doran Maillard libelous little screed, that he would not mind in the least if Mexico regained sovereignty over Texas – as long as they repaid their English loans.